make me
BELIEVE

Book ONE in the Believe Series

KAREN FERRY

This is a work of fiction. Names, characters, brands, places, media, and incidents are either the author's imagination or are used fictitiously. The author acknowledges the trademarked status and trademark owners of various products referred to in this work of fiction, which have been used without permission.

The publication/use of these trademarks are not authorised, associated with, or sponsored by the trademark owners.

No part of this publication may be reproduced, distributed, or transmitted in any form or by any means (including photocopying, recording, or other electronic or mechanical methods) without the prior written permission of the author, except in the case of brief quotations embodied in critical reviews and certain other noncommercial uses permitted by copyright law.

Thank you for respecting the author's work.

All rights reserved.

Copyright © 2015 by Karen Ferry

Stock Photos: Stocksy.com
Cover Designer: Susan Garwood © Wicked Women Designs
Editor: The Fountain Pen
Proofreading: M & M Beta Reads & Proofreading
Formatting: AB Formatting

ISBN-10: 1514867966
ISBN-13: 978-1514867969

THIS BOOK IS A SPECIAL EDITION

INCLUDES FOUR BONUS SCENES

"Meeting The Parents - & Nan"
"Tattoos & Trinkets"
"The Proposal"
&
"An Unexpected Surprise"

To love is to burn, to be on fire
Jane Austen

DEDICATION

To my grandmother, Ruth, for teaching me the love of the written word, and for being the wisest, sassiest, sharp-tongued Nan that I could ever hope for:

I miss you every day.

And to everyone who is filled with self-doubt, wondering if they will ever be able to free themselves from their pasts:

This book is for you.

Never stop believing in your hopes and dreams - or fairy-tales.
Go after your own happily-ever-after.

You are so much stronger than you think.

AUTHOR'S NOTE

While there are parts of this book that are inspired by true events, I feel that it is necessary to state that it is mostly a work of fiction. I am not Emma - nor am I Daniel. True, many events taking place in #MMB did happen to me...but I hope you understand when I say that I will not divulge which.

All of us probably have things we wish we could erase, or do over, when we think back on our lives, but what I hope that you will take to heart with my story is the fact that you must *never* stop believing in yourself or what you are able to achieve. That *you* have the ability to change your life even when you feel that it is spiralling out of control. And when things seem to go in the wrong direction, you *will* be able to find the strength from within to keep moving forward. This is your life: make the most of it.

The past is the past. There is nothing you can do about it, but it *does not* have the power to define your future unless you give it the right to do so.

Always move forward.

Make each day count.

And do not be afraid to ask for help when you need it.

Thank you for reading my book. I hope that you will enjoy Emma and Daniel's journey as they discover their paths in life.

Much love,
Karen Ferry

PROLOGUE

THE NIGHTMARE IS BACK.
It's strange: I know I'm dreaming, yet I can't seem to break free of it. It feels as if I'm standing a bit away from what's happening...It's as if I'm a spectator while at the same time perfectly aware of the fact that the little girl lying on the bed in the dream is me.

I try to reach out to the girl as I feel her petrified stare pleading with me to help her...but I can't lift my arms. I want to go to her...but I can't move my feet. I want to comfort her with my voice, but when I open my mouth to speak, no sound comes out. I'm frozen in place. I'm helpless.

When the girl begins to cry, tears form in my eyes. I let them fall, flowing silently down my cheeks. I want so much to fight for the girl, to help her in some way, but, again, I can't. As I watch the girl's struggle, my own torment sets in, and I push against the invisible bonds rooting me to the spot.

I want to be free!

I want to protect her!

A scream starts forming in my throat, and sweat breaks out on *my face. I can feel the scream building, trying to tear free. I keep trying to force my body to move, and, suddenly, the bonds are gone, and I fall to my knees. Then I look up, but it's too late...*

I scream.

CHAPTER ONE

EMMA DAVENPORT

I WAKE UP, STILL screaming, except this time in real life. My body is covered in sweat, my heart beats frantically. The familiar nausea hits me, and I try desperately to disentangle my legs from my duvet.

I finally succeed, and I rush to the bathroom, my hand covering my mouth. As I fall to the floor in front of the toilet, I start to vomit, and it goes on for a while. The images from my nightmare assault me as I throw up, but, as usual, I try to block them out. I *do not* want them! It is bad enough that they won't leave me alone at night, I don't need them to break free during the daylight hours as well.

I shudder as dry heaves take over.

Ugh, I hate this.

At last, this morning's vomiting spell is over, and I sit back on my heels, pushing my long, curly mahogany-brown hair off my clammy face. My hands are cold. In fact, now that I am fully awake, I take in how my entire body is shaking, and I am freezing. This is nothing new to me, of course, but I do not have to accept it, and I stand up and turn on the shower.

As I wait for the water to get to the proper temperature - and, mind you, it can take a while - I brush my teeth vigorously.

I don't look in the mirror, though, because I know that I won't like my appearance. My blue-grey eyes will seem lifeless, yet red from the crying. My freckles will be even more apparent than usual because my normally pale complexion will resemble that of a corpse.

I finish brushing my teeth and turn to the shower when a voice asks from behind me:

"Babe? You okay?"

I slowly turn around and take in the fine specimen of a man standing in front of me, concern evident on his face. The guy is taller than me, but most people are, and he's got wavy, sandy-brown hair down to his shoulders. He's naked, and he has a nice body covered in ink, but whatever lust I acted out with him last night is absent now.

Slowly, I can feel a bit of colour returning to my cheeks and I clear my throat to find my voice.

"Listen...," - *blast, what's his name again?* - "aah, I'm fine. It must've been something I ate. Listen, I really want a shower, so can you please just let yourself out?" I feel the confident mask slip into place, and I revel in its familiarity. It comforts me.

The guy's lips twitches and his eyes appear to be laughing at me. "You don't remember my name, do you?" he asks me, still standing in the doorway.

Now I blush, trying to ignore the fact that I'm as naked as they come, something I don't really like to be the morning after a night of sex. "No, sorry, I don't," I apologise.

He shrugs as if he doesn't mind and leans against the doorway. "Well, I guess we *were* rather drunk last night, so I don't blame you. It's Kristian." He holds a hand out to me, and I can't help but give him a small smile; this is ridiculous. Here we are, on an early Saturday morning, stark naked, having shared a very steamy night together, but we don't know each other, and we won't ever get to that point, because I won't let it happen.

Shaking his hand, I say, "Kristian. Well, it's been fun, but I feel pretty awful, so...?"

He releases my hand quickly, like he's been zinged, and runs it through his hair. "Right. I'll get going, then. Hope you feel better soon. And...thanks for last night." A wicked grin plays on his mouth as he waggles his eyebrows, and I now remember why I brought him home with me: he has nice brown eyes, and a smile that's sure to make plenty of girls' knickers fall as quick as a heartbeat.

Well, take me, for example: Exhibit A.

I move back and start to close the door. "Get home safe, Kristian. It's been...great." Then I'm alone. I quickly turn to the shower and pray there's plenty of hot water left.

As the water cascades down over my face and my body, I slowly begin to feel warm again, and the last remnants of the nightmare leave me. *At least until the next time.*

Thinking back on my hook-up with Kristian last night, I snort and shake my head. I'd been to a posh club downtown, sipping on a drink at the bar when he'd sat down beside me and told me his name before offering to buy me a new one.

"I buy my own drinks, thank you." I'd smiled cheekily at him while taking another sip of my gin & tonic.

He chuckled and waved a finger at the bartender

standing close by.

"Well, then," Kristian said. "May I join you?"

I placed a hand on his arm, subtly leaning my body closer to his, pushing out my boobs in the process.

"Of course. I like the look of you."

Kristian blinked before bursting out with laughter, and I smiled confidently at him, satisfied with my choice for the night.

He turned his body closer to mine and then asked if I wanted to dance with him. Instead of answering him, I stood up, took his hand in mine and led him onto the dance floor, picking a perfect spot amidst other young, drunk people that were out to have a good time. I turned and put my arms around his neck, shamelessly plastering my body to his, and when he wrapped his arms around my waist, I made sure to run my fingers through his longish hair as we became lost in the music pulsing around us. It didn't take long before I let the beat of the rhythm take over, and, as usual, the alcohol flowing through my body helped loosening me up, and I became bolder. When I ran my tongue lightly up his neck, he hummed, grabbing my arse while pressing his erection into my tummy, and I knew then that I'd found the man who would be able to dull the need in me for sex.

Men can be so easy. All I have to do to catch their attention is to act with confidence, bat my eyes a bit, and stop holding back from touching their bodies even if I don't particularly enjoy that part in the beginning of my seduction. Once I'm lost in the throes of passion, it's a different story altogether, because I have one goal in mind alone. Chasing the fire coursing through my veins until I reach the end, my need quenched once more.

Kristian was no different than the rest of them, but I have

to admit that he left me feeling more satisfied, physically that is, than many of them have done in the past.

I open the door to the bathroom and turn the corner into my small kitchen, and I find a note on the counter next to the coffee machine. A small sigh escapes me as I move closer, because I'm almost certain of the words I'll find jotted down there.

I continue to dry my hair with a towel as I pick up the note. It says,

"I thought you might want some coffee when you'd finished your shower.

I'd like to see you again, Emma, so please ring me.

-Kristian."

I don't even bother to look at the phone number scrawled below his name before crumbling the note and throwing it away in the bin under the kitchen sink. I know I won't see Kristian again, because that's not what I do: one night, one hook up, and that's all you'll ever get from me.

Still, it's nice that he went to the trouble of making me coffee. As I take the first sip, I imagine my mum's voice berating me, *"How on earth can you bear to drink that without any sugar or milk?"*

For the first time this morning, I feel more like myself again.

I move into my small bedroom-slash-living room, ignoring the state of the bed for now, and go to the windows overlooking the common lawn. Dawn is breaking, and I open the door leading out to my balcony, breathing in the fresh air.

As I stare at the sun and listen to the birds waking up, I

whisper, "Because tea is for the innocents, and I haven't been innocent for a really long time, mum..."

Sipping on my coffee, I think back on the past year, and a sense of contentment fills me. This small flat finally feels like a home to me even though I miss my parents back in Oxford in the UK. Deciding to become a foreign exchange student at the University of Copenhagen wasn't an easy decision to make, something that still baffles my mum in particular a great deal. Why the heck would I leave my own country and move to *Denmark*, of all places?

Good question. And I'm not too sure I know the answer myself. All I know is that I needed to leave my past behind, thus my country, but I didn't want to be too far away from my mum and dad. I mean, they're only a couple of flight hours away, so, really, it's not so bad. Plus, the university has some pretty interesting courses to a student of English such as me. The climate is pretty much the same as in the UK, so I don't really feel too homesick that often.

Leaning my back on the door to my balcony, I take in my home away from home. I rent a one-bedroom flat on the outskirts of the city centre which is owned by the university. Its best features are a) the big closet that covers an entire wall, and b) the bathroom. There's no bath, but it's newly renovated, the walls are painted a soft dove-grey, and it just feels very...peaceful. Yes, well, I do spend a lot of time there, so maybe that's just silly of me to think so. I also love the private gardens and that it only takes about 10 minutes by train to get to the city. It's easy and convenient.

Squinting my eyes, I look to the wall farthest to the right, and my good mood takes a plummet. The only downside to such a small flat is the fact that I don't have a real bed; no, instead, I sleep on a pull-out sofa. I know that it's convenient, what with my place being the size that it is, but it's really uncomfortable. I'm not too sure my body appreciates it, either, but it can't be helped. Alas, such is the life of a poor student: sacrifices must be made.

I have a brother, Steven, who is five years older than me. Growing up, we weren't exactly close; in fact, we fought like cats and dogs all the time. I don't miss him like I miss my parents, and we only exchange sporadic, casual texts every few months. In some really weird way, I suppose I feel obligated to keep in touch with him, but I'd actually much rather just forget he exists. After all, we don't have anything in common, so why bother keeping up the pretenses?

When I'm not attending classes, I spend a lot of my time with the one close friend I've managed to get here in Denmark. Her name's Suzanne, and she's my complete opposite: she laughs a lot, has the *best* fashion sense ever, and she's always on the run, busy with some kind of project. More importantly, though, is the fact that she always seems able to know when there are things I don't want to talk about. She simply lets me be even though I know it must be frustrating for her. One day, I'll explain my reasons to her, but not just yet...

Seeing as I'm mostly here on scholarships, I have to work when I'm not studying; living expenses are quite high, and I've managed to find a job in a small bookshop called "*Andersen's Books*". I work there a couple of hours every day, except on Sundays when it's closed, and I absolutely *love* it. I was a bit worried when I first got here, what with the language barrier, but after taking a couple of language courses, not forgetting Suzanne's help as well, I can really feel that my vocabulary has improved while working at the shop. Also, the customers seem to understand my need for them to ask their questions a bit more slowly sometimes, and I really appreciate it.

Kristian enters my thoughts again...he truly *was* a nice bloke. There are times, such as this morning, when I wonder *if* my single status should change, but as I take the final sip of my coffee, I dismiss it as always. I don't do relationships...It's just not for me, so let's leave it at that. I'm sure you're now thinking that my story is a typical one, but like I said earlier...you don't have a clue.

CHAPTER TWO

EMMA

DESPITE THE USUAL NIGHTMARE, and the fact that I'm a bit hungover, there's a certain air about this morning that makes me smile. I can't put my finger on it, but I can feel that this is going to be a really good day. Maybe it's just because it's summer and the weather is nice and warm without a cloud in the sky as far as I can see. I know it doesn't have to do with Kristian. He scratched an itch, nothing more.

I rush to the bus stop around the corner which will take me to the nearest train station. I could walk, of course, but I don't have the time. I *hate* being late! I can't stand it, and I usually time it so that I'm at least five minutes early to every appointment or class. If I fail in getting ready on time, I almost break out in a cold sweat. Sounds nuts, doesn't it? Well, that's me for you: a bit nutty. Bonkers. Mad. A control freak. Whatever you want to call it.

Seeing as I'm late, I only give the owner of the small pub - or *bodega*, as the Danes call it - on the other side of the road to my building a small wave, and I yell, "Sorry, Camilla, can't talk! I'm late for work!"

She waves back at me, laughing a bit, "No worries, honey, we'll talk later." She turns back to the task at hand: trying to get the resident homeless guy to eat a sandwich. His name's Fred, and he's probably got his own sad story to tell. I don't know him, exactly, but we always exchange greetings when we're at the pub, and he's a quiet man. Harmless. I'm pretty sure, however, that he's never entirely sober. I know that Camilla makes sure he gets some food in his belly every morning, and I admire her for it.

The bus driver waits for me, and I smile in thanks as I jump in and pick a seat. As I sit down, I pull out my iPod from my clutch and press shuffle. The first song that starts is *Give Me Love* by Ed Sheeran, and I snort – not very ladylike, I know – and I immediately hit forward. *Supermassive Black Hole* by Muse blares out, and I nod in satisfaction. I blame Suzy for meddling with my playlists: she's quite the romantic and completely fanatical about Ed Sheeran. Me? Not so much. If you met me on the street, you'd probably give me a wide berth because of my heavy makeup and visible piercings.

You see, I tend to wear lots of dark eye shadow, and I never step foot outside my flat without a heavy dose of either that or eyeliner. And I mustn't forget to mention mascara: that is essential to any woman. As for my style? Well, it's...different, I suppose. Honestly, I usually just put on a pair of jeans and a shirt, and I don't get what all the fuss is about. I mean, sure, the jeans almost always have a bit of glitter or sparkle on them...*and* so does the blouse or cardigan you'll find me wearing. Who cares? It may not fit with my wild, curly hair, the makeup or the piercings - one in the middle of my bottom lip, the other in my right eyebrow - but come on! Every girl needs a bit of glitter in her life...even one like me.

Today, though, I've put on a cute, flowy, red skirt with a wide black belt, and I'm wearing a loose-fitted yellow T-shirt. On my feet are a pair of my most comfortable, yet stylish, peep-toed black sandals. And yes, they do have a bit of glitter on them.

The bus stops at the train station and I quickly run up to the platform. The trains leave every few minutes, but I really don't want to miss the one that's about to shut its doors; I run faster and just manage to squeeze in, and I sigh in relief. My inner control freak nods her head, and I smile spontaneously to an elderly woman sitting to the right of the entrance. She doesn't smile back, though, so I ignore her sour stare and move further inside. I don't bother with finding a seat because I'll only be going a few stops.

The Fighter by Gym Class Heroes plays loudly in my ears, and I'm looking out the window at the landscape passing me by when I feel someone grabbing onto my arm. I startle, lost in my own thoughts, and turn around to see a somewhat cute but also disheveled bloke lying flat on his back in front of me.

I pull out the headphones and am just about to speak when he yells in Danish, "Oh, for shite's sake!" He struggles to get on his feet so I reach out to him and ask, "Are you alright?"

He grabs my outstretched hand and sighs irritably before he struggles to his feet.

"Thanks," he says, and now that he's up, he towers over me, so I quickly take a step back. "I'm fine, just a bit...clumsy," he continues, and he's got quite the blush going for him.

I try to suppress my laugh by coughing, but I don't think I pull it off, and he looks embarrassed.

"Don't worry about it," I reassure him. "Everybody's clumsy sometimes." I look down at his feet to avoid his eyes. "It seems like one of your shoelaces is the culprit."

As he quickly reaches down to tie it, his backpack slides over his head, and he curses under his breath. Now that he's preoccupied, I try to get a proper look at him: he has very dark hair, almost black, and he's a bit gangly. When he looks up at me, still blushing, I notice that he has green eyes but they are hidden behind some pretty awful horn-rimmed glasses. When he straightens again, I smile politely, and he looks more closely at me. His penetrating stare unnerves me, and I feel uneasy. I'm not in the mood for small talk, and, as if some higher being is listening in, the movements of the train slows down, and I look out the window.

I turn back to him and say brightly, "Well, this is the end of my journey."

I rush out the doors before he can stop me. I faintly hear him shout *"Wait"* behind me, but I ignore him and walk quickly away, heading for my workplace. Yes, he was cute, in some sort of nerdy way, but unnerving at the same time. Something about him tugged at a hidden place inside me - and I don't mean my lady bits, thank you very much - and I don't have the time or the desire to examine it further.

"Get a grip, Emma," I mutter to myself, "You don't need that kind of distraction in your life right now. In fact, you won't ever need it."

Satisfied with my talking-to, I force the geek out of my head and I quickly become lost in the throng of people surrounding me. Like me, they are busy with getting to their own destinations.

One of the things I love about Copenhagen is that the people you see on the streets don't shy away if you catch their eye. Instead they either smile politely, or curse, or perhaps even laugh as you walk past them. True, some people will ignore you, too, and most of them will be lost in their own thoughts, a vacant look in their eyes, but I like that the Danes have this no-nonsense kind of vibe around them. I can't explain it properly. All I know is that it seems they have an ingrained confidence, as if they don't give a toss about how the rest of the world perceives them.

I'm probably wrong about that last part, though…Most of these men and women are most likely just as insecure or as scared of failure as I am.

Nevertheless, perception is key here: where do you think I learned how to make people believe that I'm this really confident, cool chick who does not give a damn about what anyone else thinks?

Yep, I'm such a liar, but the rest of the world doesn't have to know that.

As I walk the final couple of hundred meters to *"Andersen's Books"*, I hear a ping from my phone, and I'm guessing that it's a text from Suzanne.

I take it out of my clutch and swipe the screen. Yep, I'm right. Frowning, I contemplate ignoring her, but only for a split second. Not the reaction you'd expect when getting a text from your best friend, I know, but I can imagine the contents of it. Still, she *is* my BFF, so I really can't ignore her. No, scratch that: I *shouldn't* ignore her. There's a difference. I read her text.

Suzy: You, missy, are in deep trouble!

I cringe, and quickly type a vague response to her.

Me: What do you mean???

As if I didn't know...

I walk more swiftly, and a few seconds pass before I hear another ping:

Suzy: You KNOW what I mean, Emma!!!

Ouch. Shouty capitals, exclamation points, *and* she's using my name? Oh dear, she must be so pissed off at me right now.

I stop a few steps short of the entrance to the bookshop and text her back.

Me: You're right, and I'm sorry. Listen, I'm about to head in for work, can I ring you later?

I can't help but stare at the phone in my hand, chewing and biting my lip ring - a nervous habit of mine that I've never been able to get rid of - and anxiously wait for her reply

Suzy: Don't ring me, dummy. Just come on by -- AND bring pizza! AND fries! AND Diet Coke! I'm so hungover that I need all the greasy food I can handle, and I'm thinking I'll get to that point in about 5 hours or so. ;-)

I sigh in relief.

Me: You've got it, honey. Love you! xxx

Finally, I open the door and step inside the shop. *Peace at last.* I paste a smile on my face, ready to face the day.

CHAPTER THREE

EMMA

"SORRY I'M LATE, MR. Andersen," I shout as I shut the door behind me and head to the staff room in the back. We have our own small drawers with a personal key where we can put our belongings when we're at work.

"Don't worry about it," he says from behind me, and I turn around. "But you're usually on time, so I was starting to get a bit worried about you, Emma."

Mr. Andersen is this quiet, older man, probably in his fifties, and his thinning hair is almost completely white. He tends to wear clothes that would have been better suited for a 19th century English lord. Today, he's wearing pale, almost white, trousers, a white shirt and a cream-coloured pullover as well as a black tie. He has brown loafers on his feet. It's an outfit that looks a lot like cricket attire to me, actually. Not that I play cricket, of course, but it is considered the English national sport, apart from football, so I can't help but know a lot about it. Plus, my dad watches it on the telly all the time when it's the season.

"I had a late night and overslept," I explain, and it's a total lie, of course. After having nursed my coffee and getting lost in my gloomy thoughts while listening to the birds chirping about outside on my balcony this morning, I tried to distract myself by cleaning my entire flat. "It won't happen again, I promise," I vow to Mr. Andersen.

"Now, it's perfectly alright, Emma. And when will you stop calling me *Mr. Andersen*, by the way?" His eyes always hold amusement when he asks me this, and today's no different. "I've asked you countless times to simply call me by my birth name, Andreas."

He asks me this very frequently, and my answer is always the same.

I shrug. "I suppose it's the Brit in me: you don't really call your employer by their birth name. Besides, that's not how I was brought up, so I guess it won't ever happen, *Mr. Andersen*." I beam at him.

He shakes his head, smiling wryly. "We had a new delivery come in after you left yesterday. Mind getting these new books sorted and settled in? I know you enjoy that particular part of the job." He turns to go out into the shop and I quickly follow him.

"Of course." I nod even though he can't see me. "I'd love to. And yes, you're right, I love opening the crates, seeing what hidden gems lie in wait for the world to discover." Excitement bubbles inside me, popping wildly in my tummy. "I mean, it feels like it's either my birthday or Christmas when new books arrive!"

I know I sound nuts, but what can I say? I'm a bookaholic.

Mr. Andersen laughs and pulls out his pipe from his pocket - it's not lit, of course, but you never see him without it. "Good." He turns away. "I'll be at the front desk if you need to ask me anything."

I nod, satisfied with the task before me, and I head to the storage room.

I don't know that much about Mr. Andersen even though I've worked at his shop for almost a year. I'm not even sure if he's married or not. I know that his favourite author is Sir Arthur Conan Doyle - the man who invented Sherlock Holmes – and I also know that he used to be an English professor at the university.

But I don't know the story of how he came to be a bookshop owner. I once tentatively asked him about it, but only received a cryptic answer from him: *"Life tends to offer a person certain opportunities he never even contemplated on pursuing. And sometimes you're forced to reinvent yourself and take a different path than the one you had in mind."*

A quiet and cryptic man indeed.

When I open the first box of books in front of me, the memory of the day I applied for a job here suddenly pops into my head. I was really nervous because I thought he would simply take one look at me and show me to the door.

I didn't speak much Danish at the time, so when I haltingly asked if he was looking for an employee, he stared at me for longer than is usually considered polite.

Finally, he asked me, "Do you like to read books? I mean, *real* books, and not simply graphic novels?" and I nodded. Then he said, "I need someone who loves to get lost in the world of a great novel; one who appreciates the words an author has poured out of his soul in order to write his story; and one who likes to help other people come to the same conclusion: that books are everything. *Are* you that person?" He looked at me as if he wished he could read my mind.

I was a bit puzzled by Mr. Andersen's way of thinking, but I needed money in my pocket, so I replied with confidence. "Absolutely. I promise that my Danish will improve over time, too. I've just recently moved here from the UK, but I'm a quick learner and can be a great employee, Sir."

He shook his head. "That doesn't matter, really. Actually, most of the books I sell are in English, and I have many customers who aren't Danish. The question is, plain and simple, if you are passionate about books?"

Again, I nodded.

He looked lost in thought for a moment, and then the biggest smile lit up his face as he clapped his hands. "Good!" he exclaimed. "When would you like to start?"

I began working for him the next day, and I have loved the job ever since.

The bookshop isn't big, but it's not small, either. It has a square floor plan, and all the surrounding walls are covered with rows and rows of books. In the middle of the room, there are a couple of old leather armchairs as well as two coffee tables. To me, it gives the customer the idea that you're almost in a library and that you can sit down and relax for a while before getting on your way. We even have a small vending machine offering hot chocolate, coffee, or tea.

I think the front desk is an older antique: it's huge, made of mahogany, and the most fascinating twirls and shapes can be seen on all four sides of it as well as on the legs. Even to my untrained eye, it shows great craftsmanship, and I'd love to know who the artist is. Mr. Andersen doesn't seem to have any idea about him or her, either, so I suppose we'll always be left in the dark. And maybe it doesn't really matter, in the large scheme of things, who built it.

The storage room is situated at the end of the wall to the right that's closest to the entrance. There's a door separating it from the shop, of course, and Mr. Andersen and I are the only ones who have a key.

That's where I am now, opening boxes and pulling out these beautiful books that are all waiting to find new homes. I'm pretty excited about seeing the latest book by Deborah Harkness here. *The Book Of Life* has been on the top of my reading list for a long time now, and I wonder if Mr. Andersen will let me buy a copy.

Another reason why I'm so happy to be working here is the fact that Mr. Andersen usually doesn't want me to pay for a book I take a fancy to. I mean, how many employers are that kind to their staff? Well, I do try to convince him to at least deduct the costs of the books from my wages, but he won't hear of it. His usual response is: *"Now, please don't reject a gift, Emma. It shows poor manners."* And that always makes me laugh so I give in. Can't object to that kind of reasoning, can you?

Mr. Andersen pokes his head inside the room. "It's almost lunch time so I'm just going to pop around the corner and buy a sandwich. Do you want one?"

My stomach growls loudly, answering for me, and I smile. "Yes, please. Just no -"

"No ham, I know," he interrupts me, laughter in his voice.

I give him the thumbs-up. "Exactly."

"I've never met anyone who objects so much to a piece of

pork," he says and shakes his head. "Mind the desk, please?"

"Sure." I leave the storage room, locking it behind me, before heading to the desk. There's a lull in the shop, but I know we'll be busy in an hour or so.

I go to the coffee tables and clear it. *Someone doesn't like Mr. George W. Bush*, I think to myself as I pick up a biography about him. *Well, can't say I disagree.*

As I head to the Autobiography section, the bell above the door rings, and I call out, "Be with you in a moment!" I quickly find the correct spot for the former American president and head back to the desk.

"Hello, how may I help -?" My voice falters, and I come to an abrupt standstill when I see the customer who just walked in.

Geek guy from the train? *Of all the luck...*

My defense mechanism kicks in, and I smile brightly at him as I say, "Well, hello again. Tripped over your feet some more since we last saw each other?" Oh god, I *did not* just say that, did I? Heat burns my cheeks as if I'd stood close to the fire.

I hurry to apologise. "I'm so sorry, that was really rude of me. Please forget I said that. How may I help you?"

The guy blushes – *again*! It's pretty adorable, really, but it must be so annoying for him if that happens all the time.

"Err...hi," he stammers. "I've managed to stay vertical since the train, actually. It's quite a feat for me, not having fallen flat on my face more than once today, I mean." He smirks at me, still blushing, and I snort.

"I'm really sorry," I repeat cheerfully. "Happens to me all the time, too," I try to reassure him, and I move closer to him.

"Really?" he asks hopefully.

I can't contain my mask, and I laugh. "No, not really.

How would I be able to wear high heels if that were the case?" I lift my foot and twist it a bit so that he can see my sandals.

He sighs, and you can almost see the way his whole body seems to deflate. I take pity on him and quickly add, "But I used to be a real klutz when I was a child."

He scratches his neck and looks down at his feet, mumbling, "Not really helping me overcome my embarrassment here."

"Oh." I sober a bit, clearing my throat. I can tell how uncomfortable he is and I mentally berate myself for putting my big, shiny stiletto foot in my mouth. "Of course not. Let's try this again, shall we?" I move closer to the front desk where he's standing. "Hello. Can I help you find something in particular?"

Geek Guy puffs a little, running a hand through his hair. "Is the Professor here?"

"The Professor?" I frown, confused.

"Yes, you know, Mr. Andersen?" He gives me an odd look, seemingly baffled that I don't know who he's referring to.

"Oh!" I exclaim. "Of course, Mr. Andersen. No, he's not here at the moment, sorry. He just went around the corner to buy us some lunch, though, so I'm sure he'll be back in a few minutes."

"He's my uncle," Geek Guy explains, and he extends his hand to me. "I'm Daniel."

I hesitate a bit before clasping his hand firmly in mine. "Nice to meet you, Daniel. My name's Emma."

"Emma...," he repeats my name, and I jerk my hand free of his. This is getting a bit uncomfortable for me.

"You're not Danish, are you?" Daniel then blurts out, and I give him a small smile, relieved. This is more familiar ground to me.

"No, I'm originally from England, but I've been living in Denmark and attending the university for the past year now. I hope my accent isn't too horrible?" I smile teasingly.

Daniel smiles shyly back at me. "No, it's not bad...I mean, you're actually really good at it. I hear Danish is one of the worst languages to learn. Is that true?" He leans a hip on the desk, definitely settling in to chat, and I start to fidget. I don't mind small talk, but I don't do it with guys. Even if it's one with the most beautiful green eyes I've ever seen. I wish Mr. Andersen would get back soon, and I look down at the nail polish on my toes to avoid his probing gaze.

"It is a really difficult language, yes," I answer, distracted by the bell over the door ringing and I turn my eyes to the door. *Customers, yay!*

"If you'll excuse me," I quickly say to Daniel, and he nods as I pass him.

I greet the customers - an older couple in their seventies who frequent the shop a lot - and try to ignore Daniel's stare. I can feel it burning my back, and I'm guessing that he's caught sight of the ten small stars tattooed on my lower neck. Ten is my lucky number, but it serves as a reminder as well.

"Emma, it's nice to see you again," the older man, Mr. Sorensen, says to me, and he shakes my hand briefly. I don't really like being this touchy-feely with customers, but this man and woman are old-fashioned in many ways and seem to appreciate the formality, so I try not to let it show that I'm a bit uncomfortable. His wife has already moved to the romance section, and she gives me a small, distracted wave before her eyes start to peruse the shelves. These are some of my favourite customers: they always take time to ask about me and my studies, and even though I don't exactly tell them much, they always seem glad to hear about the goings-on of my life.

"The same to you, Sir." I smile warmly at him. "Are you looking for something in particular today?"

"Well, yes, and we really need your help. You see, our son is moving to Greenland this fall – he's got a teaching position there – and my wife and I were hoping to find a really good book about the country for him. Something a bit out of the ordinary. Do you think you can help us out?"

I take a moment to think about his request. "Hmm...Well, I do believe we have a very beautiful coffee-table-book that might interest you. Let me fetch it for you."

"Ah, perfect. Thanks so much, Emma." Mr. Sorensen moves closer to his wife while I find the book I'm thinking about.

The bell above the entrance sounds again, and I quickly look up to see Mr. Andersen walk through it, food in hand. When he notices Daniel, his step falters for a beat in surprise, but then he hurries towards him.

"Daniel!" He smiles and the two men hug each other. "When did you get here?" Mr. Andersen moves back, giving Daniel the once-over, and I can tell that he's pleased to see his nephew from the way his eyes lit up when he saw him.

"Well, I've been here about 10 minutes, if that's what you meant," Daniel laughs. "Though, if you were thinking more about when I came to Copenhagen, I would have to admit that I've only been here 24 hours."

"A bit overwhelmed, are you?" Mr. Andersen asks Daniel. "Well, I'm so glad you stopped by." He turns around and calls out to me. "Emma, will you be alright for another half an hour? Need to do some catching up with my nephew here."

"Of course. Take your time." I don't look at Daniel even though I can sense his eyes on me again, heating and prickling on my skin.

Mr. Andersen takes Daniel by the arm and directs him to our staff room, and as they move past me, Daniel manages to catch my eye. He gives me a small smile, but I quickly turn away and head back to my customers, carrying the chosen book in my arms.

"Now, Mr. and Mrs. Sorensen, this is what I had in mind..."

"Thank you so much for your help, Emma," Mrs. Sorensen says as I open the door for her. "I do believe you've found the perfect present. Again! Oh, and I appreciate you getting that new book by Nora Roberts out of storage for me. You're really good at finding new romance novels for me to sink my teeth into." She laughs, and I join in.

"It's always a pleasure, Mrs. Sorensen. I hope you enjoy the rest of your weekend." I hand her the bag with the gift as well as the two romance novels they also bought. Mr. Sorensen shakes his head, but smiles affectionately at his wife.

He nods at me. "And the same to you. Thank you." He places a hand to the back of his wife, nudging her along, and she smiles widely at him as they leave the shop.

I wave at them before shutting the door and can't help but feel a bit envious when I see Mr. Sorensen take his wife's hand as they walk away. *What must it be like to feel so much love when you get to be that age?*

For once, I almost regret not being a romantic. Life has shown me too much ugliness for me to believe in fairytales, but every now and then, I wonder about the loving couples I see walking around the streets. They laugh, kiss, or simply look at each other in such an intimate way that I feel as if I'm an intruder to their show of affection. And I also feel saddened by it...because I know I'll never have that.

My stomach growls again. It's getting quite angry with me, and I hope it won't be long before Mr. Andersen and Daniel are finished with their talk.

I'm just about to leave the front desk to grab myself a cup of coffee when I hear the door to the staff room opening. Male laughter erupts, and my shoulders sag in relief.

"Emma, I'm so sorry," Mr. Andersen apologises as the two of them come closer. "You must be famished! Please feel free to take your lunch break now. I got the hummus sandwich for you, by the way."

Warmness fills me at his nice gesture. "You spoil me, Mr. Andersen. You know it's my favourite." I look at Daniel, and what do you know? He blushes again! As if he was a fifteen-year-old schoolboy.

"It was nice to meet you, Daniel," I acknowledge him politely as I pass him.

"Likewise," he mumbles, and I'm just about to shut the door when his next words halt me in my tracks. "I'll see you on Monday."

Shocked, I turn back and look at him, mouth agape. "What?" I ask dumbly.

Mr. Andersen jumps in. "Daniel here will be joining us in the shop, Emma."

I look closely at my boss, and even though I can tell that

he's pleased with this new addition to our "family", I can't quite make out his thoughts. Usually, he doesn't hide his emotions, but this time feels different, especially because he suddenly takes an interest to an imaginary thread on his sleeve, avoiding my eyes.

"Oh, I see," I mutter. Then I paste a fake smile on my face as I glance briefly at Daniel. "Well, I'll see you then." Before I say something either snarky or embarrassing - which tends to happen a lot when I feel unnerved - I shut the door quietly and blow out a confused breath once I'm alone.

Suddenly, I don't feel that hungry anymore. I can't put my finger on it, but this news screams *Trouble* to me. It's completely irrational, of course.

I sigh and head to the fridge. It's a good thing Mr. Andersen bought me my favourite sandwich. It'll help to cheer me up.

CHAPTER FOUR

EMMA

AFTER I'VE GOT SOME food in me, I feel so much more positive, and I wonder briefly why I freaked when I learned about Daniel working here. It's probably the nightmare's fault.

I'm filled with renewed energy when I leave the staff room, and I'm back to believing that it's a good day. The way I felt when I left my flat earlier in the day.

Mr. Andersen is talking with some customers, so I head back to the storage room to get the last crates of books sorted. It's nearing four pm when I finish with the last of them, and I'm glad I managed to do it before closing-time. I head back out to the shop, and I smile at Mr. Andersen who's standing by the front desk, leafing through a new John Grisham novel. He looks up when he hears me and smiles back at me.

"All done?" he asks me, and I nod. "Good. Then I guess it's time to close for the day, Emma." He moves to the entrance, and I do the same.

"Do you need me to stay for a bit, Mr. Andersen?"

"No, I'll manage," he reassures me as he locks the door and turns the sign on the door from *Open to Closed*.

"I'll go out the back, then." I head to the staff room to get my clutch and phone and I check the screen for messages, seeing a new text from my friend:

Suzy: Hurry up, honey, I'm hungry! ;-) xxx

I smile big. She really is a great friend, and my guilty conscience rears its ugly head again. Ugh.

When I get back, I find Mr. Andersen staring out the window, a pensive look on his face. His demeanor confuses me, and I can't help but feel that I'm intruding on his thoughts.

I clear my throat to catch his attention, apparently startling him.

"I'll be off now, boss," I say as I turn to the back door.

"What did you think of Daniel?" he suddenly asks me, and I stop and slowly turn around to face him, puzzled by his odd question. This is so strange.

I hesitate, jangling my keys lightly. "I didn't speak with him much," I reply.

He doesn't give up. "But what was your first impression of him?"

"Well, he seems nice." Awkward! my brain screams at me. "A bit of a geek," I try to joke, and Mr. Andersen's intense stare loosens up. Silently, I sigh in relief.

"Yes," he mumbles. "He is nice. And he is a bit of a nerd, I suppose." Now it's Mr. Andersen's turn to hesitate. "Listen, Emma, I don't mean to sound so cryptic, but I know that Daniel could use a friend - being new to the city and far away from home, you know - so I'd really appreciate if you'd make a bit of an effort and get to know him."

I'm dumbfounded. This is so unlike my boss, and I don't

know what to say.

"Well," Mr. Andersen quietly says, "Please just think about it, Emma. Perhaps..." He stops and looks down, hands in his pockets, lost in thought for a moment.

"Sure," I reply lamely.

He looks up and gives me a small smile. "Thank you. Enjoy the rest of your weekend." He lifts a hand in goodbye, and I move to the back once again.

"You, too," I say quietly, and I leave the shop, confusion and apprehension waging war inside me.

What the bloody hell was that?!

Deciding that Mr. Andersen's odd behaviour calls for something stronger than Diet Coke, I buy some white wine to go along with the pizzas. A small voice inside tells me that I really shouldn't but I ignore it. I'm pretty sure Suzy will curse at me for the way I disappeared last night, so the wine serves more than one purpose.

My best friend lives practically around the corner from the shop, and she's actually the one who made me apply for a job there when we met, so I owe her for that. Her favourite pizza place is only a stone's throw away from her home, and I make sure to order an extra pizza in case she wants it. Suzy has given me a key to her flat so I don't have to hit the buzzer every time I visit her. I love her for trusting in me, and I honestly don't know what I'd do without her.

As I walk up the two flights of stairs to her flat, almost dragging my feet, I try to practice what to say to her, but, for once, nothing really comes to mind. I guess I'll just have to wing it, and I cringe. I hate feeling this way, but I don't know what to say to her; I mean, she's heard the same excuses before, and I hate myself for lying to her.

I stand in front of the door and take a couple of deep breaths. When I feel my confident mask slipping into place, I'm relieved, and I give a quick knock before opening the door.

"Hi, honey! Don't worry, I've got lots of pizza and fries to satisfy that hunger of yours!"

Suzy comes out of the kitchen to the left of the small hall, a frown marring her face. "You look worn out," she scolds me and gives me a quick hug.

"Well, thanks for that," I reply sarcastically as I follow her into the huge living room. Her flat is bigger than mine, but it has more like an open floor plan. I know that her dad tore down one of the walls when he bought it for her, and it was a good idea: you never feel closed-in here.

"Where do you want to eat?" I ask her and throw my clutch on her big leather couch that takes up the wall to our right.

"Let's just eat here," she replies. "I can't be bothered with setting the table tonight," she sighs and slumps down in her armchair.

I take pity on her as I scurry to the kitchen. "I'll get the plates and forks". As a bonus, it gives me some more time before she launches into her interrogation. There's a certain tension in the air, and I know the storm is coming. That doesn't mean I won't try to avoid it for as long as possible, though.

"Don't forget to bring glasses," she shouts to me as I open her cabinets.

As I walk back with everything on a tray, I find her in the same position I left her in. *Damn, it's a really bad one.*

"Don't think that just because I feel as if an elephant is currently trampling on my head and I can't really move, I won't be laying into you soon," she warns me, and I sigh.

"I know," I reply quietly. "I'm really sorry, Suzy." I put the tray on her coffee table and silently set the table. I can't look her in the eye, and I know she's well aware of the fact that I'm trying to evade her.

She huffs in frustration. "I know that, Emma, but that doesn't make it okay. You're always sorry the day after. I really don't understand you sometimes."

I venture a look at her. The sadness in her eyes causes the guilt inside me to intensify. Her usual immaculate self is rumpled, and she hasn't bothered with make-up for once. Her blonde locks have been put up in a messy bun, and her tanned complexion isn't as noticeable today.

I sit down on the couch and remove my sandals before tucking my feet under me.

"Listen, Suzy, -"

"No, Emma, you listen to me for once: You drink too much, you party too hard, and you disappear when we're out. One minute, you're there, laughing with me, and the next you're just gone." I cringe as she soldiers on, "I end up spending most of the night looking for you or texting you. And I get scared, okay?" She finishes on a sniffle. *Oh no, not the tears!*

"I know you won't tell me much about your past," she whispers, and my body freezes automatically as I hold my breath while my heart rate picks up speed, racing away. I'm terrified if *this* is the moment I have dreaded for so long. Has she reached her breaking point? Will she no longer retreat? I force my face to remain blank as I wait for her to go on, yet pinch my lips tightly to keep the trembling locked down. "But

I love you and worry about you, okay? So if you can't talk to me about whatever demons that haunt you..." She hesitates, so I finally muster up the courage to meet her eyes. She's sitting on the edge of the couch, hands clasped between her knees, her brows furrowed. The hurt in her eyes pierces my chest.

"Well, please talk to someone, Em." She takes my hand in one of hers and wipes away her tears on her sleeve. "Please just think about it, honey. Like I said: I love you, and I don't want to lose you." She stares hard at me before releasing her hold on me. "Lecture over, I promise. Now, let's eat." She opens one of the pizza boxes and takes out a piece.

I automatically nod my head, but I can feel that I'm not really there anymore. My thoughts have gone down a dark route, and I feel as if I'm about to throw up.

"Hey," Suzy quietly says, and I move my eyes back to hers. She's gobbling up her pizza in big mouthfuls, and I'm happy to see some colour return to her cheeks.

"I met someone last night," she tells me after she's swallowed a piece, and I'm grateful to call her my friend once more. The tension in my body ebbs slowly. She's finished, and she's giving me space, like always.

I smile slightly. "Interesting. Who's the guy? Or is it a girl this time?" My teasing helps my body relax again.

Suzy blushes. "His name is Thomas, and he's been texting me all day."

"You know," I say, and take the fries out of the bag, "I wouldn't think less of you if it was a girl. I mean, bisexuality is really interesting; might be an idea to try it," I muse and pick up the Diet Coke.

Suzy laughs, and I'm happy to see her bubbling personality is resurfacing. "Yeah, right, as if that'd work for you. Emma, you're so straight, and you'd end up running away, screaming, if a girl put some serious moves on you." She winks. "Take me, for example."

I snort as I remember the first time we met: at a club, of course.

Suzanne laughs some more. "I remember it as if it were yesterday: as soon as I caressed the side of one of your boobs, you became stiff as a board and you almost spit out your Cosmopolitan." She wrinkles her nose. "I really thought you'd fancy me," she sighs mockingly. "And *then* you started blabbering on and on about some weird novelist in the 18th century, and I knew you were a lost cause."

I feel warmness returning to my body. "I'd so fancy you if I were gay, sweetie, you know that."

Suzy takes another piece of pizza, a smug expression on her face. "I know. I'm a hot babe." She winks lewdly at me, and I giggle.

"You *so* are, honey." I switch to English because I can feel my tired brain can't take anymore Danish for today. "I love you, always and forever."

When my throat begins to close up with suppressed emotions, I cough lightly. "Right, enough of this. I promise to think hard about what you've said. But now I need details! Who's Thomas and does he have a gorgeous friend I can borrow for a night of wild monkey sex?" I take a big bite of pizza and moan as the delicious flavours hit my tastebuds, and I lick some sauce from my lips.

Suzy smiles and picks up her glass. "Well, this is what he's told me so far…"

As my friend begins to talk about her new possible love interest, I listen attentively, but a thought niggles in my mind at the same time.

Is it time to stop hiding?

I decide to push the thought away, for now at least, and I make an effort to only pay attention to my friend's news the rest of the evening.

CHAPTER FIVE

EMMA

IT'S SUNDAY - THE BANE of my existence. I always have trouble filling the day, but it's easier to do when I'm at university and working at the book shop; now that it's summer and classes don't start up again for another two months, I have way too much time on my hands.

Suzy told me last night that she plans on seeing Thomas today, so I can't really text her and find out if she wants to meet up.

I sigh as I lie in bed. Well, at least I didn't dream last night. Hoorah! I look at the clock, and I curse at the early hour: seven am. How typical: it's summer, I'm young, and I don't have classes, but do I manage to sleep in? Nooo, of course not. I turn on the TV that hangs on the wall opposite my bed, but after zapping through the channels twice, not finding anything remotely interesting to watch, I groan and get out of bed.

The trouble with me is that once I wake up, I can't lounge in the bed for hours like some people are able to do. I have to get up, I have to move, and I really can't stand it if I don't get to brush my teeth quickly enough.

Yep, I'm weird, I know. Deal with it.

I scrutinise my makeup-free face in the bathroom mirror as I go through my usual routine. My friend's words hover in the back of my mind, but I refuse to acknowledge them. I will, however, cut back on the drinking because I know Suzanne's right: I do drink too much.

Why is it that we always seem to overindulge even when we know it's wrong? At least I don't do drugs anymore.

Okay, this morning sucks already, and I mentally slap my cheek and try to force my thoughts to more pleasant things. Such as...Daniel. *Uh-oh, not going there, either.* That intense stare of his was a bit strange, but even worse is how my belly flips wildly when I think about him. My curiosity is piqued because I have never before felt like that when I met a guy, not even when I'm on the prowl, looking for my next hook-up.

The words of my boss come to mind, and I reflect on his request. Sure, it can't hurt to befriend his nephew, and I suppose I could always use another friend. It can't be healthy that I only have Suzy to rely on, can it? And if I *do* want something to do, I guess I can always offer to be his tour guide.

Pleased with my resolve, I turn on the shower before walking to my iPod station. I can't decide exactly on what to listen to, so I press shuffle. And I immediately groan when I hear the song: *"Need You Now"* by Lady Antebellum.

"Suzy, honestly!" I mutter, but something prevents me from pushing down on the forward button like I usually do. I listen closely to the lyrics.

"Huh. This song isn't too bad," I say out loud, and

without thinking too much about it, I head to the shower, not bothering with closing the door behind me.

♡

Turning this way and that as I put on some clothes, looking more closely at my body, the thought about getting another tattoo comes back to me. I have three already: the ten stars on the back of my neck, and I also wear the Celtic symbol of the Tree Of Knowledge on the inside of my left wrist. My first tat was some hideous tribal tattoo I have on my lower back. I don't know *what* I was thinking when I got that one, though, so I plan on getting it covered up at some point.

There's a certain design I'd love to wear on my body, and I've been saving up for it for a while now. It's a dream catcher with blue feathers, and I want it on my left side, starting from the side of my breast, down my ribs, and ending at my hip bone. To tell the truth, I'm a bit nervous about having it done, because I know that the size of such a tattoo, and at that part of my body, will hurt a great deal. Yes, getting a tattoo isn't a walk in the park, I know that. But the tattoos I already have are small, and they didn't take long for the artists to make, so that's why I'm hesitating about this latest one.

As I put on a tank top, I promise myself that I'll have made up my mind about it by the end of the summer. I love the symbolism of having a dream catcher on me forever. I could use the help of some unseen force to take away my nightmares.

♡

I'm sitting outside on my balcony, enjoying my coffee and breakfast, when I hear the familiar ping of my phone I have lying beside me. I look at it and mutter, "Shite." It's from my brother.

Steven: Hey, little sis. Are you enjoying your summer?
Well, there goes my positive thinking for the day.

I know he'll keep texting me if I don't reply, so I quickly type back, my hands clammy with apprehension.

Me: Much. How are you?

A couple of seconds pass and I stare unseeingly down on the park. But then I notice a couple, obviously lovers, is sitting on one of the benches, smooching and whispering. Yuck. I turn away from them, and my heart begins to race the longer I have to wait for Steven's reply.

The ping makes me jump, though, and I swipe the screen to see what he says.

Steven: I'm good. Listen, the office is sending me on a business trip to Copenhagen in two months, so can we meet up while I'm there?

"Fuck!" I shout, and I cover my eyes with a hand. I *really* don't want to see him...but if I refuse, he'll just tell mum and dad about it, and then the shite will really hit the fan. The rift between us hurts them, I know, but that's Steven's fault. Not mine.

I take a couple of deep breaths.

Me: Sure. Just text me a couple of dates, and we'll have lunch. I'll fake some kind of illness on the day and then he won't be able to do anything about it.

I wait for his reply, sipping on my coffee. I refuse to let the nausea win this time. I chance a look down at the lovers, and both of them are so lost in each other, I very much doubt they heard me cursing before. When the next text lights up my screen, I quickly read it:

Steven: Great! I'm looking forward to seeing you. I

really want to talk with you about something important.

"Ugh," I mutter. "Yeah, yeah, you always say that, big brother."

Me: Okay, fine. See you in two months.

I hit *send* one last time and quickly stand, gathering up my things to head back inside my flat. I've left a whole piece of toast with cheese and jam, but I can't force anymore food in me.

That's what my brother does, causing me to lose my appetite.

I quickly clear away the dishes, my movements jerky as edginess overcomes me, and I know I have to get out of the flat for a while. I can't stay inside all day. Besides, it'd be a shame to do that seeing as it's another beautiful summer's day.

I stand in front of my closet, wondering about what to wear, when I hear a new text.

"Honestly?!" This day really sucks. But I relent and look at the caller ID: ***Unknown***, it says, and I frown.

I swipe the screen and read the text:

Hi, this is Daniel. The Professor gave me your number. Can I come over to your place?

"What the fuck?!" I'm completely taken by surprise, and I think a whole minute passes before I text back:

Me: Actually, now's not a good time. I'm headed out for the day. I huff, and I can't help but crossing my fingers that Daniel will take the not-so-subtle hint that I don't want to see him.

A knock follows, and I jump. What on Earth?

I look down at myself and curse: great, I'm only wearing yoga pants, and my ample bosom is just begging for a guy to zone in on it now that it's bra-less and close to falling out of my grey top. Also, I haven't even put on any of my usual make-up - blast!

I stand there for a couple of seconds, undecided, until the door bell rings, and I walk quickly to the peep hole. Who do I find? Daniel, of course.

"*Shite!*" I yell, and I cover my mouth, cringing.

"I can hear you, you know," he says, and - yep, you guessed it: a blush forms on his neck.

I frown, contemplating on being the rude Goth girl many people mistake me for, and tell Daniel to go away, but an ingrained sense of being polite takes over. Plus it's Mr. Andersen's nephew, so he'll only think my behaviour mighty strange if he hears about this.

"Sod it," I whisper, and I unlock the door and stare hard at the unwanted guest standing before me now.

"Don't you think it's pretty rude to just show up at some person's doorstep? At an address not given to you by said person?" I snap.

"Ummm..." He seems taken aback by my questions. "Didn't my uncle tell you that he'd given me your number? Or that I've moved in right next door?"

Wait, what the what?

"What?!" I shriek, and he looks even more nervous now. Then, lo and behold, his eyes zero in on my boobs. *Typical!*

I snap my fingers in front of his face, and he immediately raises his eyes, swallowing audibly.

"Hey!" I say. "My eyes are up here." I narrow my own, but then I sigh and take a step back. "Listen, Mr. Andersen told me that you'd just moved here a few days ago, but he didn't say anything about you now being my neighbour. So forgive me if I sound rude, but I'm really confused about why you're here, okay?"

He nods. "Sure, I understand." He puts his hands in his pockets, and we stare silently at each other for a while. *Those eyes*...I snap out of this unusual kind of daydreaming on my part.

"Okay," I finally say. "How about you give me 10 minutes to get some more decent clothes on, and then come back?"

I try to smile at him, but I can't. I really don't get what's happening, and I need him to let me be for a bit.

With relief, Daniel smiles at me, clasping his hands behind his back. "No problem. See you soon." He takes a step back, and I quickly shut the door.

As I lean my back on it, I take a deep breath before saying to myself, "Mr. Andersen, what are you playing at?" No voice replies back, of course, and I rush to get ready for Daniel, wondering all the time what he could possibly be doing here.

CHAPTER SIX

EMMA

I'M JUST APPLYING THE last coat of mascara when I hear the expected knock on my door. I sigh and turn my neck from side to side, gearing myself up for whatever Daniel could be up to, and I hurry to get the door for him.

"Hi," I say, and I take a step back, allowing him to come inside.

He remains silent as he walks through and into my living room-slash-bedroom. He takes a look around and I stand in the doorway, unsure of what to do. I look at the time on my phone: it's only ten am. As the silence continues, I become more and more uncomfortable, and I cross my arms in front of me.

"Do you want a soda or something?" I ask him, trying to break the awkward silence.

Daniel turns away from my bookshelf and looks closely at me. I've only put on a pair of capris and a sleeve-less black top, and I haven't put any shoes on. My hair hangs wildly around my face, and I curse at not having the time to do something about it. But then it hits me: *Why do I even care?*

"Just some water, please," he answers, and I go to the kitchen. I hear him follow me and I groan on the inside.

"Listen, Daniel, I really don't know why you're here, so..." I hint as I stand with my back to him, reaching for a glass on the shelf above the sink.

"I know...," he answers, and I can hear how nervous he is.

As I fill a glass of water for him, I turn to him. "Come on, out with it, then." I smile, but I know it doesn't look genuine.

"You put on make-up," he blurts out, and I roll my eyes, fed up with his stalling.

"Yes, I know. So what? Don't get the idea that I did it for you, though. I always wear make-up when I'm around people." I walk closer to him and hand him the glass of water.

"We can sit outside on the balcony," I tell him, and I brush past him.

I take a seat and surreptitiously look down to the hidden pack of cigarettes I keep behind the door as Daniel takes the other chair beside me. I only smoke when I drink, or when I can't fall back to sleep after having a nightmare, but I'm seriously thinking about lighting one up right about now.

Daniel takes a sip of water, and then he sighs. "I need your help," he mumbles, but he doesn't meet my eye. In fact, his entire body language seems withdrawn and definitely embarrassed.

"What do you mean?" I ask him, and I'm more confused than ever.

"Well..." He hesitates before finally manning up and meeting my stare. "I'm dyslexic," he blurts out.

I shrug. "So? Many people are dyslexic, Daniel." My voice softens. "It's nothing to be ashamed about." And it still doesn't tell me anything about why he's here.

He looks away, towards the park across from the complex, and a flush starts to spread on his neck again.

"It is when you are about to study English at the university," he answers back.

"Oh, I see." But I really don't. I mean, I can imagine that it's bound to cause some trouble, and it's far from easy being a student at all these days.

Daniel remains silent, still staring straight ahead. I allow him more time to get to the point, but, finally, I lose patience and ask him, "So why do you need my help?"

He ignores my question. "You know, I'm 24 years old, and I'm just now about to start classes. I'll be considered an "older student", and lots of people will ask me the same questions over and over again; they'll be wondering about me, because, on top of the dyslexic part, I have problems with my speech as well." He looks at me but then turns away again before continuing, "It's not easy for me to look at someone while I talk. I mean, I can't seem to focus on both speaking properly as well as taking in what the person next to me is talking about. So it's not exactly easy being around girls, either. But at least I don't stutter that much anymore." The blush deepens, and I'm beginning to understand why he won't look at me.

I look straight ahead. I might be rude and unable to keep my mouth shut sometimes, but I don't want Daniel to think that I'll just brush him off now that he's opening up to me.

We sit in silence for a while, just taking in the sounds of birds around us. I regret not pouring myself a glass of water now, because the sun is beating down on us, and I can feel small beads of sweat gathering on my neck. I really should think about buying a parasol and setting it up here; the sun can be very brutal to my sensitive skin.

Daniel takes a deep breath. "I need you t...to," he starts to stutter, and he stops talking. I wait again. "I need you to tutor me," he finally gets out, and I'm not sure I follow him.

"Sorry?" I look at him more closely, confused.

"I need a tutor, for the summer, I mean," he says, and finally turns in his seat to look at me properly. His green eyes instantly mesmerise me, but I force myself to appear calm. "Before the university starts up in September, I need a tutor to go through some course material with me." A crooked smile appears on his face, and my tummy begins to flutter. *Oh my...* "And who better to tutor me than a British girl?" he adds softly.

I quickly turn away from his gaze, my thoughts all scattered. This is *not* good! I try to reject him as kindly as possible: "Daniel, I think I understand why *you* think I would be a good tutor, but you are so wrong. I mean, I'm too impatient, I've got absolutely no filter - which, I'm sure, you've already noticed - and to top everything off, I don't have time. I'll be working at your uncle's bookshop full-time all summer." *So there*...yet I still can't look at him.

"It's actually my uncle wh-..." Daniel's voice falters, and I feel bad for him. "My uncle suggested that I ask you," he forces out. "He also said that he'd cover your wages as if you're working at the shop all day even though you'll be tutoring me from noon every day."

"He said *what*?!" I shriek and turn to take in Daniel's profile. "He can't mean that, Daniel. It'd put him in a bind if we leave him on his own." I shake my head. "No, I can't and won't do that to him."

Daniel sighs as he looks down at his slacks, lost in his own thoughts. He rubs his knee absentmindedly.

We're both quiet for some time, and I honestly don't know what to say. In some mysterious, completely ridiculous way, I want to help him, but then I shut down that thought completely. What else can I do? Being around Daniel everyday is bad enough, but also tutoring him? Definitely stupid of me to even consider the notion.

Don't say yes, don't say yes, don't say yes, I chant silently.

A thought occurs to me, and I blurt out, "Why did you move in next door? You don't own the flat, do you?"

Daniel shakes his head. "It turns out Mrs. Hansen wants to go travelling for a while, and she knows The Professor from somewhere. When she mentioned that she was looking for someone to sub-let it while she's away, he thought of me." He hesitates for a bit. "When he gave me your address, I was shocked." He chuckles and looks at me again. "If it wasn't for the fact that I don't believe in these things, I'd call it *fate*."

My mouth pops open. "*Fate*?! Oh no...no-no-no-no. Absolutely not."

Suddenly, some new-found confidence sets in because he winks at me. Um, what?

"That's what I just said. There's no such thing as fate," he replies. Then his smile disappears and he turns away from me. "If fate," he spits the word out, "truly existed, certain things wouldn't happen to really good people."

Right, Daniel is proving to be just as cryptic as his uncle. Yet, there's a small part of me who still wants to help this geeky guy while, at the same time, I feel so on edge.

I stand and walk inside to the coolness of the flat. I can't think while sitting outside in this heat anymore.

I pace the floor, looking down, pondering his request. I huff, irritated with myself, but I'm relieved that Daniel doesn't follow me inside. Somehow, he seems to know that I need some alone time.

One of my very strict rules has always been to keep away from spending too much time with the opposite sex. I don't want to get to *know* men, and yet here's one, sitting right outside on my balcony, who wants me to spend time with him every single day?

Ugh. I am going to regret this, I know it.

I stop pacing in front of my bookshelves and call out, "Daniel?"

I stand with my back to the balcony but turn around when I can hear him move towards me. He looks really nervous again.

"I need time to think about this," I tell him.

His smile is blinding. "Of course, I understand perfectly. Just text me later when you've come to a decision, okay?"

I nod and go to my front door, and he quickly follows behind me.

I turn the lock and open the door. "I will." I venture another look in his eyes, and I can feel a blush starting in my cheeks. *Hang on, what is happening here? This isn't me!*

"Thanks." He walks out, leaving me alone.

As soon as I've locked the door, I run to my coffee table to grab my phone. I swipe the screen and quickly find Suzy's number.

I type a text, my fingers fumbling.

Me: You will NOT believe what just happened!

I hit *send* and head for the kitchen. My throat is parched, and I'm dying for a drink. *This is bad, this is really bad.*

Only a few seconds pass before I get a text back.

Suzy: Well, if you're about to say you went clubbing after you left me last night and ended up drunk AND in a threesome, I'm going to be incredibly disappointed you

didn't invite me with you! ;-)

A hysterical laugh escapes my lips, easing the panic rising for a moment.

Me: NO, you tosser! No, this is WAY worse! Are you home?

Almost immediately, a reply comes back.

Suzy: For a while yet, so just come by. xx

I sigh loudly, relieved beyond measure.

Me: See you soon, honey. THANK YOU! xxx

I grab my clutch, my phone, and put on some black ballerinas, and hurry to my kitchen to find my keys hanging on the wall.

I'm out of the door before even a full thirty seconds has passed.

CHAPTER SEVEN

EMMA

"I MEAN, THIS IS the *worst* idea ever!" I exclaim as I pace in front of Suzy who's quietly watching me from her sofa, a nonplussed look on her face.

Arms flailing, I continue my rant, "Yes, it might be a good idea, as far as putting tutor on my résumé, but, personally, it's *really* bad." I take a quick look at Suzy, who's now looking as if she's holding back from laughing.

I stop and glare at her. "This is *not* funny, Suzy! I'm freaking out here!"

Finally, she can't hold back, and an honest-to-god belly-holding laugh erupts from her. I cross my arms in front of me, tapping my right foot, and wait her out. To tell the truth, I'm pretty miffed.

She wipes tears from her eyes. "Em, you ruined my make-up," she scolds me, and she quickly stands and hurries to her bathroom.

I gape at her, lost for words, before my frozen feet scurry after her. "Suzy!" I shout. "Did you not hear a word of what I just said?"

"Oh, I heard you, sweetie," she responds calmly while picking up her mascara.

I stand in the doorway, dumbfounded. "And?" I ask impatiently. "Why are you not trying to console me?"

She leans towards the mirror above the sink and begins to fix her looks. "For one thing, I'm supposed to meet Thomas in less than half an hour and I want to look my best before I leave."

Oh, bloody hell. I forgot.

As I open my mouth to apologise, she continues, "For another, I don't see why this is bad. As far as I can see, there's no harm in taking the job. I mean, Daniel sounds like a good guy, and the fact that he's your boss's nephew isn't really that horrible, is it?"

I shake my head. "You don't understand...," I begin, and she interrupts me:

"No, Em, I really don't. This might be a good thing. *Maybe* tutoring Daniel will be good for you," she says and picks up her brush.

I sigh, and I can feel my already weakened resolve slip further. Then something she just said makes me frown.

"What do you mean, that maybe it'll be good for me?" I ask her suspiciously.

"Well..." She turns to look at me closely, a thoughtful look in her eyes. "Okay, I'll just come out and say it: Maybe you and Daniel will end up *more* than friends, Em...And I actually want that to happen for you."

My mouth hangs open, and I try to come up with the right words. "What...I...eh? *No*," I finally stammer, and my sweet, romantic, *devious* friend chuckles.

Suzanne grins triumphantly. "If he didn't already have

your knickers in such a twist, you wouldn't be so flabbergasted right now."

As she moves past me and back into the living room, I follow her, gritting my teeth. "Do not think about my knickers, Suzy!"

A snort escapes her as she picks up her keys and a small, expensive-looking clutch. She turns to face me, and I hold my tongue when I look in her eyes. The laughter is completely gone, replaced with determination, and I'm scared to breathe for fear of hearing her next words.

"It's time to rethink the whole *hooking-up-with-strangers* scenario, Emma," she adds quietly. "I'm tired of it, you know. I actually want to find the man or woman of my dreams and live happily-ever-after."

I don't know what to say.

She goes on, "I know that we're young, and meant to live our lives wild and free, not thinking about settling down for at least another 10 years. But..." Suzy hesitates and looks down, fiddling with the clasp on her clutch. "All I'm saying is that I'm done with it. I want something meaningful. And I think..." As she stops again, I can't help but dread what she'll say next.

She squares her shoulders and finally looks me dead in the eye. "And I think that, deep down, you want the very same thing as me. But you're scared of going after it."

My head is reeling, and I have trouble forming words. I think a whole minute passes before I gather up the courage to whisper, "I'm so messed up, Suzy. I can't..." I swallow hard, tears gathering in my eyes. "I can't let anyone close to me. If you knew the reason why..." A tear escapes me, and even though I just want to turn and bolt from my friend's compassionate eyes, I muster up some more courage. "Well, you wouldn't want to be my friend anymore."

She gasps, and, suddenly, her arms are around me, holding me in a fierce hug. I grab onto her, finding strength in her embrace and begin to cry in earnest.

"Don't *ever* say that again, honey," Suzy whispers in my ear. "Don't you *dare* to even think that way. Please forget I said anything....or...do you remember what I told you last night?"

As my tears subside, I simply nod, afraid that I won't be able to hold any more back if I speak.

"Well, whatever it is that you can't talk with me about? It's eating you up from the inside; I can see and feel it whenever we're together," Suzy continues to whisper emphatically.

She loosens her hold on me, but I strengthen my grip around her neck; I'm afraid to let go. I don't want her to look into my eyes right now. She lets out a breath but doesn't protest, so we just hold onto each other for a couple of minutes. Finally, I feel ready to let go, and I wipe my cheeks, a bit embarrassed now.

Without looking at my friend, I urge her to leave. "You'll be late for your date, sweetie. Best be off with you." My usual mask seems unable to fall into place, and I fidget a bit, looking everywhere but at the woman standing in front of me.

"Hey." She breaks the silence, and I can't keep away from her anymore so I look up. I'm still wary, though. "Didn't you mention that this Daniel guy was cute?" She winks, trying to lighten the mood, and, despite my unhappy thoughts, a small smile breaks free on my lips.

"Yes, he is *very* cute," I sigh.

"Well, at least it won't be a hardship to be his tutor, then. He'll be your own personal man candy."

Now I *really* laugh. "Oh, dear. What's gotten into you, honey?"

She shrugs and takes a step back. "I'm just trying to look on the bright side of life," she says and turns to me. "You should try it sometime. Now..." She walks briskly to her front door. "Stay as long as you like, darling. Just be sure to lock up after yourself when you're ready to go home." She opens the door and smiles at me. "If I don't leave now, Thomas will think the worst of me."

I shake my head in wonder. "Always the optimist, aren't you?"

She smiles brightly. "Someone has to be." And with that she leaves me alone with my ugly thoughts.

♡

I ponder Suzy's words as I clean up my face in her bathroom. It feels as if my past is catching up with me; I have to admit that moving to another country, and being so far away from home, hasn't helped that much. The nightmares keep a tight hold on me, and I can't seem to break free of them on my own. Rationally speaking, I know that what Suzy told me is true: I *should* speak to someone about them. Alright, I'll just go ahead and say it: *a psychologist*. The word alone leaves a sour taste in my mouth, my head starts to spin, and it feels as if my legs drop, leaving me on the floor, all trembling and scared of the unknown.

I lie on my side, curled into a ball, holding on tight to my knees.

I can't do it, I can't do it, I can't do it...The same thought runs around and around like a broken record, and I don't know how long I remain this way. My eyes are closed tight, and maybe I even begin to drift away for a while.

Suddenly, a pair of intense, green eyes fill my mind, and my shivers subside ever so slowly; my tight grip on my knees loosen, and warmth returns to my limbs. Finally, feeling slightly more conscious of myself and my surroundings, I open my eyes and move to sit up. My body is sore, as if I'd just finished working out, and I feel slightly lightheaded. Immediately, I remember that I haven't had much to eat today.

As I get up from the floor, I hold on tightly to the sink. I can't believe I feel so weak…A spell like the one I just had hasn't come upon me in *months*.

I take a look in the mirror and wince. The bad thing about being a pale, freckled, and rosy-cheeked Brit is that it doesn't take much to look like the walking dead. I turn on the faucet and wash my face, hoping the cool water will help clear my thoughts.

My stomach growls madly, so I decide it's time to satisfy my hunger. As I gather my things, I realise that it in fact is time for me to face the music: I need help. I resolve to do a search on the internet for psychologists when I get home. I might stop by the pub and have a chat with Camilla first, though. Her upbeat attitude could be just what I need right now.

CHAPTER EIGHT

EMMA

AS I LOCK THE door to Suzy's flat, my phone rings. I quickly dig it out of my purse and check the caller ID. For the first time today, I smile: it's my grandmother.

"Hi, Nan," I answer. "How are you?" I hurry down the stairs and out the door.

"I'm fine, darling," she replies. "Not much happens when you're 85, so I thought I'd ring my favourite granddaughter and hear what's going on in her life." The humour in her voice is evident, but she also manages to convey her love for me at the same time.

"I'm your only granddaughter," I laugh.

"Oh, a minor detail," she tuts.

I laugh again, but then sigh, feeling defeated. "Actually, I'm really glad you phoned me. I'm having a bad day."

"What's wrong?" All humour has fled, replacing her voice with worry.

I sigh. "Well, I just had a bit of a...spell, I guess." I pause and quickly take in my surroundings, making sure no one can hear what I say next. "I've had the strangest morning, Nan, and I feel unsettled."

"You haven't fainted in a long time, dear. What brought this on?" she asks me.

"I..." I hesitate.

"Come on, out with it," she scolds me in that no-nonsense, grandmotherly voice that I adore.

I huff. "Okay, okay. I met this guy, and – "

She interrupts me, "Ooooh, did you now? When? Where? How?"

"Shush, Nan," I chuckle. "Please let me finish."

"Oh, fine," she grumbles. "But I want *all* the details."

"You're worse than Suzy," I protest, but I can't help but smile wider. Talking to my grandmother always has this effect on me. No matter what I do, no matter how self-destructive I used to be, I know that she loves me unconditionally; true, she *has* been known to give me quite an earful, but it was always followed by hugs and kisses.

"Will you get on with it?" she urges me, evidently impatient, but I can sense her humour has returned.

"Actually, I don't have time to tell you every single detail, Nan, but I'll email you later with them. Okay, his name is Daniel, and he's the nephew of my employer, Mr. Andersen. You do remember him, don't you?"

She puffs. "I may be old, but I'm not senile - of course I remember him. Go on."

I frown. "Well, apparently, he's also my next-door neighbour, and he showed up on my doorstep this morning - *before* I'd put on some proper clothes, I might add - and I was so distracted that I just opened the door and let him in."

"Did you have sex?" Nan interrupts me again

"NO!" I shout, quickly looking over my shoulder again.

Luckily, the street I'm walking on isn't full of people, but as soon as I see a bench further up the road, I hurry to reach it and sit down on it. That way, I can concentrate better on my grandmother.

"No," I repeat, more calm. "We *did not* have sex. I wouldn't even contemplate that notion, Nan. He's my boss' nephew, for pete's sake!"

"Oh, don't be so old-fashioned, Emma dear. But do continue, please. I need to hear what he said to cause you to faint."

"Daniel had nothing to do with the fainting part," I quickly say. *But is that entirely true?*

"Good grief, girl, you're the worst storyteller," she sighs. "When do you get to the point? I'm not getting any younger, you know."

"If you didn't interrupt me all the time, it wouldn't take me that long," I protest, frowning and shaking my head.

Silence.

"Nan?" I ask, slightly worried that I've lost her.

"I'm waiting," she sighs. "Now, carry on."

"Right," I answer, a small smile tugging at my lips. *Honestly, this woman.*

"Well, he came up with a really strange proposition, Nan. He starts at university this fall, but due to being dyslexic, he's worried about being unable to keep up with the course-load. So he wants me to tutor him over the summer, and..."

She laughs hysterically.

"What?! I'm not *that* bad," I protest.

"Oh, but, sweetie, you are," she laughs, gasping for air. "I mean, do you remember when you tried to teach me how to use your computer?"

"That was different," I reply vaguely, and I drum my

fingers on the bench, feeling a bit embarrassed now.

"A-ha, was it, now?"

I avoid her question. "Do you want to hear the rest or not?"

"Please. Daniel's dyslexic, and him asking for your help is a bad thing, because...?"

I stay quiet for a while. "He has really beautiful eyes, Nan," I finally whisper. "And although he seems very unsure of himself, when he lets go of his shyness, he has this certain smile that just...unnerves me," I finish, feeling a bit foolish.

"Aaaah," she sighs. She gets me. "So that's the problem, darling? He makes you *feel*? Remind me again why that is so wrong?"

I hesitate, unwilling to bare more of my soul for the day. But I know my Nan, and she'll keep nagging me if I don't come clean.

"I don't want to develop feelings for him. I mean, I'm not saying that I will, but, you know...I'm not *that* girl, Nan."

"What girl?" she asks, a perplexed tone in her voice.

"The girl who goes all gooey and becomes weak at the knees just because a cute and handsome bloke comes along and seems to be different from all the others," I sigh.

"Emma. The fact that you fancy him does not make you weak," she scolds me.

"Yes, it does," I whisper.

"No, it does not," she contradicts me firmly. "It simply means that you are human. And that you are, perhaps, ready to fall in love."

"Hey, wait, what?" I ask her, bewildered. "Who is saying anything about *love*?"

"No one, honey, but this Daniel does seem to ruffle your feathers somehow, and opening yourself up to the possibility of more than just a...well, a quick roll in the hay, so to speak, is good."

I can't help but laugh. "How difficult was it for you to say the last bit, Nan?"

"Very," she mutters. Then, in a lighter tone of voice, she continues, "I was rather wild in my day, as you know. But that does not mean I find it a tad strange to say...certain words."

I snort. "Of course not."

Silence settles as we both become lost in our thoughts.

"I need some words of wisdom, Nan," I finally break the silence. "Should I say yes to tutor Daniel?"

"Tell me about the fainting spell," she answers back, a sombre tone to her voice.

I look around me, not sure I have the energy left to tell her about the last part of my morning. When my stomach growls madly, I stand up and walk towards a 7-Eleven.

"I'll tell you all about that in my email later, Nan," I evade her. "I haven't had much food in me yet, and I really need to eat."

"Are you sure, Emma? I worry about you, you know. Why on Earth did you have to move to another country?" she scolds me. "I miss our Sundays together."

"You know why, Nan," I quietly answer, and I can hear her take a long inhale.

"I do."

"But I miss our brunches, too," I add, somewhat apologetic.

"Alright, email me later, darling, and about Daniel... " She stops and that grabs my attention.

"What about him?" I urge her.

"Say yes to the tutoring job, and just relax. Be young,

darling. You need to stop overanalysing everything to death and simply *be*. Those are my words of wisdom," she finishes, and I can tell that she is satisfied.

I chuckle. "I don't know if that's the kind of advice I can use, Nan, but thanks. It *was* lovely that you decided to ring me, though. I needed that." I have reached the shop but hesitate to go inside.

A thought strikes me, and I ask, "Nan?"

"Yes, dear?"

"Do you miss granddad?" I ask her.

"Every day." No hesitation, no humour in her voice. Just a sureness that I can't help but admit I envy.

"But...he's been gone for so long now, for over 20 years. If you still miss him after all this time, how can your heart bear it?" This is something I have wanted to ask her for so long, but I have not had the courage to do it until now.

I can hear the smile in her voice when she answers me. "Because I have my children and you, Emma darling. You keep me going; you always have. Besides, I know I'll be with him again. Not in Heaven, though," she mutters as an afterthought. "The way we acted in our youth? We'll probably go to Hell instead," she chuckles.

I laugh, "It's likely a much more fun place to be."

"Indeed," she chuckles, and then says her goodbyes. "Don't forget to email me, Emma."

"I'm glad Dad taught you to do that," I say, and I truly am.

"He was a much better teacher than you," she teases me. But then continues in a more sombre voice, "I love you, darling."

"I love you, too," I reply, just as quietly. "Always and forever."

"Goodbye, Emma."

"Bye, Nan."

I look down at my mobile for a few seconds before heading into the shop. My grandmother has given me even more to think about.

A perfectly nutty idea begins to form in my mind, and I can't believe I am even contemplating it. My stomach chooses this moment to make its hungry presence known again, and I almost run inside the shop to buy food.

CHAPTER NINE

EMMA

I KNOCK FRANTICALLY ON Daniel's door, my crazy, yet perfect plan, firmly in my mind.

Not much time passes, and when he opens the door, I blurt out, "I need you to be my boyfriend."

"Wh...what?!" he stutters, eyes big as saucers, and he even looks a bit scared.

I plant a palm on my face. "Sorry. That came out wrong. May I come in?"

Silently, he moves back from the entrance, and I walk past him and enter his living room. I don't really notice the way it looks, though, too focused on my plan; when I hear him following me, I turn around and smile.

"Look, I know that sounded mad, but let me explain, please."

He just nods, and I continue, "I had a crazy idea, and I'll completely understand if you don't want to do this, but...here goes." I take a deep breath. "My brother will be coming to Copenhagen soon, on a business trip, and for reasons I can't really tell you, we don't have the best relationship. However, while he's here, he wants us to get together, and I already know that I can't get out of this meeting. So I was thinking that if you *pretend* to be my boyfriend and come with me, he won't be able to ask me questions I have no desire to answer, and he'll get out of my hair and let me be."

"And why do you think he'll fall for that kind of charade?" Daniel asks me as he crosses his arms. He looks uncomfortable, and I can't say that I blame him.

"Well, we just have to act like we're dating and madly in love with each other," I answer. "I'm sure it can't be that hard to do."

"No," he says firmly and shakes his head.

"What do you mean, no?" I ask him, confused. *I don't get this guy.*

"I mean, no, I won't do it. It's got nothing to do with you, Emma," he hurries on. "But I wouldn't know how to pretend to be your boyfriend."

"Oh. I see." But I'm lying; *I don't* see why this can't work.

Daniel uncrosses his arms and looks at his feet. Even though I don't know him that well, I can tell that he's embarrassed.

"Why?" I decide to ask him, and he looks up, a pained expression on his face.

"Please don't ask me that," he pleads with me.

I know that I should relent, let him be, but the devil in me takes over, and I put my hands on my hips and ask stubbornly, "Why don't you think you can pretend to be my boyfriend?"

Daniel sighs and comes closer to me. He looks intently into my eyes, and I can't read him at all. There is a hard look on his face, but he still seems vulnerable somehow.

He looks away. "For one thing, we don't know each other _"

"Well, I expect that will change a bit once I start tutoring you," I interrupt him. *Yes, I have made my decision -- lord help me.*

His head snaps back. "You'll be my tutor?" he asks, a hopeful smile starting to spread on his face.

"Yes, yes, I'll be your tutor." I wave a hand and then ask him *again,* "What's your other objection to pretending to be my boyfriend? Is it the way I look? The piercings? The tattoos?" For once, I feel self-conscious, an emotion I'm not used to feeling, and that makes me rather angry at Daniel.

His eyes widen and he shakes his head madly. "No, no, it's nothing like that! I promise, Emma. You're..." He looks up and then sighs. "You're gorgeous, Emma." Then he sighs, still keeping his eyes from meeting my own, and he sighs, defeated. "Are you *really* going to make me say it?"

"Yes, I am." I tap my foot, becoming more and more aggravated. "I'm stubborn, Daniel. You might as well know this about me from the get-go."

"Fine!" he exclaims and then moves away from me so that I can't see his face at all. "I don't know how to be your boyfriend, because I've never had a girlfriend."

I'm stunned, speechless. *Did he just say what I think he did?*

"Say that again...?" I move hesitantly closer to him.

His words are almost a whisper, but because I so desperately want to hear what he says, I strain myself: "You heard me."

I don't know what to say. I swallow, but it is a futile attempt. My mouth has gone completely dry.

"Never?" I finally ask him. "Does that mean...?"

"What do you think it means, Emma?" he snaps at me,

clearly mortified. He doesn't turn around to face me, but he lifts his head, causing his profile to become more visible to me.

"I told you how my speech impairment did not make talking with girls easy for me - I'm a klutz, I stutter, and I become so lost in my head that when I finally muster up the courage to talk with one of them, some other guy moves in. And I've lost my chance."

"But...but you're 24 years old," I protest. "Surely, it can't be that bad." I honestly don't understand how this gorgeous guy, despite his shy ways, hasn't been snatched up by anyone yet.

Daniel moves to open the door to his balcony, and I have no trouble understanding why; it's hot as hell in the flat.

He chuckles darkly. "Yeah, I know," he says, and the sarcasm in his voice isn't lost on me. At last, he gives me his eyes, and I become lost in the vulnerability I see there; somehow, it mirrors my own, but for completely different reasons.

I take a step towards him but stop, opening my mouth but then shut it again, unsure of what to say. I decide that honesty is probably best.

"I've never had a boyfriend," I confess to him, a defiant hilt to my chin. He frowns.

"What? Why?" he asks me, a blush starting to creep up on his neck, and my tummy erupts with butterflies again.

"It's my own choice, Daniel, and I won't tell you why that is. I'm no virgin, though, if that's what you want to know." I hold his eyes, but it becomes increasingly difficult to maintain. He looks confused, lost in thought.

Another idea begins to form, and I take another step towards him. "I'll teach you," I tell him.

He frowns again. "What do you mean?" he asks me, a suspicious glint in his eyes.

The more I think about it, this plan is perfect, and I can't help but show my enthusiasm by smiling widely at him.

"I'll teach you how to interact with girls - wait, you're not gay, right?"

Damn, that would be a real shame.

Daniel lifts an eyebrow, momentarily forgetting his shyness, so I hurry on, "Of course not. You did say *girls* and not *boys*. How silly of me. Right. I'll teach you what a relationship should be like - sans the-kissing-and-getting-naked-together part, of course - and you'll then be fully prepared to meet my brother in two months. Plus, you'll also have gained some confidence - at least I hope so - about girls by then as well. It's the perfect plan!" I feel giddy, exuberant, yet I know this is definitely *not* a perfect plan - it's quite mad, actually.

"How can you teach me how a boyfriend should act when you've never had one?" Daniel proceeds to ask me.

"I guess I'll have to check my books," I mutter, a bit distracted as I try to come up with a game plan.

His voice, however, pulls me back to the present. "Your books?" he repeats incredulously.

"Yes, my books: a lot of them are love stories, you know. Plenty of research material for me. Oh, I can also just work on your skills based on the guys I've met while clubbing, I guess." I frown, and, for the first time, I become a bit worried about pulling this off.

"You're nuts," Daniel then grins, shaking his head.

I huff and cross my arms in front of me. "*No*, I'm not. I'm just...eccentric," I finish with a satisfied smirk on my face. However, my satisfaction doesn't last long. It never does.

"Look, Daniel, what harm can it do? I'll tutor you, teach you about the female mind - and I know *a lot* of guys would love to know that last part - and all you'll have to do is pretend to be madly in love with me for one afternoon. That's it. So...what do you say? Do we have a deal?" I uncross my arms and reach out my right hand, waiting for him to shake it. He looks at it for a couple of beats, and then takes a deep breath before moving closer to me.

He looks into my eyes for a while, before he rakes a hand through his hair, seemingly agitated.

"Deal," he says, and he shakes my hand, a nervous smile curving his lips.

My fingers tingle from his touch, and I can't ignore the warmth it elicits down my spine. I suppress a shiver, and I can't help but feel that this is a pivotal moment in my life. I don't know how my mind conjured up this mad idea, but maybe it was because of what Nan told me earlier. Or maybe Suzy's pep-talk? Who knows?

All I know is that the next few months are bound to be interesting.

I just hope that I'll be able to keep my distance from this charming boy.

No matter what Suzy and Nan said, I won't let my heart fall for Daniel. It's just safer that way.

CHAPTER TEN

EMMA

YOU KNOW THAT FEELING you get when you *think* you know what you're doing, but then, a while later, the reality of the situation hits you, forcing you to realise that you're entirely clueless?

That's how I feel right now.

Daniel gave me a copy of his English Literature syllabus before I left his flat an hour ago, and we agreed that we would talk with Mr. Andersen tomorrow about our work hours. I'm still not sold on the idea to only work half-days and still being paid as if I were there full time, but I'll have to speak with him about it. I don't think I want to spend every single afternoon with Daniel. That's a temptation that's bound to become too much for me.

I still can't get over the fact that Daniel is a virgin. It seems so odd. I know I sound sexist, but I'm really not. It's just surprising to meet a 24-year-old guy - and one who looks like him - who hasn't any kind of experience whatsoever.

In the last hour, I've been sitting on my balcony, chain smoking and berating myself for suggesting that ludicrous idea! How on earth can I, one of the most cynical people on the planet, profess to know anything at all about what a relationship should be like? I guess I can ask Suzy for advice....or my mum. Err, no, not mum - *worst* idea ever!

I cringe and then stub out the latest smoke before heading inside to fetch my phone. I need Suzy. A dose of her positive attitude is the perfect medicine. I look at the clock over my bookshelf: three-fifteen pm. Ugh. She's probably still on her date, but I decide to text her instead.

Me: Hey, honey. Are you free or has Thomas already persuaded you to lose the knickers? ;-) x

Almost immediately, a reply pings:

Suzy: No, you tart, he hasn't! You've got a dirty mind, my friend. But I AM still with him, and it's going really well. Are you okay?

I hesitate, then shake my head and quickly type back.

Me: Text me when you get home, okay? I'm fine. Just need a chat. Glad your date's going well. Love you. X

Suzy: Will do, darling. Love you. x

I head to the kitchen, not sure of what to do with myself.

Sighing, I lean back on the table. I feel irritated, unsettled, and even a bit scared. I look down at my feet, pondering what to do when the thought of Camilla, the pub owner across from me, springs to mind once more, and I immediately go in search of my sandals and my clutch.

This lady is just the person I need to cheer me up.
As long as I don't get tempted to drink, I'll be fine.

♡

I had my first drink when I was fourteen. It was New Year's Eve, my parents had gone to a party, and my brother was out with friends. I remember telling them that I'd rather spend the evening with my Nan - which was the truth - but I also had an ulterior motive for staying home.

Nan made a lovely dinner, and we just chatted throughout the night, watching the telly, and making jokes of all the celebrities who looked silly. She let me have one small glass of white wine for dinner, but I was feeling rebellious and didn't want to stop there.

So I faked being tired and headed home - my parents and Nan lived, and still do, right next to each other - so Nan, being responsible like always, waited by her front door until I'd waved goodnight and she watched me go inside.

I remember going straight to my parents' bar, looking through their collection of liquor, and at last settling on the gin. I don't know why I chose that one - I guess it was the only bottle open - but I picked it up, put it to my mouth, and drank most of it.

I don't remember much about what happened afterwards. I guess I passed out, because I can vaguely remember my dad gently shaking me, asking me what I'd been drinking. My mum was standing in the background, worried sick, of course, and mad as hell. They let me sleep in their bed that night because they wanted to make sure I didn't choke on my own vomit.

I woke up with the meanest hangover ever, the lecture to

beat all lectures from my parents, and, to this day, I still can't stand the smell of gin: it makes me gag.

Luckily, you don't have to smell it in order to drink it.

♡

Camilla's pub is called, well, *Camilla's*. It looks a bit rundown from the outside, but once you climb the two steps and enter her pub, it's entirely different. There are beautiful, dark-brown wooden floors, a long bar with comfortable stools opposite the entrance, and if you prefer to sit down instead of at the bar, red leather-chairs as well as couches are scattered here and there. It's a small pub, and it only offers beverages and light snacks, and Camilla runs it with her husband, George.

Camilla is a plump, red-haired woman with lots of freckles on her face and arms, and she has this knack of breaking down your defences, making you spill the beans about whatever troubles you find yourself in on that particular day. I actually think she is good at this because she doesn't *ask* you what's wrong. She greets you, of course, takes a good, hard look at you, and, depending on what she finds there, she either leans across the bar and gives you a certain look, or she continues doing what she's doing while waiting until you're ready.

She's a witch, I'm sure of it.

George is a flamboyant kind of man: loud, he laughs a lot, and he can get quite passionate about politics and religion. He can break down every argument you put up when you discuss a topic, and it usually leaves your head reeling - and confused about what you thought in the first place.

He's probably also a witch.

This afternoon, Camilla is, naturally, standing behind the bar, polishing a glass, and the stereo is playing Frank Sinatra's *Witchcraft*. I love the old crooners. I also love rock, but there's just something about this kind of music that has the ability to make me relax; I also quite often find myself wondering about what it would have been like to live in the 1930s or 1940s: in a way, life was probably a lot simpler for people. Well, minus World War II, of course.

"Hi, lovely," Camilla calls out as I walk up to the bar. "How are you?"

I stop in front of her and take a seat.

"Confused," I tell her, and she stops her movements, tilts her head and looks at me. In a move well practiced, she reaches for a glass underneath the bar, picks a Coke Zero from the small fridge behind her, and she caps the bottle. She pours some of the cold liquid in the glass and sets it in front of me. Then she looks at me again, and I cringe a bit. I know myself well enough to be aware of the fact that I can't keep myself from blurting out my troubles, but, at the same time, I really wish I could. I know I'll cave eventually, though, so I might just get on with it.

Here we go.

"A guy moved in next door," I blurt out. Before my courage abandons me, I continue on a rush, "and he's actually the nephew of my boss, Mr. Andersen." She nods, still looking at me in that particular way of hers. "Well, I met him yesterday, found out that he's my new neighbour today, and he wants me to tutor him, and I really don't want to, but, at the same time, I do, because he's really gorgeous, and I fancy him." After that fantastic case of word vomit, I take a big breath, and soldier on. "*And* it turns out that my brother will be visiting soon, and you know I'm not that keen on seeing him, but Steven, being the way that he is, won't let me off the hook, and then, a few hours ago, my brain - if I'm even allowed to call it that - popped up with this crazy idea: I need a fake boyfriend. To conclude said mad idea, I just asked Daniel, my gorgeous, geeky, new neighbour, to play along with it! And he agreed!" I don't feel right about blurting out Daniel's secret, so I hold my tongue about that part. "And...this is bad. I mean, really, really bad!" On a deep sigh, I close my eyes and hang my head.

A couple of beat pass and I keep waiting for Camilla to say anything to my peculiar tale. But she doesn't comment at all. Finally, I get tired of the silence and I lift my head again, open my eyes, and squint. What I see is definitely not what I thought I would, because she is no longer standing in front of me.

I turn my head left, then right, and almost fall off my chair when I see her right next to me, way into my personal space.

"Holy crap, Camilla!" I shriek, patting my galloping heart. "Don't sneak up on me like that!"

Camilla ignores me and simply moves even closer. *Alright, don't come closer. This is freaking me out.*

"Will you please say something?" I sputter, but she ignores me and stares into my eyes. I suddenly realise that I can't look away even though I want to. Camilla keeps looking intently into my eyes for another thirty seconds - yes, I counted them - until she beams brightly and gives me a hug. *Whoa! What the hell is happening?!*

The hug is over almost before it began, though, and as Camilla walks away from me and gets back behind the bar, she says, "Don't worry. You'll be fine." She picks up another glass and a dishcloth and gets on with her routine.

I'm gobsmacked. I feel as if I'm in a movie. *Or am I being punk'd?* I take a quick look over my left shoulder, but when I don't find a camera crew behind me, I look back at Camilla. She may be busy with the task at hand, but I can't help but notice the mysterious, secretive smile on her face.

"Fine?!" I ask her. "That's it?"

She nods. "That's it."

"Don't you think I should be admitted to a mental institution because of my stupid brain and my stupid ideas?" I sit up straighter and cross my arms across my chest, a bit defensive even though I really shouldn't be.

Camilla chuckles. "Of course not, Emma. You're not crazy, far from it. The same can't exactly be said about George, though," she muses and looks affectionately at her husband. I look closely at him: he's standing with a couple of customers, a man and a woman, and they look a bit frightened, actually. I can't say I blame them: he's making some rather wild gesticulations, and you can tell, from looking at his red cheeks, that he feels very passionately about whatever it is they are talking about.

I shake my head a bit and look back at Camilla, frowning. "You can't seriously mean that. Come on, I must be crazy. Just a tiny bit?" I raise my hand and make the universal sign of crazy: twirling my index finger around next to my ear.

Camilla huffs and puts down the glass rather forcefully and says, "Stop being silly. You're *not* mad. You're entirely normal." At that, I snort, but Camilla ignores it and continues, "The only way you would ever be considered crazy was if you had a bad feeling about Daniel but still agreed to tutor him. You don't get a creepy vibe, do you?"

I quickly shake my head. "Definitely not," I reassure her.

Not a creepy vibe...something far more pleasurable comes to mind whenever I'm near him.

I choose to not voice my inner monologue and say to Camilla, "I'm just...well, I've never been in a romantic relationship, so I guess I'm rather surprised at myself for even suggesting it to Daniel. Oh, and another thing," I suddenly remember, "he's such a geek! I mean, he has the most awful pair of glasses, he wears slacks, button-down shirts and *loafers,* for crying out loud!" A giggle escapes me, but I try to suppress it.

For once, it seems that I have caught Camilla by surprise. "How old is this Daniel?" she asks me.

"Just a year older than me, so 24," I tell her, almost certain I know where she's headed with this. She opens her mouth to speak, so I beat her to it, "I know, he needs to get a completely new wardrobe if he's to impersonate being my boyfriend. I think he gets his fashion sense from his uncle, actually." As the last line leaves my lips, I frown and I make a mental note of mentioning it to Daniel. I'd never go out with such a preppy type of man. No, I'm usually into the whole "bad-boy-guaranteed-to-make-you-come-within-five-minutes-tops" type. Having perfected the art of ignoring unpleasant thoughts - or simply thoughts I don't want to scrutinise too much - I don't exactly wish to ponder the fact that I seem to fancy a bloke so far from being the usual kind that catches my attention, yet here I am, doing just that.

"Oh," Camilla says, pulling me away from my own head. "Well, that's not so bad, is it?"

"Not really, no," I grudgingly admit, and we fall silent for a while. I sip the coke from time to time, soothing my parched throat. Suddenly, I remember that I have completely forgotten to email Nan even though I promised to do that, and

I spring up from my seat.

Camilla looks at me questioningly.

"I'm so sorry, I forgot that I owe my grandmother an email." I rummage around in my clutch, looking for my purse.

"The drink's on the house," Camilla says as I try to hand her some money. "But only today," she says, and I can't help but smile.

"For a minute there, I thought your good business sense had abandoned you," I tease her, and she smiles.

"Never." She turns to George who has snuck up behind her. "What were you raving about this time?" she asks him, and my curiosity is piqued.

He puts an arm around her waist and sighs dramatically. "The youth of today has not one tiny bit of romantic bones in them," he mutters.

Camilla pats his cheek and smiles fondly at him. "I think you need to elaborate on that a bit," she says and winks at me.

"Well...I mean, is it really such a bad idea to elope? If you want to get married, why bother spending thousands of kroners on the wedding?! It's only one day!" George turns his blue eyes to me, and I shrug, trying to let him know that I agree with him.

"Oh, how lovely, a wedding!" Camilla exclaims, clapping her hands excitedly.

"Err...maybe not quite yet," George says. Camilla and I look at each other, and I can see the same confusion as mine mirrored in her eyes. At the same time, we turn back to George, and he starts to fidget and won't meet our eyes.

"George..." Camilla places a hand on her hip. It is impossible to overhear the warning in her voice. "What do you mean? Come on, out with it."

George sighs, and then admits, "I may have failed to mention that this was their first date, but they looked to be so into each other that I found myself encouraging them to elope first chance they got."

What?! That's insane!

"George!" Camilla snaps and gives him a mild slap on his protruding belly. "That's so incredibly rude! You should be ashamed of yourself, butting in on people's conversations when they're, quite clearly, not meant for your ears!" She sighs and looks at me. "Wouldn't you agree, Emma?"

"Oh, absolutely," I reply hastily, trying to hold in a laugh. I clear my throat and look at a rather bashful-looking George. "Well, I'm sure there's no harm done."

"Maybe not," Camilla admits and picks up another glass to polish. "See, Emma? Definitely not crazy." She winks at me again, and I chuckle.

"What?" George asks, and he looks at his wife with narrowed eyes and then turns them back to me. "What does crazy have to do with it?"

Taking this as my cue to leave, I quickly say, "Nothing, George. Thanks for the drink, Camilla." I smile at her in thanks and leave the pub.

I don't feel anymore settled about the whole Daniel situation, but these strange people did manage to make me smile, and I suppose that's something, at least.

Definitely witches.

CHAPTER ELEVEN

DANIEL LARSEN

I have been thinking about Emma and her strange proposition all night. Ever since she left my flat, I've pondered whether or not I should text her and tell her that I can't go through with it at least a dozen times. But something stops me every time from actually doing it.

That girl is the weirdest person I have ever met. I don't mean that in a bad way, no...but I can't deny the fact that she is rather crazy. Or, well, like she said, *eccentric*.

All the while Emma was in my flat, I had to concentrate so much on not letting my dirty thoughts run away with me. I might be inexperienced, but I have a great imagination, polished through years of watching soft porn.

I'm a guy, okay? We all do it, even shy ones like me. Emma is a beautiful woman so it's only natural that I feel attracted to her. She's all woman, not stick and bones, and the way her perfume teased my nose made my mind wander, thinking about her in all sorts of sexual ways.

I'm lying in my bed, staring out the window to the left of

me and looking at the full moon; seeing as I'm not wearing my glasses, I can't make it out that clearly, but the light is still comforting. Even though I feel bone tired, sleep seems to evade me. I've only been in the city for a few days, so the flat doesn't feel like a home yet. I never could sleep the first night in a new place.

I move my head and glance at all the boxes lining most of the wall at the end of my bed. I guess I should get up and begin to sort through them, but I just can't be bothered with it right now. Squinting at the clock on my phone, I sigh in irritation; it's close to midnight, and I really ought to force myself to close my eyes and try to fall asleep.

I do just that, but it doesn't have the desired effect; as soon as my eyes are shut, a pair of blue-grey ones fills my mind. I remember the piercing in Emma's eyebrow, the freckles on her nose, and, bit by bit, her entire face and body have formed, and I think back on her beautiful curves: her gorgeous, rosy full lips I want to trace with my tongue before dipping it inside her mouth to tangle with hers. Her rather large breasts I just want to lick, nibble, and kiss and spend a really long time on worshipping. Her small waist I want to hold on to. Her beautiful arse that seems to be begging for a man to squeeze it tightly. Before I'm even aware of it, I've moved my hand down my stomach and my fingertips are touching the base of my cock. As the fantasy of licking my way down her body takes over, I kick the sheets covering me away, pull up my knees, and I take a firm grip on my cock and begin to stroke it up and down slowly.

I imagine Emma's fingers pulling my hair, her soft whimpers filling my ears, as my mouth teases her hip bone, and my fingers gently move down to caress her pussy.

"Fuck," I mutter aloud, stroking my cock from base to tip,

fantasising that Emma's hungry mouth and teeth are all over my body. Groaning and panting, I open my eyes to look down at my fully erected cock, and I begin to play with my balls, stroking them gently. My breaths come out in pants, and I can feel sweat form on my forehead.

Lying back, I close my eyes again, returning to my fantasy of Emma.

I imagine my hands grip her thighs before pulling them apart, and my mouth finally descends on her clit.

As I envision licking, sucking, and kissing her clit, I stroke my cock faster and faster. A familiar tingling begins to spread out from my spine, but I don't want to come yet, and I force my hand to slow down a bit. Feeling the ache in my balls, I fondle them for some time before opening my eyes again to look at my cock; watching myself jack off is a major turn on for me. Seeing some pre-come on the tip, I quickly move my hand over my cock head, smearing it all over.

Shite, I'm not going to last much longer.

Imagining thrusting inside Emma's pussy while she squirms beneath me, grabbing hold of my arms, digging her nails in, I take a firmer grip on my cock, and my calculated strokes become more frantic. All I can think about is what it would be like to hear her moan my name…to feel her lips on mine…to hear her whisper dirty things in my ears as I fuck her…to feel her pussy clamp down on my cock as she comes. Will she go wild if I pull on her lip ring with my teeth as I keep fucking her? That image alone almost makes me spill my load, and, groaning, I release the hold on my balls. Needing to come more than ever before, my left hand grips onto my sheets, and the tingling in my spine, the warmth in my body, intensify until, finally, my cock jerks in my hand once…twice…three times, and come erupts from it, landing on my stomach. Instinctively, I loosen the tight hold on it, letting my hand fall listlessly to my side.

"Holy fuck...," I growl loudly and close my eyes as my body begins to come down from the high. *Fuck, that was intense.*

I lie still for a couple of minutes, catching my breath, until, finally, I sit up. I look down at my stomach and I can't help but grin smugly.

That was just what I needed.

I hurry to the bathroom to clean up, and, as usual, I trip over my own feet on the way there. Why I can never walk on a flat surface without almost always falling flat on my arse goes beyond me. When I'm done, I hurry back to my bed and jump in. I lie down, pulling the sheet over me as I do.

With a content sigh, I close my eyes, and it doesn't take long before I drift off to sleep.

My alarm goes off and I hit snooze quickly.

Just five more minutes...

The ping alerting me to a text message, however, makes me open my eyes slightly, and my arm sneaks out from the warmth of the sheet covering me. I fumble around a bit, my hand searching for my glasses. As soon as I have found them and put them on, I pick up my phone from the floor, swipe the screen and see that the text is from Emma.

Damn, she's up early, I think, yawning, and I look at her message:

Emma: You know, the walls in this building are really thin...

I frown, confused.

Me: What do you mean???

This is weird...

Emma: Let's just say that I'm glad I won't have to teach you everything . . .

What the...? I bolt upright in bed as a feeling of dread fills my gut. Before I have the wits to form a reply, another ping alerts me of a new message. I'm almost too embarrassed to read it, but I think I have to man up, and so I take a look.

Emma: The next time you need to...err...relieve some tension? Go do it in the shower, okay? ;-)

That winky face at the end mocks me, and I can feel an embarrassing blush starting to rise on my neck. What the hell do I text back to her? This is really embarrassing. Ugh. I can't make a joke of this, but I do have to answer her, I guess. I'm quite relieved that I didn't shout out her name last night, though...now, *that* would be pretty difficult to talk myself out of. I don't want her to think that I'm some kind of pervert just because I had her in mind when I jacked off.

Me: Will do. See you at work.

I throw the phone behind me on the bed and rake my hands through my hair, all the way to my nape, holding onto it tightly for a couple of seconds. I breathe deeply a few times before loosening my hold, and I decide to try to ignore the fact that Emma obviously heard me get myself off last night. There's nothing I can do about it.

At the thought of my fantasy, I can't help but smirk a bit, but it disappears when I feel my cock begin to stir again.

"Down, boy," I mutter. "We need to behave ourselves around her, or I'm pretty sure she'll get pissed."

I have a feeling Emma is quite the ball buster, but, even so, the person she appears to be has me very intrigued. I would be lying if I said I weren't just a little bit curious about her, and the thought of seeing her again today cheers me up.

Finding out how she plans to shape me into being her pretend boyfriend is bound to be interesting.

Sighing, I decide that I might as well get up now that I'm awake, and I stand up to stretch. It's a good thing there isn't a building on the opposite side of my window, only the park, because then sleeping naked would no longer be an option for me.

♡

According to my parents, I didn't speak any proper words until I was three years old. They couldn't understand why, but it never worried them much. I suppose they thought it was only natural seeing as they had four other children all begging for attention, and the noise level in our house was quite high. There wasn't room for me to be heard. Being the quiet child, however, proved to be rather difficult as I got older, and when I eventually started school and almost stopped talking altogether, that's when my mum, in particular, began to notice how much I struggled. It would take a few years, though, before her worries were taken seriously.

The teachers made sure I was given many tests, and after some more practical sessions as well, they diagnosed me with dyslexia. Even though I was only 10 years old or so, I remember feeling relief that *someone* finally recognised the issues I had; being known as 'the dumb kid' or other such demeaning names isn't fun for anyone, but especially not when you're a young boy wanting to simply fit in...It didn't matter that I taught myself to pay attention to how the words on the pages actually *looked* like, making my almost photographic memory more evident than it already was...no, I was still different in the eyes of the other children in class.

Now, don't get me wrong: even though I struggled, and still do, with my "condition", I love books, but I have to say that audio books make life a hell of a lot easier for someone like me. People often wonder why I'm choosing to attend university at all - many seem to be under the assumption that people with dyslexia can't hold down jobs that deal with the linguistic arts or literature, but I want to prove them all wrong.

Why can't I choose something that I love, something that gives me great pleasure?

Why must I still be labelled as the kind of guy who won't be able to amount to much?

No. I refuse to let others choose for me. If I want to become a teacher - heck, if I get the urge to get a Ph.D. someday - *no one* is going to deny me that. Maybe it'll just take me a bit longer than the rest of them, but I'm fine with it.

Great things are worth fighting for - and nobody will be able to stop me from going after my dreams.

I just wish I wouldn't have to do it alone.

CHAPTER TWELVE

EMMA

I'M STANDING OUTSIDE DANIEL'S flat, arm raised and ready to knock, but I have yet to actually go through with it. My thoughts continue to wander back to last night when I listened to him pleasuring himself. I was quite shameless, actually, and held my ear to the wall above my headboard when the realisation of what he was up to - no pun intended - hit me. Hearing his moans, imagining how and where he touched his body felt forbidden somehow. I'm by no means a shy person, sexually, I mean, but I'm not a voyeur. I don't usually get aroused by watching other people jack off.

I'm quite sure that watching Daniel would change my mind about that, though.

When silence finally descended from his flat, I refrained from doing the same, no matter how turned on I was. In theory, I shouldn't have held back, but I chickened out: I didn't want to risk *him* waking up to the sounds of *my* moans.

Mentally giving my lady bits a good talking-to, I finally muster up the courage to knock and then wait impatiently for

Daniel to open his door.

When I hear his footsteps drawing nearer, I plaster a smile on my face, ready to greet him like I would any other not-so-close friend: politely.

As soon as I see him, however, my brain has a mind of its own.

"Good morning, Daniel. Feeling well rested today?" I ask, and I'm *this* close to kicking myself in the arse.

Oh, well, too late to do anything about it.

"Quite," he answers, not smiling back at me in the least. But at least he's not blushing this time.

Ignoring his stony face, I soldier on, "I thought that, seeing as we're off to work, we might as well go together. It'll give us a chance to get to know each other better, which, I might add, *is* a very vital factor if you are to be my pretend boyfriend." Pulling on the strap of my purse, I take in his clothes and sigh: another boring button-down shirt, grey slacks and – yep, just as I thought - a pair of loafers. "You know, we need to do something about your wardrobe," I continue, and shake my head.

"What?" Daniels asks me and looks quickly down and back at me. "What's wrong with it?" He frowns, and that horrid pair of glasses slips down his nose a bit, preventing me from seeing his eyes properly.

"Well, for one thing, Preppy, you dress like your uncle does: as if we're living in another day and age," I admonish him, giving him the once-over again. "And for another," I add, "it's summer. We're in the beginning of July, so how can you stand wearing so many clothes in this heat? It'll stifle you." I begin to tap my foot slightly, not wanting to be late for work, but, at the same time, not wanting to make Daniel think that I'm rude.

Daniel takes a few steps back, indicating that I should enter his flat, and after hesitating a few seconds, I do as he asks and walk inside. Taking in the flat and finding that it really hasn't changed since yesterday - there are still plenty of boxes waiting to be unpacked - I move across the living room to take a peek out of the window overlooking his balcony. It looks just like mine.

"I'm almost ready to leave," Daniel says from behind me, and I turn around to see him rummaging through his backpack as if he's looking for something.

"Not that I really care that much," he says, still not looking at me, "but why are my clothes so bad?"

Sensing that he's not altogether happy with my outspoken views on his dress code, I quickly reassure him, "Oh, there's nothing wrong with them as such - they're very fancy - but no boyfriend of mine would wear that."

He grabs his wallet and, finally, lifts his head. "Why not?" he asks me, and pushes his glasses back. He still looks a bit miffed, but it's mostly been replaced by curiosity.

"Well, I'm not exactly the...*conservative* type, in case you hadn't noticed?" I answer back teasingly and smile at him.

"Oh, I've noticed," he mumbles, and I feel the burn of his eyes as he looks me over. I'm wearing a pair of beige capris today and a black sleeve-less top that's got some glittering writing on it that says, *So I'm weird - Deal With It* right across my boobs.

"Yes, right..." I clear my throat, suddenly feeling a bit flushed myself. "Anyway, the point is that I'm more into the laid-back, doesn't-give-a-fuck, rocker bad boy, so we clearly need to take you shopping soon."

He straightens back and crosses his arms. "Over my dead body." He clenches his jaw, and, to tell the truth, he looks so stubborn.

What, is that...? Is he gritting his teeth now?

I blink. "Excuse me?" I ask incredulously.

"Under no circumstances whatsoever will I go shopping and buy some clothes that I am quite confident I will never wear again. Nope. No way."

I blow out a disgruntled breath and mimic his posture. We stare each other down, neither of us willing to stand down, for almost a minute, and then an idea forms in my head.

Slowly uncrossing my arms from under my boobs, I sigh rather dramatically. "Well, if I can't persuade you, I guess that's that."

"Exactly," he nods, and a smirk begins to form on his face.

Ha! He thinks he's won!

I put my hands on my hips and sashay towards him. I put a bit more into swaying my hips, as if I was dancing, and I place my hands behind my back, subtly pushing out my breasts. Noticing how his eyes zero in on them, taking in the way they strain against my top, I try to hold back my triumphant smile. As I slowly move closer to him, he swallows, and his cheeks are looking slightly flushed. He uncrosses his arms, letting them fall down, but I can't help but notice how his fists close tightly, and his knuckles turn white.

When I'm standing quite close to him, I look down and say, "I guess, if you don't really want to, I can always ask someone else to pretend to be my boyfriend."

I'm staring at his chest, and it's clear to see how his breathing has picked up: it comes out more quickly now, and I really don't understand how my little show can seem to turn him on so much. It's evident that he's affected by my actions, and, just to see how far I can push him - because I'm just too bloody curious for my own good - I place my hands on his biceps and squeeze them a little. Now that I am touching him, I am able to take in that he's actually not as skinny as I'd thought he was; no, there's some muscle to this geek. I move my hands up and down a bit up, caressing them, and I take the tiniest peek down to see if I'm turning him on. I avert my eyes after a beat. *Yep, the flag has risen!* And it seems to have a good size on it, too.

Setting my plan aside for a minute, I allow myself to take in the firmness of his arms, and I enjoy the silence, interrupted only by his shallow breathing. The warmth from his body feels inviting: it's as if it is calling for mine to come closer, and for me to put my arms around his waist, but I dare not give in to the temptation. I need to keep my distance, but I can't ignore the small voice inside my mind, whispering to me, urging me to look up and meet his gaze. For once, I'm not listening to this voice, because it has a tendency to get me into trouble. My heart was locked away a long time ago and I have no intention of finding the key to unlock it anytime soon.

"Don't do that," Daniel suddenly says, his voice sounding hoarse and slightly out of breath.

"What?" I whisper back, and I berate myself for sounding almost as breathless as he is. I imagine myself throwing caution to the wind...to unbutton his shirt to find out what his body looks like underneath it. I wish I had the courage to simply say *Sod it* and allow Daniel to touch me. I have never wanted to feel a man's touch as much as I do now.

"Don't ask anyone else," he replies, close to a whisper.

I don't respond for a few moments, but, eventually, I tell myself to release my hold on him, and I take a few steps back.

"I won't," I whisper, and, finally, dare to let my eyes meet his. The pure need radiating from his almost makes me stumble. But I do not close the distance between us. I need it now.

Awkwardly, I clap my hands together, feeling rather foolish, but I ignore my red cheeks. "Good. We'll go shopping next weekend, then." I give him my most fake smile, and walk past him.

"You're quite dangerous, Emma. You know that, don't you?" Daniel asks, and I stop at the entrance to his kitchen and look back at him. A small smile graces his mouth, and he has a twinkle in his eyes that I haven't seen before.

I lean against the doorway and look up at the ceiling, pretending to be lost in thought. "Oh, I don't know...," I ponder loudly before moving my eyes to his. "I prefer the word *"devious"*, actually."

He grins and mutters, "Yes, that, too." He sighs, and I know he's relented. "Fine, I'll buy some new clothes. *But...*" he holds up his index finger, looking so severe and grown-up that I almost giggle. "...no one says I have to wear them until the day we go see your brother. Is that understood?"

I raise my hand and give him a mock-salute. "Yes, Sir. Understood."

Daniel sighs, and, scratching the back of his head with his right hand, he mumbles, "What have I gotten myself into?"

I push out a breath and answer, "Into a world of fun. Now, Daniel, I think you need to start thinking about something else, because your...err...*manhood* appears to not settle down, and we really need to get a move on."

Daniel quickly turns around so that I can't see him, and now I really can't suppress a snort. *This guy is too strange.* I hear mumbling come from his direction, though, and I strain my ears so that I can hear him better.

"Is that...? Are you...*counting*?" I ask him, my voice disbelieving, because I'm sure I must have misheard him.

"Shh, you're distracting me," he mutters, and, sure enough, he continues to count. I'm standing there, staring at his back, gaping, and my curiosity about this geeky virgin is almost begging for me to ask him a ton of questions. I manage to contain myself, though.

Finally, I hear the number twenty, and I shut my mouth and pretend to be examining my nails when I hear him say, "Right. Let's go."

Still not looking at him, I turn towards the doorway, pretending not to hear the heavy sigh behind me. Rather pleased with myself, just before opening the door I say, "You know, Daniel, you really should get used to girls standing so close to you. We'd best practice some more later."

"Shit," he mutters, and I turn around to wink at him before opening the door. The expression on his face surprises me, though, because, despite his outburst, he has a huge smile plastered on his face. It is infectious, and I don't quite manage to stop my lips from smiling back.

CHAPTER THIRTEEN

EMMA

WE WALK DOWN THE stairs in silence and out into the beautiful summer's day. I briefly look up to take in the blue sky and breathe deeply before turning left to walk in the direction of the bus stop. Daniel walks beside me, not speaking, but the silence does not feel awkward at all. In fact, it is quite comforting. As much as I prefer to listen to music when I'm walking, Daniel's presence seems to quiet my usually rambling thoughts instead of enhancing them.

My good mood takes a plummet, though, when he asks, "So...what did you do last night?"

"Oh, this and that," I hedge. There is no way I am going to tell him that I spent most of my evening scouring the internet for psychologists. That would only lead him to ask me a load of questions I have no intention of answering.

I see the bus coming to a standstill at the stop and lengthen my stride. "I just watched some TV for a while. But I also took a look at your syllabus, by the way. I can see you're starting off with all the classics; *"The Canterbury Tales"*,

"Wuthering Heights", "Pride & Prejudice"..." I chance a peek at him, and seeing him so much more relaxed from what I have come to expect from him calms me.

As we enter the bus, I ask him, "Have you read - or tried to read - any of these books?" I politely nod at the bus driver and move to the end to take a seat.

Daniel doesn't answer me until he is seated beside me.

He sighs. "Well, I have tried on my own, of course, but I *really* need some help." He laughs, but it's not a happy sound. "Obviously," he mutters. He pushes his glasses up his nose and crosses his arms, looking straight ahead.

I puff, a bit irritated, and lean closer to loosen his tight grip. "You need to relax, Daniel." *Damn, his hold is almost unbreakable.* "Being dyslexic is not something to be ashamed of! Honestly." At last, he relents, and I grumble, "For a skinny guy, you do have a lot of strength packed away." I scoot back in my seat again and look out the window.

"I'm not skinny," he tells me, affronted. "If you must know, I keep in shape by swimming several times each week."

I shudder. "I hate the water. It's too...unpredictable," I say quietly. Trying to lighten the mood, I turn back to meet his gaze. "Anyway, I was just teasing you. From what I felt back at the flat, you've got some muscles hiding away in that...err..." I give him the once-over again. "Well, those preppy clothes you like to wear."

He chuckles, and the warmth in his green eyes makes my stomach flip. "I've already agreed to go shopping with you, Emma, so there's no need for you to mince your words."

Unable to hold his gaze any longer, I force myself to turn away, and I end up staring straight ahead. Noticing the train station in the distance, I say, "This is our stop."

"I know," Daniel says, and the amusement in his voice does not go unnoticed.

Deciding to ignore that last bit, I stand up, and shoo at him. "Well, get up, Preppy."

He holds up his hand and gives me that stern Professor look I have already seen once today, and an explosion of butterflies begins to flutter in my stomach. *Oh my...who'd have thought I'd fancy that?*

"On one condition," his voice interrupts my wayward thoughts, and I blink and focus on his mouth instead.

"What?" I ask, distracted and slightly turned on at the same time.

"That you never call me *Preppy* again," he tells me, trying to hide a smirk.

I roll my eyes. "Fine! Now, *Daniel*, will you please get up?" Placing a hand on my hip, I tap my foot; the universal sign of a woman impatient with a man.

"But of course," Daniel relents and quickly grabs his backpack.

I glare at it, and as soon as we move to leave the bus, I mutter, "You need a new bag, too."

I'm pretty sure he heard what I just said, but he pretends to ignore me; silently, we hurry up the stairs to get to our train.

♡

DANIEL

I'm finding it increasingly difficult to keep my eyes from lingering on Emma's lips whenever she talks. This girl is making my head spin, and I can't fathom why that is. Yes, she's beautiful, and yes, last night will definitely not be the last time I fantasise about what I'd like to do to her - and I have plenty of ideas - but she's so confusing.

I *am* surprised that I feel so at ease in her company. My tongue doesn't tie itself into knots whenever I speak, and that's definitely a first for me. Her voice calms me somehow. She hasn't said a word since we got on the train, though, and I wonder what made her clam up like that. One minute we're talking, and the next...nothing. Zilch. Except this strange silence. I can't keep my curiosity in check; this girl fascinates me to no end, and I want to get to know her better.

And I don't just mean in the biblical sense - though I'd gladly give up my virginity to Emma if she asked me - but, somehow, I get the feeling that sex won't be enough for me. I want to know who the real Emma is...the one I know is there, hiding behind all that heavy makeup and the piercings.

Who is this girl?

When she gripped my arms like that back at the flat, I had to force my body to keep still. My cock was more than up for the wicked idea that popped into my head, but acting on it would most likely have ended up with me being kneed in the balls. No, instead of pulling her to me and kissing her senseless, I remained stock-still; my willpower was the only thing that kept me from doing just that.

Just now, thinking back on her warm touch makes my cock twitch and I quickly remove my gaze from those perfectly full lips - *Stop thinking about them!* - and I look at the other passengers. There aren't that many on the train, but a man sitting on the dirty floor a ways from us with a cardboard sign in his hand distracts me from my dirty thoughts. I can't read the sign from this distance, but it's pretty easy to see that he's homeless: clothes wrinkled, worn, and a bit dusty; hair and beard seem unkempt, too. And then there's the general manner of him which appears hopeless. It exudes exhaustion. This is a man who has given up.

I know this may not exactly help, but that doesn't stop me from walking towards him. As I draw nearer, he looks up at me, the hopelessness catching me off-guard and it reminds me of such a dark time in my life. I crouch down in front of him, probably garnering a lot of attention, but I ignore the hostility I can feel surrounding me.

"What's your name?" I ask the man.

He narrows his eyes at me, unwilling to answer, but then he coughs and says, "Carl."

I nod and reach out my hand to him. "I'm Daniel."

Carl hesitates for a couple of seconds, but just as I think that he won't shake my hand, his right one reaches to mine, and he grips it.

His grip is firm. Not what I expected.

"Hi, Daniel," he says, his voice gruff. Maybe he doesn't speak much?

We nod at each other, and I loosen my hold from his before standing up. Seeing the confusion in his eyes, I quickly pull out my wallet, grab a couple of notes, and hand them to him.

"Nice to meet you, Carl," I say, patiently waiting for him to take the money. When he doesn't, but merely keeps looking confused, I bend down on my knees and put them in the small tin canister in front of him.

Just before I move to straighten up again, my eyes meet his, and the shock I see in them embarrasses me.

"I hope you have a good day," I say quickly, and then walk away from him. I haven't moved more than a few paces before I hear a quiet, but heartfelt, *"Thank You"* behind me. I half-turn my head and nod, acknowledging him, but I don't slow down. I look down as I move closer to Emma, and once I'm standing next to her, I sense her gaze lingering on me. Crossing my arms, I ignore her and stare straight ahead, my jaw clenched.

"How much did you give him?" she asks me quietly.

I shrug. "It doesn't matter. He needs the money more than I do."

"It matters a lot to him," she replies, but I don't answer. What is there to say, anyway? There's a part of me that wants to satisfy her need for answers...but I'm still feeling rather embarrassed. I don't want Emma to think that the gesture I just did was more than it was: one human being kind to another...to one less fortunate in life than me.

Silence descends on us again, and I'm glad that's the case. I don't want to answer all her questions right now. Even though it feels as if they're screaming at me, demanding me to pay attention.

CHAPTER FOURTEEN

EMMA

THOUGHTS RUN WILD IN my mind as Daniel and I leave the train and walk towards the bookshop. This boy puzzles me more and more, and even though a small part of me - the cynical part - scoffs at the gesture Daniel just showed to that homeless guy, another part of me is going all soft and gooey. And that's the part of me that I need to watch out for; it doesn't matter how attracted I am to him. I have to remain firm and stand my ground, keeping emotionally detached.

Because if I don't, and we end up becoming involved - as in, dating each other - I have a feeling that when I share all of me with him the disgust on his face will break me. Yes, here's a guy who will have that kind of power over me. And I won't risk my heart. I have to remember to keep it under lock and key.

A particular calm settles over me when we draw nearer to the shop. It always has that effect on me, because I feel safe here: I'll be at work, and no one is able to tell anything about me for as long as I'm here. There'll definitely not be any uncomfortable questions for me to answer. Here, I'm simply an employee, and, at the end of the day, the goal is to keep the customers walking away happy and satisfied with their purchases. Nothing more, nothing less. It's simple, really.

I have a feeling, though, that today won't be like that because of Daniel.

Mentally shaking my head, I open the door and call out, "Hi, Mr. Andersen." Checking the clock on the wall above the desk, I sigh quietly in relief. Five minutes before we officially open. We made it.

Mr. Andersen looks up from the till and smiles warmly at us. "Emma, Daniel...hi. Daniel, are you ready for your first day?" he asks him eagerly. It's nice to see him so enthusiastic about the fact that he now has two young people instead of just me, but it's still strange he didn't tell me about Daniel being my new neighbor before I left on Saturday.

I quickly look at Daniel who smiles and nods at his uncle and I walk closer to my boss.

"Mr. Andersen, I'm sure you're aware of Daniel asking me to be his tutor, and you should know that I've said yes." I hesitate but find my courage when Mr. Andersen just keeps smiling at us. "However, I don't feel comfortable being paid as if I were here full time when, in fact, I won't be. So we need to work on our schedules."

"Now, Emma," Mr. Andersen begins, but I don't let him finish.

"I'm sorry, Sir, but it just doesn't sit well with me," I try to explain, straightening my back.

Mr. Andersen frowns for a while, but finally relents. "Alright, Emma. Why don't the two of you have a chat about it and then let me know your decision by the end of today?"

I smile, relieved, and answer, "Thank you. We will."

A bit of an awkward silence descends, and I'm not entirely sure why that is. Maybe it's just me, so I turn to Daniel.

"Ready to get started?" I ask him expectantly.

I can't quite understand the closed-off expression on his face, but at least he answers me, saying, "Sure."

"Let's get our things put away, and I'll show you around, then?" I continue, and he nods. Turning back to Mr. Andersen, I say, "We'll be out in a few."

He picks up a stack of books. "You know Mondays are usually pretty quiet, Emma, so take your time. I'll call out for you if I suddenly find the shop filled with customers, all here to be guided to the lands of glory," he answers brightly, and I laugh.

"Right," I chuckle, and leave him with his books. Daniel follows closely behind me, and I really need to talk to him about the appropriate kind of space the rest of us prefer to have around people, but I hold my tongue. Usually, it bothers me to no end when people can't seem to understand that standing too close to another human being is far from polite, but, somehow, feeling Daniel's warmth behind me isn't so bad. Maybe it's because of the delicious manly scent I can smell; it's hard to define, but it's kind of woodsy and warm...comforting, I suppose.

Maybe it's just your hormones running amok, the small voice inside admonishes me, but I ignore it. I prefer my other theory.

Opening the door to the back room, I say, "Okay, this is off-limits to all customers. Well, you already know that, of course." I walk the few steps along the narrow entrance before it opens up to the small room. I point to the left, and explain, "As you can see, we have a small kitchenette here where we can make a pot of coffee or tea whenever we feel like it. There's also a small refrigerator for our lunches or...you know, whatever." I walk to the round table standing at the end of the room with four chairs surrounding it, and after I've put down my clutch, I look over my shoulder to find Daniel perusing the small bookshelf situated on the far right wall.

"Sometimes, publishers send us an early printed copy of future releases so that we can read them and decide if we want to feature them in the shop. It's a nice benefit, really. It also gives us the chance to service our customers better," I explain when I see him holding a copy of the highly famous - and notorious - *Fifty Shades of Grey* by E. L. James, and he looks up at me, a small smile on his lips.

"I didn't know my uncle read romance novels," he murmurs, before he puts the book back on the shelf.

I hesitate but then blurt out, "He doesn't. I do." Seeing the question in his eyes, I amend, "Well, sometimes I do. I may not be a romantic as such, but I do like reading about it from time to time. Fantasy and historical thrillers are what I prefer, though."

Liar, liar, pants on fire.

Avoiding his gaze, I look down and pull out my keys from my clutch, pretending to find the right one to my small compartment.

"Hmm," Daniel muses, but I still don't look up. I feel embarrassed, when, in fact, there's no reason to be. Everyone needs a bit of romance in their lives. I just prefer to keep it in the fictional world instead of the real one. It's nice reading about true love, the strife the characters in books go through in order to get their *happily-ever-afters* when the actual reality is that people rarely find it - and then keep it - in this modern day and age.

"I can't say I've read many romance novels," Daniel's voice breaks through my inner musings. "But at least now I know who to ask if I want some recommendations."

Hearing the teasing note in his voice, I narrow my eyes before raising my head to glare at hm. "Well, I'll ask my friend Suzy: she's a romance addict."

"Mm-hmm," he simply hums, but I don't take the bait.

"Okay, we leave our bags, and whatever else we want to, here and have a key to lock it. You never know if anyone wants to try their hand at shop lifting," I tell him and gesture at the ugly, white closet taking up the most of the wall to the left. I shrug. "It's not exactly a beauty to look at, but at least our things aren't easy to steal." Reaching my right arm towards him, I continue, "Give me your backpack and I'll get our things locked away."

Daniels does as I ask, and after it's taken care of, I put my keys in my right back pocket. "Right then. I'll give a tour of the shop." I smile reassuringly at him, and he walks closer to me. So close that I have to tilt my head back to keep my eyes on his. *What is he doing now?*

His face moves closer, and I widen my eyes, surprised by his bold move.

"Please go easy on me," he finally says, and I cannot overlook the nervousness emanating from his body. He's wound so tight I am pretty sure that one false movement will make him explode. In what way, I don't entirely know, but I don't want his first day here to be a bad one. Surprisingly, despite the fact I don't really know him yet, I'm beginning to realise how important this is for him. I want to see him succeed, and I will do what I can to help him.

"Don't worry," I answer quietly. "I don't bite." *Well, not if people don't want me to,* but I don't voice that little morsel of information out loud.

Daniel takes a deep breath, holds it for a couple of seconds, before finally releasing it.

"Good," he says and nods once. "Then please lead the way, Miss," he says, and holds out his left arm towards the door to the shop, indicating that I should go first.

"My, my, my, I'm quite impressed with your gentlemanly manners," I tease, trying to lighten the mood, and it seems to work, because he chuckles. Warmth spreads in my body, because when he does that? His eyes get a certain twinkle in them, and I find that I'm almost unable to resist the pull of them. *Almost.*

As I turn to leave the room, he mutters, "Yeah. That's what they all say."

My step falters, but I pretend to ignore what I just heard. My curiosity is piqued, though: who are *they*? I don't have time to ask him, so I decide to let it go for the rest of the day. I'm quite sure, however, that I won't be able to keep my stupid mouth from doing just that at some point. And soon.

Curiosity may have killed the cat, but I never followed the rules, anyway. Why start now?

It's been a few hours, and Daniel seems to be happy about working at the shop. Well, it's hard to tell, really, because as usual, he doesn't say much. I'm starting to get used to it, though, and it's quite nice. The fact that he isn't a chatterbox but only speaks when he has something he feels is important to say relaxes me, actually. I'd like to know what goes on inside his head, though, because he may not say much, but that doesn't mean he hides his emotions; he's like an open book. When I showed him the bookshelf with literature of all the classics, his eyes lit up like a Christmas tree, and it was difficult to pry him away from them. I have to admit that seeing this made my lady bits tingle a bit.

Yes, guys who love books are, apparently, also quite a turn-on for me. Who knew?

It's getting close to lunchtime, and I'm trying to come up with some sort of excuse about why we shouldn't have lunch together when Mr. Andersen unknowingly comes to my rescue.

"Daniel, what do you say the two of us go over the business side of the shop while Emma takes her lunch break?" he asks Daniel from the front desk.

Daniel's sitting in one of the armchairs, his nose stuck in a book, and I can't stop my lips from pulling up in a smile. He looks so cute.

Hang on. I don't do cute, do I?

Mr. Andersen frowns, and repeats, "Daniel?"

Still no reply. Wow, that boy definitely knows how to keep the world from interrupting when he's absorbed. Shaking my head, I walk to him and tap his shoulder with my right index finger. He jumps, and I snort.

"What?" he asks, looking from side to side before tilting his head back to find me standing behind him.

I smirk. "Your uncle asked you a question, Daniel. Don't you know it's rude not to respond?" I ask him teasingly.

Half turning in his seat, he looks around my body covering his view, and he apologises, "Sorry, Prof, I got lost in a book." His ears turn red, and upon seeing that, my stomach does a scary flip. My body seems more and more eager to get to know Daniel on a more intimate level, but that wouldn't be wise of me. I can't deny, though, that experiencing these feelings - no matter how much they unnerve me - is kind of uplifting.

It gives me hope that maybe, one day, I will no longer be so afraid of intimacy.

"No worries, it happens to us all," Mr. Andersen beams at him. He's been quite chipper today, and I'm guessing it has a lot to do with Daniel being here.

"What did you say?" Daniels asks him and stands.

"I merely suggested that we should let Emma take her break now and go over a few of the business things being a bookshop owner entail," Mr. Andersen replies.

Nodding, Daniel answers, "Sure," and, giving me a small smile, he walks to the front desk, the book he was so absorbed in tucked to his side. I tilt my head a bit, trying to see the title, but his hand and fingers cover most of it, and I can't make it out. I'll have to ask him later.

"I'll just grab my purse, and then I'll be off," I say to them and move quickly to the back room. I hurry to unlock the door and head inside to do just that. Opening the closet to retrieve my purse, I can't ignore the butterflies erupting in my stomach. Quickly scanning the contents, I find the folded note I wrote last night, and a sense of dread overcomes me.

I can't avoid it anymore. Inside that piece of paper may be the answer to fixing me.

Satisfied, and, strangely enough, feeling less anxious of what I am about to do, I close the closet doors, lock them, and leave the room. Walking quickly to the entrance, I glance at the two men, and when Daniel looks up from some papers lying on the desk, frowning, I give him a small wave, but I don't stop.

I don't have time.

If I stop, I'll chicken out, and I mustn't do that.

I have an appointment with a psychologist to make.

CHAPTER FIFTEEN

EMMA

SETTING UP THE APPOINTMENT with the psychologist - one Katherine McGregor - was easier than I thought it would be. And yes, I like the fact that, based on the name alone, I will be pouring out my thoughts, my life, really, to someone who seems to be British. That'll probably make it easier for me. I hope. Seeing as it's the summer holiday for many, she is able to fit me in for later this week.

Shite. I'm really doing this.

Well, I have to. If I don't, I'm pretty sure the nightmares will end up taking over my life completely, and I can't say I'll enjoy that. I won't like having to spill my secrets to a complete stranger, either, but maybe I'll feel differently once I get started. One can only hope that she'll be able to help me.

And if she can't? Well, then I guess that's that.

Walking back to the bookshop with a small skip to my steps, I can't deny that taking this first step is a relief. I guess I should thank Suzy for that. Munching on a sandwich, I sit down on a nearby bench and pull out my phone to do just that.

Me: You're the best friend ever. xxx

It doesn't take long for her to respond.

Suzy: Not that I would ever disagree with that sentiment, but what brought this on? xx

Me: I did like you asked: I have a meeting with a psychologist this week...x

She doesn't text back right away, but I can't really say I'm surprised by that. Checking the clock on my phone, I quickly eat the rest of my lunch before I have to head back to work. Finally, I see the screen on my phone light up with a new text.

Suzy: I'm glad. And maybe, once you've had a few sessions, you'll stop avoiding your issues and talk to me as well. ;-) x

I smile. How can I not?

Me: I promise I will. Got to get back to work now, lovely. TTYL. xx

As I finish typing my last text, I realise how frustrating it must be for Suzy to be my friend sometimes. For her to stick around, to keep from asking me any sort of questions about my past must be more than a little annoying, and I resolve to ask her out for dinner soon.

All sorts of emotions seem to wage war inside me: anger, trepidation, relief, fear, all leaving me unsure about how to handle them, so I stop a little distance from the bookshop to put myself together; I take a few deep breaths, let them out slowly, and shake my head. I have to get a grip before seeing Mr. Andersen and Daniel again.

The sound of a new text message distracts me and I quickly open it and smile when I see Suzy's sent me a big heart emoticon with the words *I love you -- Always & Forever* xx on it.

"Damn it," I mutter, and quickly put my phone back in my clutch. I don't need more of that touchy-feely stuff right now. But seeing and reading these texts warm my heart. Why that girl is still single, I will never know. She has the biggest heart in the world.

Grabbing the door handle, I push it open and walk inside my favourite place in the world, ready to face whatever the rest of the day has to offer once again. Satisfied to see quite a lot of customers, I hurry to the staff room to get rid of my things and back outside to help Daniel.

♡

The rest of the day has been quite uneventful, and I'm glad to see Daniel seeming to fit in so well. He's been a bit quiet and shy when customers have approached him, but I've never been far away from his side, able to step in if he needed a hand with anything. I don't quite know if his speech impairment has been a problem for him, because, to be perfectly honest, I don't notice it much anymore. Strange how I have already become so used to his company, isn't it?

We're just about to close when a group of giggling teenage girls enters the shop, and I suppress the groan rising up in my throat. Just what we needed: customers who'll take forever to browse around but probably end up leaving again without having made a purchase. Yes, that's part of running a shop, I know, but it's been a really long day, and I just want to go home. Daniel and I managed to come to an agreement on how often I'll tutor him every week, and I'll be spending my evening going through some of my notes on the first book we'll be reading together: *"The Canterbury Tales"*. That should be interesting.

Trying to appear the professional I am, I walk towards the annoying girls, but before I have even taken a few steps, one of them – a pretty blonde who can't be more than eighteen years old – heads straight for Daniel standing behind the front desk, about to sort through the till. He's frowning at the receipts, seemingly oblivious to the Man-Eater-In-Training approaching him, but some small evil part of me wants to see how he handles her. I know he's told me about getting all flustered and tongue-tied around girls, but surely not this one? I mean, she's so young! He can't be intimidated by someone like her?

"Hi," she greets him exuberantly, and I want to roll my eyes when she strikes quite the pose: tilting her head to the side, pushing out her boobs in her already pretty daring pink top, the fingers of her left hand fiddling at a necklace she's wearing, but then I frown. When did I become such a prude? Hell, I tend to wear even less when I go out clubbing! Clearly, I need to have my head examined. Realising that the clenching in the pit of my stomach is rather uncomfortable, and that it could very well resemble the feeling of possessiveness, I take a step back. Surprised at this very unwelcome notion that Daniel is mine, and that I do not particularly like seeing this blonde girl trying to catch his attention, I turn my back on them and make it seem as if I am busy sorting out some books on the nearby coffee table. My ears, however, work really well.

"Err...hi," Daniel answers her, and although I cannot see him, the uncertainty in his voice isn't difficult to notice.

"Do you have any naughty books?" she asks him, and I want to cringe. Even I wouldn't feel comfortable with a customer asking me that. It's just a tad too blunt.

"Ex...excuse me?" Daniel's stuttering starts back up, and

a small sliver of sympathy for his bad luck grabs me in my soft spot.

"Yes, you know...books about sex? Or any romance novels that are quite racy?" comes the cheeky reply from the blonde.

"Um...well, I...I don't r-really know..." My shoulders shake with suppressed laughter. Poor guy, he's in way over his head here. Deciding to come to his rescue without making it seem too obvious, I clear my throat as quietly as I can, and meander over to the desk to stand close beside Daniel.

Smiling, I ask the blonde, "Can I help you? My colleague here doesn't read many romance novels." I place my hands on the desk, and subtly allow the pinky on my right to touch Daniel's left one. Such a small touch shouldn't really zing through my body, but it does, and even though a part of me wants to put some distance between us again, another part revels in the pleasant feeling that soars through me.

The blonde squints her eyes and answers me curtly, "Actually, I think your colleague here is more than happy to help me instead of you."

Ouch. The cat's come out to play, I see.

I try a different tactic. "Well, you see, Daniel is new to the shop, and we're about to close, so I just thought that in order to help you, it'd be easier if I did just that instead of him." Looking up at Daniel, who, surprisingly hasn't uttered a word, I look adoringly at him - at least, I hope that's what my eyes convey - and continue talking to the little man-eater, "Also, my boyfriend and I would like to go home soon and have some...alone time together." Turning my eyes to the blonde, I want to laugh at the sour expression now covering her face, but I keep my impulses in check. Unable to let my triumph go completely unnoticed, however, I wrap my arm around Daniel's waist, stand up on my toes and give him a lingering kiss on his cheek. As soon as my lips come into contact with his skin, he jolts, but I ignore it; instead, I focus on the way his stubble seems to be coarse and soft at the same time, and I revel in the tingle left on my lips as I slowly move back on my feet. As if having a mind of their own, my eyes immediately look into Daniel's, and the intensity and lust I find there almost cause my knees to buckle.

It's just a small kiss. It shouldn't affect me so much.

My lips part on a whoosh, and I wrench my gaze away from his.

The blonde huffs and grumpily says, "Never mind. I'll come back another day." Turning on her heels without saying even a goodbye, she waves at her friends, and they all hurry out of the shop, leaving us free to close down for the day. As soon as they're out the door, I rush to it, flip the sign over, and lock it.

"What was that?" Daniel asks from behind me, and if I'm not mistaken, he sounds almost angry.

Turning around, I reply vaguely, "Nothing. I just wanted them to go so we could shut down for the day. No big deal." Crossing my arms in front of me, I look at him, and yes, he does look rather annoyed.

"No big deal?" he sputters. "You kissed me!"

I sigh. "On your cheek, dummy. It's not as if I stuck my tongue down your throat." I walk past the desk he still hasn't moved away from, and continue towards the back room. "Besides, if we're supposed to impersonate a couple, we both need to get used to acting like it once in a while."

"But...," he protests quietly, and instead of just ignoring him, I stop in my tracks and look over my shoulder, raising an eyebrow. I want to know what he feels is important to say.

"Well, just...some fair warning the next time would be nice," he mutters, looking down at the papers in his hands. The unhappy frown on his face puzzles me, but before I can question him further, Mr. Andersen comes out from the back room, and the moment is lost.

"Sorry, guys. Time ran away from me," Mr. Andersen says as he closes the door, and I can't help but notice that he seems rather distracted.

"No worries. I'll just grab my things. Are you coming, Daniel?" I turn fully to both men, and I guess I have my answer when instead of Daniel, Mr. Andersen replies for him.

"Actually, Daniel and I will get everything sorted for the night, Emma. Have a few things left to show him. There's no need for you to be kept from your plans." He smiles at me, and the kindness in his smile suddenly reminds me of my dad. It's been a while since I last talked with my parents, actually, and I miss them.

I shrug. "Okay." Moving my eyes to Daniel, I tell him, "Have a good night."

"You, too," he murmurs, but he still refuses to meet my gaze, a fact that is beginning to annoy the crap out of me. The ease and camaraderie we have shared all day is gone now, and the old Daniel is back: the one who doesn't - or won't - say much...the one who seems to flick a switch from one moment to the next, leaving me wondering why he does that.

Is it just me? Am I letting my imagination run away with me? And why do I even care when we've only known each other for a few days? It baffles me.

Quickly, I grab my things, and, without a backwards glance, I call out a "goodnight" and leave the bookshop. My usually safe haven no longer feels so safe. Not with Daniel's eyes burning a hole in my back as I walk away.

CHAPTER SIXTEEN

EMMA

ONCE I ENTER MY flat, my unusually crappy mood still evident, I pull out my phone, find the number to my parents, and hit the green button. Listening to it ring, I toss my clutch on my kitchen counter and remove my shoes.

It keeps ringing for a long time, and just when I'm about to give up, my mum's voice fills my ear: "Hello?"

"Hi, Mum," I greet her.

"Emma!" she squeals, and hearing her excitement instantly makes me smile. My mum, Julia, doesn't usually squeal, except when speaking with her children or other loved ones. She's 55, works as a barrister, and she can be quite scary, actually. Having a temper on her, but claiming that she doesn't, made growing up rather interesting. She can't cook, so it's a good thing my dad loves to do it.

"Oh my gosh, darling, so lovely to hear your voice," she continues. "It's been too long since we chatted. How are you?"

Sighing, I sit down on my bed. "I'm okay," I reply.

"Only okay?" she asks me, confused, and I mentally shake my head.

"No, I'm more than okay," I hurry to reassure her. "Just got home from work and I'm a bit tired."

"Oh, I see. Well, tell me all about what you've been up to lately." Hearing her concerned mum-voice kick in, I think I manage to satisfy her curiosity for the next few minutes by telling her about Suzy, and my job, but it doesn't take long before she interrupts me.

"Honey, something is bothering you. I can hear it in your voice. Now, tell your old mum all about it and let it out."

Rolling my eyes, I say, "How is it you immediately come to the conclusion that something is off when I ring you?"

"Because you only ring us when you're feeling low, sweetie," she admonishes me, and her words make me stop and examine them more closely.

"Do I?" I ask her quietly.

"Yes," she replies firmly, and I cringe. "Your dad and I worry about you, you know. It's been so long since we saw you. Are you eating properly? Sleeping?" Her concern is evident in her voice now, and I feel guilty for having kept silent for so long.

"I'm sorry, Mum. Yes, I'm eating. As far as the sleeping goes..." I hesitate but then soldier on. "Well, that's debatable, I suppose."

"You still have those...nightmares?" she asks me tentatively. Usually, this is the part in our conversation when I'll change the subject, refusing to speak of them, but even though I feel sick to my stomach right now, this is my mum...and she deserves the truth.

Feeling a little teary, I whisper, "Yes. Every night." *Well, apart from one,* I think to myself, but seeing as I don't know why that is, there's no reason to tell her that.

"Oh, sweetheart," my mum sniffles, and I can't stand hearing the tears in her voice.

Hurriedly, I say, "Please don't cry, Mum. I'm okay, honestly."

"I want you to be more than *okay*, Em, I want you to be happy," she says, the fierceness in her tone not lost on me.

"I'm working on it," I try to reassure her.

"Working on it? What do you mean?" she asks me, puzzled, but thankfully no longer sniffling.

"I've..." I take a deep breath, and then force the words to leave my mouth, "I've set up an appointment with a psychologist."

There's nothing but silence meeting my statement, and dread fills my stomach.

"You've what?" Mum whispers, and the disbelief and hurt in her voice don't escape me.

"I'm having my first session on Friday," I reply.

"You're telling me that you're perfectly fine with talking to some random *stranger* about your dreams, yet you're not comfortable with telling *me*, your own mother, about them?!" she asks, openly crying now.

"Mum!" I protest. "This is a professional! Someone equipped to help me move on!" Standing from my bed, I start to pace from one end of the room to another, agitation filling my limbs.

"But why can't you talk to me instead?"

"Because I just can't, Mum!" I snap at her. "Don't ask me to do that!"

"Emma, darling, I'm your mother. I want to help you, don't you understand that?" she says, and the despondency in her voice isn't lost on me.

Sighing, I quietly answer, "Because they're not your burden to bear."

"Don't be daft, girl. Of course they are! Ever since you were born, all your heartaches, and your joys, have been meant to be mine to share with you. That's a mother's job, Em," she sighs.

"Maybe I shouldn't have told you," I backtrack.

"Don't you think like that, Emma. I want to know what's going on. I just wish you felt that you could talk to me about everything," she sighs dejectedly, piercing my heart. But this is one thing I vowed a long time ago that I would never divulge; she doesn't need the same kind of dreams haunting her at night.

Mum continues, "Just promise me that if you ever do decide to let me in on these things that you won't keep parts of them to yourself; you have to tell me every single detail, you hear?"

"I hear you," I murmur.

"Good."

An uncomfortable silence falls between us, and I don't have a clue on what to say to break it. It turns out that I won't have to because I hear the voice of my father in the background:

"Julia, let me talk to Emma, please."

Mum sighs and then says, "Your dad would like a word with you, sweetie, so I'll put him on. However, I want to speak with you again afterwards, so don't ring off, okay?"

"Got it," I agree.

A few seconds pass and then the soothing voice of my dad fills my ears.

"Hello, darling."

Immediately, I want to cry, but I refuse to let the tears fall.

Instead, I just say, "Hi," leaving it at that.

"Are you enjoying your summer holiday?" he asks me, and the relief I feel at hearing him ask something so normal after the bout I just had with my mum relaxes me. Soon after, we're lost in the usual kind of chit-chat, but it doesn't bother me in the least. My dad, Ralph, is a quiet, taciturn man, but I've never doubted the love he has for his family. He's a professor in geography at Oxford University, and, as far as I know, nothing short of dire illness will ever force him to retire. He loves his job, and I know he wants to keep teaching for as long as possible, because as soon as he retires, mum will have a very long list of things she wants to have done around the house. And let's just say that my dad's clutter will be first order of business to attend to; mum loathes it with a vengeance, and she's never hidden this fact from anyone.

After a few minutes, my dad says, "Alright, love, it was good to hear your voice. Your mum is standing here, giving me the evil eye, so I'd best let you go now. But before I do..." For once, my dad hesitates, causing me to take notice, but the reason becomes clear when he goes on saying, "Please ring again soon, okay? We miss you."

A lump forms in my throat, but I push past it. "I will, dad. Promise."

"Good, good. Well, here's your mum, darling. Bye."

Hearing the phone crackle in the other end, followed by my dad's chuckles, I can almost picture my mum wrenching it away from him.

"Emma, you still there?" she asks me.

"Yes," I reply and walk to my kitchen.

"Okay, I just wanted to ask you if Steven texted you yet?"

Hearing my brother's name makes my body freeze up, and I curse inwardly, damning Steven to the pits of hell for telling mum that.

Knowing she'll only start asking questions if I don't answer her, I reply casually, "He did, yes. We've arranged to meet when he's coming to Copenhagen in a couple of months."

"Oh, good," she says, relieved, and she doesn't have to elaborate on that. The rift between us has always bothered her, and even though I'm aware that's only natural, it doesn't stop me from being more than ticked off by his actions.

"Well, I'm glad," mum's voice pulls me away from my musings, but I don't comment on it. Why should I?

"Mum, I have to go now," I tell her instead. "I promise I'll ring again soon."

"That would be lovely, sweetie. Take care, and don't work too hard, yeah?"

"I won't, I promise," I reassure her.

"And...well, please let me know when you've been to that psychologist next week, Emma. It'd mean a lot to me."

"Sure, mum. Love you."

"Love you, too, darling. Bye."

"Bye."

Pressing the red button, I end the call on a deep sigh.

That went well.

Throat parched, I throw my phone on my bed and walk into the kitchen to pour a glass of water. As I guzzle it down, I try not to worry about my mum's distress. My mum doesn't cry much but when she does? It breaks my heart. She's such a strong woman, but very sensitive underneath her tough exterior. Nevertheless, I won't ever divulge the details of my nightmares...I can't. Because I was telling her the truth when I said that it isn't her burden to bear; it's mine and only mine.

CHAPTER SEVENTEEN

DANIEL

I DON'T KNOW WHY I freaked out when Emma kissed me earlier. I mean, a small kiss like that shouldn't mean anything, and I know she only did it to stop that blonde from pestering me, but it's the first time a girl outside my family has done that. And having Emma's lips on my skin, even for such a short time? It burned me, and not in a bad way at all. Oh no, it was entirely pleasurable.

Even now, hours later, as I sit here on my balcony, I only have to think back on that moment when she put her arm around me, leaned up, and placed her full lips on my cheek, and warmth spreads in my entire body. I want to whip out my cock right now and jack off, not caring in the least if anyone sees me. But I'm not brave enough. And I honestly don't have time for that as I have so many boxes that need unpacking. If I don't get them sorted, this will never feel like a home to me.

I desperately want that: to feel as if I belong here, in this big city, living next door to a woman who has already become a permanent fixture on my mind. On one hand, she annoys me with her sometimes insensitive questions, but on the other, I find her very fascinating. Probably because she is so closed off herself. Why does that turn me on to no end?

Hint: because she is gorgeous, and I'm horny.

Despite the fact that she showed up on my doorstep this morning, wanting us to get to know each other, she didn't ask me any questions at all throughout the day. To tell the truth, we didn't have much time to do that seeing as it was my first day in the bookshop, so maybe it isn't that odd, after all.

I wish I was the kind of guy who could simply man up, go to her, and kiss her senseless. But I'm not. That isn't me. I'm quiet, introspective, and let's not forget the clumsiness and how uneasy Emma makes me feel. If I do that, she'll most likely kick my arse, and that's the last thing I want. For one thing, it'll hurt, and I just know that I'm not into that kind of pain; for another, I want her to come to *me* first.

Selfish? Perhaps. I want her to show me if this almost unbearable attraction I harbour towards her is reciprocated.

Also, I'm pretty certain that I'm a coward, and I can't handle the rejection right now.

What I *can* do, though, is try to get beneath her skin and find out as much as I can about her.

Setting aside my cold beer, I pick up my phone and text her.

Me: When's your birthday?

Taking a sip, I wait. And wait. It takes a while, but then the screen lights up with her name.

Emma: June 1st. When's yours?

Satisfied that she's decided to play along, I hurry to respond.

Me: December 1st. What's your favourite colour?

This time, it doesn't take long for her to answer.

Emma: Hmm...I don't really have one. But I like green and blue the most, I suppose. What about you?

Immediately, her eyes materialise in my head, and I text back:

Me: No real preference, either. Off the top of my head, I'd have to say grey...or blue.

What else should I ask her? I know she has a brother, of course, but I can't really see her revealing much about him at this stage. The whole *'fake boyfriend'* thing already tells me there's a story there, but I sincerely doubt that Emma will open up to me about it.

Me: What're the names of your parents?

Leaning back in my chair, I take another sip of my beer, waiting for Emma's response, but it doesn't come. I wait some more until, finally, I text her again:

Me: Are you there?

Finally, she replies.

Emma: Sorry, was just about to take a shower.

Groaning, I hang my head. Is this girl trying to kill me already? Imagining her body, slick with water and soap, is going to do my head in.

Taking a deep breath, I text her again.

Me: Sorry, I didn't mean to disturb you. Just wanted to get to know you better. You know, so that I can act like I'm your boyfriend.

I can't sit still anymore. Standing up, I gather my beer and then I head inside, eyeing the boxes containing all my belongings. Frowning, I sigh, but then I mentally shake my head and move to the first one. I've only just opened it when a ping from my phone lying on my bed alerts me of a text. Quickly, I pick it up, swipe the screen and read it.

Emma: You couldn't know so there's no need to apologise. My mum's name is Julia -- my dad's is Ralph. Next month, it'll be their 35th wedding anniversary.

Looking up, I mutter, "Wow." Immediately, I type a new response.

Me: That's very impressive. I'll let you get to your shower now. Got a lot of things to unpack, anyway. See you in the morning.

Moving back to the box, I notice all the books inside, and then close the lid again. I don't have any bookshelves yet so it's probably better I leave that one for last. As I move to another one, a new text arrives, and I read it.

Emma: Sure. See you tomorrow. Sleep well.
Me: Thanks. You, too.

I place my hands on my hips and scan the room, trying to get my butt in gear, but it's futile. It's impossible to ignore the hard-on tenting my pants now, knowing what Emma is about to do, and I quickly tear off my t-shirt and push them down.

"Guess I'll take a shower, too," I mutter, and, palming my balls, I walk to my bathroom.

EMMA

Pursing my lips, I send a final text to Daniel:
Me: Don't forget we're having your first tutoring session tomorrow. Should we do it at my place?

I stand there, holding my towel loosely around my body, and a sliver of disappointment courses through me when, after some time, I still haven't received a reply. Shaking it off,

I place my phone on my kitchen counter and go inside my bathroom. Hanging up the towel on the back of the door, I reach out my arm to gauge the temperature of the cascading water, and satisfied that it's to my preference, I move inside and shut the sliding doors behind me.

Tipping my head back to let the water run through my hair, I pick up the shampoo. As I lather my hair, I think back on the short text exchange we just had and find that I liked it. I mean, apart from Suzy and my mum, I don't text with other people, but getting to know Daniel even just a little bit feels nice. Normal. Non-threatening, even. Probably because it was done through texting instead of, say, sitting opposite each other in some café or in one of our flats.

Not having those intense eyes on me, scrutinising my every move as we get to know each other better is safer.

I rinse out my hair, grab some conditioner, and after having put it in, I pick up my soap and pour it on a small sponge. As soon as I let it glide over my breasts, a set of intense, lust-filled green eyes spring to mind, and I feel immensely turned on. Slowing down my movements, I move the sponge to my right nipple, causing it to perk up instantly, and warmth settles in my lower abdomen. Moving the sponge to my other nipple, I put pressure on it which gives the same result as before, and while I continue to massage my body with the sponge, going lower, the index finger and thumb on my right hand close around my nipple. Feeling the sting, a small sigh escapes my lips, and I close my eyes.

Imagining that it's Daniel's hands caressing my stomach, holding onto my hips, a moan escapes me, and I can feel the wetness gathering in my pussy. I want to feel his lips on me...His tongue dipping into my navel as he kneels before me, one hand moving up to my breast, pinching my nipple...his lips teasing my hip bone as he grabs onto my arse cheeks, fondling them, moulding them…his hands moving to my thighs, putting pressure on for me to spread my legs some more…his hot breath fanning above my clit, teasing and torturing me.

Continuing to pinch my nipples, I drop the sponge, hardly noticing the *plop* it makes, and I tease my clit with my fingers.

Shite, I'm horny.

Feeling the tingle in my core, I finally dip a finger inside, and I moan more loudly. The wetness there spurs me on, and I slap my clit once, allowing the tingle to spread. As I finger myself, I imagine Daniel's tongue doing it. He licks, sucks, even bites gently, maintaining the perfect rhythm, and I'm panting, spurring him on.

Spreading my legs further, I put another finger inside my drenched pussy, curling them up to reach my sweet spot, and I can't hold back anymore. My thumb rubs my clit over and over until, finally, the most intense orgasm erupts, and I come loudly. Just before the name Daniel erupts from my mouth, I clamp it shut, biting my lower lip, and I sag back to lean on the cool tiles covering the wall.

"Wow," I whisper, keeping my eyes closed for a while longer. When my legs no longer seem to be mere limp noodles, I straighten up, quickly rinse away the conditioner still in my hair, and I turn off the water. I open the sliding doors to grab my towel, dry off before getting another one for my hair, and then I walk into my room to put on my yoga pants and a tank top to sleep in.

Pulling my clothes on, I feel unsettled. I don't think I've ever come that hard, not even when being with one of my hook-ups, and the intensity scares me a little.

I'm not ashamed of it, no.

Only...surprised. Uncertain about what it means. And I don't like uncertainty...not knowing what to expect is not something I relish at all. And I have a feeling that Daniel is a factor that will leave me rattled and insecure, and I can't say I'm looking forward to that. I can't deny, though, that the way he looks at me thrills me. He makes me feel desired...wanted. And not just for my body, no. He actually seems to want to get to know me. But what will it mean in the end? Am I brave enough to let him in completely?

Sighing at my jumbled thoughts, I pull back the duvet from my bed and begin to settle in. Remembering I left my phone in the kitchen I get up immediately and head to fetch it, and I can't resist swiping the screen to check if Daniel replied to my last message. When I find none, disappointment settles within, but I try to ignore it, and walk back to my bed and jump in. Reaching beside me where my always present ereader lies on my bedside table, I switch it on, determined to become lost in a book for the next few hours.

Yet even though I'm enjoying it, a pair of green eyes is never far away from my thoughts.

CHAPTER EIGHTEEN

EMMA

"HELP ME," THE LITTLE girl whispers, her frightened eyes filling up with tears.

I can't move my body, and my lips are unable to form words. Trying to tell her how much I wished I could help her with my eyes alone, I don't even dare blink in case she can't see the sincerity in them.

"Please," she begs, openly crying now. I push and push, trying to break free from the bonds holding me, but, as usual, I can't. I'm being held captive by my own body. I hate this weakness.

A shadow looms over the little girl, and, for once, she sits up and skirts to the other end of the bed, trying to get away. Tucking her legs under her, clasping them tightly with her arms, she tries to appear smaller. But it's no use; the shadow moves closer and reaches its arms out to her.

She turns her head to me and screams, "Help me! Please!"

At last, my voice breaks free, but my body is still useless. "How?!" I cry out to her. "I can't move!"

The shadow draws ever nearer, and the girl is openly sobbing now. "Just... speak up," she whispers.

As the bonds loosen from around my body, I fall to my knees, and I scramble to get up again. Frantically pushing my hair from my face, I look towards the bed, and my steps falter. The shadow has engulfed the little girl – me – and I can no longer see her at all.

I scream.

Waking up, I clutch my head, and the nausea sets in right away. Kicking away the duvet covering my legs, I hurry as best I can and, finally, I storm into the bathroom and pull up the toilet seat. I only just manage to pull my hair away and collect it in my fist on the nape of my neck when the sickness overtakes me, and I throw up. Shutting my eyes tightly, I wait it out until only dry heaves are what's left in my stomach.

Sitting back on my haunches, I lean my head back and scrub at my face, wiping away my tears.

Why the fuck can't Tom leave me alone?! Why must he haunt me after all this time?

Grabbing onto the sink, I pull my weakened body up, and just when I'm about to turn on the faucet, banging on my front door interrupts me. Pausing and slightly panicking as well, I hold my breath, which, to tell the truth, is kind of silly, given the circumstances. I quickly grab my toothbrush, put it in my mouth and scrub vigorously, hoping the mint will get rid of the nasty taste, and I turn and leave my sanctuary.

"Emma! Are you alright?!" Daniel shouts from behind the door, and hearing his muffled voice fills me with warmth. Not thinking twice about it, I hurry to the door, stubbing my toe in the process, and skipping a bit, I finally manage to grab onto the handle, turn the locks, and I wrench the door open.

Whoa...be still my beating heart.

Standing before me is definitely not a gangly geek. Only

clothed in a pair of sweatpants is my neighbour, looking all disheveled and flushed...and lickable.

"Emma! What the hell just happened?" he asks me, but I can't tear my eyes off this chest. A small smattering of hair covers his chest, and my gaze wanders down his abs – *yes! Abs!* – following his very happy trail down his navel and disappears in his pants.

Oh...my...god. He has a 'V'?!

"Emma?" Daniel's concerned voice halters my silent perusal of his body, and my head snaps up to lock my eyes on his. He's wearing his glasses, of course, and a frown mars his face, but even though he's obviously tired, he's the most beautiful sight I've ever laid my eyes upon.

"Gorgeous," I croak out.

"Excuse me?" he says, frowning, and my befuddled brain finally catches up.

Clearing my throat, I quickly say, "Nothing. Absolutely nothing."

Crossing his arms, he gives me a quick once-over before pulling his eyes back to mine, and then he asks me, "Why were you screaming?"

My body freezes automatically. "Erm...what screaming?" I ask him and avoid his gaze. Not a good idea, actually, seeing as it's now focused on his lips. *Uh-uh.*

He sighs. "Come on, Emma, don't play daft. I woke up to your horrible screams and instantly thought that someone had broken into your flat and was assaulting you! Are you okay?"

Taking a more defensive stance, crossing my own arms, I answer irritably, "Well, as you can see, I'm fine. Sorry I woke you up."

Disbelief and hurt flashes in his eyes, but it's only there

briefly, leaving me wondering if that's actually what I saw.

Raking a hand through his already messed up hair, he looks away from me, not speaking a word.

"Thanks for checking up on me, though," I say quietly, and take a step closer to him. I'm not entirely sure what to do, but before I even know it, Daniel's taken my arm and is pulling me to him and into a tight embrace. I barely avoid hitting my forehead on his chest, turning my face at the very last moment, and as soon as his arms wrap around me, my body relaxes, and my toothbrush slips from my fingers.

I feel...*safe*, actually. A feeling so foreign to me, yet I know instantly what it means, and I don't want to lose it; I quickly manage to wrap my own arms around his waist, holding on tight, and I never want to let go.

"Scared me," Daniel murmurs into my hair, his face bent down close to my own. If I turned my head now, I'm sure our mouths would be perfectly aligned. The longing to feel his lips on mine for the first time is close to overwhelming me. The warmth of his breath on my neck instantly covers my entire body with goose bumps. Unable to ignore the flush on my cheeks, I remain silent, willing it to go away on its own without Daniel noticing it.

"I'm sorry," I whisper, my hands grabbing onto the waistline of his pants. I don't want to move out of his embrace. I think I could live here forever.

"Don't be," he replies gruffly. "Did you have a nightmare?"

Tensing a bit, I say vaguely, "Yes...I have them now and then."

"I see," he whispers, and that's it. He doesn't ask any more questions...there are no demands coming from his mouth, and for that, I'm grateful.

Knowing how late it must be, I pull back slightly, but his arms only strengthen the hold they have on me. Instinctively, I'm aware that this means he doesn't want to let me go, and thinking, *Sod it*, I relax further into his arms.

We stand just like that, reveling in the silence, for I don't know how long. Eventually, though, a certain hard object begins to poke me in my stomach, and a snort erupts from me.

"Err...Daniel?" I say quietly.

"Yes?" he answers, and I can tell that he's some place far away from reality. When he turns his head and buries his nose in my hair, inhaling deeply, the butterflies intensify and they're no longer fluttering; no, they're doing somersaults. *Wait...did he just sniff my hair?*

"I think junior wants to come out and play," I tease.

His body stills for a heartbeat, but then he moves so suddenly, wrenching his arms from around me, that I almost fall flat on my face.

"Sorry, sorry," he stammers, reaching a hand out to my shoulder to steady me, and laughter erupts from me.

"It's...no...problem," I gasp, and although I'm trying to hold it back, I just can't. It must be the fatigue causing this fit because there really isn't a reason to laugh.

"I'm...sorry." I hurriedly wipe tears from my eyes. "It's not funny, I know. Just...please give me a minute."

Daniel has moved to stand directly behind the doorjamb, only his head peeking around it, and the flush on his face intensifies the need in me that appears to grow stronger each time I am near him. I want to reach out to him, yank him inside my flat, and violate him and have my wicked way with him.

Looking into Daniel's embarrassed, yet amused eyes, I

smile a little, hating how awkward the situation has become.

"It's really late...," he murmurs, his gaze zooming in on my mouth, and I instinctively lick my lips. Daniel takes a deep breath and lets it out slowly.

Nodding, I ask him, "What time is it?"

"Around three am," he answers, still holding my gaze.

We stand there, just staring at each other for a while. The reluctance to let him go is almost staggering, and the longer he stares so intently at me, the ability to breathe becomes more and more difficult.

Finally, he asks me, "Are you sure you're okay?"

"Yup. Fit as a fiddle," I reassure him and take a few steps back, forcing my body to be released from the spell his gaze has on me. Reaching for the door, I move to close it, and when he doesn't say anything else, only keeps on watching me silently, I say, "Thank you for coming to my rescue, my white knight," and I wink at him.

Laughing, he says, "I'll be your knight anytime, sweetheart," and butterflies flutter in my stomach.

Get a grip, I admonish myself, but, obviously, I don't say that to him. Instead, my lips pull up in a cheeky smile and just as I shut the door, I say, "Goodnight, Daniel."

"Goodnight," he whispers.

As soon as I've locked it, I turn around and lean my back on it, sighing deeply.

"Wow...what the heck do I do now?" I mutter to my small hallway, but it doesn't have any answers for me. Of course it doesn't.

Feeling the urge for a cigarette, I quickly pick up my toothbrush from the floor and head to my bathroom to rinse my mouth properly. Once that's done, I move to open the doors to my balcony and I slip outside. Taking my small stash from the ground, I sit down on one of the chairs, and I remain there for the rest of the night, contemplating what just happened.

And all the mysteries of Daniel...

Who'd have thought that all *that* deliciousness was hidden beneath his clothes? It kept my thoughts away from my nightmare, that's for certain. I'm actually grateful for him coming to check up on me, however embarrassing it was that he heard me, and the way his actions make me feel? Well, let's just say that I'm starting to become one of those heroines I always read about in my romance novels.

I guess miracles *do* happen.

There is *one* part about the nightmare I can't keep away from my mind: the fact that the little girl tried to call for help. That's definitely a new development, and I can't help but wonder what it means?

I don't get an answer, however, and I remain in my seat, staring unseeingly at the park across from me until the birds begin to wake up and the sun rises.

A new day...a new beginning, perhaps?

DANIEL

I'm lying in my bed, one arm supporting my head, and the urge to get up and go to Emma's is almost unbearable.

Waking up to her screams easily stole five years from my life...they were that horrendous and chilling. Not being a stranger to nightmares, I keep wondering what past events could be the reason for them, because I'm absolutely certain that something happened to Emma to cause her such night terrors.

When I saw her standing in the doorway, her tear-stained face evident for all to see nearly made me pick her up and take her back to my flat. I didn't do that, of course...but now that I'm back in my own home, still thinking about her an hour later, I vow to do exactly that the next time she has a nightmare.

Because I'm sure there'll be a next time...and when she breaks, I'll be there, helping her stand tall and proud again. Seeing her tears, the sadness and fear in her eyes nearly unmanned me. The intensity of our growing connection scares the ever-loving crap out of me, but I can't keep my curiosity in check. Somehow, some way, Emma has managed to dig herself deeper and deeper into my soul - and now I sound like a pansy.

Frustrated and, as ever, rather turned on by the thought of my evasive neighbor, I fluff my pillows, turn to my side, and close my eyes. Sleep is necessary...yet it eludes me, and I end up lying awake all night, wondering if Emma has fallen into a more peaceful sleep than the one I heard.

CHAPTER NINETEEN

EMMA

STAYING UP THE REST of the night was clearly a very bad idea. The pounding in my head and the way the sunlight only seems to intensify my headache are almost enough to make me consider the idea of calling Mr. Andersen and telling him I am sick. But my stubbornness kicks in; I will not let those blasted nightmare win. They will *not* have the power to rule my life. They are not worth it.

The day starts very much like the day before. I knock on Daniel's door, and together we take off to work at the shop, none of us mentioning what happened during the night. As we walk to the bus stop, it almost seems as if I dreamt the whole thing.

We're a bit early today, and apart from playing with his phone, Daniel is awfully quiet. I've already become used to feeling his eyes meeting mine, and the fact that he withholds them today is disappointing. I do love his emerald-green eyes. It makes me wonder what is on his mind. I don't have to wait long to get my wish granted.

"Sorry I didn't text you back yesterday," he says, only looking at me briefly.

For a moment, I can't remember what text he's referring to, but then it hits me: our first tutoring session.

"Oh, no worries," I answer quietly. *Shite, this headache is killing me!*

"All my books are yet to be unpacked, so is it alright if we do it at your place?" he continues, staring straight ahead at the playground across the road. No children are there, and my gaze turns to the swings. For some reason, the lack of children, the way there are no sounds surrounding us, makes me a bit despondent, but I shake it off.

"Sure, no problem," I tell him and give him a small smile. I can see the unsaid question in his eyes; he wants to ask me if I am okay, but he's too polite to say anything.

I break eye contact, and silence descends upon us again. I'm grateful when I see the bus arriving in the distance so we can get on our way.

In a move that resembles very much that of a gentleman's, Daniel steps back immediately as the bus opens its doors, and he holds out a hand, indicating that I should go first.

I may be a modern woman and everything, but I do appreciate his gesture and smile more genuinely at him when I pass him and climb the steps to head inside. As usual, not many passengers are present. Once we're seated, I take a deep breath, lean my head on the headrest and close my eyes.

"Are you alright?" Daniel whispers from beside me. His breath causes my skin to break out in goose bumps again.

Here we go.

"Just a headache," I mumble, keeping my eyes shut.

Daniel doesn't respond, and I find comfort in that. In my

sleep deprived state, I don't think I'll be able to keep my wayward thoughts about him in check if I speak too much with him today.

"Do you want to cancel this afternoon?" he suddenly asks me, surprising me, and I turn my head closer to his, but I daren't open my eyes yet.

"Don't be silly, Preppy. I can handle it. One small headache won't defeat me."

"You promised not to call me that," he scoffs, and I mentally bite my tongue.

"Sorry," I apologise. "But now that it's stuck in my head, I kind of like it."

He chuckles. "Strangely enough, so do I."

I don't answer that - what is there to say? I've already said too much. Suddenly, I'm unable to open my heavy eyelids, and my busy thoughts seem to have quieted down a bit.

I need sleep.

"Don't let me fall asleep, please?" I mumble.

"I won't," Daniel promises me, but his voice seems far away. In no time at all, I drift off into a deep slumber, only vaguely aware of someone putting an arm around me, and I snuggle closer, inhaling deeply. *Mmm... nice.*

♡

I wake up with a start, cuddled close to a warm body, and when my sleepy eyes fall on my arm around a very manly chest, I panic. Shooting up, my head collides with a sharp object, making me see stars, and hearing a pained grunt forces me to scoot back in my seat and I look up and beside me.

Oh...Daniel. One who's currently rubbing his chin, eyes

squinting with the discomfort my hard head must have caused him.

"What the hell, Daniel?" I sputter, and immediately rub said head. *Dang it, that hurts.*

"What?" he asks, abandoning the pain to his chin to lean further into me. Automatically, I shrink back until the cold glass from the bus window makes me too uncomfortable and I ease up a bit.

"I told you not to let me fall asleep!" Clearing my throat, I look around me, and find the bus empty. Frantically pulling out my phone from my clutch, I check the time and almost have a heart attack. *Eleven am?! I've slept for an hour?!*

"We're late for work, you nutter," I explain harshly, and Daniel grits his teeth, bristling at me.

"Well, you needed the rest, you stupid girl," he seethes, causing me to wince. I don't get a chance to rip into him for calling me *stupid*, before he continues, "Don't worry, I already texted the Prof, and he knows we'll be there soon. For your information, he actually told us to take the day off, but I knew you wouldn't approve of that fact. Yes, we're late for work, but it's not the end of the world, Emma. It's clear you needed the rest, and I do apologise for allowing that to happen. I won't let it again."

Pulling his backpack from the floor, he leaves his seat to stand at the doors of the bus, not looking at me, and I feel like I've just been scolded as if I were a child. And I'm embarrassed that I couldn't keep my sharp tongue in check.

Seeing that we are now close to the train station, I pick up my things and leave my seat. My headache is gone, and I do feel thankful for the way Daniel took care of me. I suppose I'm just so used to being in charge - living in a foreign country will do that - but that isn't an excuse. I shouldn't have lashed out the way I did.

I walk slowly towards Daniel who stubbornly avoids my gaze, instead looking straight ahead out of the window. Jaw clenched, frown drawn, he suddenly looks so much older than his twenty-four years, and I can't say I like that.

Hesitating, I open my mouth, but no sound comes out, and I turn away from him and stand at a safe distance, leaning against one of the seats so as not to fall.

"How's the headache?" he asks me gruffly, and I let out a big sigh, feeling relief beyond measure.

"All gone, so...thank you," I reply, finally venturing closer.

He gives a curt nod, and I don't have time to ask him about his chin before the bus is at a standstill, and we step off and walk hastily towards the station.

The rest of our journey is made in silence once more, me busy wracking my brain for coming up with a proper apology. But no words feel good enough.

It's ironic: words are a huge part of my life, yet I cannot seem to find the right ones at this very moment.

♡

After I apologised to Mr. Andersen and he, in turn, kept telling me that it didn't matter, Daniel went to the front desk to work alongside his uncle, making it clear that he didn't feel like spending more time with me, and the past couple of hours have dragged. Being in the shop hasn't had the calming effect it normally has, and I've found no joy in my usual tasks. I don't like feeling so unsettled, and now that it's close to lunchtime, I vow to get the chance to apologise properly for my behaviour earlier. It's evident that it's still bothering

Daniel, and the fact that we're also leaving early today for our tutoring session forces me to break the tension.

Because spending the rest of the day with a disgruntled guy is not my idea of having a good time. And I want...no, I crave seeing Daniel smile at me again.

I've gone quite mad.

Since when have I let a guy's mood dictate my own? Answer: never. But...well, Daniel is different.

Not wishing to examine these unusual thoughts further, I walk briskly up to Daniel, who's just finished serving a customer, and when his blank eyes turn to mine, I stand taller.

"What do you want for lunch?" I ask him. "My treat."

Putting his hands in his pockets, he purses his lips for a minute, leaving me just standing there, and I cross my arms.

"A ham sandwich sounds good," he finally relents, and I can't keep the grimace from my features. He chuckles.

"I take it you don't like ham?" he asks me, smirking.

"I hate it with a vengeance, but, luckily for me, I don't have to eat it," I return and walk to the back office where Mr. Andersen has been avoiding us for the past hour, clearly hiding from the tension that has cloaked us.

After he tells me what he would like to eat, I grab my purse and leave the shop to buy lunch at the supermarket right next door. The way Daniel tries to hide a cheeky smile isn't lost on me, however, but I refuse to acknowledge it.

I need food. Now.

♡

As soon as I get back, I hurry to Mr. Andersen to get him his food and to tell him that Daniel and I will be eating outside today. I almost don't hear his reply before rushing out and over to Daniel. I grab his hand in mine and practically pull him out of the shop, walking briskly around the corner where a small park with benches is situated. For once, there is no wind, and I want to feel the sun on my face while we eat.

"Hey, slow down a bit, Emma," Daniel says from behind me, but I ignore him and keep up the pace.

Soon, we're at the park, and I quickly spot a set of benches with attached tables another young couple is about to leave. Perfect. I drop Daniel's hand when we reach it, place the bag with our food and drinks on the table, and turn around to face him. Grabbing his hips, I don't comment when his eyes widen, but instead manage to push him in the direction I want, forcing him to stumble around a bit. When his back is to the seat, I place my hands on his shoulders and push lightly, causing his knees to buckle, and he's finally sitting down.

"Emma, what are...? " I hold up my right index finger, silencing whatever he's about to say.

"Now, please just listen, Daniel," I say, and he nods, accepting my request.

Clearing my throat, I feel a bit nervous, but I force out what's on my mind anyway. "Okay. I'm very sorry for the way I treated you earlier. It was very considerate of you to let me sleep, and I just want you to know that I appreciate it. Even when it didn't seem like it at the time." Holding his gaze for a while, and seeing the acceptance there, I let my arm fall to my side. "Right, then. Let's eat."

Walking to the other side of the bench, it isn't lost on me that Daniel's eyes follow me the whole time; my body feels heated up from within, leaving me small pinpricks all over, but not in a bad way. I can practically *feel* his gaze zeroing in on my arse, and another kind of tingling spreads throughout my body.

When I turn around, he has a thoughtful look on his face, and a smirk covering that handsome face of his.

As I sit down, I ask him, "What? See something you like?" and I grab the sandwich I bought for myself: grilled slices of chicken with tomatoes, pesto and garlic.

"Hmm," he ponders, and I start to unwrap the food, my mouth salivating at the thought of the first bite.

"Well," Daniel continues, "that would be telling, wouldn't it?"

Stopping with my mouth hanging open, the sandwich halfway to it, I'm quite taken aback by his brazen comeback to my question. I brush it off and dig into the food instead. The moan erupting from me is loud, but I don't care, and I close my eyes and lean my head back to soak up the sun. This is just too good!

A strangled groan coming from Daniel instantly makes me reopen them, and I find Daniel's gaze locked on me, his food clearly forgotten, and his face is flushed.

"What now?" I ask him, but I can't keep a knowing smile from forming on my lips. Oh, I know exactly what's causing this, and I'm enjoying it immensely.

Daniel swallows and places his food back on the wrapping.

"You're cruel, Emma," he answers, his voice husky and low. He leans closer towards me from across the table separating us, and hearing those words wipes the smile from my face.

"Why?" I croak, mouth suddenly parched, and my heart begins to beat faster and faster. My heart wants Daniel to stand up and come closer...yet my head is screaming at him to keep his distance. *I'm not ready!*

Once again, it feels as if Daniel has an uncanny ability to understand what I need, because he leans back in his seat and breaks eye contact with me. When I see him reaching for his sandwich again, I breathe a small sigh of relief.

Taking a huge bite of my own, I am determined to stop this kind of *cat and mouse* game that always comes over me whenever he is near. Because that is not fair...not to him or to me. Still, it *is* very flattering to see how my words and actions affect him so much. It's a great boost to my confidence.

When he speaks again, I jump a bit, startled after having been so lost inside my own head.

"You're a cruel woman for toying with the virgin in such a public place, Em," he says, and I don't know what to say.

Oh...my...God...did he just say what I think I heard him say?

"I didn't do anything!" I sputter, and I can feel the blush creeping over my cheeks.

"Oh, but you moaned, and it sounded beyond sexy," he continues, and I narrow my eyes at him when I see the smirk reappearing on his lips.

Balling my napkins in my hand, I say, "You better be careful or I'll throttle you." My threatening words seem to have the opposite effect, though, because Daniel's smirk transforms into a beautiful smile, and his eyes twinkle with suppressed laughter.

"That might be interesting, but you can't do that in a public place," he says, grinning, and my lips pull up in a knowing smile.

"Oh, can't I?" I threaten, causing him to pause and look at me thoughtfully.

"You don't embarrass easily, do you?" he asks me, and I pause, mulling his words over.

"Well, no, not really...Actually, the only times I have been embarrassed have been when I was sober," I tell him, and the admission makes me frown.

Hurrying on, I say, "I mean, I've probably done a lot of strange things while out clubbing."

"You go dancing a lot?" he asks me, and I nod and take another bite.

"I have in the past, but not anymore," I answer vaguely and hurry to change the subject. "Oh, remind me to introduce you to Suzy, by the way. She's my best friend. She might be good to practice on," I muse, and Daniel coughs.

"Get your head out of the gutter," I reproach him and pull out a bottle of water from the bag placed on the table between us. I hand it to him and watch as he guzzles it down. *Never knew Adam's apples could be so fascinating...*

Moving on.

"What I meant," I continue, "is that seeing as I'm supposed to help you get over that...err...awkwardness you experience while in the presence of the opposite sex, I could call Suzy, let her in on what we're trying to do, and she could go out with us one evening. What do you think?"

Frowning, Daniel says, "I really hope you're not setting me up for embarrassment, Emma."

Shaking my head, I answer, "Oh, no, not at all. I wouldn't do that, I promise."

Some time passes in silence, but then he nods, acquiescing. He doesn't look convinced, though.

"Well, it doesn't have to be decided on right now," I tell him and check the clock on my phone. Our break is almost over, so I hurry to eat the rest and take a few large gulps of my water.

"Why are you so obsessed with the time?" Daniel asks me as I stand up and clear the table.

His question makes me pause, considering it.

"I...I don't know," I answer hesitantly and look away, taking in the rose bushes blooming not that far away. "I guess I don't like losing control," I finally admit to him.

Standing up to gather the waste, Daniel peruses me for some time. *What is he thinking?*

"Control is important to you?" he asks, yet it sounds more like a statement instead of a question.

"It is to a lot of people," I reply, and even I can detect the defensive tone of my voice. "Look, enough with the psychoanalysis, Preppy. We should head back."

Grabbing the bag, I gather our water bottles and walk briskly away from him.

"I'm just trying to get to know you, Emma," Daniel yells from behind me, stopping me in my tracks. "And will you please stop calling me that?" he continues. The irritation in his voice makes me smile a little, and I turn around to watch him draw nearer.

"Why should I?" I ask him. "It's fun to rattle you a bit from time to time."

Coming to a standstill beside me, he huffs, placing his hands in his pockets again. Squinting his eyes, he gazes intently into my own for a while, and I can feel how I become lost in the depth of them with each second that passes.

Finally, he relents and asks me quietly, "So what does it take to make you stumble?"

What an odd thing to ask.

Taking a deep breath, I take in his boring, black button down shirt he has chosen to wear today, and I frown.

"Men who don't know how to dress," I blurt out.

Daniel rolls his eyes and then walks away from me, shaking his head. *Ooops.*

CHAPTER TWENTY

DANIEL

LEAVING EMMA BEHIND ME, I feel slightly affronted, yet amused at the same time. What's wrong with my clothes? I don't get it. Still chuckling, I enter the bookshop to find my uncle busy manning the desk. Nodding at him, I walk over to stand beside him and take in the older couple standing in front of me. Listening to them chatter away with the Prof quickly tells me that they come here often.

"...I can't tell you how fantastic Emma is," the woman gushes excitedly to my uncle as he hands her over some change. "That book she found for our son made him so excited!" she continues.

Hearing the *ping* coming from the door, I look over and watch as Emma walks inside the shop. When she sees the customers, her eyes light up, making me wonder how well she knows these people.

"Mr. and Mrs. Sorensen, how lovely to see you," Emma says and hurries over to them.

"Oh, Emma," Mrs. Sorensen says and grabs her hand.

"You're a lifesaver! The book we bought the other day, the one about Greenland?" Nodding, Emma smiles, and Mrs. Sorensen continues, "It was the perfect present. Our son was over the moon about it, dear. Thank you."

"I'm so pleased he liked it," Emma says and turns to Mr. Sorensen when he snorts.

"You could say that," he responds. "He hasn't stopped perusing it, exclaiming about this and that, doing my head in."

Despite the harshness of his words, the twinkle in his eyes belies them: it's evident how pleased he is.

Emma laughs and says, "Always nice to hear from satisfied customers."

Mr. Andersen holds out his hand to Mr. Sorensen and they shake quickly. The formality puzzles me a bit, but I guess that's just the way of the older generation; politeness is not completely lost even in this day and age.

Emma moves to pull away from his grasp, but stops when Mr. Sorensen doesn't release his hold on her hand. Frowning, because I don't understand why he won't let go, I walk around the desk to stand beside her. I needn't have worried, though.

"Mr. Andersen," the man turns to my uncle, still holding onto Emma who seems just as confused as me. "If you let this girl return home to England, you'll be daft. We need to keep her here," Mr. Sorensen says.

Chuckling, my uncle says, "I'll do my best. But you know as well as I do that if Emma decides to leave us, I won't be able to stop her." Leaning a hip to the desk, he crosses his arms and looks at Emma who seems to get more and more uncomfortable about the situation. For some unfathomable reason, this pleases me to no end.

Another piece to the puzzle: she doesn't like to be the cause of too much attention.

My uncle says, "However, I have a few ideas that might make her stay in the cold north." Now *I'm* the one who's confused, but I don't get to voice my questions because Emma laughs beside me.

"Listen, my scholarship doesn't end until next summer, gentlemen, so don't talk about me as if I'm about to vanish into thin air, please."

Smiling, Mr. Sorensen releases her hand. "Well, that's good, then. Remind me when we need to have this discussion again, my dear," he says to her. Before Emma has the chance to agree, he turns to me, the smile fleeing his face immediately.

"And who might you be?" he asks me gruffly, his scrutinising gaze causing my breath to still for a moment.

Where has the jovial old man gone? This one is rather frightening.

I reach out my hand to him and clear my throat. "Daniel Larsen," I reply.

"Hmm?" he says as he takes my hand. *Ouch.* He's got some strength in him.

Nodding, I explain further. "Mr. Andersen is my uncle."

"Ah, I see," he says and releases my hand.

"Oh, are you working here, too?" his wife asks and comes closer, beaming smile in place.

"I am, yes. I've just moved here," I tell her, careful to not stumble over my words, wishing with everything that I am that meeting strangers didn't make me so nervous.

"Oh, how splendid," she exclaims, looking from Emma to me. "Emma, how nice for you to be around someone a bit more your own age," Mrs. Sorensen turns to her. Leaning closer to Emma, she whispers, "He's quite handsome, isn't he?"

Smiling, Emma nods. "Very handsome," she chuckles.

"Now, come, come, woman," Mr. Sorensen butts in. "Enough of that. We need to get home. You've got a new book to read." Nodding at me, he takes his wife's hand and begins to walk closer to the door.

"Sorry we can't stay and chat," Mrs. Sorensen says as she is being pulled away. Just before her husband opens the door, she pauses to take a final look at us.

"Such a beautiful couple," she says, beaming again, and I can feel the flush in my cheeks. Hearing a strangled noise coming from Emma, I look at her beside me. Her befuddled expression causes me to smile widely. This is fun.

"Bye, Mr. And Mrs. Sorensen," she manages to get out. "See you soon."

We watch the couple walk out the door, and I don't move for a few beats. Thinking, I finally turn to Emma.

"What a nice couple," I say.

"Hmm, yes, they are," she replies, looking at the tattoo on her wrist, avoiding my eyes.

"I hope they come back soon," I persist, leaning down to catch her eyes, but trying to get her to look at me seems futile.

"Yes, well, they stop by the shop every week, so I'm sure you'll see them again," she answers, then abruptly turns her back to walk to the desk where my uncle is still standing.

"Mr. Andersen, is it alright if I go in the back room for the rest of my shift?" she asks him. "Some books ordered specifically by customers arrived the other day, and I need to ring them to let them know that they're ready to be picked up."

"Of course, Emma," he replies, and she hurries to walk

away, still not meeting my gaze burning a hole in her back.

I'm interrupted in my musings by my uncle. "Well, Daniel, why don't you just browse for a bit and become better acquainted with the stock we have?"

Glad for the opportunity to spend a few quiet moments alone with my thoughts, I nod.

"Sure," I answer and immediately head to the bookshelf containing the classic literature.

But even though I try to take in what's there, I can't help but wonder why Emma just felt the need to flee from me.

EMMA

"Such a beautiful couple..."

The seemingly innocent words replay like a bad record in my mind as I stand in the storage room, sorting the books I need with the lists of customers lying in a tray on one of the shelves.

I hate the fact that those words have the ability to freak me out like that. I hate that I seem unable to keep from running away from Daniel, putting more than there is into some words spoken by an old woman who, I know, is such a romantic that she probably can't help herself. I hate that I seem to keep changing my mind about how to handle my attraction towards Daniel.

One moment, I want to jump his bones, throw caution to the wind and ravish him. And next thing I know, I want to run away, remain in my bubble of safety and never let the attraction amount to anything.

Rolling my eyes at the way I all of a sudden appear to

have become one of those annoying and indecisive heroines that I find so often in the books I read, I sigh and pick up my phone. Taking the first note and making sure that the book the customer ordered has arrived, I dial his number.

Work is probably the best approach for me right now. This is an easy, but important, task, of course, and immediately calmness fills me up from the inside. Knowing that if I simply concentrate on this for the next hour, I won't have to delve too much into my reactions - or actions - when I am around Daniel relaxes me.

Denial is a beautiful thing, isn't it?

After an hour or so, the door opens and Daniel pokes his head inside the storage room where I've been hiding.

"Are you ready to go?" he asks me, looking rather unsure. The worry in his eyes is plain to see, and when I glance down, his hands are clenched. His body seems wired, strung out somehow. I suppose this tutoring thing isn't exactly something that thrills him.

"Absolutely," I answer him, smiling at him, and sounding oh so optimistic and positive. *Ugh. I need to let go of this bad mood I'm in.*

Putting the tray with the notes back on the shelf it belongs to, I say, "Just give me five minutes to grab my things, okay?"

"Of course," he responds and ducks out again.

It doesn't take me long to finish putting everything in place, and I walk outside and lock the door. I don't want to keep Daniel waiting and seeing him talking quietly with Mr. Andersen by the entrance to the shop, the worried frown on his face doesn't escape me. A sliver of sympathy about how it must be like to struggle so hard with an ability that merely seems like second nature to me runs through me, and I become determined to be the best damn tutor I can be.

And if I fail and can't help him? Well, I'll just have to help him find a person who can. Simple.

Picking up my purse from my compartment, I quickly lock it again and walk outside.

Standing close together, talking in hushed voices, my gaze turns to Mr. Andersen, and I become confused when I see the angry look on his face.

As soon as Daniel spots me nearing them, he takes a step back from his uncle, clenching his teeth. Mr. Andersen turns to me and quickly smooths out his features. His lips may be smiling, but it doesn't reach his eyes.

What's that all about?

"I'm ready," I tell Daniel, not commenting on the behaviour of my boss. It's not my place, after all. "Have a good evening, Sir," I tell him instead.

Daniel opens the door for me, and as I walk through it, I hear a muttered, "You, too," coming from Mr. Andersen. I turn my head and smile faintly, and Daniel closes the door behind us.

We walk in silence towards the train station, and deciding I don't like the heaviness in the air, I ask him, "Please bear in mind that I have not been a tutor before, okay?" Glancing briefly at him, I explain further. "I mean, I'm not too sure of how to go about this, but I have found all my old notes from my classes last year, and we'll take it from there if that sounds good to you?"

Nodding, he replies, "That's just fine. Basically, my...challenge is the reading and understanding part of the different texts. Once we've gone over each one, I think I'll be able to cope. You know, because of my photographic memory."

"Sorry?" I ask him as we walk up the stairs to get to our train.

He looks nervously at me. "My photographic memory. You do know what that is, don't you?" He trips, and I reach out my hand to take a firm hold on his arm.

"Of course I know what it is. I just didn't know that it applied to people who're dyslexic," I answer him when we reach the top of the stairs. I check the billboard up ahead on the platform, finding that there are still a few minutes until the next train arrives.

Meandering down the platform, I look questioningly at Daniel when he doesn't say anything.

"So?" I push him. "Please explain."

"I don't know if I can," he answers slowly and we stop walking.

"Please try," I ask him, my patience running a bit thin.

He looks across the platform, seeming to be lost in thought, and I wait.

"You know how you learned to read and write?" he starts and I nod. "You were taught the spelling of your name, how to add each word in a sentence so that it made sense?" Looking briefly at me with a frown, he continues, "Well, my teachers did the same, of course, but unlike the rest of my classmates, the way a certain word was spelled did not make sense to me at all. I couldn't recognise the word, no matter how many times the teacher spelled it out, writing it on the blackboard. The word just looked like gibberish to me. However..." he pauses and looks pointedly at a man standing to my left who's holding a newspaper but is clearly listening in on our conversation.

Rolling my eyes, I grab Daniel's hand and we walk further away from the unwanted spectator.

"Please go on," I urge Daniel when we stop again, and I quickly release his hand.

"Well, this happened for a long time," he tells me and takes off his glasses to rub his eyes. Putting them back on, he says, "One thing I'll never understand is why my teachers didn't catch on about my problems or disability or whatever you'd like to call it, but I guess it just didn't occur to them. No, instead, they just thought I was slow," he spits out the words, making it clear that this is an old wound of his. And I can't say I blame him even though I don't understand it at the same time; reading is second nature to me. If I couldn't read, I don't know what I'd do.

"Never mind them," I quickly say. "What about the photographic memory part?" I ask him. This is the fascinating part.

"I guess that over the years, once my teachers gave me some learning techniques and showed me how to cope, some of my other senses took over. Now, once I get what a text or book means, and I *hear* the words on a page instead of struggle through spelling them out, because that clearly doesn't work, I remember everything of said text or book. I can recite it by heart. It's just the first part – reading it – that I struggle through and that I'll need your help with," Daniel ends and looks at me again.

"So what we'll be doing today, for instance, is that I'll read the book aloud to you and then we'll analyse each chapter together?" I ask him slowly, wanting to be sure I understand what he means.

"Exactly," he confirms and scratches the scruff on his

chin, looking a bit unsure of himself.

"I see," I say brightly, because it really does make sense. "Thank you for explaining how your mind works," I add, bumping my shoulder lightly on his. Or, well, his arm seeing as he's so much taller than me and I can't reach it.

Hearing the train approaching, I say, "Reading *"The Canterbury Tales"* aloud should be an interesting experience," I grin at him, and he returns it immediately, causing a tingle in my lady bits.

Not today...I don't need all those kinds of thoughts when we're about to spend all afternoon together. I'm actually starting to get excited about this tutoring job...as long as I can keep my dirty thoughts to myself, that is.

Once the train stops, we stand aside and let the passengers leave. There's always so many at this time of the afternoon, and it takes a bit. All the while, I can feel Daniel's reassuring presence at my back, and that certainly doesn't help the tingling in my body. It does, though, make my heart soften even further towards him. Shocking, isn't it?

CHAPTER TWENTY-ONE

EMMA

BACK IN MY FLAT, we end up deciding on sitting outside on my balcony because the heat of the sun has made it almost unbearable to stay indoors. While I gather my notes from last year and fix us some drinks, Daniel leaves me alone to get his books and sunglasses.

Sitting down to my right, Daniel notices my secret stash behind the door and asks, sounding surprised, "You smoke?"

I shrug as if it's no big deal and respond truthfully, "Only when I'm stressed out or when I'm clubbing."

He frowns, but doesn't say anything else. It annoys me, but obviously I know that smoking is bad for me. Well, it's not as if I'm addicted to any dangerous substances.

Grabbing my water, I take a large gulp and ask him, "Are you ready to get started?"

He nods, a worried line forming on his forehead, and I continue, "Just remember that you're the pupil; if there's something you need me to explain, tell me to stop, okay?"

"Right," he responds, and opens what appears to be a

brand new copy of *"The Canterbury Tales".*

"Okay, then. Let's begin."

And we get down to business.

♡

An hour has passed, and the lack of sleep is starting to get to me. The headache hasn't returned, thankfully, but I really need a break.

"Do you mind if we take a breather for ten minutes?" I ask Daniel.

"Not at all," he answers and closes his book, but not before marking the page with a post-it. Stretching, he yawns, and I can't keep my eyes from admiring his arms and the veins that are slightly visible there.

Good lord...never knew those could be such a turn-on.

I snap out of it when Daniels asks me, "Do you mind if I use your bathroom?"

Shaking my head, I stand up. "Not at all."

We both walk inside and I grab my clutch I tossed on my couch to get my phone to check if I have any messages. I didn't want to be rude seeing as Daniel is here, and I have a job to do, so I set it to silent when we got back from the bookshop.

"I won't be long," Daniel says from behind me, but I don't answer. A chill runs through me when I see that I have three missed calls - and all from my brother, Steven.

Ugh. There goes my good mood for the day.

As I stand there, holding my phone, and contemplating whether or not to just ignore him, karma seems to be out to get me, because as soon as the thought of forgetting that I ever saw his missed calls sets in, my phone rings.

Closing my eyes briefly, I swipe the screen and put the phone to my ear.

"Hello," I say, and even my voice doesn't sound right: it's weak, not strong. And I can't have him sensing that.

"Hello? Who's this?" I hear coming from the other end, and my grip tightens painfully on my phone as I hear his voice.

"Well, who do you think it is?" I ask Steven, relieved that some of my usual spunk has returned.

"Emma," he reproaches me. "Still your charming self, I hear."

"Hey, you rang me, brother dear, so why don't you just get on with it?" I ask him, so pissed off by the condescending tone of voice that seems to be the only one he knows.

"Temper, temper, Emma," he goes on, and leaning my head back, I close my eyes as I wait for him to say what he wants. It must've been important since he rang three times the last hour.

"Okay, so the reason I rang is to give you those dates when I'll be in Copenhagen," he then proceeds to tell me, and I frown.

"I told you to just text them to me, Steven," I tell him.

"Yes, I know, but..." For once, my brother hesitates, and it causes me to take notice. My brother *never* sounds like he does now.

"But what?" I prompt him, feeling tension gathering in my neck from keeping my head back. Opening my eyes, I try to relax and not move too quickly, and when I turn around and see Daniel standing patiently in the doorway to my living room, I jump. I didn't even hear him come out from the bathroom. I can't quite figure out why he's looking at me so puzzled.

"Emma, I just wanted to hear your voice," Steven says, pulling my attention back to our conversation. If you can even call it that.

"Well, that's...unusual," I respond.

Laughing nervously, he agrees, "True."

Silence descends between us, but I'm not going to be the bigger person here and try to fill it with some inane chit chat that none of us could give a flying fuck about.

"So...How are you?" Steven asks me at last.

"Good. Busy. You?" Some small, evil part inside me takes joy in being so abrupt with my big brother, but I don't care.

"Good, good...I'm the same," he weakly responds.

Becoming impatient, I say, "Look, Steven, I'm really busy at the moment, so will you please just text me those dates?"

Clearing his throat, my brother asks me, "Why can't you chat now?"

Smiling deviously, I look deep into Daniel's eyes as I reply, "Because I'm about to have wild monkey sex with my boyfriend, that's why."

"Em!" Steven exclaims horrified at the same time Daniel laughs loudly, quickly covering his mouth with a hand, and I wink at him.

"Why do you have to be so...so...crude?" Steven hisses in my ear, and I can't keep the snort from erupting from my mouth.

"Why do you have to be such a prude?" I counter his question with one of my own.

Ignoring it, Stevens demands, "Who was that?"

"My...boyfriend," I answer slowly, as if I'm talking to a child who has no idea what that is.

"You don't have boyfriends," Steven says suspiciously, and I roll my eyes even though he's right.

"Well, now I do. *And* you'll be meeting him yourself when you get here."

"Is that really necessary?" he asks me, irritation oozing from his words.

"Of *course* it is," I answer, sounding all bubbly and excited even though I'm a nervous wreck on the inside. "It would seem silly if you didn't," I continue, looking down at my bare feet, willing him to end the call sooner rather than later.

"Hmm...you're probably right," Steven says quietly, and the change in him surprises me; my brother isn't exactly known to agree with me.

"Well, I'll let you go, then," he says.

"Just text me those days and I'll see if any of them works with Daniel," I say.

"I'll do that," he says briskly. "Goodbye."

"Bye," I tell him, remove the phone from my ear and quickly press *End Call*. I toss it on my bed, run my hands through my hair, and when I've gathered it in a messy bun on the top of my head, I inhale deeply and let myself settle. I handled that phone call better than I thought I would, actually, but I can't say I enjoyed it much. And why did he act so peculiar? Strange...

"Wild monkey sex?" Daniel's voice interrupts my thoughts, and I look at him. He hasn't moved, but there's a delightful blush rising on his neck now.

Letting my hair fall down my back, I shrug and smile. "I had to say something to get rid of him," I explain. "Besides, now he knows I won't be meeting him alone."

Daniel nods once, uncrosses his arms and walk towards me. "It's a little strange hearing you speak English," he says, stopping very close to me.

"Oh?" I'm surprised. "In what way?" Preventing my fingers from reaching out to touch his stubble - it looks so soft and inviting - I cross my arms.

He shrugs. "Just different, I guess. Actually," he chuckles, "you sounded so proper, yet it seems you've also picked up a bit of a Danish accent while you've lived here."

Smiling crookedly, I answer, "I suppose you're right...about the last bit, I mean. My Nan always says that to me when we're chatting on the phone. But I guess it's inevitable when I don't really speak my native language much."

His eyes light up with humour. "Maybe we're rubbing off on you and you'll end up deciding to stay here on a more permanent basis."

Shaking my head, I uncross my arms and move past him. "I doubt that." In need of water, I walk to my kitchen, leaving Daniel in my living room.

"Never say never," he yells behind me, making me pull my lip ring and suck on it for a bit.

As I release it, I yell back, "True, but no need to get into that today."

Turning on the tap, I pick up a glass and quickly fill it before guzzling it down in one go.

"I'm sorry that our break was so long," I say and turn around, only to find Daniel right behind me now.

"What are you, a cat?" I ask him, surprised I didn't hear him come in.

He grins. "I'm not wearing any shoes, you know. It's not my fault your hearing is so bad."

Narrowing my eyes at his cheeky response, I poke a finger in his chest. "You, Sir, need to mind your manners."

"Oh, really?" he retorts. "Like you just did while on the

phone with your brother?" His grin widens and I have no answer for that.

"Well," I huff, placing my hands on my hips. "That was different."

Now he's full on laughing and although the sound is so very pleasant, we need to get back to work.

"Are you done?" I ask him, raising an eyebrow, and his laughter dies down. Seeing the twinkle in his eyes, the warmth mingled with humour, can't make me stay annoyed for long, though.

He opens his mouth, no doubt to answer, and then I hear a rattling sound coming from my front door. Turning our heads at the same time, we watch as my best friend enters my flat.

"Men are pigs!" Suzy shouts, looking mad as a hatter, and she slams the door shut.

Oh dear...

CHAPTER TWENTY-TWO

EMMA

The minute Suzy sees us standing right in front of her, she stops...and stares. Neither of us says a word for a few moments, and when I notice the tears on Suzy's cheeks, my protective instincts kick into gear.

"Not that I don't disagree, sweetie, but what happened to make you barge in like a mad woman? What's wrong?"

Hastily drying her cheeks, she waves me off and walks closer, her hand outstretched towards Daniel.

"We can talk about all that later," she says, a small smile now grazing her lips. "Hi, I'm Suzanne," she greets my clearly uncomfortable neighbour. "You must be Daniel."

"I am," he replies, and they shake hands. "How do you know my name?"

Tucking her hair behind her ear, she says, "Oh, Emma tells me everything...including that she has a new hunky neighbour."

Clearing his throat, Daniel takes a step closer to me. "Well, err...thanks, I guess."

"Oh, you're more than welcome," Suzy replies, a small twinkle in her eyes.

Briefly narrowing my own, but thinking that I can't stop Suzy from being her usual flirtatious self when she sees something she fancies, I turn to Daniel and apologise, "I'm sorry, Daniel, but can you give us a few minutes alone?"

Shrugging, he says, "No problem," and he walks briskly outside and closes the balcony door behind him. I wait until I watch him sit down, and then turn to Suzy.

Grabbing her hand, I yank her with me and we take the few short steps into my kitchen.

"What's going on, honey?" I ask her and squeeze her hand.

She huffs and rubs her forehead. "I'm sorry about just turning up like this, Emma, but I really needed a night with my best friend." She crosses her arms and leans a hip against the kitchen counter. "And to answer your question: Thomas is a rat bastard! He just texted me, *but* I don't think it was actually meant for me." She uncrosses her arms and takes out her phone from the side pocket of her jacket. She pushes a few buttons and hands it to me.

"Go on," she says when I fail to take it from her immediately. "I don't mind, just read it."

Tentatively doing as she tells me to, I look down and read the text:

Thomas: I want you to fuck me in my arse while I suck off Alex' cock, baby...

A startled snort escapes me, and I bring a hand to my mouth. *What...the...hell?*

"Obviously, we haven't known each other for that long, so I texted him back, saying that I thought he was getting a bit ahead of himself but that I wouldn't be opposed to some kinky sex if our relationship progressed," Suzy explains, and I hand her the phone and look at her, taking in her lopsided smile.

"What did he text back?" I ask and turn to grab some tissues to wipe away her tears with.

"Oh, he didn't. In fact, he still hasn't," she replies, sniffling. "So, you know, I don't think that text was to me."

Cautiously, I ask her, "Sweetie, don't you think it's too soon to be crying over this guy? I mean, like you just said; you've only just met him."

She dabs her eyes and sighs briefly. "I know, I know. You're right, of course. But I had *such* a great time on our date…it just felt as if he completely *got* me. But now? Well, he can piss off." Making herself at home, she takes a glass from the cupboard above the sink and turns on the tap, filling it with water.

Pausing before she takes a sip, she muses, "It's not as if I'm a prude, Em. I don't mind the occasional backdoor action, but being the one to do it? And to a guy? Uh-uh, I can't see myself doing that."

Mouth hanging open, I stare at her. *TMI!*

Breaking free from my momentary lack of speech, I say sharply, "Suzy, that's *way* too much information, even between friends."

Chuckling, she gives me a hug. "Oh, don't be such a moralist," she scolds me affectionately. The conversation I just had with my brother fills my mind, and I cringe. Ugh.

"Alright, never mind. Listen, I can ask Daniel to leave and then the two of us can open that bottle of wine I have chilling in the fridge."

"Good lord, I'd completely forgotten about him!" she exclaims and waggles her eyebrows playfully at me. "He is one fine specimen of a man. But why's he here?" she whispers, looking puzzled.

"You interrupted us in our first study session," I explain, and seeing her face fall, I quickly reassure her, "I don't think we would have stayed at it for much longer, honey, and we were just taking a break when you came by."

"I'm sorry," she says. She leans towards me and whispers conspiratorially, "Does he still make your belly flutter?"

All the freaking time!

"On occasion," I reply vaguely and move to walk past her.

Sighing dreamily, she ponders, "I wonder if those full lips of his are good at kissing...?"

"Suzy!" I snap, a flare of jealousy sparking in the pit of my stomach.

"What?" she protests and places her now empty glass on the counter. "Just because he's yours doesn't mean I can't look and appreciate what I see, Emma."

"He's not mine," I retort, but even I can hear the lie hidden in those few words.

Suzy raises an eyebrow and searches my eyes for a few seconds. "Don't lie to me," she states emphatically. "He may not be yours *yet*, but that doesn't mean you haven't claimed him already."

"*Claimed him?*" Flabbergasted, I put a hand on my hip. "Don't compare me with one of the heroines from those romance novels you love to read, Suzy."

"Don't deny that you read them, too!" she replies, a smug smile spreading across her lips.

Not having a quick comeback for that one, I quickly say, "Look, I can't keep Daniel waiting any longer, so please...just stop, okay?"

Hearing the quiet plea in my last words, her smile disappears and she nods briskly. "Of course."

"Thank you."

Leaving Suzy in the kitchen, I walk through my living room, open the door to the balcony, and apologise to Daniel.

"I'm so sorry for keeping you waiting."

Looking up from his book, he smiles briefly. "It's alright. I gather Suzy's a close friend?"

I nod. "She is. And she needs some girl time..." My voice trails off and I look down at my fidgeting hands. I quickly place them behind my back and ask him, "I'm sorry, but I think we need to call it quits for today."

He grins. "From the way she walked in, shouting about men being pigs, I kind of already knew that, Em. I have four sisters."

Whoa...I didn't know that.

He closes the book and starts to sort out his notes on the table. "I'll be out of your hair soon."

"I'm really sorry," I say quietly, but he just shakes his head.

"To tell the truth, I don't think I could've handled more today." He smiles apologetically at me, and it's not hard to notice his tired eyes.

"Tomorrow's a new day," I reply quietly, and then hurry on, "I hope you're satisfied with my tutoring skills? I want you to be happy..."

Winking at me, he stands up. "Oh, I am." He looks at his watch before we both leave the balcony and walk inside my flat.

"I need to get to the supermarket and grab a few things for dinner, anyway," Daniel says from behind me.

"Well, at least the shops don't close until late," Suzy

responds from her seat on my couch. Smiling friendly at Daniel, she continues, "Welcome to the big city, Daniel."

"Thanks," he says, and as he moves past me to walk to my front door, Suzy cranes her head, checking out his arse. My steps falter and I shake my head affectionately when she gives me the thumbs-up and winks at me.

Daniel's voice makes me turn my head and concentrate on him again. "Well, I'll talk to you later, Emma." Giving Suzy a chin lift, he tells her, "It was nice to meet you."

"Oh, the pleasure is all mine," she trills at him.

"Bye, Daniel. Have a good night," I say, and he's gone.

Locking the door, I can't help but notice that his scent lingers, causing a shiver in my body. *Holy heck...what's happening to me?*

Mentally giving myself a good talking-to, I look at Suzy who, still beaming at me, is taking off her jacket.

"I think I need that wine more than you do," I murmur, and she laughs.

"Maybe. You get the wine, and then I'll order some food for us. Pasta sounds good?" she asks me and pulls out her phone.

"Perfect," I respond, and I leave her to do as she says.

"We need a gay best friend in our lives," Suzy says from beside me.

Pausing with my drink halfway to my mouth, I ask her, "What?"

"You know," she explains, taking a sip of wine. "Someone who'll satisfy our curiosity about men and the inner workings of their minds, but one who'll be beyond excited about shopping for shoes as well." Seemingly satisfied with her own logic, she nods at me.

Frowning, I take a large gulp of wine, enjoying the buzz currently coursing through my body.

"Hmm...," I muse, thinking.

"I say we get one," she persists, and it causes me to snort loudly.

"Suzy, darling," I say, "we're not talking about a dog here! We can't just go out and get a gay man, as if he's someone we can buy, you know."

Crossing her arms, she leans back in her seat and grins at me. "You'll see...just leave it to me."

I shake my head at her silliness, and we're both quiet for a while, drinking in the sunset and listening to the French music crooning from Daniel's flat. His windows must be open, and although it's not exactly the kind I usually listen to, it relaxes me. My one bottle of Frascati was replaced by another one by the time our takeaway dinner arrived, and I think it is fair to say that we are both feeling the effects of it now. But I'm probably worse off than her. *I need to have sex soon.*

For probably the millionth time, Suzy picks up her phone to check it for messages, and I purse my lips.

"Still nothing from Thomas?" I ask her, careful to keep my tone of voice neutral. Inside, though, I feel so sad for her: if anyone deserves a man - or woman - to dote on her, it's my best friend.

She slams the phone back on my table and responds dejectedly, "Nothing."

Clinking my glass to hers, I urge her, "Forget him, love. He's not worth it."

"Why are men such...such...?" She falters, probably

searching for the most offensive word to use.

"Pigs? Bastards? Sons of whores?" I suggest.

"Exactly! I mean, *why* do they play with our feelings like that? And..." She sits up straighter in her seat, pointing at me. "*Why* do we let them?"

"No idea. Well, I don't do that, actually," I tell her. Because it's true: I never let guys get to me. I don't want them to call me the day after we've hooked up because I don't want to form any kind of emotional attachment with them.

Immediately, Daniel's face - and his abs - pop up in my head. *Or at least I haven't until now...*

Searching for a way to distract her from the current bastard occupying her thoughts, I quickly change the subject.

"Girls are probably not better than men," I tell her and wink at her.

Snorting, she says, "Well, some are...and some aren't. I guess I was just tired of going to the same gay bars and wanted to be...*normal* for once." She sighs and finishes off her wine.

"Hey," I admonish her. "You are normal, honey. Don't you ever feel as if you aren't, you hear me? Besides, what's normal? I may not be gay or bi, but I don't care one bit about labels. Love is love, Suzy...and whoever ends up loving you will feel lucky to have found you."

"Aww..." She smiles wobbly at me.

As I feel a lump begin to form in my throat, I quickly say, "See? I'm definitely not a *prude*."

Suzy giggles, her eyes dry once more. "Still thinking about that, are you?"

I huff. "Well, yes...that was really such an impolite thing to say."

She shrugs. "We're friends. Which basically means that

politeness can take a hike; we don't have to sugar-coat what we think and feel and wrap it up in a parcel with a nice bow on top of it. We just come out and say what's on our mind, no matter what. Don't you agree?" Smiling softly at me, she looks me over.

I close my left eye, because it kind of seems as if she has two heads right now. "You've become awfully *deep* all of a sudden, haven't you?"

Chuckling, she shakes her head slightly. "And you're quite drunk, aren't you?"

"Why, yes, ma'am, yes I am," I nod vigorously, but quickly stop when the spinning in my head makes me feel slightly sick.

Rolling her eyes, Suzy stands up and reaches down with a hand. "Come on, my dear. Let me put you to bed."

"But I don't want to go to bed," I whine and swallow the rest of the wine in my glass in one large gulp.

She sighs and takes a firm grip on my hand and pulls me up. "You, sweetie, are completely sloshed, and it's my duty as your best friend to see that you don't have more tonight."

I follow her into my flat, dragging my feet, and she leads me to my bathroom.

"Brush your teeth, do what you have to do, and I'll fix the bed for you," she orders and closes the door in my face.

"You're so bossy!" I yell at her.

"I know!" she shouts back at me. I realise that I won't win this argument and do as she says. When I've removed all my makeup and brushed my teeth, I open the door and walk to my bed. It looks heavenly, and not caring one bit about the way I look, I walk to the end of it and do a face plant.

Suzy laughs as she tugs at my right foot. "Sweetie, you need to get undressed. Or would you like me to do it for you?"

"No," I groan. "You'll only feel me up."

Clucking her tongue, she says irritably, "No, I won't. Do as I say, Emma. Get undressed. Now."

I turn to my side to find her standing at the end of my bed, arms crossed and a stern look on her face, and I sigh, defeated.

"Okay, okay, I'll take off my clothes."

She nods once. "Good. I'll clear the table outside and tuck you in afterwards."

Snorting drunkenly, I reply, "I don't need you to do that, you know. You're not my mum, hon."

Stopping in her tracks, she turns her head and looks thoughtfully at me. "You're right, I'm not. But we all need to be cuddled once in a while, no matter how old we are. Even a kick-arse girl such as yourself." And with that, she leaves me alone.

"Huh," I grumble, but take off my clothes. Once I'm practically naked, only wearing my bra and knickers, I grab my duvet and tuck myself in. Curling into a ball, I close my eyes, and I sigh, content and, for once, unafraid to fall asleep. The last part, though, might be the wine in my system lulling me into a false sense of safety.

I feel a soft kiss on my cheek and Suzy whispers, "Goodnight, sweetie."

"'night," I murmur, already half-asleep. "Love you..."

"Ditto."

Finally, sleep claims me, and I don't even hear Suzy letting herself out of my flat.

CHAPTER TWENTY-THREE

DANIEL

AFTER LEAVING EMMA'S FLAT earlier, I unpacked my docking station from one of my boxes, and then went out to shop for food; when I came back with enough to last me for the rest of the week, I set it up and I have been listening to the relaxing voice of Charles Aznavour most of the evening.

Music makes me relax. It stops me from thinking too much on the past and allows me to focus on the present instead. I've spent too much time dwelling on things lately, and I need to stop doing that.

I'm now cooking dinner – an easy stir fry, nothing too fancy – when a knock interrupts me. Turning down the heat a bit, I walk to my door and look through the peephole. When I find my uncle standing on the other side, surprise fills me, and I hurry to open the door.

"Prof! What are you doing here?" I ask him, surprised, but I quickly take a step back, indicating for him to come inside.

"I was in the neighbourhood," he responds vaguely, stepping over the threshold, and he sniffs the air. "Something smells nice," he says enthusiastically.

Just in the neighbourhood, my arse.

Shutting the door behind him, I quickly lock it and walk past him and into the kitchen opposite the entryway.

"You're welcome to stay for dinner," I tell him and turn up the heat again. Looking to my right, I grin at him. "And I doubt very much that you were nearby, Uncle."

"Ah," he muses and looks down at his feet, his hands in his pockets. Glancing up at me, he continues, "I just wanted to see your new place, Daniel. I hope you don't find it offensive that I drop by unannounced?"

Shaking my head, I look down at the food and stir the wok. "No, it's no trouble, just a surprise. But as you can see, I have hardly unpacked my things yet, so I'm afraid we'll have to eat here in the kitchen."

Grimacing, he asks me, "When will the rest of your furniture arrive?"

"They should be delivered tomorrow. Don't worry, I won't be living like a heathen for much longer," I tease him.

"Am I that transparent?" he chuckles and walks closer.

Shrugging, I say, "It's your own fault for showing up so soon after I've moved here."

Nodding, he looks at the food and smacks his lips. "True. But this looks positively delicious, Daniel. I suppose it won't kill me to eat standing up...just this once, mind you. Can't make it a habit, though; it's unhealthy for one's constitution to not sit down and eat properly on a permanent basis."

Grinning, I shake my head silently. My uncle and his old-fashioned ways is a riot, and it's clear that he was born in the wrong century because of the way he acts sometimes.

While we eat our dinner, we talk about this and that, nothing too heavy, and I am thankful for it. It feels...*normal*. Not being scrutinised or asked questions with hidden meanings is a reprieve, and I appreciate my uncle for it.

"So...What do you think of Emma?" my uncle suddenly asks.

Swallowing my food quickly, I try to make my answer as vague as possible. "She seems...nice, I guess."

Nodding, he takes another forkful of food, and we eat in silence once more. This is my uncle's usual tactic: he asks me a question that seems perfectly innocent, but before I know it, I open up and elaborate further. *Damn him.*

"We had our first tutoring session today," I tell him and take a sip of water. "She's good, I think. Very bright."

"Oh yes, that she is," my uncle concurs, shifting a bit on his feet. He doesn't meet my eyes, and I can't help but wonder why that is.

"She's also very guarded. She doesn't talk much about herself," I muse loudly. "She's interesting...a bit quirky...and she doesn't have a filter at all," I finish off, slightly embarrassed that I have revealed so much about what I think of her.

Chuckling, he says, "True. She's a funny little thing. But..." Putting his fork down on his plate, he finally looks me in the eye, a sombre expression in them that I can't quite understand. "She's a great employee, and she loves books," he then says, "and I don't want to lose her, Daniel. She's a great asset to the shop, you know."

I still don't get what his point is, so I reply, "I get that, Uncle, I do. But why are you telling me this?"

"Because, my dear boy, I want to let you in on a little secret and you have to *promise* me that you won't reveal anything to Emma."

Shrugging, I say, "Sure," but he holds up his index finger in that professor kind of way that always makes you take more notice.

"No, Daniel. Promise me: under no circumstances will you tell her about my plans, okay? You have to swear that you won't say anything. Can you do that?"

Frowning, I respond, "If it means that much to you, then fine. You have my word."

"Excellent!" Beaming at me, he leans closer and says in a conspiratorial whisper, "I want her to take over the book shop once she gets her degree."

Baffled, I open and close my mouth a couple of times before blurting out, "What?"

"You heard me, boy. I want to retire in a year or so and travel to France. Maybe I will even invest in or buy a vineyard, who knows? Either way, Emma is perfectly capable of running the shop, and I know that, despite your love of books, you have other plans, and I respect them." Pausing, he reaches for his glass of water and daps at his mouth with a napkin before taking a sip.

"But why are you so sure that she will want it?" I ask him and place my plate of food on the kitchen counter beside me. "She could have her own plans, Uncle. Maybe she'll want to move back to England. Her family's there and I'm sure she misses her parents," I explain when he only stares blankly at me.

"Oh, I have no doubt about that, Daniel. However, I don't think she would be that unwilling to settle down in Denmark. Something tells me that her past in England is what led her here, and now that you're here, too, I'm sure that'll be another reason for her to stay."

I shake my head, not following his logic at all.

"Err, what? How...? I mean...what?" Narrowing my eyes, I ask him, suspicious as hell, "Uncle, are you playing matchmaker now? What on earth are you talking about?"

"Well, you like her, don't you?" he asks me and sets down his food.

"Yes," I answer curtly.

"And I bet you find her attractive, am I right?" he questions me further, putting his hands in his pockets.

"Well, of course I do."

Oh boy, if only you knew...

"And I'm sure she thinks you're not hard on the eyes, either," he continues, seemingly astounded that I'm still not following him.

"Get to the point, Uncle," I tell him, really getting annoyed now.

"You're a boy, she's a girl...you're both good-looking, young people, both unattached - why are you looking at me like that?" he asks me, squinting his eyes at me.

I'm not about to come clean about my agreement with Emma, so I huff and say, "Uncle, just because we're both attracted to each other - and I don't even know if that's how Emma feels - doesn't automatically mean that we'll end up dating each other."

He rolls his eyes, something I have never imagined seeing him do, and it almost makes me chuckle.

"Good lord, the youth today...," he grumbles and takes a sip of water. "In my day, things were not as complicated as you lot seem to make it, Daniel."

I snort. "You aren't that old. I would venture a guess and say that you're wrong, though."

Suddenly, he winces and leans heavily on the kitchen

counter, causing me to take a step forward in concern. The plate clatters on the counter as I put it down.

"Uncle, are you alright?" I ask him, alarm evident in my voice.

He waves me off. "Yes, yes, I'm fine, Daniel...just a bit lightheaded."

"Are you sure?" I persist, not believing him.

"Of course I am," he snaps back, and I take a step back, surprised of his reaction.

Sighing, he straightens, and apologises, "I'm sorry. I'm just tired, Daniel."

"I see." But I don't, not really.

We stand there, the previous conversation lingering heavily in the air, until his whispered words take me back even further.

"Daniel, you forget that I, too, was young once. I have loved and lost...and I merely want you to understand that if you don't go after your desires - if you refuse to grab hold of them, and hold on tight, you will live a life of loneliness and regret. And I'd hate to see that happen to you..."

Thinking on his words for a while, I answer carefully, "Uncle, I understand what you're saying. But playing matchmaker when you're not even aware of the feelings of one of the parties may not exactly be..." I search for the right word. "...wise. Yes, I find Emma attractive - everything about her interests me, and I'd like to get to know her better. But..." I pause as he takes a step back with sorrow etched across his face, clear for any to see. "But we're both young, and who knows if we'd even make a good fit?" I ask him and run a hand through my hair.

"You may well be right, Daniel," he says quietly. "All I'm saying is that there's no harm in exploring your feelings for

Emma - and I can see them written on your face, my boy, so don't you dare deny them - and perhaps try to make her see that her future could very well lie here, in Copenhagen, instead of at home, in Oxford. That's all, I promise you."

Crossing my arms, I think hard about what he's just told me. Finally, I tell him, "Alright, then. I gave you my word, so I won't tell Emma anything about your plans, Uncle. And I can't deny that I'm...errr...very *keen* to learn more about her, find out what makes her tick, you know?" Looking into his eyes, I feel rather foolish for having such a serious heart-to-heart with none other than the Prof, but seeing his satisfied expression spurs me on. "Just don't start imagining a big, fat wedding and Emma with a brood of children surrounding her, please. One step at a time, okay?"

Backing off, he nods and replies, "Of course."

"I never knew you were such a romantic," I mutter, trying to lighten the mood, and it seems to work when I see the grin on his face.

"Aaah, Daniel, if only you knew...," he murmurs and looks as if he's about to start telling stories again.

I hold up my hand and interrupt him, "Please don't. I wish to remain in my innocent bubble for a while longer, thank you very much." I do *not* want to hear any details about my uncle's youth. *Ack!*

He chuckles and resumes eating. "Very well then, I'll keep my silence. For now, anyway."

Giving him a warning look, I say, "Good," and we finish eating our dinner.

I can't deny that the old chap has managed to surprise me a lot this evening. And while I know that he's right, and that I have every intention of getting beneath the armour Emma carries around her, the fact that he just had a dizzy spell in my presence takes up my thoughts more than his attempt at matchmaking.

I can't help but wonder if he was telling me the truth or not before. The nagging feeling in my gut tells me he didn't, and worry fills me for the rest of the evening.

CHAPTER TWENTY-FOUR

EMMA

As I stand in front of the old, nineteenth century building where I'm to have my first session with the psychologist, I want to run away and hide. I'm so nervous I almost look around for a bin to throw up in.

What the hell am I doing here?

Is this really the best course of action for me to take? I feel so uncomfortable about spilling the sordid details of my past to a complete stranger, no matter how nice she sounded on the phone. I wonder if she has a couch for her clients to lie on. In movies, they always rest there, spilling out their guts, and I am so not going to do that. That's way too strange, even for me.

The sound of a text momentarily breaks my thought process, and I pull out my phone from my clutch to read it.

Suzy: Break a leg, honey! Or, well, good luck...Love you! xx

I smile as I put it away again. I was freaking out so much last night and ended up ringing Suzy; I couldn't keep such a significant moment in my life from her, after all, and she's been nudging me about seeing *a professional*, as she keeps calling it, about my issues the past few days. I mean, she's my best friend, right? And I need to let her in. So I told her, and she was so supportive right away that I almost started to cry.

I'm turning into such a sap.

Resolved to get this first meeting over and done with, I square off my shoulders and walk the three steps up to the front door and ring the bell. As soon as I'm let inside, I hurry up the three flights of stairs. I don't want to risk changing my mind about what I am about to do, but maybe it would've been wiser to take the lift instead because my legs are killing me right now. When I reach the top, I find a door slightly ajar and glance at the letterbox to be certain I am at the right place. I take a deep breath before knocking calmly.

Light footsteps draw nearer as I wait to be let in - my mum taught me *some* manners, at least - and I don't have to wait long. A woman in her forties with blonde hair pulled back in a ponytail greets me, hand outstretched to shake mine.

"Hello. You must be Emma. I'm Katherine McGregor. Please come in." She takes a step back, and I follow, a bit hesitantly, because there's still a slight chance that I'll regret coming here and bolt out and leave whence I came.

I follow Katherine along a short, narrow hallway and through a door to the left that opens up into what appears to be a living room. The light, hardwood floor is bare apart from a few rugs placed here and there under the furniture, and what looks to be a comfy sofa is placed up against the wall to my right, with a small, rectangle coffee table opposite it that is filled with different types of magazines. I turn my head to my left where a white shelf filled with books is situated against the wall and some fancy light bulbs in the ceiling shine down on them. Even though I can't exactly make out the titles, it makes me less nervous, somehow, to find that Katherine appears to be a book lover such as myself. The sunshine from the huge windows directly opposite me gives the room a welcoming air of sorts, and the tension in my body dissipates slowly. In the middle of the room, there are two black leather armchairs with high backs that look very inviting, and there is a small round table with glasses and a few water bottles placed upon it between them.

Katherine moves to one of the windows where, just below it, stands a lovely vintage desk that, despite its beauty, appears to be so out of place considering the fact that the rest of the furniture is more modern. She pulls out one of the drawers and takes a pen and notebook before turning back towards me once more.

She smiles briefly at me and takes a seat in one of the armchairs, and I guess that is my cue to do the same. I shut the door behind me first, though. I don't want to risk anyone eavesdropping on our session.

"Is this your home?" I ask her and sit down opposite her, holding on tight to my clutch in my lap. Anxiousness flares up again, and I can't seem to relax despite the softness of the leather.

She nods. "It is, yes. I have worked from home the past few years but have recently let offices closer to the city that will be ready for me in a few months. I have come to realise that separating my home from my business will be best for me and my family."

I don't know how to proceed and we stay silent for a bit while I try not to stare too much at the woman before me. She's dressed in a flowy, white summer dress that falls below her knees and some peep-toed flat white sandals. Very classy, yet casual; I like that.

"Emma," Katherine says, and I tense. "Seeing as this is the first time you're here, let me tell you the same thing I tell everyone who comes through my doors, okay?" Her smile seems genuine, understanding even, and I nod.

"Anything and everything you say stays here. That means that our conversations are confidential, and that I am bound by law to not reveal anything you divulge to anyone. Unless, of course, you give me permission to do it. That's the first rule. The second one is that I am not a psychiatrist, meaning that I am not able to nor will I prescribe any kind of medicinal drugs. And the third rule is that if you do not feel that I am the right 'fit' for you, or that I simply can't help you, please tell me so that I can refer you to a colleague." She lets her words sink in, and I am, once again, reassured by her words. Then she goes on. "Do you understand?"

I exhale and while I still don't feel entirely at ease, I sit back in the chair and relax my shoulders a bit.

"I understand," I say. "Do you mind if we speak English?" I blurt out, and I cringe a bit. *Me and my mouth!*

Katherine smiles widely before answering, "Not at all. In fact, it's not often that I have the chance to speak my native language, so I'd like that. And," she continues, leaning forward to take a bottle of water and hands it to me, "if it makes you feel more comfortable, then by all means, let's do that."

Hearing my own language leaving her lips makes me smile lightly, and I shrug. "I just think that it will be easier for me, coming here I mean, if I don't have to worry about the language barrier as well."

She chuckles slightly and pours some water for herself.

"True, I understand that."

We sit back and sip our water, and I wonder what I am to do.

"You should also know, Emma, that you don't have to tell me every single detail of your reasons for coming here today," Katherine says, her tone of voice soothing, and I nod, lost in thoughts.

"So do I just start talking about whatever I want?" I ask her, a bit confused.

"Why don't you start by telling me a little bit about what prompted you to contact me? You didn't give me many details over the phone when you rang the other day. And we'll take it from there," she answers and opens her notebook, finding a blank page.

Unable to keep eye contact with her yet again, I turn my head to look outside the window. The leaves on the trees outside sway slightly, giving in to the warm breeze, and their movements come close to hypnotising me.

"I have nightmares," I say quietly, my eyes caught in the light shining through the leaves.

Katherine's voice filters through the images in my head as if it's coming from somewhere far away.

"How often?" she asks me quietly.

"Almost every night," I whisper, a lump forming in my throat.

"I see. Can you tell me a little about them?" she asks me, her voice low, gentle, and it gives me the strength to do just that.

I tell her about the little girl on the bed...about the looming shadow...about my desperate wish, no, my *need* to go to her but how I can't move...and that I can't speak. Not until the very end when it's already too late. Without even realising it, the more I tell her, the details pour out of my mouth. I even mention *his* name, but only briefly. While it feels cathartic, invigorating even, to *finally* share my deepest, darkest secret with someone, the nausea returns, holding me captive, until I can't go on.

Placing a hand over my mouth, I gasp, "I think I'm going to be sick."

Not missing a beat, Katherine tosses her pen and paper to the floor, stands up and grabs my hand, pulling me up from my seat. Briskly, we walk out of the room, turn left and, lucky for me, there's a door that opens up to a bathroom right next to the living room. I release Katherine's hand and rush to the toilet, and just barely manage to fall to my knees before the sickness overtakes me.

Fuck this shit!

I can't keep the tears from falling while I throw up, and even though I appreciate Katherine's soothing voice behind me as she pulls my hair back from my face and rubs my back in gentle circles, I want her to go away at the same time. I'm so embarrassed and angry at myself; why am I so weak? It disgusts me.

"I'm so sorry," I cry after the ordeal is over. "I hate this!" I want to smash something, anything…The rage inside me builds and builds until I scream, "Make it stop! Please!"

Anguished, I put an arm to the seat and put my head down, shaking and sobbing, nose running, and I don't think I'm completely in the present anymore. The images run through my head like a loop, never ceasing their torment on my heart and mind, and I wonder how long I can keep going on like this.

Is it time for the loony bin?

I feel a gentle but firm grip on my arm and slowly lift my

head to find Katherine kneeling beside me.

"Emma, try to calm down," she says firmly. "Take a deep breath in...and let it out. Come on, do it now."

I follow her instructions, not knowing how long we sit there, but ever so slowly, the tears subside and although I'm left completely exhausted, I am calm once more.

"Are you feeling a little better now?" Katherine asks me, and I nod. We stand up and she hands me some toilet paper.

"Now, wipe your nose, wash your face, and then join me in the living room once you feel more settled, okay?" Thankful for the chance to have a few moments of privacy, I nod again, and after smiling reassuringly at me, she pats my hand and leaves me alone. As soon as I hear the click of the door closing, I turn to the mirror above the sink.

Ugh. I look absolutely disgusting - again. My hair is matted from sweat, my eyes look puffy and swollen, and my complexion is deadly pale, causing my freckles to stand out even more. Not to mention that all my makeup is no longer on my eyes but have fallen to my cheeks and neck. Sighing dejectedly, I wash my hands and face, quickly redo my hair, and I take a deep breath, praying for courage, as I leave the comfort of the bathroom behind me.

I hurry back to the living room and find Katherine scribbling in her notebook. As I walk closer to her, though, she looks up and asks, "Better?"

She pours some water into my glass and hands it to me. My throat is parched, and icky with the aftertaste with vomit, and I hurry to drink every drop, still standing.

Finally, I sit down and answer, "Well, yes. Pretty embarrassed, though, and I'm almost certain that I'm rather crazy. " I look down at my lap, unsure of what to do with my hands so I end up sitting on them to prevent them from fidgeting.

"Let me ask you something...Is this the first time you have recounted your nightmares to anyone?"

Clearing my throat I raise my eyes to hers, and again only find them to be filled with interest and kindness.

"I haven't told anyone, not even my parents," I answer her and sit back in my seat.

She closes her notebook and smiles at me. "Well, in that case, let me reassure you right away: you are *not* crazy, Emma. It is only natural that telling me, a stranger, about them would cause you to have a mild anxiety attack, notwithstanding the fact that you have kept your silence about them for so many years. You are dealing with haunting memories, and while they may seem as if they have the power to take over your life, I will do my best to help you overcome them. That is, if you feel comfortable with continuing to see me?"

She raises her eyebrows, and I consider her words for a few seconds. So far, Katherine has been wonderful, and while I don't know her at all, a sixth sense tells me that I really do believe that she is able to help me.

Nodding, I say, "I'd like that."

She beams at me. "Excellent. I'm glad you think so. It's really important that you trust me and my abilities, Emma." She sets aside her things and picks up her water.

"I can guess that you feel rather spent now, so would you like to stop for today? We only have fifteen minutes left anyway."

Wow, where did the time go?

"I don't mind continuing," I answer, and it's actually true. I don't. There's something about Katherine that makes me relax, despite the serious nature of why I'm here...In a way, I'm also rather impatient because I am desperate for these nightmares to go away.

"Okay, then," she replies. "Aside from those nightmares of yours, is there another reason you have chosen to seek counseling?"

"Actually...," I start to say, and then shut my mouth firmly. Katherine waits patiently for me to go on, but the words are difficult to come by.

"I've never had a boyfriend," I blurt out and hurry on. "I mean, I've had sex, of course, but I've never wanted to experience that kind of relationship. I don't want some guy to declare his everlasting love to me, or to get married and have ten children, or something like that. Isn't it weird?" I ask her, watching her hide a smile with her right hand.

She shakes her head. "No, not if your nightmares are a reflection of past experiences, and you've already said as much; and even though I haven't got all the details yet, I'm inclined to agree with you. But we'll get to that part later in our sessions. Why do you think it's so unnatural? Plenty of people don't want that type of relationship, especially not when they're as young as you are."

"Well, because..." I open and close my mouth, frantically searching for the right words. I feel a blush creeping over my cheeks from what I'm about to tell her. "Because I have never kissed a man, either. I like sex - heck, good sex is the best - but the thought of kissing? It's always made me feel sick to my stomach. Until recently..." My voice trails off, and I take a large gulp of water. The thought of Daniel's full lips and bright, green eyes make my belly dip pleasantly.

I really need to have sex soon...

She frowns at the *'no kissing'* part, and tilts her head a bit to the side, a thoughtful look in her eyes.

"Why do you say *'until recently'*? What's happened?"

"I've met someone, and even though we barely know each other, I have this almost unbearable wish to feel his lips on mine." She has to be able to hear the need in my voice, but I am no longer embarrassed about it. This is part of the reason why I'm here, after all.

"And he's *really* gorgeous, you see. He's so not my usual type, though - in fact he's so far from it that I've wondered if I needed my head examined based solely on this fact instead of my other issues!" I exclaim, so confused and, to be perfectly honest, truly annoyed at myself right now.

Katherine laughs and immediately puts up a hand. "I'm so sorry, Emma, but the way you're recounting all this is a bit funny." Her laughter dies down, though the corners of her mouth remains tilted upwards.

"Let me ask you something," she continues. "Why does it sound like you want answers all at once? Why can't you just let the questions rest for a bit and see where this attraction takes you?"

I rub the back of my neck and reply sheepishly, "Because I need them now so that I know I'm not mad as a hatter."

Katherine shakes her head a bit. "I can't tell you all you want to know right now, Emma, because I don't even have those answers. I don't have all the facts yet. *But* one word of advice..." When she pauses, I lean forward in my seat, eager to hear what she has to say.

"If meeting this man has forced you to view new, *positive* emotions regarding sex and all it entails, then I would say that exploring them might not be such a bad thing. *However* - and this is important, Emma - you are in a vulnerable state of mind, so don't rush into things. Granted, I don't know you all that well yet, but I have a feeling you have a tendency to act before you think. Am I right?"

There's a twinkle in her eyes, so I'm not offended at the least by her words.

"True," I concede and sigh. Pondering her words we sit in silence for a while until the sound of a low bell pulls me back to the present.

"Our time's up," Katherine says and stands up, so I do the same. "How often would you like to see me?"

"I can only meet once a week because of my job," I reply regretfully. Now that I've taken the first step, I just want this process to hurry up.

"Okay then. Same time next week works for you?"

"I think so, yes. But I'll ring you if something comes up," I inform her, and we walk out of the room. I put my hand on the doorknob of her front door, but hesitate and look at her.

"Thank you," I tell her, all of a sudden feeling shy.

Smiling gently, she stretches her hand to me, and we shake hands.

"Try to be patient, Emma. I know that you've reached the stage where you're tired and anxious and just want to move forward in your life, but these things take time. And until we meet next week, try to take things as they come without overanalysing them. You're too young for that." She opens the door for me and I smile in thanks, walking slowly down the stairs.

I stand outside for some time, taking in the sun and thinking back on the past hour; while I still don't have all the answers that I had hoped for, I feel lighter somehow. As if this is the first time in a really long while that I am able to breathe properly. Darkness doesn't cloud my thoughts, not right now at least...And I take comfort in that. The road ahead may still be long and winding, and I'm sure there'll be plenty of times when I'll feel lost and confused again...but at least I've taken the first step to move forward, and that's what matters for now.

CHAPTER TWENTY-FIVE

EMMA

THE REST OF THE week passes in the same way, and a pattern forms: either I walk to Daniel's door or he comes to me, and we head to work together before coming home to study. I suppose it should bother me to work so much, considering it's our summer holiday and everything, but I like the routine. In fact, I rely on it. I may be wild and spontaneous when I'm clubbing, but that's definitely not the case when it concerns my day-to-day life. The routine relaxes me, keeps me centred, and I confess that gaining small pieces about Daniel and his sisters every day is quite interesting. Hearing his stories about what it was like growing up with four older sisters, I can't keep a small touch of envy from working its way through my system. Because I wish I'd had that instead of Steven...Maybe things would've been different if I'd been blessed with sisters instead of a brother?

I know there's no sense in dwelling on such things, of course, but I can't help but wonder if - had my parents chosen to have more children - life would have been so much different for me than it turned out to be? Would I have dabbled in drugs if I'd had *someone* to talk to?

Daniel doesn't talk much about his dad, though...or why, exactly, he hasn't started attending the university before now. As far as I can tell, he isn't nearly as bad at reading or writing as he thinks he is. In fact, now that we've completed *The Canterbury Tales*, I'm kind of in love with his brain. I have also been so knackered from our studying sessions that I have not even suffered much from my usual nightmares.

It's a bit odd, but I haven't minded sharing a few things about myself with Daniel, either. Even when we haven't been together, he's texted me a lot, asking me normal, everyday questions, and I've even caught myself grinning stupidly after having read his texts. He seems to enjoy stories about my Nan the most, actually, and I haven't been able to stop thinking about them meeting one day, either.

What's that all about?

To top it all off, the tingling I always feel in my body whenever Daniel is close to me has intensified, and I think I'm close to reaching my breaking point. Every time he's left my flat, I've been a hot, quivering mess, and I've had to use my vibrator to keep my lady bits happy each night, but I can just *feel* that a substitute for the real thing won't be enough for me for much longer. But what to do about it? A random hook up would be my usual approach, but I don't feel right about using another guy for sex when all I imagine is Daniel on me, in me, *with* me.

However, I *have* to do something about this, because if I don't, I'll be horrible to be around. Women who are horny are worse than when they're PMSing...at least, that's my opinion.

Mr. Andersen has been acting rather strange this week, though. I've caught him staring at Daniel and me more than once, either grinning mischievously or with a speculative look in his eyes, and I honestly don't understand why. Does he think there's more to our relationship than that of work colleagues and neighbours? It's made me rather uncomfortable, that's for certain, but I can't exactly ask him what's on his mind. Maybe he's just glad to see his nephew making a friend? I'm also a bit worried about him, because he's been looking rather pale lately. On one hand, I want to ask him if he's alright, but on the other, I know that we don't have that kind of relationship that makes me free to ask about his health.

It's Friday afternoon and I've finally managed to persuade Daniel to go shopping for some new clothes after work. That should be fun. Or not. Seeing as he hasn't stopped grumbling about it, I have a feeling it won't be as enjoyable as I'd originally thought.

"I honestly can't see why it matters so much what I'm wearing," he complains, probably for the hundredth time today, as we walk to the train station after work, causing me to stop on the sidewalk.

"Because it's important to make Steven believe that you truly *are* my boyfriend," I huff, glaring at him. "Not an impostor."

When he merely sighs and rubs his eyes, I take in his appearance. He looks flushed, but not in the usual, adorable way I've come to think of as uniquely his own, and his eyes are a bit puffy as well.

I take a step further, getting as close as I can, and reach up to his forehead, placing my wrist on it.

"Whoa, you're burning up, Daniel. Why didn't you say anything?" I shake my head at the stupidity, grab his hand and pull him with me to catch a taxi.

"What are you doing?" he asks me weakly, and I glance briefly at him.

"You're clearly sick, so I'm getting us a taxi so we can get home more quickly," I answer distractedly, still searching the traffic.

"I can't afford that," he protests feebly, and he's starting to lean heavily on my right side.

Releasing his hand, I wrap my arm tightly around his waist, trying to catch the eye of a cabbie when luck finds me, and one pulls over. Giving him our address, I push Daniel inside it and follow him quickly.

"Is he going to puke?" the driver asks me, and I frown when I catch his annoyed eyes in the rear view mirror.

"He's not drunk, just sick," I answer irritably.

The driver shrugs and we're on our way. Daniel has leaned back in his seat, and it looks almost as if he's sleeping, because his eyes are closed. All the way home, we keep silent, and I just hope there's nothing seriously wrong with him.

The ride doesn't take long, and after I've made sure that Daniel won't fall flat on his face - I've pushed his body into the brick wall, right next to the main door of our apartment complex - I pay the taxi driver and rummage through my clutch to find my keys. For a split second, I debate whether I should take Daniel to his own flat or mine, but as I feel his heavy body pressing in on my back, my mind is made up.

After lots of pulling and cursing - from my part, not Daniel's - we're inside my flat. As soon as I've shut the door, Daniel moves sluggishly into my room and lies, face down, on my bed. For once, I didn't make it this morning, and I'm happy about that; it would've been a mess, trying to keep him conscious while getting it ready.

"Hey, big guy, don't fall asleep on me just yet," I scold

him quietly and quickly walk towards the bed. Starting with his shoes, I untie the laces and remove them, before climbing up behind him, settling between his spread legs.

"I can't believe you didn't take off your backpack before you collapsed on my bed," I mutter, but I don't get a reply from the very affected guy on my bed. Well, nothing but a grunt, anyway.

"Shite, this is going to get awkward." Sitting back, I plant my hands on my hips, blowing a stray lock of hair from my face, wondering how I'm going to get his backpack off. He suddenly raises his right arm, and I'm glad he isn't that far off in neverland just yet.

As quickly as possible, I pull off the annoying bag and slip it off his back. "Roll over, Daniel," I tell him as I try to wrestle the duvet from under his heavy body, and I stub my toe on the bedside table in the process.

"Fuck," I curse quietly, hopping on one leg, and I catch Daniel looking at me, his head raised the tiniest bit and his glassy eyes trying to focus on me.

"Are you...hurt?" he asks me weakly.

"No, no, not at all. Just almost broke my toe, but nothing majorly alarming," I reply, and even in his fever induced state, the sarcasm isn't lost on him.

"Sorry," he sighs, leaning back on my pillows briefly before he rolls over like I requested.

"God, I hurt everywhere," he moans.

"How on earth were you able to work all day like this?" I ask him, astonished and, quite frankly, a bit angry with him. Clearly, he should've stayed in bed this morning instead of coming with me.

"It just...just snuck up...on me," he groans, and I roll my eyes at his stupidity.

"Well, lie back, try to get comfortable, and I'll just fetch my thermometer and some water for you. Don't want you to dehydrate on me," I tell him and hobble out to my kitchen to get the water before finding my thermometer in my small medicine cabinet. When I get back, I find him unbuttoning his shirt, and despite the fact that he's obviously not making an attempt at being sexy, watching him doing it causes me to halt in my tracks. The last time I saw him without a shirt on was when he came knocking on my door after hearing my screams, and I would be lying if I said I haven't missed seeing that smattering of chest hair...or his abs.

Stop drooling, Em, I scold myself and briskly resume walking.

"Here, let me help you with that," I say quietly, and place the glass on the nightstand next to the bed. He lets his arms fall and slumps over on a sigh, so I make quick work of the rest of the buttons and tug the shirt off.

"Drink the water and lie down, please," I tell him and once he's done as I've asked, I place a hand on his shoulder, nudging him down. A zing pangs through my entire arm when I feel his smooth skin, but I try to ignore it, not allowing him to see the reaction touching him emits in me.

He can't seem to get comfortable, though, because he keeps twisting and turning, and I sit down on the side with a frown.

"What's the matter?" I ask him, and he sighs.

"My pants are digging into my side," he complains, and puts a hand under his head.

"Ah, I see..." Taking the thermometer from the nightstand, I put it in his mouth. "I need to check your temperature."

We sit in silence for the next few minutes, and I

contemplate whether or not I should just tell him to lose the pants if they make him so uncomfortable. I mean, it's not as if I haven't seen my share of scantily clad guys before. Why should it be different now?

A small voice inside me whispers, *Because it's Daniel*, and I can't deny the fact that seeing him almost completely naked is a major turn-on - even if he is sick as a dog at this very moment. I remove the thermometer from his mouth, and a small gasp escapes me when I see how high the fever is.

"Okay, Daniel, I think it's safe to say that you won't be leaving this bed for the rest of the day."

He opens one eye to peek at me.

"Bad?" he asks me.

"Well, nothing too alarming, but you need to rest," I reassure him, giving him a small smile. "I'll wake you up in a couple of hours and force some more fluids in you." Standing from the bed, I take the glass and head towards the kitchen.

"Oh, feel free to take off your pants, by the way," I say in an offhanded tone of voice, not letting him see the blush in my cheeks.

"Are you sure it's not...too weird?" he asks, raising his voice a bit so that I can hear him from the kitchen.

"Not at all," I shout back. "It's not as if I haven't seen guys without their clothes on before," I joke, more than glad that he can't see me.

When I don't hear an answer to my last remark, I quickly wash the thermometer and go back to my room. On the floor beside the bed lies Daniel's slacks, and as I walk to pick them up, I can't help but hear the faint snoring coming from the bed. As I bend down to pick up his clothes, I look at him, and almost giggle when I see him passed out, mouth open, and his glasses dangling from his left hand, followed by his arm hanging limply over the side of my bed.

Shaking my head, I tiptoe closer to him, take the glasses and put them gently on the bedside table. I pick up his shirt, and I fold the rest of his clothes, all the while contemplating what I should get Daniel to eat later.

"The one time I need to cook, and I have no idea what to do," I mumble. Sighing, I finish sorting out his clothes and place them on a chair in my small kitchen before searching for my clutch to get my phone.

Nan will know what to do.

I walk quietly through my room, phone in hand, and out on my balcony. I don't shut the door completely, though, as I want to make sure I can hear Daniel if he wakes up.

I quickly find my Nan's phone number, press the green button, and wait impatiently for her to answer. As soon as I hear her voice, I jump right in, "There's an almost naked, sick man in my bed, and I don't know what to cook for him. Help me, please?"

She's silent for a few seconds, and then she laughs loudly. "Hello to you, too, Emma darling," she chuckles. "That sounds very interesting. Poor chap. What's the matter with him?"

"I think it's the flu. Before he fell asleep, he complained about his body hurting all over, and he has a fever as well."

"Do you know if he has a sore throat?" she asks me briskly.

"No, sorry, I don't," I reply, kicking myself for not asking Daniel some more questions about his symptoms.

"Well, the one thing that always seems to do the trick is some kind of soup, Emma," she tells me. "Chicken soup would be my recommendation," she continues. "May I ask who this man is?" The amusement in her voice isn't lost on me.

"It's my neighbour-slash-pupil-slash-colleague, Daniel," I reply and turn to check on him through the window. He hasn't moved at all.

"Nan, you know I can't cook," I whine. "How the devil am I supposed to cook chicken soup?"

"Well, isn't there a restaurant nearby that does takeaways?" she asks me.

"Hmm, probably," I mutter and sigh, annoyed that I didn't think of this myself. This is *not* how I imagined my afternoon: taking care of a sick guy while keeping my libido in check.

"Remember to wake him up every few hours *and* get some water in his system, and be sure to keep an eye on the fever as well," Nan tells me.

"I know, I know," I reply.

"Now, best get back to him, then. But keep me posted, and don't hesitate to ring me if you need more help," she says matter-of-factly.

"I will. I'm sorry I can't chat more today," I apologise truthfully.

She clucks and it makes me smile. "Don't you worry about that, my dear, we'll talk another day. Or email," she adds, almost as an afterthought.

"Okay, Nan, love you," I tell her and we ring off.

I get up from my seat and walk back inside, though I don't shut the door completely; the weather is still so warm and I don't want it to become stifling in the flat, especially not now there's a big, hunky guy in my bed.

Daniel still hasn't moved and if it weren't for the fact that he's still snoring, I'd be a bit worried. His breathing seems laboured, and it concerns me a bit, so I walk closer and put a hand to his forehead again. I don't think the fever has risen, however, but I look at the clock on my phone and make a mental note of waking him up in an hour.

It feels odd to have him in my bed, but strangely pleasant at the same time. Watching him sleeping, I take in his appearance; he looks younger, more vulnerable, especially now that those hideous glasses aren't covering the majority of his face. Gently, I sit down beside him, careful not to disturb him, and my eyes wander shamelessly across his features. The sun has given him a few freckles on his nose, and there are a couple of lines in the corner of his eyes, probably because he tends to squint a bit when he's outside. His cheeks are flushed because of the fever, obviously, and there's stubble on his chin again. Despite his preppy look, he obviously doesn't like to shave much, and I wonder, as ever, if his facial hair is as soft as it appears, and I reach out my fingers to touch it lightly.

A bit soft, yes, but also prickly.

I wonder what they'd feel like running against my thighs.

As soon as that thought hits me, I jerk my hand back as if I've burnt my fingers, and I stand up faster than you'd be able to say Bob's your uncle.

Thankful that he hasn't woken up from my nosy perusal of his face, I turn back to the kitchen to find the takeaway brochures. I know I should learn to cook, but it doesn't interest me, so I just can't be bothered with it.

Leafing through them, I find one from a Chinese restaurant just around the corner, and I look at their soups. There aren't exactly any with chicken, but maybe the Wonton soup will do the trick - at least it's not spicy or lumpy, something I very much doubt the poor guy will be able to swallow.

Satisfied with my choice, I put the brochure on the kitchen counter, walk to my nightstand to pick up my e-reader, resolving to read for a while outside until it's time to wake up my patient.

♡

Reading is my escape. It allows me breathing room whenever I feel as if the outside world becomes too much. I have Nan, and my parents, to thank for my love of books and reading because they always encouraged me to read as much as possible while growing up. They never minded what kind of books I read, as long as they were age appropriate, of course, and something my Nan once told me has stuck by me: *You're never bored when you lose yourself in a great story.*

She was right. I never have trouble finding out what to do with my time, and once a book catches my interest, I am able to stay in that other world for as long as I want. There are no ugly memories assaulting me when I read. There is no past and no future...only the present. I take comfort in that.

The fact that I enjoy romance novels the most seems so very ironic when I am not a born and bred romantic, doesn't it? Well, I may not believe in fairytales or the happy-ever-afters, but, for a time, I like to pretend that the story I am reading is the truth: that the girl gets the boy in the end, and that they ride off in the sunset together, ready to take on the world.

Very poetic, eh? True, the books I read now are a lot saucier than they used to be, but I like that many authors are not afraid to breathe life into their fantasies these days. There is a certain freedom in them that I appreciate, especially given the fact that I enjoy sex so much. Or my body seems to, anyway.

Fantasies cost nothing. And I, for one, like to stay in the fantasy world from time to time, finding a reprieve from my past.

Is that such a bad thing?

♡

I've been checking up on Daniel every hour as the afternoon wore on, and evening is setting in. It's getting so dark that I won't be able to stay outside reading my book for much longer. He didn't eat much of the soup I ordered, but at least he's been drinking a lot of water, and I can always try to force some more into him later.

After yet another hour has passed - it's eight pm now - I go to wake up Daniel. He's lying on his stomach now, his head on an arm, turned slightly on the side, and I become lost in the sight before me once again.

That sinful body of his can only be described as a work of art: the curve of his spine, the long, lean muscles in his arms...and who knew that the veins there would turn me on like that? I just want to lick them! A lock of his thick hair has fallen, almost concealing his eyes completely, and my fingers are itching to brush it aside, allowing me to see his face completely.

Suddenly, his eyes open, and I gasp; they are not as glassy anymore, and the intensity in them takes me by surprise. I can't pull away from the heat in his gaze, nor do I wish to. The green colour pulls me in, and I take a few more steps closer until he has to shift back to keep his eyes locked on mine.

In order to keep my body in check, I place my hands in

the back pockets of the jeans I'm wearing today, and I clear my throat that feels awfully dry now.

"How are you feeling?" I croak, my breaths picking up speed.

"Awful," he grumbles. His surly reply breaks the heaviness in the air, and I chuckle.

"Well, that's honest," I say and move to sit beside him. He shifts a bit on the bed, making more room for me, and I appreciate the gesture.

"I don't tell lies, Emma. I never do," he answers; the flush is back in his cheeks, and I lean forward to place my hand on his forehead once again. He lets me do it, keeping his silence, and as hard as I try, I can't tear my eyes from his once more. Vaguely, I notice that he doesn't feel as hot as before he fell asleep, but he's still too warm for me to believe that he's completely fever-free.

The air becomes electric as we stay like this, locked in each other's gaze, and as if in slow motion, I move my arm away from his fevered head and turn my hand so that my palm rests on his cheek. His eyelids flutter closed, and he leans into my hand, sighing deeply. My thumb caresses the stubble, absorbed in the texture as if I'm in a trance of some sort.

"I need to get you some water," I murmur distractedly, because I really should.

"In a minute," he whispers, and nuzzles closer, as if he were a cat or a dog who wants to cuddle. "This is too nice...I can't move yet."

"Okay," I whisper back, and my eyes linger on his lips. Suzy's words from earlier in the week come to mind...What would it feel like to kiss those lips of his? Will I feel repulsed like all the other times guys have attempted to do that?

Shit, I hope not...because I want to run my tongue across them so much right now that it physically pains me to hold back.

However, that is just what I do. I retreat like the coward I am, slowly removing my hand from his cheek, and, as he feels the loss of it, he opens his eyes immediately. I move to stand up, but he grabs my hand, preventing me to leave his side and the strength in his grip causes my body to tense up automatically.

"Emma...," he says softly, and the way he says my name - so tenderly, so reverently - cracks my heart open wider and the ache in my body intensifies. "Don't pull away from me," he continues on a whisper. The plea in his voice is evident, but, somehow, I can't do as he asks me to. My fight or flight instincts kick in, and I tug my hand from his and stand.

Backing away, I murmur a feeble "I'm sorry," and I hurry to the kitchen to fetch the thermometer. Leaning heavily on the kitchen counter, my outstretched arms feel shaky and weak, and I let out the huge breath I've unknowingly held in since leaving Daniel in my bed. Angry at myself, I shut my eyes tightly, willing my body to just run back to him and explain why I can't let go.

But how do I do that when I don't even know why that is?

I release the tight hold on the counter and take a step away. Realising that I need to get back to Daniel, I grab a new glass, fill it with water, and take that, along with the thermometer, and begin to walk out of the kitchen. I lean my head back to stare aimlessly at the ceiling for a few seconds when the devil takes over me, and the seeds of a delicious idea take root in my mind.

Maybe I don't need to let go completely...? Maybe, just maybe...there's a way for me to keep my body happy without having to relinquish the tight control I have on my emotions?

Feeling the beginnings of a devious smile to form on my lips, I take a few deep breaths in order to psych myself up for what I'm about to do. When I feel confident that I can pull this off, I straighten my back, and I turn to walk back into my bedroom.

Here goes nothing.

CHAPTER TWENTY-SIX

DANIEL

EMMA IS, WITHOUT A doubt, the most infuriating woman I have ever met.

If my legs didn't feel like jelly right now, I'd toss the sheets aside, march out in the kitchen and just grab her. However, some small and powerful voice inside me still wants for her to make the first move.

I must be a masochist. My cock thinks so at least.

Feeling the ache for release in my cock - because even in this sorry state I'm in, it quite clearly still believes it's ready to play - I bundle the duvet around me quickly so that Emma won't notice the bulge in my boxers when she comes back.

It's been a difficult week in many ways. Spending time with her every day, getting to know her better, and definitely becoming turned on whenever she's been close to me - but without having the balls to do anything about it - has made me cover the bulge in my pants so as not to reveal the effect she has on me when I've left her flat. I've definitely been showering a lot more than usual. What can I say? My cock needs release more than once each day.

My head is hurting like a bitch right now, and I lie back down on my - well, Emma's - pillow on a heavy sigh. The first time I'm in Emma's bed is not exactly going according to plan.

See, the plan was to go shopping for clothes - and I have to admit I'm not too sorry about missing out on that - followed by me persuading her to go back to my place so that I could cook her a proper meal for once, and *then*...Okay, I hadn't planned that far ahead, to tell the truth. But now those plans will have to be set aside for another day.

But, fuck...those lips of hers...what I wouldn't give to have them on mine right about now...to taste, lick, and bite them and crush her soft body on top of mine, pressing her pussy into my cock.

Groaning, I place my right arm across my eyes, but it's no good; the hardness in my cock just won't settle down, and I clench my hand in a tight fist.

"Okay, Daniel, here's the thing," Emma says, and I move my arm from my eyes to take her in. She looks...determined. And a bit scary, actually, with the way her hands are firmly planted on her hips as she stands next to the bed, looking down at me. Glancing at the bedside table, I notice the fresh glass of water. *How the heck did that get there?* My eyebrows raised, I reach out for it and swallow down every drop, almost forgetting a certain female waiting for me to pay attention to her once more. I can't see her properly without wearing my glasses, though, so I hurry to put them on, finally giving her my undivided attention.

Head held high, she looks me straight in the eyes and says, "I like you...and it's clear we're very attracted to each other, am I right?"

Not seeing where she's headed with this, I simply nod.

"You're hot in that preppy, geeky kind of way many

women appreciate, and I think you already are aware of the fact that you're not my usual type, correct?"

Gritting my teeth at her words, and close to getting pissed at her, I grunt. "Correct."

She nods, turns her head slightly to the side, revealing her long neck that I, right now, just want to take a bite out of.

"Despite that, I have an idea that I think will work splendidly for both of us," she says cryptically, and I wait for her to go on. She keeps silent, though, and I motion with my hand for to get on with it, tired and cranky as hell right now.

"Okay, what's this idea of yours?" I ask her, and I watch as she moves to release the hair band and let her long curls run free down her back.

"I have a proposition for you," Emma says as she backs away from me, and she begins to tug her top from the waistband of her jeans.

What...the...hell?

Feeling slightly panicked my cock will weep with frustration if she doesn't stop what I think she's doing, I rise up on my elbows and ask her sharply, "What are you doing, Emma?"

"My idea," she says in a low voice, "involves you, and me, and getting to know each other in the biblical sense - without any kissing on the lips, mind you - and without having actual sex, Daniel." And off is her top, leaving her in a very low-cut, very sexy blue bra, and my cock throbs.

Swallowing hard, I say hoarsely, "Why?"

"Because I'm horny as hell, and I fancy you," she replies quickly and starts to unbutton her jeans.

Fuck, that's hot.

"And..." She hesitates, and I can't move my eyes from her hands on the last button, but when she doesn't unfasten it, I manage to tear my gaze away and look into hers. Seemingly satisfied with me, she nods once and smiles.

"And I don't want to take advantage of you, so that's why I won't be your first shag, either. But you told me not that long ago that you wanted me to help you become more...well, relaxed around girls, remember?"

Still unable to form proper words, I nod again, certain I'm drooling.

"So I thought that if I *show* you how to pleasure a woman's body, that might help...as well as keeping my pussy happy."

Shit, I love that she doesn't mind talking dirty.

Based on the way she smiles at me just now, I can only imagine what I must look like.

Like it's my birthday and Christmas and that I won the lottery all on the same day, probably.

"Am I hallucinating?" I ask her.

Please, for the love of all things holy, don't let that be, I beg silently to the powers that be, and she chuckles.

"Most definitely not," she tells me, finally allowing her pants to drop, and letting me see the incredibly sexy lacy thong covering her pussy.

"I promise I'll go easy on you today," she says and stills. When I see the sincerity in her eyes, I know deep down to my bones that I already mean more to her than just a boy toy for her to play with. Because the way she's looking at me right now? Yes, there's lust in her eyes, her cheeks are flushed, and her breathing has become heavy...but there's also tenderness hidden behind it all, and I'm dying to see more of that coming from her.

"Are you serious?" I ask her, not caring one bit that I sound both greedy and horny right now. This is definitely not what I had planned, but what warm-blooded male could say no to the vision standing in front of him, all able and willing to teach him how to make a girl go wild with passion?

Not me.

She licks her lips, pulling her lip ring between her teeth, and nods.

"Then I do believe we have a deal," I say, almost growling, and her eyes widen. She likes that. *Good to know.*

She places a hand and knee on the bed and crawls towards me, her eyes never leaving mine. I feel as if I'm the lamb being prepared for slaughter, but I can't say I mind that at all. As she comes closer, I tear the sheets hiding my lap away, and when she notices the big bulge in my boxers, I smirk. However, when she licks her lips and smiles secretively, the smirk leaves me and I become fascinated with the way her boobs look in that tiny bra. I love the curves on this woman, and I'm such a guy for being unable to tear my gaze away from the handful currently nearing me.

Strangely enough, I don't feel that nervous yet. Emma may be about to devour me in some way, but I know this girl. If she tells me that she'll be gentle with me, she will. Lightheaded, flushed, and massively turned on, I spread my legs further apart as she continues to crawl towards me. I pull up my knees and palm my cock, putting mild pressure on it. Sadly, I don't think I'll last long for this first time fooling around with a woman who's every fantasy I've ever had, and then some, come alive right before me.

She stops her feline movements and sits back on her knees, her hungry gaze taking me in. Her eyes burn me, inside out, and I feel tiny pinpricks on every part of my body she shamelessly peruses. My breath speeds up, and I'm not sure of what she'll have me do right now. Do I wait? Do I move towards her?

As if able to hear my thoughts, her gaze lifts from my lap, and she smiles gently.

"You should know, Daniel, that most women, including me, like it when the guy makes the first move, but I'll start this time." Her voice is low, husky, and I grip my cock more firmly in my hand. It's almost painfully hard, and pre-come wets my boxers.

She reaches an arm behind her and removes her bra, the movement forcing me to hold my breath in until her breasts are completely visible to me. They're pale, but covered in freckles, like the rest of her skin, and I just want to lick and kiss each and every one of them.

"Foreplay is really important," Emma whispers, her breathing almost coming out in large puffs, and when she raises a hand to suck on her finger, a moan escapes me, and she smiles knowingly at me.

"Patience," she whispers around the thumb in her mouth, and once it's licked to her satisfaction, she begins to fondle her left breast, moulding and massaging it. Her fingers then circle the hard nipple and she pulls on it. I clench my fist around the sheets on her bed when she moans, as turned on as I am.

Her other hand moves towards my lap and as she lifts the waistband of my boxers, she commands, "Take these off." I happily oblige her, doing what she wants as fast as I can. My cock springs free of its confinements, and I sigh in relief: equally hoping that her hands will pay attention to it soon, yet praying that she'll draw out this seduction as long as humanly possible at the same time.

She licks her palm and I watch, mesmerised, as she reaches down; but instead of fisting the base of my cock like I expect her to, she takes a firm, yet gentle, grip on my balls, and I can't hold up my head any longer.

"Look at me," she tells me firmly, and the way she is taking control right now makes it hard to breathe. Again doing what she asks, I take in the way she looks at my balls as she emits just the right pressure on them and pulls at them. Tearing my gaze away, I focus on her fingers and hand still caressing her breast, taking note of the way she does it for future reference.

"Tell me what you want," she murmurs, and the nervousness sets in now, mingling with the anticipation of what she'll do next.

"I...I don't know," I stammer out, slightly embarrassed at her request.

"Please?" she asks me, and there's no hesitation in her eyes when she looks at me: only desire and, again, tenderness.

I shake my head: this is too much for me.

She relents and straightens slightly, losing her hold on my balls, before she moves even closer on her hands and knees.

"I'll just have to play it by ear, then," she whispers, her lips closing in until they're a mere hairsbreadth from mine. The thought that she may kiss me after all strikes me, but, at the very last moment, she moves her head to the side and, finally, her mouth rests lightly on my skin just below my ear. The touch sears through me, and I can't keep my eyes open any longer. Applying pressure, she begins to nibble and lick her way down my neck, and it feels incredible.

"Fuck," I groan, and she chuckles a bit.

"Do you want me to stop?" she asks me teasingly, and a breathless laugh escapes me.

"Fuck no," I answer.

"Just checking." She continues her sensual assault on my body, moving lower and lower until I can feel her heavy pants just above my right nipple.

"Bite it," I blurt out, and I feel her mouth descend on it, and I hold in my breath once more. Her tongue laves my nipple before she gently bites down, and, on a heavy whoosh, I breathe out.

"Harder," I grind out, and she doesn't even hesitate for a second. Forcing my eyes open, I find her lying half on top of me and half on the bed, holding her body up with her left arm as she tends to my needs. Her warm breasts rest against my side, and forgetting about being nervous, I release the tight grip on her bed and begin to caress her thigh. As she presses closer to my side, I take that as confirmation that she doesn't mind, and my hand wanders up, up, up until, at last, it rests just below her right breast.

Releasing my nipple from her teeth, she lifts her head and when I see the lust in her eyes, I become bolder, more intent on not letting her do all the work after all. Holding her gaze captured in mine, I place my hand on her breast, and I resolve to learn every contour of her body properly.

We don't speak, only look at each other as I caress her breast, applying pressure on her nipple and repeating her motions from earlier. I shift to lie on my side, the aches and pains in my body forgotten in this very significant moment, and we're face to face. She places her head on the pillow next to me, no doubt getting more comfortable, and the burning need to kiss her comes pretty fucking close to unmanning me...But I respect her wish...for now, at least.

She scoots a bit down on the bed and her hand finally - *thank fuck* - closes around my cock.

"Holy shit," I curse loudly, a shudder coursing through

my entire body, and she smiles wickedly at me.

"I know," she says with a twinkle in her eyes, and we smile at each other. Because although I'm so turned on right now that I doubt it'll take more than a couple of strokes from her hand for me to come, I relish the closeness we're sharing.

Whatever she says, this right here? It matters. And I'll be damned if I won't wear her down with time.

I growl when I feel her starting to jack me off, and I lick my lips and watch as she does the same.

"I don't...I don't think I'll last much longer," I pant, my voice filled with regret, and she rests her movements right away. It almost makes me weep, losing her touch like that, and my cock agrees wholeheartedly.

"Well, we can't have that," she says and she lies down on her back before taking my left hand in hers, guiding my palm firmly down her body from the base of her throat, between her breasts, down across her soft belly until she stops just above her panties hiding what I'd do *everything* to see right about now. For a few seconds, my fingertips rest just above her slit, and I can actually *feel* the warmth coming from it. Still holding my hand, she presses it down on her panties, applying pressure on my index finger, and...at last, I know what her clit feels like.

Panting, she says, "Rub it gently for a bit," and being the good pupil I am, I do as she says. Her clit feels hard, yet soft, and I lean closer down on the bed to watch my finger pleasuring her. I can *smell* her arousal, and it's like an aphrodisiac to me. She moans more loudly, grips her panties with her hands, forcing me to stop my movements for a few seconds as she tears them off. Seeing the small, trimmed strip just above her pussy, I inhale sharply, finding it hard to breathe again, and I lift my head to glance into her eyes. They are closed, though, her mouth open, and she's starting to make some small sounds I can only describe as whimpers.

"Slap my clit lightly," she orders me, and I feel more pre-come leaking out of my cock. Again, I do as she asks me, and when she groans loudly, I do the same.

"Fuck, you're gorgoeus, Em...So sexy...I love watching you like this," I growl, and she opens her eyes.

"Thank you." The lust I find there, as well as something else - I can't put my finger on it - make me long to feel her lips on mine more than ever, but I force the thought away.

"If you don't hurry up, though, I'll come all over your sheets," I warn her, and she smirks at me, clearly reveling in the power she has over me.

"Put your finger inside my pussy and reach up until you feel a rough spot," she breathes and lifts her hips so I have better access. When I feel her walls clamping down on my finger, I watch her writhing on her bed, almost there. My thumb finds her clit again, rubbing it harder and harder until she clamps a hand over her mouth, masking her screams as she falls apart on my hand.

Palming my balls, I try to be patient and watch her come down from her high, and, luckily, I don't have to wait long. Hand to my chest, she pushes me until I'm lying on my back once more, and without saying anything, she takes a firm grip on my cock before leaning down...and her mouth closes around the tip.

"Fuck, fuck, fuck," I chant when she sucks on the tip before swallowing my cock as far as she can. Her mouth is...incredible, hot. Like I predicted, it doesn't take long before I feel an all-consuming heat begin from my spine, and as she sucks me faster and faster, I grab a fistful of her hair, moving it away from her face so I can watch her finish me off.

"Yeeees," I hiss, "shit, yes, that's it, baby!" Pushing my hips up, I find my release and come in her mouth. Caressing her cheek with my thumb, in my own way trying to thank her for what she just gave me, I sigh deeply and enjoy the aftershocks running through my body before falling into a deep, dreamless sleep.

CHAPTER TWENTY-SEVEN

EMMA

I WAKE UP SLOWLY, feeling the sunlight filtering through the white curtains covering the door to my balcony warm my entire being, and I revel in the knowledge that I have not had to suffer through yet another nightmare during the night. In fact, this is the best night I have had in *forever*. Now, as I lie on my side in my bed, I become conscious of a large, warm hand covering my right breast. Blinking the sleep away, I become even more aware of the firm body pressing into my back...and there's definitely a familiar, yet foreign, hard object prodding my spine at this very moment. It takes some time before my sleepy mind remembers what happened last night, and when it does, I feel slightly embarrassed. But also incredibly turned on at the same time.

Who'd have thought that taking control like *that* would leave me feeling so empowered? So...satisfied and safe?

I'm not usually the one to take charge while having sex. True, when I see a guy I'd like to shag, I do tend to make the first move, but once we're at my - or his - flat, I just let the guy do his thing. Sometimes, I have to guide him a bit, and I'm most definitely not opposed to talking dirty, but once I sense he's with me, and knows what he's doing, my mind shuts down and I concentrate on the moment...It's all about catching the pleasure wave, ride it hard, and end it with the both of us reaching the high we've sought.

Nothing more, nothing less.

Sex is merely a physical need, and one we all have to tap into from time to time in order to not fall into an endless pit of either lunacy or depression.

However, I'd usually also wake up in a fright panic if I found some random hook-up spooning me the way Daniel is doing right now, but panic is certainly not the emotion I'm feeling. Rather, being intimate like this with him feels natural...safe...and incredibly sensual.

What do I do now? Wait until he wakes up? Or disturb him in his sleep?

Before that last thought has even taken root, Daniel's hand on my breast twitches and takes a more possessive hold on it. Soon after, I feel small, feather light, hot kisses trailing across my neck and down my back, causing me to stretch languidly, as if I'm a cat that can't hold back purring from the pleasure of them.

"'Morning, sweetheart," Daniel murmurs sleepily behind me, and alarm bells start to go off in my head.

"That's the second time you've called me that, and you have to stop doing it," I reply, a bit more sharply than I'd intended. I can't let him forget our deal, though, no matter how much it leaves a sour taste in my mouth when I think about it...yet, I have to. For now, at least.

His lips leave my body, but I can still feel his breath fanning across my skin, and it makes me break out in goose bumps.

"What?" he asks me, and picks up his sensual assault on my body again.

"*Sweetheart*," I say quietly, biting down on my lower lip to prevent a moan from escaping me. I can't keep the shiver down, though, and I just know that he felt that, too.

Daniel chuckles and murmurs, "Sorry, it won't happen again." There is not one ounce of truthfulness in his voice, but I let it go for now.

"Good. What are you doing?" I can feel his thumb and forefinger pinching my nipple and wetness begins to gather between my legs. I quickly become lost to his touch...it feels like magic.

"Shhh...just relax and enjoy it," he whispers, his voice husky and filled with desire.

"Relax?! You've got to be joking," I protest meekly, and I can feel a rumble in his chest.

Great, now he's amused...

His cock makes small, thrilling circles on my lower back, causing more wetness to pool between my legs. He kisses the stars on my neck, and small shock waves wrack my body as I count his kisses silently.

One...two...three...four...five...six...seven...eight...nine...ten.

With each kiss he bestows upon my body, he soothes the darkness in my heart a little bit more.

It fades but it isn't gone completely.

Not yet.

A mewl leaves my lips from the havoc he stirs in my body and mind, and the arm I'm resting my head on shifts until I can feel his hand on my throat pressing down lightly, and I instinctively tilt my head back, surrendering to his command.

"You like my mouth on you, Emma?" he asks me on a

low growl, and I press my arse against him, silently giving him my answer. Hearing him groan causes me to smile in satisfaction. Knowing that I have this effect on him is like an aphrodisiac.

"Say it," he demands gruffly, tilting his cock closer to me, and his thumb caresses my lower lip.

"Yes," I gasp, giving him what he craves. How can I not? This feels beyond hot...it's heavenly.

"Good," he murmurs, and his right hand leaves my breast, almost causing me to whimper in protest. I don't, though, as I feel his fingers trailing down my rounded belly, closer and closer to my pussy, and I wait impatiently for them to reach his goal.

"How can you be so good at this?" I ask him, voice devoid of breath as I revel in his touch.

He chuckles again. "I may be a virgin, but I pay attention...And you, Emma, have captured me completely. Now, hush...allow me to pleasure you. Let all your thoughts, apart from me and what I'm doing, leave you for a while..."

Gripping the sheets, I close my heavy-lidded eyes, and I do as he asks. I allow him to take control over my body and even over my mind. His fingers crawl lower and lower, until one rests lightly on my throbbing core. I open my legs wider, giving him further permission to possess me, and when he starts to rub my clit, I moan loudly. My mouth wide, I instinctively search for something to heighten the pleasure he's giving me, and when I locate his thumb, I grab onto his wrist, pull his hand closer, and suck it inside my wet mouth.

"Fuck," he hisses, and I can feel his laboured breath against my neck. "Shit, Em, that feels fucking fantastic...Your pussy is so wet, I have to taste you." Hearing those words, my eyes pop wide open, and I raise my head just as his fingers leave my clit, and I watch, mesmerised, as his mouth closes over his fingers, tasting my arousal. I shudder from the state we're both in, and my breath picks up speed.

He groans, eyes closed in bliss, and grunts, "Sweet…Just like I imagined."

I almost come from his words alone.

"Shit, that's hot," I gasp, keeping my eyes open, and I watch his fingers return to my throbbing clit. His movements are less gentle now, more hurried, but I don't mind that at all. I'm so wet with need, longing for release, but I don't feel it's fair to come before giving him something in return. I reach behind me, fumbling blindly, until my fingers close around the base of his cock, and he grunts.

"Yeeesss," he growls as my thumb finds the pre-come on the tip and smears it around it. As I jack him off, he moves his hips, matching my rhythm. His mouth closes around my earlobe, sucking the small studded earring inside, and the tingling in my pussy intensifies.

"Fuck, Em, I'm getting close…," he pants, and puts two fingers inside my pussy, searching for the right spot that'll make me go wild.

"Me, too," I moan and release his thumb from my lips, and just when I am so close to hitting the pleasure wave, I feel his mouth on my neck. He bites down, not gently, but as if he's a lion staking his mate: possessive and impatient.

"Daniel!" I scream as I come, so overcome by the intensity of my orgasm that I am forced to shut my eyes, and I see stars behind the lids.

The extent of the power this man has over me is almost frightening.

He releases my neck on a loud groan, licking the sting from his teeth away, and as his cock jerks in my hand, I feel his come on my back.

"Holy fuck," I whisper when I finally catch my breath and the pounding of my heartbeat has settled down a bit. How is it possible that he can possess me so powerfully? We haven't even kissed yet!

Hang on...Yet? Where the hell did that come from?

"You could say that again," Daniel breathes from behind me, and I gently loosen the hold on his cock. His fingers don't leave my pussy, though, and it makes me wonder if he's reluctant to let this moment pass. Eventually, though, he pulls back, and I open my eyes just in time to see him wiping his fingers on my sheets.

We lie in silence for some time, and although I don't want to lose this moment between us, I know I should.

I need to remind him of our deal.

I need to remind him that this is only sex...well, not even that: just fooling around, giving and receiving pleasure from each other.

I need to tell him that this is only a temporary arrangement.

Yet...my mouth remains silent, unwilling to let reality set in.

"Your thoughts are practically screaming at me." Daniel's amused voice breaks me from my indecisiveness of what to do, and I sigh.

"I don't know what you're talking about," I respond and move to get up from the bed. His hand touching my back stops me, however, and I hold my breath.

"Don't worry, Em, I haven't forgotten what you told me last night. So relax."

A pang of hurt pierces right through me, but I don't allow him to see it when I turn my head to look into his eyes.

Smiling brightly, I say, "All's good. Thanks for the orgasm, Preppy." I wink at him, and, as I see the satisfied smirk crossing his face, I roll my eyes and stand up.

"Men," I mutter, shaking my head as I walk towards the bathroom. The stickiness of his come on my back doesn't feel uncomfortable, but I need a shower.

"Doesn't mean I won't do my best to change your mind, though," his raised voice sounds from behind me, causing me to a standstill.

What...the...hell?

Placing my hands on my hips, I turn around and arch an eyebrow at him. He's put on his glasses, and the heat in his gaze almost sends a punch through my stomach: it's wild, possessive and determined. For once, I don't feel like I have the upper hand anymore, and it makes me uneasy. He's lying on his back, arms behind his head, not caring in the least that he's stark naked or that, by the looks of it, his cock is more than ready and willing to get started on round two.

"Excuse me?" I ask him.

He shrugs, grinning, and I narrow my eyes at him while trying to ignore the fact that my nipples have hardened.

Blimey, he's sexy.

"Just telling you that I'll do my hardest to win you over, and that you might as well get used to it," he replies flippantly.

"What...? Why...? Come again?" I stammer and close my eyes briefly.

"You heard me," he says, and I look down at his lap.

Yep, definitely ready again.

I shake my head and cross my arms, forgetting that will only draw attention to my boobs, and I watch his gaze zero in on them.

"You do realise that that's for me to decide, don't you? Or has the bug you caught yesterday addled your brain?" Cocking my hip, I place my hand there and push out my boobs because I just can't keep my body from teasing this man.

"Keep telling yourself that, Em. I'm stubborn, just like you. I can wait you out."

I snort. "Right, well, in your dreams, Romeo." Feigning amusement, I turn around and walk the few short steps to my bathroom and shut the door firmly behind me. My body deflates immediately, and I lean heavily on the sink as I scan my face. For once, I'm not pale, but flushed; my eyes shine, not with tears, but with the afterglow of my orgasm; my hands shake, yes, but not from fatigue: no, from excitement.

Most importantly, however, is the fact that my lips are pulled up in a wide smile, and my belly is fluttering with butterflies.

"Shit," I whisper to myself. "What the hell have you gotten yourself into now?"

My reflection doesn't give me an answer and the smile on my face fades ever so slowly as the enormity of Daniel's words hit home.

If he *was* saying what I thought he was...does that mean he'll want to know every little, single detail about my life? Will I have to tell him what happened? About *him*, the man who broke a part of me that I'll probably never get back?

"Fuck...I'm in so much trouble," I whisper and sigh, the high leaving my body, suddenly feeling cold, and I turn on the shower.

How will I find the courage to let Daniel in completely? Do I even want to?

Yet again, my mind doesn't have an answer at the ready,

but I force the gloominess that's this close to take over my fragile head away and decide to take Katherine's advice to heart: I try not to think and overanalyse things to death.

Taking a deep breath, I nod once, and then step into the shower to wash away more than my body: I'm cleansing my mind from the darkness.

♡

DANIEL

I hear the shower go on and take a deep breath, letting it out slowly while thinking back on what just happened. That went well. Never in a million years would I believe that my first sexual acts would be the likes of which I've experienced in the past 24 hours. Am I confusing my overwhelming lust for this woman with love? I mean...*damn*! She's every guy's wet dream come true, but, underneath her hard mask Emma carries around with her is a woman I'm desperate to get to know. Not just in the biblical sense. Not being allowed to kiss her physically hurts me. Those lips...Who'd have thought that all the while I was pleasuring her, I had to keep myself in check, preventing myself from slamming my mouth against hers, swallowing her moans and cries, and concentrate on the rest of her body instead? Not that it was a hardship – her body is made for sin, and I'm more than willing to be corrupted by it.

I'm gobsmacked, maybe even still under the influence of whatever bug I caught, but I don't feel feverish anymore. And I'm starving.

What the hell was I thinking, blurting out those things to Emma just now? She's bound to run screaming for the hills.

Shaking my head, I push up on my elbows and stare out her windows for a while. What is my next move?

Pretend to play along with that game of hers and take it easy...

Satisfied with my plan, I toss the sheets from my feet and stand up to stretch. My body still aches a bit, but not too bad. In fact, I feel a whole lot better than I thought I would.

Grinning, I run a hand through my dishevelled hair. I could get used to waking up like this every day, but I vow to not voice that to the stubborn girl behind the bathroom door. No, I will let her believe that she has the upper hand and simply wait her out - just like I told her. Eventually, she'll come around, I'm sure of it.

In the meantime, there's nothing wrong with enjoying her and all the things she's bound to teach me.

My cock stirs, and seeing as I'm a guy, thus unable to let it rest, I stroke it lightly a few times until I hear the shower turn off. That's my cue to get dressed and sort out some breakfast for the two of us.

CHAPTER TWENTY-EIGHT

EMMA

I OPEN THE DOOR to the bathroom and stop as soon as the smell of bacon frying hits my nostrils. Looking to my right, I see Daniel standing in front of my stove, only dressed in his slacks, and he's cooking.
This day is too bizarre.
"How do you like your eggs?" he asks me, breaking me free from my shock, and I take a few steps closer to him, holding the towel covering my body wrapped tightly around me.
Mouth salivating with the sight before me - and not just from the food - I answer, "Scrambled, please."
Daniel nods and continues cooking, and it annoys me when he doesn't even take a peek at me. Which, I know, is completely irrational...
"The coffee is ready if you want any," he proceeds to tell me and takes two cups from the cupboard above the stove. I'm still just standing there, taking in the contours of his body, his long, lean muscles, his abs...

Hell, that V is going to be my downfall.

I finally come unglued from the spot when I find him, cups in hand, waiting for my answer, an arrogant smirk on his lips, and I narrow my eyes, annoyed that he's caught me staring - again!

"I'll put on some clothes first," I tell him and quickly leave him to his task. Somehow, I sincerely doubt that he'll listen if I argue about him cooking for me, and I don't want the hassle because it'll be stupid of me to say no to a free meal. Plus, it's *home cooked*, for pete's sake! I haven't had that in a while, and I miss it.

I grab some clothes from my closet and hurry to put them on. Underwear, a tank top, and yoga pants will have to do for now - not that I actually do yoga, but the clothes are so comfortable, I don't care.

"Where did you find the food?" I yell at Daniel, pretty sure I didn't have any of the ingredients hiding away in my fridge.

"While you were in the shower, I went next-door and got them from my place," he shouts back, and while I really *should* argue about that, I don't bother; again, what's the point?

I walk back to the kitchen, combing through my hair with my fingers, and almost run into him and a really hot cup of coffee.

"Careful there," he murmurs and hands me the nectar to feed my soul. He raises his eyes when I practically yank the cup from him.

"Hush...coffee is my addiction. Thanks," I answer in a low voice and take the first sip. Immediately, I feel more refreshed and I close my eyes for a few seconds.

His voice breaks me from my reverie, though. "What's on the agenda for today?"

I open my eyes and give him a quick once-over.

"How are you feeling today? Still sick?" I ask him and lean a hip on the kitchen counter.

He shakes his head. "Naah, I feel good. Well, actually, I feel great, and I guess I have you to thank for that." He turns his head and smiles gently at me before reaching for the eggs.

I shrug. "I was just being a good neighbour."

He stops in his tracks, eggs in hand, and smirks at me. "I'm pretty sure not every neighbour would help me get better by choosing...err...sexcapades as the medicine."

I almost choke on my coffee, burning my tongue in the process, and cough.

"I'm pretty sure it was the sleep and soup that cured you," I wheeze out.

Pursing his lips, Daniel breaks the eggs and doesn't answer me until a fair dozen is in the bowl. "Maybe so," he muses, adding milk, water, salt and pepper to the eggs, then grabs a whisk from one of my drawers.

"I'm pretty sure it was the sexcapades, though," he suddenly says, and I snort.

"You could be right," I murmur, smiling briefly at him when he turns to me. "I had to ring my Nan and ask what to do with you, so you should probably thank her as well."

Abruptly, he stops whisking away and looks at me, horror clearly written on his face.

"Your Nan told you to seduce me?" he asks incredulously, and it causes me to burst with laughter.

"No, you dimwit," I force out between breaths. "She just told me about what food to give you!"

He chuckles, and I can't help but notice his ears getting red.

"Oh," he comments faintly, embarrassment covering his

features, and my heart flutters.

Too adorable.

"Okay," I say, quickly changing the subject. "Seeing as you're much better, I'd say we stick with our original plan."

"And what's that?" he asks, frowning at me before pouring the eggs in the pan.

Beaming at him, I reply, "Why, go shopping, of course."

He groans and leans his head back, looking as if he's in pain.

"Must we?" he asks me, turning his head to look at me with the most pathetic expression on his face, making me chuckle.

"Of course. Now, I'll set the table outside while you finish preparing our food, and once we've eaten, we can take off." Placing my cup on the counter beside me, I quickly get some plates and cutlery and move to leave.

"I think I'm still sick," Daniel mutters surly from behind me, and I turn my head to smile cheekily at him as I walk away.

"Too late, Preppy. We've got work to do, and not a lot of time left to do it."

Leaving him to sulk, I don't give him the opportunity to see the enormous smile on my lips as I walk away.

♡

After we've eaten - and wow, this man can cook! - Daniel goes to his flat to grab some fresh clothes, and I do the same. I've picked a long, boho, black skirt, a red t-shirt, and some flat red ballerinas with black rhinestones to wear. After I've applied some makeup, I put my hair in a messy bun on top of my head. I make sure to have all I need for spending the day away from home, grab my black clutch and leave to knock on Daniel's door.

It feels rather strange to still do that, given the events of last night and this morning, but I don't feel comfortable just barging in. Besides, I'm not his *real* girlfriend, so knocking it is. It's still imperative to keep some sort of distance between us, no matter how much the lines seem to have blurred between us.

The distance is necessary for the sake of my sanity.

Daniel opens his door at once and I take in his clothes: white button-down shirt - *again* - but at least he's rolled the sleeves up to his elbows. And *again* he is wearing grey slacks and loafers.

I shake my head and frown. "It's definitely good that you're no longer sick. Right, let's get going," I smile brightly and turn around to walk down the stairs.

"Please promise me that this won't take long," Daniel begs as he follows behind me, causing me to roll my eyes.

"Relax, Preppy, we'll only be gone for a few hours," I answer, lying through my teeth. This is going to take all day, but he doesn't need to know that.

"How come I don't believe you one little bit?" he grumbles behind me. I pretend to ignore him, and we walk outside and down to the bus in silence. I keep some distance between us, though, because while Daniel didn't utter one single word about his *intentions* all the time we had breakfast, I don't want him to think that I've forgotten about it.

Because I can't. The words run around and around in my head like a broken record, and I'm merely waiting for him to make another move. I can't let down my guard and let him blindside me.

Not until I'm ready.

♡

"Will you *please* stop doing that?" Daniel asks me and pushes my hands away from the waistband on the denim shorts he's currently trying on.

"Oh, stop being such a baby," I mumble. "You need a bigger size, or that cock of yours won't be able to breathe in these."

A strangled laugh sounds from above me, and I smile deviously, enjoying myself immensely, and reach for the pants again. We're in a dressing room inside *H&M* by the Gl. Kongevej, and we've been shopping for a few hours now.

"Well, my *cock*," he hisses, "can't take this anymore, Emma, so stop. *Now.*"

Sensing that this is a guy close to breaking point, I do as he says and take a step away.

Putting my hands in the air, I look into his eyes, grinning. "Okay, okay. Don't get your knickers in a twist."

Disbelieving, he rakes a hand through his hair and shakes his head.

"You're cruel, Emma, you know that?"

"Oh, don't be such a *Debbie Downer*, Daniel," I admonish him and cross my arms, feigning annoyance, and he narrows his eyes at me.

Without uttering another word, he closes the distance separating us in the dressing room, towering over me, until I have to lean my head back so as to not lose his eyes. He keeps moving closer, forcing me to move back, until his hard body is pressed into mine, holding me prisoner.

So far, I've avoided any kind of intimate space between us, but now I can't. The fact that we're in a public place, with other customers surrounding us, able to hear our every move, is strangely arousing, and my breathing speeds up from the naughtiness of the situation. That's what this is: it's forbidden, unheard of by many...yet it excites me to no end.

Surely he wouldn't try anything here, would he?

I watch, mesmerised, as his head moves closer and closer, the look in his eyes keeping me spellbound. They are a bit angry, but there's more to them than that; they're also heated, and when he leans his arm above my head, his chest brushing mine, my nipples harden immediately.

He turns his head and I can feel his warm breath on my neck - it's not unpleasant, of course, but it unnerves me, not knowing what he's about to do, and, for once, I'm speechless. The anticipation is searing through me, and I feel wetness gathering between my legs. Balling my hands into tight fists, thus preventing myself to reach for him and crush my mouth to his, I wait...and wait.

He has a few freckles on his neck, and it makes me remember what the skin there tastes like.

"Now," he whispers - *finally!* - and I can feel his lips resting lightly on my ear, sending a shiver straight through me. "Have you finished tormenting me for the day, or do you have more plans for me?" he asks me, and I can hear the strain in his voice as he pushes his pelvis into mine, making me feel the hardness of his cock through his clothes.

"I think I'm done," I breathe out, relishing the warmth of his body.

"Good," he says curtly, but he doesn't move away from me.

"Are you going to step back?" I ask him after more than

ten seconds have passed, even though I don't really want him to. The air seems electric, ready to burst somehow, and the dampness in my panties is evident, even to him: if I can smell my arousal, I'm almost certain he can, too.

"Not yet," he groans, pressing even further against me, and a soft moan escapes me.

"You have to," I urge him, but then I feel his other hand trailing up, up, up my skirt, taking it with him, until my left thigh is exposed. The coolness of the air-con makes my skin break out in goose bumps, and my legs seem like jelly.

"What...what are you doing?" I hiss, but there's not much strength behind my rebuttal.

"Shhh...you'll give us away," he whispers, and I hold my breath when his lips descend on the sensitive skin beneath my ear. His fingers trail the edge of my knickers, and I spread my legs a bit, giving him better access. A low growl sounds from his throat, and holy shit, it's hot when he does that. Wetness pools between my legs, my clit throbs, and I can't keep my eyes open anymore.

"I just need...a small taste...," he pants as his fingers rub my clit lightly over the fabric covering my pussy.

I breathe hard, but try to keep it down, afraid others may hear us...I bite my lip, my aching nipples hardening further.

Daniel keeps trailing hot, open-mouthed kisses along my neck as he rubs my clit, and I can't stand it anymore. I loosen my right fist and clamp a hand over his, preventing him from keeping up his sensual assault, and I open my eyes.

Moving up on my toes, I whisper in his ear, "I know a place not far from here where we'll be able to play for a while."

He keeps silent for a few heartbeats and catches his breath. When he nods once, jaw clenched, I kiss the freckles on his neck, biting down lightly, and he breathes hard.

"Em...," he warns, and I rest a hand on his chest, pushing him slightly away. He removes his hand from beneath my skirt, and although I miss his touch immediately, the fire in his gaze tells me that it won't be for long.

Rearranging my clothes quickly, I tell him quietly, "I'll go first," and he nods once and adjusts the bulge in his pants. Knowing what's hiding there, I lick my lips, and he can't hold back a low groan.

"Hurry," I whisper, draw the curtains aside and leave him alone. I'm positive that my flaming cheeks give away what I've been up to, but I don't care.

I need Daniel. And I need him now.

♡

I've never felt such desire before. As I sit here in this secluded park on Daniel's lap, my skirt covering his right hand while he fingers me, I don't give a toss if anyone sees us. My arms are around his neck, my lips peppering his skin with wet kisses, and my thighs tremble so much I'm almost scared I'd fall off if I didn't feel his other arm wrapped tightly around my waist, his fingers digging sharply into my skin.

They're going to leave a mark.

The thought of Daniel branding me only makes me wetter, and I ride his hand harder, moaning loudly from the pleasure soaring through me.

"Emma," he groans. "Fuck, this tight pussy feels like heaven. I want to make you come so bad." His lips fused to the hollow beneath my neck, his teeth nibbling the sensitive skin there immediately sends a shockwave through my entire body, and I hide my face in his neck so my lust-filled moans become muffled.

"Ride my fingers, baby," he whispers, putting two fingers inside me while his thumb puts more pressure on my clit. "This pussy needs my mouth soon..." As I imagine him licking my taste away, the orgasm slams through me, and I come, groaning out his name.

Small tremors run through my body. I love the way Daniel's fingers keep caressing my sensitive clit ever so softly, and the way he waits me out even though his cock must be bursting at the seams for release only strengthens my feelings for him.

Because this isn't just lust...this is *more*. Daniel makes me want to believe in fairytales again even if I did give up on them many years ago. Now it's his turn to ride the wave, and I give him a small, lingering kiss below his ear before slipping down to kneel before him.

He's breathing hard, and his cheeks and ears are flushed. His eyes never leave mine as I hurry to unbuckle his belt so I can free his cock. He sits back and moves his hips slightly, helping me with my task, and the way he remains silent, focusing only on me, and doesn't seem to care that we're in a public place - in broad daylight, no less - makes me long for his touch again.

I'll have to wait, though...but I'll definitely have to teach him how to make me come with his mouth and tongue soon.

Freeing his cock from his boxers, I lean closer, never losing eye contact with Daniel, and, just before my mouth is about to close around the tip, he licks his fingers, tasting me again. His pupils are dilated with want - want for *me* - and it only spurs me on even more. This man is about to be blown away...and in more ways than one.

As soon as I taste the small beads of semen on his cock, I

hum in pleasure, rubbing my thighs together to alleviate the hot throbbing between my legs, and I take his cock further in my mouth.

"This is too good, Em...Please don't stop," Daniel croaks out, and I keep my eyes on his as I suck gently on the head. Hearing the need in his voice only drives me to please him even more. I grab the base of his cock with my right hand and suck him off, my mouth and tongue eager to make him come undone. His musky scent fills my nostrils, the taste of him overwhelming, and I pick up the pace when I feel his hand cupping my chin. He doesn't push down or tries to take control, which, to me, speaks volumes, and I love it. I can't take him all the way to the root, he's just too big for my mouth for that, but I go as far as I can manage. He continues to whisper dirty things as I increase the pace, and I want to reach down and touch myself, but refrain; this is about him, after all. It's about driving him wild, about making him realise that I have the power - not him. And that I'll decide when he's allowed to take over. That moment is not now.

"Shit, shit, shit," he growls as come spurts in my mouth, and I swallow every last drop of it, satisfied and, I'll admit, pretty turned on once again.

I sit back on my haunches and quickly look around to check for unwanted witnesses, but we're still alone. As I turn to smile at Daniel, I find him buckling his belt again, and I stand up and walk to sit beside him. We're both silent for some time, our hands resting on the seat between us. I don't reach out to touch him, though...that would make this too intimate a moment. Once Daniel's breathing has levelled out, he takes off his glasses and polishes them by using the end of his white shirt. I watch him silently, taking in his sharp features, and I wonder why he doesn't get contacts. Actually, there are a lot of things I can't quite understand about him or reconcile myself with.

Deciding it's time to get some answers, I say quietly, "You confuse me, Daniel..."

"What?" He puts on his glasses and looks at me, clearly taken back by my admission. Suddenly overcome by shyness - something, I might add, that seems so illogical given the hot and heavy situation we've just been in - I turn away from his scrutinising gaze and pretend to take in the park instead.

"What makes you say that, Emma?" he persists and cups my cheek, putting pressure on it so I have no choice but to meet his eyes. He's frowning, and I guess I do owe him some sort of explanation.

"It's just that..." I hesitate, searching for the right words. "You told me that you didn't know how to act around girls...that you became tongue-tied, nervous...and that's the reason you're still...well, you know, a virgin." Rolling my eyes, I feel rather foolish, but he simply nods, and I go on. "Yet you aren't the least bit embarrassed or nervous when you're around me. In fact, you're the exact opposite: you're quite the dirty talker, aren't you?" I waggle my eyebrows on the last bit, and he chuckles, his thumb rubbing my jaw in small circles.

I shrug. "I guess I feel...intrigued by you." Yes, that's it; on many levels, Daniel is like an open book to me. He doesn't hold back. But I can't make the pieces of what he told me when we first met fit now that this shift in our relationship has occurred. It unsettles me, yet the many facets to his personality make me curious to learn more about him. A novelty thought, given my past.

Clearing his throat, he sits back and turns away, a thoughtful expression in his eyes, and I wonder what he's about to say.

"I guess I'm more at ease when I'm with you." His answer takes me by surprise, and I tense up. "With you, I don't have to pretend that I'm someone I'm not. I'm just Daniel; I'm normal. And I guess there's freedom in that." Finally, he shifts his gaze to mine, and the vulnerability there comes close to melting the ice surrounding my heart. Ever so slowly, he leans closer to me, and I can't keep my body from mimicking his movements. It's as if he's a magnet, the opposite of my own, and it's completely futile to try to resist him. He just has this *pull* over me.

"And as far as the dirty talker you think I am...," he murmurs, his nose running along my chin, before he kisses my neck sweetly and nibbles on it. "That's entirely your own fault, you know," he whispers. "You're so sexy all the time I can't rein it in. You consume me every time you're near... My main focus is on you and I don't care where we are. You bring out a side of me I never knew existed, and I just want to...*claim* you in some way."

Holy...fuck!

"You're becoming very dominating," I whisper softly. "I kind of like it."

Like it? That's the understatement of the year. It's hot as hell!

Daniel hums low in his throat and then inhales deeply. "I want to taste your pussy, Em...soon. But not here. When I finally get you in my bed, I want you to teach me how to go down on you...and I can't wait for the day I'll have you writhing beneath me, calling out my name in ecstasy as I lick you out..."

His words conjure hot images in my head, and my core throbs from his promise.

"Now, though," he goes on, "I think we need to leave. I

don't think we're alone anymore."

I jump up and search frantically around me. Daniel's right: what seems to be a family of four - two adults with a young girl and toddler trailing behind them - have entered the park, and they are headed our way. I grab a couple of shopping bags from the ground and wave a hand at Daniel, letting him know that it's time to go. He shakes his head but does as I command.

"Where to now?" he asks me, sorting out his pants, and we begin to walk out of the park.

"Home, I suppose," I mutter. "I think that all you bought today should last you for a while. Oh, but I need to stop at the supermarket on the way home. My fridge is...well, devoid of anything edible," I joke, but it's true. I need to start taking better care of myself.

"Yes, I couldn't help but notice that," he replies drily, and I chuckle.

"I can't cook," I admit sheepishly, and he stops in his tracks.

"At all?" The look on his face is priceless! He looks absolutely flabbergasted, and I laugh heartily.

"Nope," I chuckle, and we resume walking.

"I guess that means I'll have to teach you a thing or two, then."

What?

"Errm, Daniel, that's sweet of you, but it's not really necessary," I reply cautiously, not wanting to appear rude.

He waves off my protests. "Nonsense. Look at it this way...We spend practically every day together, either at the shop or studying. We might as well have dinner those nights...before we get down to the fun stuff."

The last part he says makes me stumble, surprised.

"What do you mean, *'the fun stuff'*?" I ask him

suspiciously, peeking at him.

He takes my hand and pulls slightly, forcing me to stop walking. He wraps his other arm around my waist and grabs my arse, and I gasp at his cheekiness.

"Don't think for one minute that I'll be able to keep my hands off you, Em," he warns me, grin in place.

Narrowing my eyes at him, I ask testily, "Meaning?"

"Meaning that my mouth or my hands will be on some part of your delectable body every single day," he says and presses my bottom into his crotch.

My, my, my...hello, there.

"Cocky, aren't you? What makes you think that I'll even want you each day?"

Smirking, he leans closer, his lips hovering above mine, and says, "Oh, you bet the fuck I am. And don't lie to me, or to yourself, and pretend that you won't want it."

"I've changed my mind. I think I prefer the shy, preppy boy I met a few days ago instead of the dominating alpha male you're turning into," I snap, trying to pull out of his arms, but they only tighten around me.

He chuckles. "Oh no, you don't. You like this side of me...probably more than you're willing to admit, even to yourself."

Damn him! How can he know me so well already?

I huff. "Well, we'll see about that, won't we?" I ask and smile sweetly at him, but even I can tell that I don't pull it off that well.

Daniel shakes his head, clearly exasperated, but releases his hold on me, and we walk in silence the rest of the way to the train station.

I have a nasty suspicion, though, that I've just put myself in a situation I can't get out of without losing my footing.

CHAPTER TWENTY-NINE

EMMA

AS WE DRAW NEARER to my flat, Daniel's phone starts ringing, and he searches through the pockets of his slacks and pulls it out to answer it.

"Hello?" he says, and when he hears the voice on the other end, he breaks out in a wide smile. "Hi!" he exclaims, and I become curious as to whom the caller is.

He hurries on, "Hang on, please." Covering the mouthpiece with a hand, he turns to me and whispers, "It's my mum."

I nod, understanding, and then indicate I'll leave him for now. His attention focused on his mother, he waves distractedly at me and unlocks his front door.

Once I'm alone in my hallway and have set aside my own bags - because I just couldn't resist buying a new pair of shoes - I take a deep breath and remove my hairband, letting my unruly hair hang loose down my back. Threading my fingers through the curls, I think back on the events of the day.

How did Daniel manage to completely blindside me like

that? He acts as if he doesn't care one tiny bit about the rules I've set up, and it causes unease to surge through me. Yes, I *really, truly* want him, but some small part of me just can't let go completely...I dare not tear down my walls yet... Not until I know for a fact that I'm in the right frame of mind, that is.

Wow, I'm acting like an adult now...

I walk to my kitchen to get some water, feeling all kinds of hot and bothered but too stubborn to let Daniel win, so I decide to text Suzy. So much has happened in the past 48 hours, and I need her to cheer me up. Her positive, upbeat personality always manages to make me put things in perspective. On second thought, it might be better to just text her and ask if I can come over for a chat.

Me: Hey, are you home?
She responds soon after.
Suzy: Yep, and I'm SO bored! What's up?
Me: I have LOTS to tell you so is it alright if I stop by?
Suzy: Of course! Please do! ;-)
Me: Okay, see you soon. X
Suzy: Fab! X

I don't text Daniel before leaving my flat. I can't have him believe that I'll all of a sudden be available to him whenever he fancies some *sexcapades*.

"...so, as you can see, I'm more confused than ever, and I want you to tell me what to do," I finish my tale, a glass of Diet Coke in my hand. I've just spent the past hour going over my first psychology session - skipping a few details, though - and how my relationship with Daniel has shifted. When I showed up at Suzy's, she had just finished making us popcorn and, without even saying a proper 'hello' first, she ordered me to start talking. And that's what I did, occasionally munching on my snacks while Suzy listened, hanging onto every word coming out of my mouth.

Now, though, she sits on the couch opposite me, keeping her silence while looking at me with her head tilted to the side a bit, a thoughtful expression on her every feature.

I wipe my sticky fingers on a napkin and ask, "Well?"

She frowns. "I can't *believe* it's taken you two days to tell me all that's happened!"

Flabbergasted, I exclaim, "I *have* been pretty busy, you know."

"Uh, yes, seducing your virgin neighbor, I know," she murmurs, but I can tell that she isn't really offended at all.

"Don't make me regret telling you about that part," I warn her.

She sits back and laughs. "I promise I won't divulge Daniel's secret, Em. Don't get your knickers in a twist."

I sigh loudly. "What do I do, Suzy?" I ask her quietly.

Crossing her arms in front of her, she shrugs. "Why not just enjoy it?"

I huff. "Because I *need* to keep my wits about me, that's why. I can't just let Daniel take over, and wait for things to progress naturally. I need to be two steps ahead of him all the time."

Suzy frowns. "I don't get it, Emma. What's so bad about letting go of your precious control every once in a while? And I don't mean in a sexual way?"

I look down at my lap, really thinking her question through.

Yes, why can't I do that?

I don't have the answer.

Finally, I look back into her eyes and say, "I don't know. I just can't."

Shaking her head at me, she says grumpily, "You have some serious trust issues you need to get sorted, Em."

Smiling a little, I nod. "I guess you're right about that."

We sit in silence for some time, lost in our own thoughts, until Suzy whispers, "Does he make your belly flutter with butterflies?"

I fan a hand across my face. "It feels like they're doing cartwheels all the bloody time."

She bursts out in laughter and I have no choice but to wait her out. Although I do it while looking rather irritated, I can't prevent the blush in my cheeks from transforming, and it only emphasizes my annoyance.

Suzy rubs her hands together. "Oh, this is fantastic," she utters gleefully.

"Oh, really?" I snap at her. "Why is that?!"

"Because it means that, hopefully, you'll get your act together soon, and I can't wait to see you happy," she replies, her good mood evaporating rapidly.

I can't beat that kind of retort. Because she's probably right.

"It's not as if I *want* to be alone and miserable all my life," I say, trying to defend my reasons. "I just can't seem to get past this..." I lean back in my seat, all of a sudden so sick and tired of myself.

What does Daniel see in me? I'm so fucked up I can't even understand why I'm holding back.

Suzy gets up from her seat, walks toward me and sits down next to me, wrapping her arm around my shoulders. I sniffle a bit as I place my head on her shoulder, yet I'm determined not to cry.

"There, there," she whispers, rocking me gently back and forth.

"My head's messed up, Suzy...I don't even understand why I'm reacting like this," I whisper, and the first tear trickles down my cheek, followed by another soon after.

"Listen, Em, I'm no psychologist, but I'm almost positive that it's because you're scared of how much Daniel will be able to change your life. Or, rather, the way you see yourself and the world. Besides..." She leans away from me, and I meet her cheerful gaze, eager to hear what she has to say next.

"Look at it this way," she continues, "at least you'll be able to teach Daniel all the things we wish men did to please their women. That's a great thing, right? If people knew, they'd take classes from you, I'm sure of it."

A giggle bursts free from my throat, and I grin at my best friend.

"Oh, another thing...," Suzy says before I have time to talk. "How's his cock?"

I snort, blushing wildly.

"Eerrm...it's...perfect: long, thick, and beautiful," I sigh as I envision it before me, and it causes tingles to erupt in my body. I don't lie; Daniel's cock is definitely perfect.

"I'm so jealous of you right now, you dirty cow," Suzy teases me, and I hug her affectionately.

"Thank you for clearing my head," I tell her as I sit back. "I don't know what I'd do without you."

She winks at me. "Lucky for you, you won't ever have to. But promise me this..." She waits, watching me with a cheeky expression in her eyes, and I wave my hand at her to simply get on with it.

"You *have* to ring me the minute you've kissed for the first time. I need details!"

Sighing, I vow quietly, "I promise."

Yet I don't tell her that it'll be my first kiss...I'm too embarrassed to admit to even my best friend about that part. It'll only get her started on another kind of interrogation, and I don't have the strength in me to confide in her yet.

Maybe I'll tell her everything once I've kissed Daniel.

The more I think about it - which is approximately every five seconds - the more I crave it.

Problem is, however, if, once I feel his lips on mine, I'll feel what every normal woman feels when kissing someone she's attracted to?

Or will the fears I have become true?

Will I bolt, consumed with nausea, like I have done before?

It's been three years since I lost my virginity. Well, perhaps '*lost*' is the wrong word; actively pursued getting rid of it would be more accurate, I guess. I'd hoped that somehow forcing myself to be physically intimate with a man would help, sort out my fears, and so I went out clubbing one night, found a guy I fancied, and it didn't take long to convince him to take me home to his place and...well, you get the idea.

It didn't matter, though, and I can't say I really enjoyed it while it lasted, but at least it didn't hurt like so many of my friends had told me it would. After he fell asleep – I can't even remember his name – I just stayed there beside him for a while, hoping against hope that *this* was it: the moment when my life would take a turn to the better, and that'd I'd no longer wake up screaming with fright each and every night.

How naive of me to think that.

It didn't have the desired effect, of course.

The nightmares continued...they even became worse for a while.

With each hook-up I had thereafter, though, I became aware of the fact that sex is just sex; an impulse in our brain that makes itself known from time to time. It tells you that you need to seek release of one kind or another. And at least it's better than doing drugs.

Lucky for me, then, that I'm at least not afraid to get down and dirty whenever I need that particular itch scratched.

And, to tell the truth, sex is *great*: there's no better thing than finding a willing participant, state what you are after in no uncertain terms, and then chasing the fire together before you explode and you're able to quiet the cravings again. At least for a little while.

It seems cold, doesn't it? It doesn't have to be. So many men do this - why is it such a taboo if you're a woman looking for the same thing?

The double standards of society is mind boggling, to say the least.

And yet...Sometimes I wonder what it'll be like to have sex with someone you actually have feelings for?

What will it feel like to be with Daniel?

Our attraction only strengthens each day, and I know I can't avoid the inevitable for much longer.

I'm not sure I even want that. I'm an impatient person by

nature, and I want him.

I want him in every way I can get him – and it has to be soon.

♡

I haven't seen or heard from Daniel ever since his mother rang him when we'd just got back from the shops on Saturday afternoon.

It's been five days since then, and I have to admit that I'm a bit worried now.

I ended up staying over at Suzy's, and I mostly did it because I wanted to avoid Daniel, but it was lovely being alone with my friend for once. We always seem to be so busy with other things that we tend to forget to relax, only the two of us together, and I could tell that she enjoyed our girl time as much as I did. On Sunday, we went out to brunch, then headed to a spa and got pampered, before we went out to eat at our favourite Italian restaurant, *Vivaldi*, in the evening. Then we took off to the cinema to catch a late film at *Palads*. I was so exhausted when I got home that I didn't even text Daniel to find out if he'd had a good evening.

Come Monday morning, I knocked on his door when it was time to go to work, but when he didn't answer and I was simply met with silence from his flat, I didn't think much of it and simply took off to the bookshop alone. However, when he didn't show up, I finally asked Mr. Andersen if he knew anything – I tried to make it appear as if I was just being a friendly neighbor, asking if Daniel was okay. Mr. Andersen didn't really say anything, just mumbled that Daniel had phoned him during the weekend, and told him that he had a family matter to attend to. I didn't want to come off as too nosy and make him suspicious about my questions even though that was exactly the case, so I left it at that.

But now it's Thursday afternoon, and I *still* haven't heard anything from him. My casual texts to him have all gone unanswered, which is so unlike him that I don't know what to make of it. I hope nothing too serious has happened, of course, but I don't feel comfortable to merely ring him, demanding answers. That's too pushy, even for me.

I have another appointment with Katherine today. She phoned me on Monday, asking if we could move it up a day because of some school event her daughter wanted to take her to, and I don't really mind it. At least it gives me something to do instead of waiting around at home like some lovesick teenager – how depressing.

I sit down in the armchair across from her like I did the last time, and she pours me some water.

"How have you been since we spoke last week?" she asks me and opens her notebook.

In order to gather my thoughts, I take a sip of water.

"Confused," I finally answer, but smile to make the sting caused by my answer less evident. At least I hope it does.

"In what way?" she asks me, her face mirroring one big question mark.

I hesitate for a few seconds but at last simply blurt out all that's happened with Daniel as well as his disappearing act.

"Wow," she answers. "You've been quite busy, haven't you?" I don't take offense, because she's obviously right, and I don't mind her bluntness at all. In fact, I find it quite refreshing.

Nodding, I clear my throat, and she goes on, "What about your nightmares? Have they increased in nature, or...?"

"I'm still haunted by them, but actually not every night: only three times since I saw you, and I see that as a good thing," I answer her truthfully. "Do you think they'll ever vanish completely?" I ask her, hope evident in my voice.

She shrugs. "I hope so, but it's difficult to say when I don't have all the facts yet." I frown, disappointed to get that kind of answer, and she smiles gently. "Emma, do you think you're ready to tell me about what they are about? I mean, whatever happened to you that caused them to start?"

I tense, my whole body locking down, and I feel coldness seeping in every part of me.

This is it. The moment I knew was coming ever since taking the plunge to see Katherine. But now that it's here, I feel as if the time has arrived too soon.

I'm not ready...Or am I?

Katherine leans forward in her seat and says, "It's important that you give me as many details as possible, Emma. Without them, I won't be able to help you."

I force my hands gripping the armrest to relax, because I know she's right. Logically, that is. Emotionally, though? Well, that's a completely other matter.

I exhale slowly, actually praying for strength, and answer wobbly, "I'll try..."

Katherine sits back and hands me some Kleenexes which, quite unexpectedly, makes me smirk. She winks at me.

"Good. Please begin," she urges me, and I sit back in my chair.

"I was ten years old when my parents and I went on a small trip...," I begin, and the next hour is spent telling my tale.

DANIEL

Friday morning, and I'm back in Copenhagen at last. This week has been hell. There's no other word for it, really, and not a day has gone by when I didn't pick up my phone and came close to phoning Emma.

Close...yet I never went through with it. Not even when I could tell that she was getting concerned about my silence, even if her texts didn't outright say so.

I'm such a bloody coward.

What must she think of me, disappearing like that?

When my mum rang me, I didn't pick up on her mood right away. I was just pleased to hear from her – and still flying high on my day with Emma – but once she started talking, I knew something was off. It didn't take much probing from my part to get her to open up, and then I knew I had to go home.

I love my mum, of course I do, but I also resent her. Why am I always forced to be the grownup when it in reality is *her* role to play?

I sink down on my bed and rub my face after having just taken a quick shower. My jaw is covered with stubble, but shaving is so far from my thoughts right now, and I feel so tired that I just can't be bothered with it. I haven't been able to breathe properly for the past few days, and now that I'm back, I just want to forget they've ever taken place. I wish I could erase the stench of my mother's house from my memory, but I know it'll take forever for that to happen.

I want Emma to help me forget about the dumpster I grew up in, but will she forgive me if I knock on her door now?

Only one way to find out.

I grab one of the black t-shirts and a pair of blue, loose fitted jeans I bought on our shopping spree, quickly pull on a pair of sandals and grab my keys. I lock my front door and turn to hers, taking a few fortifying deep breaths, and before I lose my courage, I knock lightly, praying that she's home. When I hear the faint tones of *Clair De Lune* by Claude Debussy sounding from behind the door, I take a step closer, and relief fills my body.

Thank God.

Footfalls draw nearer, and I hold my breath, nervousness and desire raging war within me, and, soon after, my wish of being near Emma is granted when she opens her door. When she sees me, she blinks a few times and quickly takes a step back, motioning for me to come in, and I swallow audibly from the sight of her, rooted to my spot. She's wearing a grey, form fitted dress covered with lace, black stilettos on her feet, and the light shining from the window in her kitchen behind her makes her dress almost see-through.

Suddenly, my throat is parched, and I still haven't moved at all.

Instead of apologising to her like I had originally planned, I blurt out, "My mum's a drunk. I had to go back home to try...just *try again* to make her see reason and get help."

I have to admire Emma for her quick thinking, because she simply answers, "Did she?" I'm grateful for the lack of pity in her eyes. I don't want pity from anybody.

Feeling a lump in my throat, I only shake my head.

She never does.

Emma takes my hand in hers and pulls me inside her flat, shutting the door quietly. I wait in her small hallway, unsure of what to do, and I'm completely taken aback when I feel her arms surrounding me from behind, her body pressed flush to mine.

For the first time since I last saw her, I can breathe freely again.

Shite...I'm going to bawl like a baby soon!

Emma's lips press against me, and although I can't feel them on my skin, they're burning me.

"I'm sorry, Daniel...," she whispers softly, and I'm grateful when she leaves it at that. Reaching my hand upwards, I place it on top of hers briefly before turning in her arms to wrap my own around her.

I need her so fucking bad right now.

I squeeze tightly, wishing more than ever that she would allow me to kiss her. But if she won't let me pour out how much she means to me with my mouth, at least I am able to use my hands, mouth, and my tongue on her body. Maybe it'll even force her to open her eyes and truly see how I need her so much.

It would seem that Emma has another plan in mind, though, because she wriggles gently out of my grasp, takes my hand again and leads me inside her living room. She stops next to her CD player hanging on the wall to the right just above her small TV and turns up the volume a bit. Smiling shyly at me, looking cute as hell, she backs away from me, and I have no other choice but to follow her. The next song starts, and I'm surprised when I hear a French woman singing a cover of *"Someone Like You"* by Adele. I like it, and I like to see yet another side to Emma.

"I thought you weren't a romantic," I murmur, keeping my voice low for fear of breaking this strange spell she has me under, and she shrugs.

"Dancing isn't necessarily a romantic act," she mutters.

Bloody hell, she's stubborn.

I want to disagree with her but I don't want to lose this moment we're having right now. Because this feels significant, somehow...The air is charged with electricity, my stomach is wrapped up in knots, and I honestly don't know where this is going.

But I know I'll follow this girl everywhere she goes.

It's as if she has woven a web around my entire being...She's never far from my thoughts, my attraction to her has not died down while I was away these past few days - quite the contrary, in fact - and even though I don't believe in some higher deity, I thank them for bringing this girl into my life.

Emma accepts me for who I am, no matter where I come from.

I'd be lying if I said I'd want to break free of the bonds she has wrapped tightly around my heart.

I don't. Not now. Not ever.

This is *it*: the moment I hand over my heart to her, unafraid of what the consequences might be.

And she seems to want to dance with me. Well, then...who am I to deny her? I just hope I don't step on her toes too much.

I place my hands on her waist and practically yank her to me, causing her to stumble into my chest.

"I don't dance," I warn her as she puts her arms around

my neck, my eyes never leaving hers.

A small, contented sigh leaves her lips. "Don't worry, I won't break."

I chuckle. "Maybe not, but your feet might."

She rolls her eyes and shakes her head at me, clearly not believing me, before placing her head just above my heart. Can she hear how loudly it beats? Can she feel the tremors coursing through my body from feeling her soft curves molding around the hard planes of my own?

We start swaying gently to the music, and my tense muscles loosen up after a few moments when I feel confident that I won't accidentally step on her feet. I kind of wish we'd never stop dancing, but my cock clearly disagrees with me. From the minute I stepped over the threshold, I've been raging one hell of a hard-on, and I'm sure she can feel it pushing against her stomach. I don't care, though. She ought to know by now that I only have to see her, not even touch her, and I become turned on instantly.

I'm a guy. That's just how it is.

Emma moves her head a fraction of an inch and places her lips over my nipple, and when she starts to suck it through my T-shirt, I can feel the tight leash on my control slipping away. Her mouth is warm, wet...and hungry.

A low growl rumbles through me, and my already pounding heart beats faster.

Shite, this feels amazing.

Wrapping my arms even more tightly around her, I bend my knees and lift her up, walking backwards until I'm stopped by her closet. She moans, her legs holding on like a vice around my hips, and I do my best to support her weight by grabbing her arse firmly with my hands.

"Off," Emma demands huskily, panting, and pulls up my

T-shirt. I turn around, reversing our position, and yank it off. Once I throw it on the floor, Emma's lips return to explore my chest, and my abs contract from feeling her mouth on me again.

It's as if I've been away for five years instead of merely five days – I'm that desperate to become close to her, even if it's only on a physical level. Momentarily forgetting about her rules, I cup her cheeks, and lean down to kiss her. I pretend to not let it show how it pierces through my heart when she turns her head at the very last moment, pressing her lips to my neck, so I continue to pepper her face with hot kisses instead. I'm not even listening to the music anymore…there's only this tormenting need inside me to make her become wild for me. I trail the curve of her shoulder with my mouth, stopping when I reach the fabric covering her shoulder, and I don't know what kind of beast takes over me, but before I know it, I've grabbed the front of it and pull hard, tearing it in two.

"Sorry," I growl, even though I'm not.

"Fuck my dress," she moans, getting rid of the remains of it until it pools at her waist.

"I need you," I pant out, my eyes raking over her gorgeous breasts now visible before me, barely concealed by another lacy thing, and my mouth latches hard onto the nipple once I've yanked down her bra, causing her tits to perk up at me. "I ache for you, sweetheart…"

"Oh, god," Emma moans loudly and grabs my head, pulling hard on my hair. The pain doesn't matter, though, as I'm too busy focusing on sucking her hard nipple into my mouth, biting down before soothing the sting from my teeth with my tongue.

I pull impatiently at her dress covering her crotch, and I

don't know how I'll be able to stand up for much longer. My knees are shaking so badly, my brow is covered with sweat from the amount of need I have for her right now.

"Are you wet for me, Em?" I groan out, longing to hear her answer. "Does your pussy want my mouth?"

"Yes, yes, yes," she chants, and she reaches down to rub her clit with a finger.

"Fuck, you're hot...Perfect," I gasp, mesmerised by watching her teasing herself, but I tear my gaze away and look up to find her eyes. Her pupils are dilated, only affirming that her need for me is as powerful as mine. Her fingers thread through my hair, caressing me softly, and the scent of her arousal fills my nostrils. I crave the taste of her on my tongue. *Now.*

Grabbing the back of her knees, I pull them gently, but firmly, away from around my waist. Emma moves her right arm and places it on my shoulder as she glides down my body achingly slow. She stops, and I wonder why until her pussy rubs against my cock, the friction sending thrills down my spine, and I hurry to unbutton my pants once she's standing before me.

"You're a tease, Em," I ground out as I free my cock from my boxers, stroking it up and down slowly. I need to make this last for a long time.

She puts her chin out and places her hands on her hips, watching me with a lust filled gaze.

"Don't pretend you don't love it," she purrs and licks her lips before her eyes lock on my hand jacking off.

"Oh, I love it, that's for sure," I grit out and drop to my knees before her. "Spread your legs for me, baby," I demand harshly, and satisfaction seeps through me when she hurries to obey me. Her arms fall limply to her sides, and I can't help but wonder if she, despite her precious control, secretly revels in submitting to me.

"Pull down your panties," I continue, my voice hoarse, my chest heaving with anticipation, and sweat gathers on my spine. When she, once again, does as I ask, I lick my lips and grin up at her.

"Don't forget to tell me how you like it, sweetheart," I tell her, a bit nervous if I'll be able to bring her to ecstasy like I hope.

She smiles widely, settling my nerves, and whispers, "I won't forget." Gently, she removes my glasses, and I squint automatically when I can no longer see her clearly.

I really need to get contacts.

"Best be careful with these." Emma's voice breaks through, and I straighten my back, bringing my face closer to her crotch. I grab her right leg and place it over my shoulder, baring her pussy before me completely, and inhale deeply.

Heaven.

Meeting her eyes one last time, I smile at her.

"Hold on to something, baby. I want you to unravel completely on my mouth," I say and, *finally*, my tongue meets her clit for the first time.

If ever there was a thing such as heaven, I believe this is it: her, me, our desire for each other palpable, and her scent permeating her flat. As I listen to Emma's instructions, I revel in the scent and feel of her taste wetting my chin, proud that I can make her so hungry for me. I lick gently at first, my tongue flat, holding her up by grabbing her hips, and her whimpers only push me to take my time with her. I force myself to hold back, focusing solely on making her abandon the precious control she wears like armour.

"Daniel...," Emma repeats my name over and over,

completely forgetting to guide me, but it only makes me bolder, hearing how my pleasuring her affects her. I suck on her clit while putting a finger inside her wetness, finding the spot that'll drive her over the edge. She puts a hand on my head, and I press my mouth closer, lapping her flowing juices up, and the taste...*fuck me*, it's sweet, hot, and I never want to stop.

Feeling the ache in my cock, I reach down to jack off, smearing the pre-come over the tip, but Emma's voice penetrates and makes me slow down again.

"Don't. I want to suck you off," she pants, and I pull away from her pussy and shake my head.

"No. Not until you've come all over my mouth, Em. You taste unbelievably *fucking* good."

Denying her wish I move back to finish her off, stroking my cock in earnest now. I blow on her clit first, though, registering how that seems to please her when she whimpers incomprehensible words at me, and then start to lick her again, all the way from her clit to her slit. Putting another finger inside her pussy, I finger fuck her, faster and faster until she comes all over me, just like I wanted. Flattening my tongue again, my licks become slower, gentler, and I focus on holding her limp body up before removing my fingers from inside her.

When she seems able to stand on her own again, I release my hold on her arse, but not without stroking a wet finger gently over her puckered hole. I'm not too shy to admit that I'd like to explore that area of her body as well, but that's something to leave for another day.

Licking my lips, I wipe my chin and grin up at her. "I take it you liked it?" It's not really a question, and Emma knows it as well as me.

Without answering me, she gets down on her knees and straddles me. Feeling her pussy just above my cock causes me to lose my breath entirely. I look down to watch her as she takes a firm hold on the base of it, and the pleasure when she rubs the head over her clit, still wet and glistening from her orgasm, becomes almost too much for me to handle.

"Fuck...me," I growl loudly, and at last admit defeat by closing my eyes, taking in the fire raging through me by her torment.

"No...But I *will* fuck you with my mouth," she chuckles, and I open one eye to glare at her. I don't think it possesses that much power, though, because she simply smirks at me and puts a palm to my sweaty chest, pushing slightly.

"Just lie back and enjoy it...," she whispers, her eyes twinkling with mischief and she removes her bra. She's keeping her black stilettos on, though, and my cock hardens further from the sight - it's such a turn-on.

What am I to do, really? Refuse?

Definitely not an option.

So I lie down on the hard floor and let Emma finish me off, still tasting her pussy on my tongue.

CHAPTER THIRTY

EMMA

Nighttime has fallen, and we're lying in my bed. Again. And we're spooning. Again. I can't believe I let Daniel talk me into this, but when he asked me if he could stay over, I didn't have the heart to tell him no.

"I need you," he said. "Please let me hold you tonight."

What kind of heartless cow would he take me for if I'd said no?

It's not as if I *truly* wanted him to go after our hot and heavy sexcapade, but the walls I've spent more than a decade building up around my heart are being torn down, little by little, and so much faster than I ever thought would be possible. I'm so frightened that he's going to despise me if I ever tell him everything that's happened before I came here. What if he finds me weak, unhinged even?

What kind of girl allows her assailant to go free like I did?

I can't relax at all now, but it almost feels as if the man behind me is an octopus because he has me wrapped up tightly in his embrace, his arms and legs curling around mine.

It's as if he's a cocoon, my own personal safe haven...And he wants me to feel comfortable with relying on him.

Can he feel that I'm wound up so much that I'm about to burst from the bed, untangling myself from within his grasp?

"Shhh, relax, Em. I'm not going to attack you in your sleep," Daniel whispers sleepily, hugging me closer to him.

Well, there you have it: he can read my mind. I've officially gone off the deep end now.

I sigh and try to will my tense body to do as he says, and once I hear the faint snoring from my sexy prep boy, it becomes easier for me to finally let go. Yawning widely, sleep overtakes me, allowing my mind respite.

At least for a little while.

♡

I bolt upright, gasping for air, a scream lodged in my throat. Despair, anger, and hurt overwhelm me, and a torrent of tears start pouring down my face.

Not again! Not tonight of all nights!

"Shh, shh, I've got you, sweetheart," Daniel whispers from beside me, and it takes my befuddled brain a few seconds to realise that he's holding me. Next thing I know, I'm lying on top of him, chin pressed into his neck, my hands in his hair, all the while huge shudders break through my body, preventing me from hiding my distress from him. His soothing voice whispers sweet nothings in my ear, all the while his hold on me never lets up, and, ever so slowly, my sobs subside, leaving only silent tears in their wake.

"Just hold onto me," he croons, leaving small, lingering kisses on my cheeks, my hair, and, lastly, on the corners of my mouth. And so I do just that. I hold onto him, never wanting to let go. His kisses burn me, make me catch my breath for fear that he'll try to go for my lips...the last thing I want right now is to feel that part of him against me. Yet...he never does. Instead, his sweet caresses force me to focus solely on them instead of the never-ending nightmare until it finally fades away.

Their aftermath, however, is the same as always: I need a shower, and I think I'm about to get sick.

I don't want Daniel to become suspicious of anything, though, so I try to concentrate on him, his voice, and his arms holding me in a vice like grip until my eyes are dry again. It almost feels like he's afraid that *now* is the time I'll choose to run from him.

I can't say he's wrong about that part. I do want to escape him this very moment...but only because I feel beyond mortified about him seeing me like this: weak, broken, *ugly*, and undesirable.

Praying that he won't ask me any questions, I untangle my hands from his hair and clear my throat quietly.

"I...I need a shower. Let me go, please...," I ask him in a small voice. There's no strength behind them, no fight within me, but, somehow, he seems to understand because he loosens his arms slowly and sits up, and I have no choice but to straddle him.

Averting my gaze, I move to leave him, but his hands on my chin makes me pause. I refuse to meet his eyes even though I feel them trying to penetrate me until he leans down and look up at me. A worried frown mars his face, and my lips automatically pull up in a small smile. He doesn't buy it.

"Do you need any help?" he asks me softly, bringing me

close to tears again, and I shake my head adamantly at him.

"No."

He hesitates and opens his mouth as if to say more, but apparently thinks better of it because he shuts it almost immediately and grits his teeth.

"Please don't ask me any questions," I beg quietly, and he nods once, understanding that I don't need them right now.

Again, I move to leave his lap, and this time, he doesn't stop me. He just keeps holding my hand until I'm standing firmly on the floor, and then squeezes it once before releasing me. I hesitate briefly, but then go with my instincts and lean down to brush my lips across his, and it causes him to jolt as if I've marked him in some way.

"Thank you," I whisper and then practically run to my bathroom, open the door and lock it behind me. The shivering begins again and I hurry to turn on the shower, silently praying that it'll warm up soon.

I step under the showerhead, and, for once, the nausea has left me. Instead, the tingling in my lips reminds me of what I just did, and that's what I choose to hold onto all while the hot water does its job.

I kissed Daniel. And I didn't flee from him.

Granted, it wasn't what I'd call a proper kiss involving lots of tongue, but that's not important.

What's important is the fact that I no longer feel so terrified of what'll happen once we *do* finally kiss. And that's an encouraging thought.

One that, even in this sorry state I'm in, causes me to smile.

DANIEL

Emma kissed me. It may only have been a small kiss, one that so many other guys would scoff at, but this is *huge*. Maybe...just *maybe*...this means that she's finally beginning to realise that there's more to us than merely a physical relationship. If I hadn't heard the soft click of the lock on the door, I'd be tempted to go after her, but even I know that she needs to be alone.

Her nightmare woke me up before she did, her frightened whimpers and thrashing about on the bed making me worried that she'd end up hurting herself and fall down on the floor. She scared me, and I was just about to shake her awake when she pulled out of it.

The way her eyes looked when they sought out mine...*shit*. Rage unlike any I have ever felt before surged through me, but I hid it from her the best I could.

What the hell happened to her?!

I can't fathom it. I mean, I could ask her, perhaps even force an explanation out of her, of course. Somehow, I doubt she'd tell me the truth, though, and it's imperative that I gain her trust.

Without it, she'll never become mine. Not completely.

My mum always told me that I'd know it deep down to my bones when I'd found the woman I'd want to spend the rest of my life with. Even when drunk, she'd be adamant about this fact, not letting my skepticism about the validity of her words take root. Needless to say, I never believed her...until now. I felt it earlier when I knocked on Emma's door, but I feel it even stronger now. Another important moment in my life, and I never really saw it coming.

Is it irrational and completely messed up having such strong feelings for her so soon after I've met her? Probably...but who cares? I want the chance to get to know every single detail about this woman, to protect her from all harm, and I just *know* that she'll never stop intriguing me. True, I'd also like to do all sorts of wicked things to that body of hers, but I can wait. I mean, I've waited this long to lose my virginity - what's a couple more months?

I may not be a real knight in shining armour, but I'll be Emma's whenever she needs one. I'll be damned if she tries to stop me, but even if she does? It won't matter. I can be just as stubborn as she is.

For now, though, I won't voice how desperately in love with her I am. Now, I'll take care of her, whatever she needs, and just be there for her, tending to her every wish.

I rub my eyes and search for my glasses on the floor before putting them on.

This situation calls for hot chocolate, cuddles, and caresses, and I'm just the man to provide that for Emma. I pick up my jeans from the floor, not bothering with my boxers at all. Checking that the keys to my flat are still in one of the pockets, I leave Emma in order to fetch what I need from my fridge as quickly as possible.

It's time I take care of my girl.

My girl. Has a nice ring to it.

The high from officially staking my claim on Emma, albeit silently, makes me grin widely. She is at a bad place right now, I know that, and clearly marked by her nightmare, but maybe some special attention will help her overcome it for now.

At least she'll know that I won't abandon her.

EMMA

Scrutinising my reflection in the mirror above the sink, I shake my head at what I see; once again, I look ghastly. Granted, it *is* the middle of the night, and nobody really looks their best at this ungodly hour - not even Michael Fassbender, I bet - but, even so, it is clear that the shower hasn't really helped. Except from causing the bone-deep coldness the nightmare always leaves me with disappear.

Now, though, I wish I'd thought of bringing some clothes with me, because I feel too exposed with only a towel wrapped around my body.

Vulnerable.

Broken.

Empty.

Now that I have thought more about it, I feel kind of silly for making the small kiss I gave Daniel a bigger deal than it probably was. Still, it was important to me - and it still is.

Taking a fortifying breath, I finally muster up enough courage to unlock the door and leave the confines of my safe haven to get back to Daniel. The scent of melted chocolate that seems to be wafting out from my kitchen teases my nostrils, halting me in my tracks halfway through the door to my living room, and I back up a few steps to look in the direction it is coming from.

There he is: Daniel, my sexy-as-sin-virgin-neighbour. And he's cooking for me again. From the looks of it, he's making me hot chocolate, and I have to swallow hard for fearing the emotion welling up inside me will burst free. The enormity of what he's trying to do hits me smack dab in my heart, and my resolve to keep away from him dwindles further.

He wants to help me.

He's trying to put the broken pieces back together, bit by bit.

Will he be able to succeed?

I doubt I'll ever be altogether healed, and, logically, I know that I will have to heal myself...that only I hold the power to do that.

Still...it feels wonderful to know that he cares enough about me to make hot chocolate - and is that marshmallows? - at four am in the morning.

Daniel looks up from the stove as I move further towards him and smiles gently at me. He's only wearing his jeans, and they're hanging loosely from his hips, leaving me with a perfect view of that delectable V and happy trail. I can't decide if my mouth waters from the sight of him or because of what he's cooking, but I don't care. Seeing him here, relaxed and at ease in my flat, makes me happy, and I smile back at him.

What he says next surprises me.

"My mum wasn't always an alcoholic, you know." He looks down and stirs the pot, his tone of voice not giving one tiny hint of how he must feel about his mother and her illness.

"I can't pinpoint when she started drinking more heavily, though," he continues and starts pouring the chocolate into my largest mugs. "One day I came home - I think I was around 12 or 13 years old - and found her passed out on the living room couch, TV blaring with some god-awful show." Pausing, he opens the bag with the marshmallows and put a generous amount of them in the mugs. They make a soft plop, and I watch, mesmerised, before he hands me the mug.

"Do you want to sit outside?" he asks me and blows on the steam of his.

I break free of my stupor and nod. "Yes. But I'll just put on some clothes. Do you want me to bring your T-shirt?"

He nods and takes a sip of chocolate. The drop left on his upper lip is calling me to lick it, but I ignore it. Daniel is in a conversational mood, and I want to hear his story. Even if it is an ugly one.

I just hope he doesn't expect me to reciprocate tonight.

"I'll take care of our drinks," he says quietly and follows me into the living room. Without saying another word, his hand brushes mine, and he leaves me alone. I do my best to hurry up and pull on my beloved yoga pants and a jumper before joining him on my balcony. I hand him his T-shirt and hope that he doesn't clam up on me now.

Once we're seated, Daniel watches me silently as I pick up a cigarette and light it. He doesn't reproach me for needing it, and I'm grateful for his silence.

I pick up my mug of chocolate, and take my first sip.

Mmm...divine. And just what I needed.

"What did you do when you saw your mother like that?" I ask him, glancing at him briefly.

He leans back in his seat and looks over the park, taking in the beautiful sunrise before us for a minute, before continuing his tale.

"I panicked, of course. Tried to shake her awake and then phoned my dad at work. I begged him to come home, and he did, all the while I stayed by her side." He shrugs. "At the time, I didn't think of ringing 1-1-2, even though both of my parents had drilled it into us children from when we were quite young that that's the first course of action in case of an emergency."

I take a final drag of my cigarette before flicking the butt away with my fingertip, and we both watch it as it sails through the air and then lands on the grass below us.

Daniel inhales deeply, warming his hands on his mug, his face still turned away from me. It's clear that he needs to distance himself somehow while unveiling such a horrible memory, and it makes perfect sense to me.

"When Dad got home, I couldn't help but notice the grim set to his mouth or the way he didn't really seem to be that surprised. I guess my mum had been good at fooling her children and that she'd been doing it for a long time," he adds, his voice showing the first hint of bitterness and anger.

"Eventually, he managed to rouse her, and then put her to bed, almost dragging her...He ordered me to stay away for the rest of the night, said that he and mum needed to have a *chat*...," he spits out, and my heart hurts for him.

"So...," he continues after he's gathered himself. "I went to a mate's house, and I guess my sisters did the same, or I can't remember...Anyway, when I got home the next morning, dreading what I'd see once I got there, I found my mum sitting on the couch in nothing but a robe, beer in hand..." He hesitates, gritting his teeth so hard I can almost hear them grinding. On a loud whoosh of his breath, he finishes his tale. "She was sporting a black eye and two broken ribs, drunk off her arse."

Scooting my seat closer to him, trying to show him my support, I put my hand on his thigh and squeeze it lightly. I hope he's aware that I do not pity him and what he's had to endure.

"I'm so sorry," I whisper, unshed tears clogging my

throat.

He snorts. "Yeah, me, too. The day I found her? That's the last time I ever saw or heard from my dad."

I gasp. "What?"

He chuckles grimly. "You heard me. He was just...gone...vanished. After that, my mum didn't seem to care at all about us, about anything at all, besides her precious alcohol. She disappeared into the bottle, and no matter how many times she's promised us that she'll get better...that she'll seek counselling...she never does, and she never will."

Daniel leans over and rubs his face harshly, despondency and anger radiating off him.

"Not one word from him? Not even on birthdays?" I ask him, even though I already know the answer. "How did you manage?"

Sighing, he sits back and entwines his fingers with mine, and I look down at our hands but don't refuse him this sign of intimacy. I don't believe I am able to refuse this man anything.

"Nope. You learn to get by the hard way when you are five children desperately searching for a way to survive without the system finding out. None of us wanted to go away, to be separated from each other, so we lied a lot, I guess. Well, I kept silent most of the time which is part of the reason I didn't graduate from school until two years after anyone else. Therein lies the explanation, or some of it, as to why I'm not already at university."

"It makes sense. I just can't fathom why your teachers didn't make a better effort. What about your neighbours, the rest of your family?"

Daniel looks at me, his eyes shifting, as if there's more to his story than what he's told me so far.

"You don't have to answer," I hurry to say, wanting him to relax while he's with me. It's the least I can do after the way he's taken care of me, making me forget about my own troubles for a while.

We sit in silence once more, and I notice how the birds are waking up now. Their cheerful voices take the last shreds of the night away, carrying it away on the wind, and I hope I won't have another nightmare for a few nights.

"Do you want to watch a movie?" Daniel surprisingly asks me, straightening up in his seat.

I blink at him, wondering if I heard that right.

"Now? At this hour?"

He nods enthusiastically, and the way he looks right now - tired, yet hopeful - almost makes me want to agree with anything he suggests, just to see the shadows of his past leave his eyes for another while.

"Sure...But I'm choosing the movie, alright?"

Curling his lip, he frowns unhappily. "Not a chick flick, please?"

I chuckle and stand up, my fingers still wrapped around his.

"How does *Back To The Future* or *Indiana Jones* sound?"

"Perfect." His beaming smile almost knocks me off-kilter, and a sharp pang hits me right in the centre of my heart.

Shite. I think I'm in love.

Trying to hide my reaction from him, I look down at my feet and lead him back inside to grant him his wish. None of us are working today, so there's no harm in spending the day together, I suppose.

Daniel's story keeps swirling around and around in my mind as we watch the movie, though, and if his father were here right now, I'd knee him so hard in his balls for leaving his children like that.

No one, least of all your parents, abandons a child. It's unacceptable.

CHAPTER THIRTY-ONE

DANIEL

B LOODY HELL, WHERE DID *that come from?*
I didn't set out to tell Emma so much about my past, but before I knew it, words spilled out of my mouth, and I couldn't stop them. It took a great deal out of me to let her in on what happened, but I don't regret it. Deep inside me, I hope that she'll realise that she can confide in me when she feels ready for it. I want, no *need* her to know that she can trust me. And baring some of my dirty laundry to her felt liberating in a way: I feel freer now than I did before.

The way she let me tell my story? How she kept her silence and didn't try to make me divulge more than I was ready for only intensifies the burning need I have for her. I crave her, and not only on a physical level. I love the way she crinkles her nose and frowns when she thinks I'm not watching her and she becomes lost inside her own head; I love the way her eyes light up when she lets down her guard and allows herself to *feel*.

And I love her laugh because she doesn't let go easily.

True, I would love for her to laugh more often...but at least for now, I know that when she *does* laugh, it's because she truly means it.

There's nothing fake about this girl.

I love that about her, too.

I just...love her.

Full stop.

The end.

I pray that our real beginning - the one that will *truly* matter - will come soon.

I'm near desperation with want for kissing her lips...and if it doesn't happen soon, I fear that I am going to explode.

We ended up watching all three movies of *Back To The Future*, and I can't remember the last time I felt so relaxed. It was comfortable, but the ever present attraction between us never simmered down. I don't doubt for a minute that she noticed my hard-on more than once - and I went back to my flat with a serious case of the blue balls - but she didn't bring it up. Not once. And I saw no reason to do it, either.

What kind of an arse would I be if I tried something with her when she, quite clearly, wasn't in the mood for it?

I hope she'll confide in me soon. Those nightmares of hers...they're beyond horrible. I'm not the one suffering from their attack on the mind, but having witnessed them twice now - especially the one last night - frightened the ever-loving shite out of me. I'm not an idiot; it's clear that ghosts haunt her.

I wish that the ghosts will be eradicated so that we both can put our pasts behind us for good

The problem is, though, if Emma will allow me to help her get rid of hers?

Or will she push me away, running as fast as she can in the opposite direction?

EMMA

The weeks pass. My mum rings me every Friday, asking me about my latest session with Katherine. She tries not to probe me with too many questions, but I know it's costing her to hold back.

My mum is definitely not one to restrain herself, hence the reason she chose criminal law at university: she can be quite scary at times.

And every week, I try to open up more, to let her in on my innermost thoughts and feelings, but it is just so damn *difficult* at times.

I mean, I pour my heart and soul out in my sessions – why do I have to do it twice every week?

Some people go on and on about their *emotions* all the time, but I favour my dad, I think: a man of few words. I prefer to *act*, not *talk*.

Which, come to think of it, is probably why I've got into trouble so many times in the past.

Daniel has been staying at my place a lot the past two weeks, and I'm not sure what to make of it. Katherine keeps telling me to take things slow, and I agree with her. I'm not ready to take things further, despite our hot and heavy shenanigans in private and in public.

Yes...*in public*.

I can't believe the way I let reason fade away whenever

he's near me. Only yesterday, we decided to go out to dinner after our study session, and it was absolute *torture* sitting beside him at the restaurant we chose and try to ignore the way his hands and fingers would tease me underneath my summer dress. And he was oh so subtle about it, keeping a straight face all the while he did the best he could to make me come then and there, and plain for all the other guests to see.

Now, *that* would have been so embarrassing.

Before I knew it, I'd dragged him to the ladies' room, told him to go down on me, and then commenced to suck him off once he'd finished licking my pussy with so much vigour and passion, I was feeling completely lightheaded for a while after we got back to our table.

Knowing how much he loves to go down on me, as if he can't get enough, is a truly powerful thrill, and one I take advantage of as often as possible.

Daniel, being a man, kept looking at me with such cheeky smugness for the rest of our evening, not caring in the least bit about everyone else.

What the heck is wrong with me?

I must be hormonal or something. It's either that, or I just don't care what people think when they see us together.

Honestly, I don't *think*, full stop.

The other strange part is how I'm becoming even further relaxed and simply enjoy spending time with him, or how I've noticed that I grin like a goon whenever he texts me another one of his random questions. I'm even becoming addicted to seeing him each day.

I've introduced him to *Camilla's*, of course, and he seems to enjoy rattling George with some wild conspiracy theories from time to time. Needless to say, George lets off every time, not even picking up on Daniel pulling his chain, while

Camilla and I watch our men fondly as we chat about this and that. He's clearly been given the stamp of approval from my friend - even though I didn't ask her for it, of course - and I have to confess that it thrills me to no end having it.

We went clubbing with Suzy last weekend, which, to tell the truth, did confirm that Daniel's definitely not a dancer. Even though I told him that we only went so that he could become more comfortable around girls, I hated seeing them flock to him like bees to the honey. I ended up sitting at the bar, sulking, at the other end from him, all the while Suzy kept snickering at my jealous behaviour.

I didn't find it remotely funny. Not. One. Bit.

Daniel didn't drink any alcohol - which is kind of understandable - but that didn't prevent me from holding back. I did imbibe less than I usually do, thereby keeping my promise to Suzy to take things slowly, and I hope she took notice. Well, the times she didn't have her tongue stuck down some blonde bombshell's throat, that is.

At some point or another, I was being chatted up by a blue-eyed bloke that I'd definitely never have passed up before I met Daniel, but all of a sudden, he was gone, and Daniel was pulling me from my seat. In no uncertain terms, he demanded that it was time to leave, and so we did. In my drunken state, I didn't really protest that much. After we got back to my place, he told me to find my secret stash of toys, and he ended up pleasuring me in all sorts of naughty ways that night.

Phew. Mind. Blown.

Ever since he told me about the situation at home, and about his dad walking out on him and his family, it seems as if he's let go of his own ghosts. He's more relaxed, happier even, from when we first met. Or maybe that's just my lovesick feelings overanalysing everything to death as usual.

Yes, I said the word: *love*. The one thing I have never believed in - or believed I would ever have the desire to experience - has befallen me.

I love him.

He makes my heart soar whenever he's near. I miss him on the nights we don't spend together. And I long for him and his familiar touch when I wake up in the morning and he's not there, spooning me.

How is it possible to love someone you haven't even *kissed* yet?

It's so bizarre. Completely irrational.

Yet...it's also true.

Needless to say, I'm yearning for that kiss with every fibre of my being even though I feel so conflicted about it at the same time. I hope it'll blow my mind...that I'll see stars and fireworks and all that crap once I muster up the courage to pick up my big girl knickers and just go for it.

♡

It's Thursday, and both Daniel and I are at the bookshop and busy going through our stock. A big, annual book fair is happening this week at The Bella Center in Copenhagen, and Mr. Andersen always makes sure we have enough of the current Danish bestsellers available.

Being in this close proximity with him is wreaking havoc with my libido, though, but I'd be lying if I pretended not to enjoy it. Because I do...and so does Daniel, I'm sure of it. He keeps giving me those intense, scorching hot looks that almost make me completely forget where I am, making me imagine all sorts of crazy ideas that urge me to take off, him in hand, and ravage him somewhere nearby.

I don't want to be responsible right now.

However, I have another appointment with Katherine later today so, obviously, I have to at least act like a grown-up and attempt to get some proper work done before I have to go soon.

The thought hasn't even really left my mind before a pair of very familiar hands finds their way to my hips, firmly gripping me and keeping me in place.

"What are you doing?" I ask Daniel softly, my heartbeat picking up speed as his warm breath meets my burning skin until his lips find the sensitive spot just below my ear.

"Nothing," he murmurs, but his actions clearly belie his words. I lean back until our bodies are perfectly aligned, and I sigh softly...content, happy even.

"That's not true, you know," I whisper, reaching an arm up to curl around his neck, and he chuckles.

"Well, you're right, of course. But, technically, we ought to be working. I just couldn't resist your neck...you taste like melons, my favourite fruit."

A tiny shiver runs through me as I become lost in his caresses...his right hand loses its grip on my hip and moves scintillatingly slow around my soft belly and down the front of my dress until he's cupping my pussy.

"Aren't you being a bit too...forward?" I ask him teasingly, short of breath.

His lips leave the curve of my shoulder, and he growls seductively, "If you didn't want me to take advantage of you in some way every time you're near me, you shouldn't have worn a skirt today."

Dang it...and I thought I was being so subtle about it.

My fingers thread through his hair, and I widen my

stance a little.

"I love it when you go all hot alpha on me," I whisper on a sigh, and it's true.

"I know," he replies smugly, and I laugh at his forwardness.

"Are you going to ravish me now?" I ask him seductively, revelling when I feel the way the fabric of my skirt brushes my legs as he pulls it up. When his fingers begin to tease my clit, I can't hold back a moan.

"Fuck it...you're already wet for me, sweetheart...Always ready for me, aren't you?" The dark growl in his voice turns me on even more, and I roll my hips in time with the movements of his fingers. He pushes his erection into my back, and I reach a hand behind me to unbuckle his belt.

"Yes," I gasp. "But...the door...we need to lock it. What if someone comes in?"

"Don't pretend the idea doesn't thrill you in some way," he answers, and he's right again: it does.

"Maybe so...but..." I hesitate, biting my lip for fear of revealing my desires.

"But what? Answer me, Em," he orders and grips my ponytail in his left hand, pulling lightly yet just enough to make me realise that his dominant side has come out – and that he's in charge completely.

"I don't want to share you," I groan out, submitting to him once more.

He bites my earlobe lightly. "Don't worry, I won't ever share you with anyone else...However..." It's his turn to hesitate, and I hear his sharp intake of breath when my hand finds his ready cock and I start to stroke it earnestly.

"You were saying...?" I tease him, reassured and beyond thrilled that he feels the way I do; that we're exclusive.

"The thought of having an audience while we're consumed with each other is something I'd like to try sometime," he replies huskily. His words make my pussy even wetter, and he hums in pleasure, no doubt feeling it, too.

"We'll have to look into that," I whisper and close my eyes when he puts two fingers inside me and begins to finger fuck me thoroughly. I place my head on his chest with abandon, so immersed in his ministrations that I almost don't hear his reply.

"Shit...Fuck, Em, I want to kiss you so badly," he groans out.

It feels as if a bucketful of cold ice douses me when I hear the desperate plea in his words. The lust quickly abandons my body, stilling my movements when the impact of them pierces my heart.

"What's wrong?" Daniel asks me, voice devoid of the dominant male I have come to know so well.

Yes. What is wrong with you, you idiot?!

"I...I'm sorry, Daniel. I have to go," I mutter and pull out of his embrace, straightening my clothes quickly.

"What?!" he asks me, disbelieving. I can't meet his gaze, though; I'm too embarrassed about my reaction.

"Hold up," he says and takes a firm grip on my shoulders, preventing me from running away.

"Emma?" He leans down, trying to catch my eyes, and I squirm in his arms, trying to break free of him.

"Let me go," I demand harshly, but, for once, he doesn't do like I ask him to.

"Why?" he demands, and I glance briefly at him. He's frowning, frustration and concern clear in his eyes, and I can't blame him.

"I forgot that I have an appointment today and so I have

to leave now," I try to placate him, but it only seems to backfire at me.

"I know," he replies, the sarcasm hitting me right in my heart. "It's Thursday, Em, and I'm not stupid. It's the same bloody thing every week! You make up some vague excuse and then you disappear for the rest of the day."

Mouth hanging agape, I place a hand on his shoulder, but he shakes it off. I wince from the hurt his action causes me even when I know that I have no right to feel that way.

He sighs and finally releases his hold on me. As he takes a step away, he quickly rearranges his own clothes, all the while his eyes remain steadily on my face.

"Why won't you trust me?" he asks me quietly, and hearing the sadness in those few words make my eyes well up.

"I don't know," I whisper hoarsely, trying with all my might to hold back the tears.

Daniel closes his eyes briefly, clearly hurt, and I wish more than anything that I wasn't the cause of it.

"Go," he finally says and rubs his neck. "I don't know what you're doing, and I don't care; I don't want to pry. But, Em..." He moves back into my private space, forcing me to lean my head back in order to hold his gaze.

"Sooner or later, I'm going to start asking questions, because I'm in love with you."

I think I stop breathing altogether.

His declaration of love simultaneously makes me long to throw myself at him and run screaming in the other direction.

"I. Love. You," he continues, enunciating each word clearly, and I can see his love for me mingled with the hurt from before shining in his eyes. "I've tried to hold back, but I can't do it anymore. I want you so much, every *single* part of you – the light, the darkness, and the in-between. It'll hurt me beyond measure if you refuse me, and...Well, now you know the depths of my feelings for you. It was never only physical between us, sweetheart. I even told you that when we first started out, but you refused to listen. So..." He cups my cheeks, caressing them with his thumbs. "Please think about what I've said. Go to your meeting, or wherever the hell it is you have to be, and then text me when you're home later."

Not even giving me time to respond, he gives me a quick kiss on my forehead and opens the door to the storage room.

I turn around, crying, "Wait!"

He pauses in the doorway and only looks at me briefly.

"How can you love me, Daniel?" I ask him, my voice hitching on his name.

Shaking his head, he answers quietly, "We'll talk later."

He leaves me, and I'm alone once again. I stand there for a while, staring after him, my head filled with confusion, before I finally pull myself together.

Taking a deep breath, I walk out of the room to pick up my things, barely avoiding running smack dab into Mr. Andersen.

"Are you okay, Emma?" he asks me, clearly concerned, his glasses perched on the end of his nose. I don't want to explain my haste, though.

"I'm fine," I hurriedly say and then leave the shop as quickly as possible. As I open the door, I almost trip over my own feet, but thankfully manage to right my body before falling headfirst down on the sidewalk.

I can't get to Katherine fast enough.

"Daniel told me he loves me," I blurt out when Katherine

opens the door to let me in. I ran all the way here and I'm suffering from an annoying sting in my side because of it.

She blinks slowly and says drily, "That boy works fast."

Her statement causes a hysteric giggle to erupt from my mouth, and I wipe away the perspiration from my forehead as I enter her flat.

"I know I'm here early," I apologise and wait for her to lead the way like I usually do. "My mind is running amok at the moment, and I just wanted to get to you as soon as possible," I explain further as she walks me to the living room. She sits down in her armchair across from mine.

"It's alright, Emma," she responds calmly and pours me some water. "Here, sit down, and have a drink. It looks like you need it."

Thankful, I do as she says, and a huge sigh of relief falls from my lips before I take a sip of the heavenly cold drink.

"Now," Katherine says quietly and opens her ever present notebook. "Initially, I wanted to discuss something else today, but seeing as you're here early, we'll save that for later. So...Daniel..." She looks closely at me, her familiar thoughtful expression in place, and her eyes assessing me. "How do you feel about it?"

"*Feel?!* I'm scared to death!"

She chuckles. "Well, yes, I gathered that, but try to explain to me why that is?"

"I would think that it's pretty obvious why I'm freaking out right now, but okay, I'll say it out loud for clarification," I answer, a bit annoyed at her for forcing me to spell it out. "What if he'll be disgusted with me for not speaking up about Tom? What if he won't understand?"

She tilts her head to the side. "Do you have so little faith in yourself?"

Gaping at her, I wave my hands wildly around. "Katherine, what do you mean?"

"What I mean is just that: why do you think he'll even care about that? Don't you think he'll stand by you? Do you find him weak?"

"No," I scoff and shake my head, denying that notion immediately. "Someone who's had to endure what he did as a child can't be weak."

"Exactly!" She snaps her fingers at me, the movement startling me because it's such an uncharacteristic thing for her to do.

"Emma," she sighs and sits back in her seat. "No one will blame you for making that decision because you were a *child*. You were only ten years old. Should your parents have taken action?" she asks me, tilting her head to the side. I shake my head vehemently before she goes on. "Maybe they should. Maybe not. The point is, though, that I have no doubt in my mind that you chose to do what was best for *you* at the time. And should you ever wish to change that, nothing is stopping you. Only yourself. I'm sure that having a man such as Daniel standing beside you would only be an asset for you - and something tells me that he's strong enough to have your back should you stumble on your way."

I don't have a retort for that one last statement, and she knows it, too. Deflated, I lean back in my seat, head in hands, and try to calm my nerves.

"Emma," Katherine calls me, and I take a peek through my fingers and watch her lean closer in her seat towards me.

"Besides your concerns about confiding in Daniel, what stops you from telling him the truth about the true nature of your feelings towards him?"

Blowing a loose strand of hair from my face, I let my arms

fall to my lap.

"What if I'm a terrible kisser? Or a terrible girlfriend?!" I wail at her, and Katherine erupts with laughter and throws her head back. I'm about to blow up with panic and abruptly leave my seat to pace back and forth in front of her. I know that the order of my world is crashing down around me at this very moment, leaving a clear path for me towards a much different future than the one I had originally planned.

"Gosh, Emma, slow down, will you?" Katherine says, and I really do try to do as she asks me to, albeit it is near impossible for me.

"Emma, trust me on this: you won't be a terrible kisser or girlfriend," Katherine tells me, remaining in her seat. I glance at her and almost want to poke out my tongue at her, just to be hard-headed like usual.

Almost...but I obviously can't do that.

"Your first kiss will probably be one of two things: it could be absolutely wonderful, or..." she pauses, and I hold my breath until she goes on, "It could be a disappointment."

Blast!

"But only if you think too hard about it, my dear; you'll just have to trust your instincts on this one."

Rubbing my forehead, I think about her words, and slowly walk back to my chair.

"But what if...what if I'll run the moment his lips touch mine?" I ask her, close to tears again, and she looks warmly at me.

"*If* that happens - and I very much doubt that it will, given the nature of your...err...chemistry, shall we say?" She looks cheekily at me, and I can't hide the blush that sets my cheeks on fire from her words. "Like I said, should you feel uncomfortable at any moment, try not to panic. Just end the kiss, and do your best to not hurt his feelings too much, okay?"

I nod, absentmindedly looking out of the window to my left. The leaves on the trees are such a bright green, and they remind me of the colour of Daniel's eyes. Just thinking about him makes my heart pick up speed.

"I don't believe I'll panic, not really." I turn back to Katherine, and she smiles at me. "I truly so want to kiss him, it's just that..." My voice trails off as uncertainty about the unknown grips me again: the strength of its leash is not as pronounced as it usually is, and the knowledge furthers my resolve.

"You're scared, which is perfectly understandable," Katherine finishes the sentence for me, and I shrug, conceding with her words.

"I'd be mortified...sad...and probably also angry for hurting him," I murmur and look down at my hands.

"Try not to overthink things," Katherine warms me, and I meet her gaze again. "Just allow yourself to truly *feel* for once...and listen to what your heart tells you," she continues.

"That doesn't sound like something a psychologist would say," I accuse mildly, and now it's her turn to blush.

"Well, maybe not. What can I say? I'm also an incorrigible romantic," she answers and takes a sip of water.

We sit in comfortable silence once more, and it suddenly occurs to me that I like it. The fact that there's no noise to distract me at all - apart from the faint sounds of cars passing by outside - soothes me instead of making my head spin.

"Do you think you're ready to move on?" Katherine asks me, pulling me out of my stupor.

"Of course. What do you want to talk about?" I reach for my own glass.

"About Tom."

I close my eyes when I hear his name once more and wait for the familiar fear and anger to return to my heart and soul. Strangely, though, they don't arrive, and a whoosh of air leaves my lungs when I realise that I only feel resentment and sorrow: resentment for what he put me through, and sorrow for the little girl - *me* - and the loss of her childhood.

Sitting back slowly, I look questioningly at Katherine. "Okay. I can do that."

She beams at me, clearly very pleased to hear that kind of response before looking down at her notebook.

"Have you forgiven him for what he did to you?" she asks me, returning her eyes to mine. Her question surprises me, and I concentrate on her words for a few moments as my eyes take in the pattern of the rug underneath my feet.

Have I forgiven him?

"No," I answer her slowly and release the tight grip of my clasped hands for the first time; my fingers are beginning to become numb and, one by one, I force them to relax.

Squaring my shoulders, I meet Katherine's kind eyes with a hard stare of my own. "No, I haven't. I don't think I ever will. But..." Pausing, I search for the right words to describe the unknown emotions coursing through me at this very moment.

Suddenly, they are clear before me, falling from my lips so easily. "But I have accepted it. And that's a step in the right direction, isn't it?" I can't keep the hope from my voice. I yearn to *finally* move on so very badly.

Katherine smiles at little, eyes remaining calm and understanding, and nods satisfied at me.

"Very much so."

"I still feel weak, though..."

She frowns at me. "How so?"

"Because...because what happened to me is far less serious from what other girls - and boys - have gone through. I guess I don't feel...right about having so many issues when I compare them to others. Or what I can imagine other people to suffer through."

Katherine lifts her hand, and I stop blathering.

"Now, Emma, you are *not* weak. Every person is different, and how they react to actions befallen on them through *no fault* of theirs is subjective. You understand? *How and why* your issues have had an effect on your adult life is just as valid and important as the next person sitting in that chair. Those thoughts about your situation being less horrible from other survivors of abuse? You have to try to let them go."

Not bloody likely.

Yet out loud, my answer is completely different. "I will."

Katherine doesn't seem to believe me if the scepticism in her eyes is anything to go by, but she doesn't have to agree with me on this. She only has to accept it and help me move on in other areas of my life. She definitely already has.

Have my fears suddenly been vanquished, vaporised into the thin air?

Of course not.

However, I'm no longer as terrified of them as I was before I started coming here.

I can't wait to get home and see Daniel.
I'm ready for that kiss. To let him in.

CHAPTER THIRTY-TWO

EMMA

ON MY WAY HOME, butterflies flutter madly in my stomach and excitement fills me. I'm in equal parts nervous and anxious, but the one emotion overriding them is anticipation. I take out my phone to text Suzy; I should let her know what's about to happen because I promised her that. With a ridiculous smile on my lips, I jab the buttons:

Me: I think it's time to kiss Daniel... ;-) x

I hit send, and, just like I thought, my phone rings shortly after.

"Hello?" I answer and quickly remove the phone from my ear when a shrill shriek bursts from the other end.

"Oh my god! Oh my god!" Suzy yells, and I laugh loudly when I feel it's safe to put the phone back so that I can hear her properly without having my ears begin to bleed.

"This is huge, sweetie, so stop laughing at me!" she scolds me, laughing excitedly.

"I'm so nervous," I confess.

"Don't worry, you'll be fine. Wow, wow, wow," she

chants incessantly, and it causes me to giggle again.

"I'll text you later or tomorrow, honey," I reassure her.

"Oh dear, to be a fly on the wall," she mutters. "Listen, Em, just take a few deep breaths and then go enjoy yourself."

"Oh, I intend to," I tease her.

"Damn, this has got me all hot and bothered," she laughs.

"Suzy!" I snap affectionately.

"What?! I haven't indulged in any hanky panky for *weeks* now! I'm getting horny here!" She laughs, and I shake my head at her candidness.

"Well, then go out tonight, find a man or woman that'll help you with your urges."

"Oh, I will, you can count on it. But don't forget to text me! I want details!"

"I will. Any tips for me?" I ask her.

Surely, they can't hurt.

"Wet your lips, remember to swallow your spit, and, above all, *don't* stick your tongue down his throat: you'll make the poor guy gag," she advises me.

Great. Maybe I shouldn't have asked her.

"Got it," I reply, blowing out a long breath. "I'm almost home, so we'll talk later, darling."

"I'm so excited! Yay! Love you, bye!"

I press the red button to end our call and remain rooted to the spot outside the duplex where we live. I still feel nervous, but now that I've made up my mind and am less scared of the unknown than I was a mere month ago, I can't wait. I just hope that I won't panic or freak out when I kiss Daniel...

"No time like the present," I mutter to myself and finally open the front door and walk upstairs. I know that Daniel wanted me to text him when I was on my way, but a part of me wants to surprise him. I'm not going to throw myself at him the minute he opens the door, though; besides, something tells me that he'll want us to talk first.

Knocking on his door, I listen to the soft tunes of some sort of piano music sounding from behind it, and then wipe my sweaty palms on my skirt. My whole body is now tingling with anticipation, and I wait impatiently for him to let me in.

I don't have to wait for long.

The minute he stands before me, a strange calm settles over me, and I ask quietly, "May I come in?"

He nods once and takes a step back, his face unreadable for once. There's a strong set to his jaw, but his eyes remain blank, guarded even.

I hate that I hurt him.

I hate that I'm the cause of that.

I walk slowly past him and into his living room. It has become so much more habitable the last month; it feels like a home now instead of merely a place to crash at night. One whole wall is covered with black bookshelves, but one of them serves more as a place for his flat screen TV and DVD player; he doesn't have a dining room table, but the corner farthest to the left holds a few bar stools and a high table in the middle where he's able to sit and take in the view over the park below us. The walls are painted a warm brown colour, and a few watercolours hang in frames here and there; they aren't arranged as such, but I like that.

Turning around to face him, I find him remaining in the doorway to the hallway, keeping his distance, and I'm saddened by it. Usually, he's never far away from me, and suddenly I realise how much I've come to depend on his small acts of affection. The way he'll kiss my cheek or nose when he tells me goodbye in the morning... how his hand will brush my arm lightly when we watch a movie...and how his arms and legs surround me at night, holding me close to his body...as if he never wants to be away from me.

"Why are you standing so far way from me?" I ask him, clasping my hands behind my back.

He remains quiet for the longest time, perusing my face, and I wonder if he'll ever give me an answer. For once, I can't read him at all, and it only makes me more scared.

"Because if I come closer, I won't be able to keep my hands to myself," he finally mutters.

"Is that such a bad thing?"

"If you're about to break my heart into a million pieces, then yes; I have to keep my distance from you, Emma, or you'll completely wreck me once you tell me that we're...over." His voice breaks on the last word, and I flinch. It physically pains me to hear it.

"That's not why I'm here, honey," I retort and walk slowly closer to him, killing the distance one step at a time.

"No?" he asks me, and the hope and yearning in that one tiny word pierces through my heart.

I shake my head vehemently. "Absolutely not."

He swallows loudly, emotion clear for me to read. He doesn't believe me, and it *kills* me.

Have I lost him before I've even truly had him?

The thought is unbearable.

When I stand before him, as close to him as I can get without touching him, I try to tell him with my eyes how much he means to me. His intense gaze doesn't waver for a moment, and it gives me the courage to open myself up to him.

"I'm seeing a psychologist every Thursday." I place my hand above his heart, holding my breath, afraid of what he'll say to that admission.

He blinks, surprised, and I hurry to go on whilst I still can. "I don't think I'm ready to tell you exactly why yet, Daniel, but...please know that I'm alright. I'm...better, more whole than when you met me a month ago."

I pause and wrap my arms around his waist, tucking my head under his chin and take a fortifying breath.

"Please be patient with me, Daniel," I whisper, my lips quivering with suppressed emotions. "Maybe I'm asking too much of you, but I'm begging you...don't leave me."

Swiftly, his arms are around my shoulders, and he's holding on tightly. I don't care that I'm hardly able to breathe: having his touch on my skin once more is heaven.

I'm safe. Home. And I don't ever want to leave.

"God, Emma, I could *never* let you go," he whispers fiercely, releasing a long exhale. "I'll wait until you're ready. I *promise* you this: nothing you say could ever make me love you less."

A sob escapes me and Daniel begins to rock me gently in his arms. The music is still playing softly in the background, and I move slowly back from him, smiling wobbly.

"Please dance with me," I urge him and pull on his hand.

He laughs once, clearly confused. "What, now?"

I nod. "Yes. Now."

Tongue in cheek, he follows me further into the room, and once I have him right where I want him - next to the window to his balcony - I put my arms around his neck and move into his welcoming body. I love the way his hands immediately grip my hips. It seems possessive somehow. As if he's claiming me, even.

"Now," I whisper and move up on my toes to be closer to his lips. "Once this tune is over, I think I'm in need of some

TLC from my man."

He grins and nods. "That I can do."

"Good," I murmur, and we begin to move to the music in earnest. I can feel the way his heart beats madly in his chest as we sway to it, and now that the crisis of sorts is over, I feel nervous once more. I'm still dying for that kiss, but the question is if he wants it now, too?

Does he think I feel more time should pass?

Shite, I hope not!

I'll lose my mind if that's the case.

No longer feeling so relaxed as I did when we first started dancing, I stop abruptly, causing Daniel to stumble. The pain from his feet doesn't bother me, though.

I can handle physical pain.

I'm not so sure about the emotional one, though.

What should be my next move?

In the far recesses of my mind, I notice that the music has stopped playing, but I can't find the strength to unwrap my arms from around Daniel's neck. Being so close to him, looking into his beautiful eyes hiding behind his glasses just feels so...*right*. I can't explain it properly. My senses are not dulled by alcohol for once. My sight is not blurred...my nose is not tingling...my lips are not numb. This is the first time in a really long while that I have been completely sober when in the arms of a man, and I find that I don't mind it at all. But that's only because Daniel's the one holding me wrapped up tight in his arms.

He leans closer and, for a split second, I panic, because this is usually where I pull away; but at the very last moment, he moves so his cheek is resting against mine. The stubble on his chin is familiar...safe...and highly intoxicating.

"What are you doing to me, Em?" Daniel whispers in my

ear, his voice...sad?

"I...I don't know what you mean...," I breathe, my entire body pressed into his. Feeling his desire for me against my stomach causes a flutter in my belly.

"You know the power you have over me, sweetheart," he whispers, and hearing his endearment causes havoc in my entire being.

"Why can't you trust me with your secrets? I've touched and tasted almost every single inch of your body, and yet you still deny me your lips? " The frustration in his voice is palpable and it causes me to press my face into his neck, inhaling his scent deeply. *He smells so good.*

"I'm scared," I admit on a broken whisper, and it's true; I am. As much as I crave him with every fiber of my being, and as much as I want to kiss him right now, I'm petrified of how I'll react.

I don't wish to hurt him ever again.

His hands roam my back, trailing a whisper-soft touch down my spine until they land on my butt. When he squeezes the cheeks tightly, I can't hold back the low moan that breaks free from my mouth, but I don't even want to. For once, I want to be free of everything...my past...my future...but definitely not my present.

"What are you so frightened of?" he asks me and buries his head in my hair. Hearing him inhale deeply makes my skin break out in goosebumps.

"That you'll push me before I'm ready and I'll end up spilling all my sordid secrets to you...," I confess on a tremor that I have no doubt he can feel. My palms sweat. My core clenches. My heartbeat quickens. Everything inside me feels as if it is being awakened from a deep sleep, allowing me to truly *feel* everything for the first time.

He moves slowly away from me, but not so far that I can't feel his minty breath fanning across my lips. He hesitates for a few beats before growling, "I'm going to kiss you now, and don't you dare pull away and run away from me. We clear?"

Hearing the sudden demand in his voice, I simply nod, slightly surprised by the change in his manner, and I wet my lips. Agonisingly slow, as if he wants to savour this moment, he draws ever nearer until, finally, his lips brush against mine in a featherlike touch. As soon as I feel them on mine, my body erupts in a powerful flame, and the tingling from before intensifies. His lips brush mine once...twice...three times, lingering a bit longer each time. When he ends the last one by sucking my lip ring into his warm mouth, allowing my lips to taste more of his, I can't stand the gentleness any longer. Wrenching my arms free from around his neck, I stand up on my toes, and grab his face, needing to be kissed by this man so desperately. Finally, I slam my mouth onto his, close to combusting with longing for a taste.

Ho-ly...fuck!

Groaning, Daniel crushes me to his chest, angles his mouth to fit better to mine, and when I feel his warm tongue probing my lips, asking for permission to enter, I open my mouth on a deep sigh, allowing his tongue to find and tangle with mine. I'm not sure who first sighs in passionate relief, him or me, but all thoughts evaporate when he starts sucking on my tongue, and I'm burning up from within.

Then we become lost in each other and the pleasure, both giving and taking in equal measure. All that matters is our mouths, our tongues, our teeth, and we can't seem to get close enough. Nothing but this immeasurable heat touches us. We're in our own small bubble, drinking from one another, and I don't think I want to come up for air ever again.

Daniel moves one hand from my arse, across my hip, and quickly pulls up my top until he's touching me, skin to skin. His touch sears through me, making me tear my mouth from his on a gasp. Breathing heavily, he doesn't stop his sensual assault but merely trails open-mouthed kisses all the way from my chin to my ear and back again. He repeats this over and over before gently sucking on my ear-lobe, causing my knees to buckle, and I grab onto his arms to hold on for dear life. In a bold move, his right hand moves from across my waist to my navel and up my ribcage until his hands brushes the underside of my breasts. Feeling my nipples harden, I lift my right leg and wrap it around his hip, causing my pussy to rub against his cock straining against his jeans. Pressing into me on a deep growl, he kisses down my neck, and I tilt my head to the side, allowing him better access. My eyes feel so heavy that I have no other choice but to let them fall shut, fully immersing myself in the pleasure coursing through my entire being at this significant moment of my life.

My first kiss...Yep, there's fireworks, the angels are singing, and all that crap. Just like all the books say...

My senses are on overload. My pulse beats frantically. My pussy begs for release. Deep inside my head, I know I'm not ready to take this all the way - this is Daniel, after all, and not some random one-night-stand. I want this...whatever *this* is to be significant. To not be some quick shag only meant to satisfy a physical need for a few minutes.

With Daniel, I want...more. I want the fairytale...the happy-ever-after I have never, not once, believed in since I was ten years old...until now.

As soon as this realisation takes root, Daniel once again proves that he has this uncanny ability to read me and my moods at once, and he stops his roaming hands just beneath my breasts. His mouth becomes gentler, slower, and he merely traces his lips from my neck until they rest on mine once more. Ending the kiss the way he started it, he brushes his lips over mine three times until, at last, he kisses the tip of my nose and my forehead. Keeping my eyes closed, I revel in his touch, and the way he slowly lets his hands caress my skin from my ribcage to my hip, allowing his thumbs to linger, almost makes me forget myself and the fact that I don't want to rush into anything with him. Yet...I have to. For both our sakes.

Forcing my eyes to open, I look straight into his. The burning I find in them makes my hardened heart melt a little more. "That was one hell of a first kiss," I croak out, and Daniel chuckles smugly. *Men!*

His smirk disappears quickly, though, and wrapping his arms loosely around my waist, making me place mine on his biceps, he scrutinizes my features for a while, not speaking, and it makes me more and more nervous. *Oh dear...what if I'm a terrible kisser?!*

When I can't stand the silence any longer, I ask, "What is it?"

"Thank you," he simply says.

Puzzled, I frown. "For what?"

"For letting me be your first kiss even when it's clear I didn't know what to do," he replies, and the most adorable blush spreads on his cheeks. *Is he nervous?!*

"I love that you were my first kiss," I tell him quietly, and it's the truth. I can't imagine anyone else I would ever trust enough to kiss me. The smile that lights up his face just now by hearing my words is priceless...and one I'll tuck away for later when I'm alone.

Sighing in a way I can only describe as in male

satisfaction, he admits, "That kiss was beyond my wildest dreams, Emma. And..." Tongue in cheek, he grins. "I wouldn't mind if you stayed here so that I could spend hours on end kissing every inch of your gorgeous body, *but*...Well, perhaps it's not the best idea. I have a feeling I wouldn't be able to hold back from sinking my cock inside you anymore..." Sobering, he adds quietly, "I don't think either of us is quite ready for that yet, anyway."

How is it possible that this guy knows how to read me so well?

"Don't you believe I'm able to keep myself in check? I mean, I've managed to resist you for some time now," I tease him.

"True, very true...I have to confess that I love waking up beside you, Em...that way, you can't escape me."

Fiddling with one of the buttons on his shirt, I admit shyly, "I don't want to escape you tonight..."

Daniel leans down and whispers, "I don't want that, either, sweetheart...But are you sure?"

As always, hearing this particular endearment for me falling from his lips sends a thrill through me, and I place my arms around his neck, silently giving him my answer. I am completely unable to keep my distance from him more than a few moments at a time.

He straightens a bit, the smirk firmly back in place. "I'd definitely not mind to practice some more," he says, and I roll my eyes for good measure. Secretly, though, my heart soars at hearing those words leaving his mouth.

"Practice makes perfect," I muse and grin a bit cheekily at him. The soreness in my lips feels...heavenly. He stays silent for a heartbeat but then barks out a laugh, pulling me closer, and wrapping his arms around me, he answers, "I think I need lots and lots of practice..."

"Oh yes, most definitely," I concur, and, sighing happily, I become lost in his embrace once more. I don't know how much time passes this time but once we come up for air again, Daniel takes my hand and leads me to his kitchen.

"Come on," he says. "Time for your first cooking lesson."

I groan, slowing down my steps. "Must I?"

Grinning at me, he nods. "If you want to keep taking advantage of me, then yes."

I gasp mockingly. "Well, when you put it that way..." I can't resist pinching his butt and he yelps, causing me to laugh. His eyes remain warm and tender on mine, and he almost trips over his feet from not watching where he's going.

So adorable.

For the first time in years, I'm happy. And I intend to keep it that way.

CHAPTER THIRTY-THREE

EMMA

COOKING WITH DANIEL IS an experience. Well, more like a mess. Apparently, he wanted to show me how to make real, Danish meatballs - *frikadeller* - but he kept distracting me with kisses and other...err, actions (*lord, that boy and his magical fingers*) that I must have miscalculated the flour or something else from the recipe, because the end result wasn't exactly edible. What should have been small, round and spicy meatballs ended up becoming one giant meat pancake of sorts: it took up the entire pan and looked rather disgusting.

After Daniel deemed that I'm no cook - a fact I've warned him about for weeks now - we decided to ring for a pizza instead, so I made a salad with fresh lettuce, peppers, tomatoes, cucumbers and salted cashews, to be served with a apple vinegar/olive oil and crushed basil dressing. At least I can be trusted in a kitchen when it comes to side dishes - it's the main course I have trouble with. I just don't have a knack for it. Daniel watched the news until our pizzas arrived.

Like me, Daniel doesn't have room for a proper dining table or chairs so we eat on his unmade bed, trying not to make a mess of things. I kind of wondered if things might be a bit strange between us now that we've kissed, but I needn't have worried. They are just the same as always - apart from the fact that Daniel leans over to peck my lips as often as he can, of course, leaving them tingling and hungry for more each time. Some people would perhaps scoff at the fact that I feel so comfortable with him, but not me. There are plenty of sparks between us just like always, clearly evidenced by the bulge in Daniel's shorts.

Let's be honest here: a monster cock standing at attention the way his does can't be hidden away. Nor would I want it to, at least not when we are alone like we are right now.

Licking some pizza sauce from my thumb, I glance at Daniel. "May I ask you something?"

He leans back and looks briefly at me before scooping up some salad and waves with his fork. "There's nothing you can't ask me about, Em."

Hesitating, I take a sip of my Coke Zero. "Okay, thanks. How do your sisters cope with your mum and her illness? I mean, do they visit her sometimes like you did a few weeks back?"

Daniel gives me a small smile and rubs his neck. He looks a bit uncomfortable, actually.

"Well...they have thicker skin than I do," he answers cryptically.

I frown. "Please elaborate. You can't say something like that and not explain it further."

Nodding, he sneaks a peek at me, his eyes now apologetic. "I suppose you're right. It just makes me a bit...well, embarrassed." He wipes his mouth with a napkin before he sets his now empty plate on his nightstand. Leaning back against the headboard, he wraps an arm around my shoulder, and we lay back, snuggling. Placing my right hand above his heart, I wait for him to open himself up to me again.

"Okay, my sisters don't speak with my mum at all," he starts and then sighs a little, the sound sad but accepting nonetheless. "After our dad left, we all helped out at home - you already know this - but the minute my oldest sister, Maria, turned 19, she left to travel to Australia and never looked back. The same thing happened with Annette, Karina, and Laura: as soon as they had finished school, they were out of there, as quick as a lightning bolt."

Daniel pauses and looks at me. "I don't blame them for leaving, you know. They wanted better lives, and at some point, they realised that if they remained at home, they'd never get the opportunity to meet their goals and dreams. I had to respect that, and I still do."

I cuddle closer to him, playing footsie with him, and reply quietly, "I understand. Well, a part of me does. But why did you stay there for so long?"

He turns his eyes to the ceiling, thinking. "For a long time, I never stopped hoping that she'd finally pull herself together and seek professional help. She kept promising that she would, and I wanted so desperately to believe in her. But...eventually, I lost hope, too. I dropped out of school - I wasn't there much anyway - and then I ran away from home."

"What?" I sit up and stare at him. "You ran away? Where did you go?"

"I roamed the streets in our city, became a homeless amongst many," Daniel explains, still not meeting my eyes.

"Oh, Daniel," I whisper, my heart hurting for him. "How old were you?"

"The first time, I was 15. My mum did ring the police, made them look for me, but I ran away again after they brought me back. This time, they didn't catch me until I had been gone for six months."

"But...how did you survive?"

He shrugs. "I begged on the streets. Stole from the shops. You'd be surprised how often the people who run shelters for the homeless don't ask you any questions," he adds drily. "My mum gave me quite a beating for that, but..."

I interrupt him, "She *beat* you?! That's despicable!"

He rubs my arm soothingly, but I shake it off and stand up to pace around in his flat.

Holy fuck! If I ever get to see that woman, I'm going to slap her!

"Emma," Daniel calls from his bed, but I wave a hand at him.

"That's...it's just...I mean, how *could* she?!" I stutter, wiping a hand across my forehead. "*She's* the one who deserves the beating for being such a sorry excuse for a mother."

"Em, please stop, you're making me dizzy with all your pacing back and forth," Daniel chuckles from the bed, but hearing the amusement only makes me glare at him.

"Excuse me, but there is nothing remotely *funny* about this, Daniel," I scold him.

So quickly that I don't even realise how he's doing it, he grabs my arm and pulls, and I find myself lying on the bed again, his body covering mine.

"Will you please listen?" he pleads with me, and the tone of his voice finally grabs my attention, causing me to set aside my murderous thoughts and concentrate on him.

I huff. "I'm sorry, Daniel, but I really, *truly* don't think I'll like your mother."

He smiles gently at me, his thumb brushing my cheek. "I don't like her much, either, but that's beside the point. Now...will you let me finish this as quickly as possible so that I can start kissing you again?"

"Oh, okay," I grumble, my hands rubbing up and down his back. "You may continue."

"Why, thank you, my lady," he responds cheekily. "Right. I'll spare you the details of the severity of her disciplining me," he continues, but I draw in a breath.

I don't like the sound of that.

"Suffice it to say that I woke up in the hospital and found Andreas sitting beside me. After he'd given me some water to drink, he sat down, gave me a long look, and then said, *"I'm taking you away from Karla if you promise me to finish school and work towards a proper future. Are we clear?"*

Daniel seems so far away, lost in his memories, and I wrap my legs around his, silently showing him my support until his gaze becomes focused on my own again. The hurt and vulnerability that meet me is staggering.

"I didn't have to think twice about that. I accepted his offer, and as soon as I was fit to leave the hospital, I was sent off to boarding school."

"*Boarding school?!*" I shriek.

Daniel frowns at me. "Is this how our future will be like? You interrupting me all the time when I have something important to say?"

Oopsie.

Smiling at him, I roll my eyes, but pretend to zip my mouth closed, tossing the key away, all the while Daniel looks at me with an amused grin on his face.

"Okay then. You have to understand that boarding

school was the best thing that ever happened to me, Em," Daniel says and kisses my cheek. "It's not all bad, and definitely not the way Hollywood depicts that kind of life in movies. Well, I can't speak for all, of course, but Danish boarding schools are probably a lot different from others."

Raising my hand, I wait for him to grant me permission to speak.

"But why couldn't you just have lived with him here, in Copenhagen?" I ask him.

He shrugs. "The Professor likes and needs his own space, sweetheart. Besides, I needed so much help - what with my dyslexia and speech impairment - and he didn't have the knowledge, or the time, to do that."

"I see." And I do, I get it. Still...I wonder if Daniel was ever lonely while he was away.

"I went home every holiday, of course, and even went to see my mum a few times, but...well, that is a lost cause, I guess."

"Why would you even want to keep seeing her, honey?" I ask him, threading my fingers through his hair. "She doesn't deserve your kindness."

He shrugs. "I know that. But just because you want to stop loving someone doesn't mean you can," he replies and grits his teeth. "Trust me, I have tried, but..." He stops and inhales deeply before he lowers his head until our mouths are perfectly aligned.

"Now," he murmurs and carefully removes his glasses, "can we start practicing kissing some more?"

My mind is swirling with hundreds more questions, but I don't want to ruin our night by bringing up more painful memories. Besides, I can sense that he isn't up for talking anymore, and I have to respect that. I nod and lick my lips, catching his in the process. I watch in fascination, my lips tingling, as his green eyes grow more heated.

"By all means," I reply, voice husky. I push my crotch closer to his, and he gasps. I revel in the power I have over him and close the distance between us.

There's plenty of time for more talking...but now? Now I want to feel his need for me. It's like a drug to me, but this is a habit I have no wish to ever break free from.

DANIEL

I watch Emma sleeping peacefully in my bed, sated from our unbelievably hot make-out session, and maybe it's a bit creepy, but I can't stop. I'm overjoyed, yet anxious, and, to tell the truth, quite turned on. I love that she never puts on PJs and feels comfortable sleeping in the nude with me because it shows that, in some way, she does trust me.

Will she trust me with her heart?

Telling her the last bits of my past was difficult for me to do, but I didn't want to keep her in the dark anymore. If I expect her to confide in me, I can't very well hold myself back, now can I? So I didn't. And while I feel better for it, I just can't fall asleep again.

Careful so as not to wake her, I remove my arms from her sleeping form and go to the bathroom. I take a good, long look at my face while my mind runs amok with thoughts I have difficulty putting into proper words.

What's wrong with me? I have the girl of my dreams lying in my bed, and even though she hasn't said so in that many words, she *must* feel the same way about me, right?

Those three little words - *I love you* - shouldn't be that important for me to hear.

And yet...they are.

I need to hear them fall from her lips...Otherwise, I won't know that she truly belongs to me and no one else, but I'll wait a bit longer.

The last thing I want is to scare her off.

I can't help but wonder if she'll finally relent and tell me everything before our meeting with her brother, Steven, in a few weeks?

Or will she prefer to keep me in the dark?

Rubbing my eyes, I sigh, but then my body locks in place when I smell her perfume. Soon after, her arms are wrapped tightly around me, and her warm, inviting body is pressed flushed to my back.

"Come back to bed," she whispers, sleep clear in her voice, and I smile a little and rest a hand on top of hers.

"I will, sweetheart. Did a bad dream wake you up?" I ask her.

She places a lingering kiss on my spine, and it sends shock waves throughout my body.

"No...not feeling you behind me did," she whispers, her hot mouth now moving further down, and I groan loudly and let my head fall back as I take in the warmth her pleasure gives me.

"Damn, Em...," I growl when her hands close around my cock that's now become fully erect.

Her throaty chuckle comes close to unmanning me completely.

"Hungry for more?" she asks me and pushes her tits closer to my back.

"For you, I'm always famished for more," I admit.

Her strokes on my cock speed up a bit, and she pants out, "Then why don't you do something about that?"

Yes...why don't I?

I turn around in her arms and place my hands on her cheeks, taking in her desire for me burning in her eyes, before I slam my mouth on hers. She opens up for me on a gasp, clearly inviting me to take imminent control, and my tongue quickly sweeps in to find hers.

I'm drowning in her warmth, her desire. But I need more. So much more.

Wrenching my mouth free, I bend down, take a firm hold on the back of her knees and heft her up until she's hanging upside down my back as I carry her to my bed.

"Daniel!" she squeals and smacks my arse. "Put me down!"

"Quiet," I order her and then bite her left arse cheek in warning. When she gasps and squeals again, I slap it gently, but firmly, and when she can't keep a moan from her lips, I quirk an eyebrow even though she can't see me.

Interesting.

I toss her on my bed and watch her bounce up and down once, surprise coupled with heat written as clear as glass all over her face.

"That wasn't nice," she snaps, but there's no real heat behind her words. Her eyes reveal the true nature of her feelings.

I stroke my cock slowly, licking my lips as I watch her take me in, her hand creeping up her rounded belly and closer to her tit.

Fuck...

Finally finding the ability to speak, I growl, "Maybe not. But I don't want to be nice tonight, Em."

Her breath hitches and she rubs her thighs together. "Then...what do you want, Daniel?" she asks me, and I take a step closer to the bed, my eyes never leaving hers. I can tell that she's as hungry for me as I am for her, and tonight, I won't hold my desires back.

"I want to kiss you so hard our lips will be sore, painful even, while my fingers play with your pussy until you beg me to fuck you. But I won't. No, instead, I'll go down on you and lick you out until you come all over my face, your voice hoarse from screaming my name. And then I want to fuck your arse with my fingers and lick your pussy again while you suck off my cock. How does that sound, Emma?" Tilting my head to the side, I grab a firm hold on my balls, waiting for her answer.

It's not exactly a question I don't already know the answer to because her actions speak louder than words right now. She's sitting on her knees, one arm stretched out to me while the fingers of her right hand plays with her clit, and I don't think I'm able to hold myself in check for much longer.

"Well then...," she breathes. "I like the sound of that. Why are you still standing there?"

In a flash, I'm on top of her, kissing her senseless, not holding back at all.

I keep my promise. Before I'm done with her, her voice is hoarse from me bringing her - and myself - to the brink of ecstasy and beyond.

CHAPTER THIRTY-FOUR

EMMA

"I CAN'T MOVE MY legs," I tell Suzy when she opens her front door to let me in. "Whoa! What the hell happened to your hair?!" I blurt out, astonished that all her golden locks have disappeared since I last saw her, leaving her with a cute, but so different pixie cut.

She bursts out in laughter and hugs me. "Well, hello to you, too, sweetie. You like?" she asks me while casually threading a hand through it. "I needed a change. Now, sounds like you've got lots to talk about. Do come in and tell me all about it."

"I love it. It's very chic."

I do as she says, almost dragging my feet until I finally collapse on her couch, arms and legs dropped to my sides, and I blow out a deep breath.

Gosh, I'm so exhausted.

Suzy jumps down beside me, still highly amused, and rubs her hands together in glee.

"Honestly, that boy...well, man, I should say," I correct

myself, staring off in space.

"Did you two *finally* stop fooling around and have sex?" she asks me and takes my hand. "Come on, don't hold back from me, Em. I need to live vicariously through you."

I turn my head and frown. "Didn't you go out last night?" I ask her, confused when I see her sad face.

She huffs. "Uh, yes, but...well, no one caught my fancy so I went home alone. A-freaking-gain."

"I'm sorry, honey," I tell her gently.

She waves it off and pastes a smile on her face. "Enough about that. Now, *please* tell me why you look and sound as if you've run a marathon."

I snort.

That'll be the day.

"Okay. No, we didn't have sex..."

"Shoot," she mutters and falls back dejectedly.

"*But*," I go on, and a giggle erupts from me when I see her face light up, a bright and genuine smile on her lips. "We did so much more..."

Recounting the way Daniel completely took control last night and how he made me experience the kind of pleasure I have, despite my hook-ups, only ever read about in romance novels, I can't keep the blush from spreading across my entire body.

Once I've finished giving Suzy almost all the details, I watch in fascination as she repeatedly opens and closes her mouth, speechless for once.

"Holy...crap!" she shouts at last. "Where do I find a guy like him?"

"On the train, apparently," I answer drily, but soon after, we're both cackling away like madwomen.

I wipe away a few stray tears and try to pull myself

together.

"Oh...One other thing...," I muse, deliberately drawing my other news out. Suzy looks at the split-eating smile I can't keep hidden, and sobers immediately.

"What is it?" she whispers and leans closer towards me, her eyes as big as saucers.

"Daniel told me he loves me," I reveal, and she squeals excitedly before hugging me tightly.

"Oh, wow...I'm so happy for you," she whispers, but then pulls away from me, a worried crease between her eyes. "Wait, this is a good thing, right?"

I nod, still grinning like a fool. "Yep, a very good thing."

"Phew!" she lets out, and dramatically wipes imaginary sweat from her forehead. "For a minute there, you had me worried, you know." She winks at me and I toss one of her throw pillows at her.

"Come on, Suzy, stop worrying about me."

"So," she persists, "you are *truly* happy?"

"Yeeeess," I repeat slowly. A thought niggles at me, and the urge to confide in her about my past overwhelms me.

"I never thought...," I start, but then hesitation strikes as usual, and I look down at my clasped hands. I'm tense all over, terrified that she'll reject me, but she deserves to know.

"What, lovely?" she asks me and rubs my shoulder soothingly.

I take a couple of deep breaths before revealing my past hurts to her a bit more. "I never thought that I'd like...Wait, that's the wrong word for it...Never once did I believe that I'd want to expose myself like that - you know, indulge in back-door play?" I sneak a peek at her, and seeing her look at me with such tenderness gives me the courage to keep pushing on. "Yet to experience that kind of intense, all-consuming pleasure with Daniel last night was..." I pause and fan my face. "It was *mind* blowing, Suzy. Out of this world!" I move in my seat so that we are now facing each other on her couch and move closer towards her, wanting to explain further. "Usually, whenever a guy tried to go down that route with me, I'd freeze up before hurrying the fuck out the door."

"Why?" she asks me gently. "I mean, it's not for everyone, but doing it with someone you trust with all your heart matters, of course."

"Well..." I look down at my lap, wetting my lips and take a few fortifying breaths once more. "The thought has been a sickening one to me because of what happened when I was...when I was ten years old. I was hurt deeply by someone I trusted, and...what he did to me has been haunting me ever since."

Suzy gasps loudly, the sound reverberating throughout her flat. I don't have to look into her eyes to know that she immediately understands what I am unable to put into words, and although there's a hint of nausea by the memories that always follow me when I think of *him*, it isn't as all-consuming as usual.

Suzy tightens her grip on my hand, and I finally venture to gaze into her tear-filled eyes. The pity I dreaded seeing there is nonexistent and I take heart from this fact, because it means that she doesn't find me weak, and I love her for it.

"I'm so...so sorry, Em," she sniffles, and I squeeze her hand, silently thanking her while a lump forms in my throat.

"You don't have to tell me anything more if you don't want to," she says and wipes her eyes. "I mean, I understand if you'd rather not."

Clearing my throat, I croak, "Thank you. One day, I will...but..."

She waves my hesitation away and smiles wobbly at me. "I know. But I'm here for you, you know that, right?" Her eyes are now clear of tears, and there's a fierceness to them I have not encountered before.

"I do," I smile at her, thankful to have her in my life.

"Good." She nods once and leans back in her seat. "Well, I don't know about you, but I could use a glass of wine."

Her statement surprises me, but then I laugh loudly, and Suzy follows after soon after. My laughter is filled with relief, love, and...yes, happiness. I'm on cloud *frigging* nine, and it's all because of Suzy and her acceptance of me.

Oh, yes, Daniel may have a thing or two to do with it as well.

Maybe I'm not as broken as I was a mere month ago.

"Frascati good with you?" Suzy asks me and leaves her seat beside me.

"But..." I glance at her clock. "Suzy, it's not even noon yet!" I protest, but it sounds kind of feeble...and moot, seeing as Suzy has already pulled out the corkscrew from one of her drawers.

"Oh, nonsense!" she says loudly, and the sound of the cork popping a cheerful sound makes me shake my head.

"This is a day to celebrate," she clarifies as she reaches for two glasses from the cupboard hanging above her stove. "It won't hurt to bend the rules a bit today, Em."

"I love you," I tell her.

She blows a kiss at me. "I love you right back," she answers and starts to pour the golden liquid into our glasses.

I smile at her briefly before turning to watch the sun filtering through her curtains paint the floor in hues of yellow and gold. Now that I have let Suzy in, I feel stronger than I thought I would...

It's time to tell Daniel about my past so that we can move forward.

In more ways than one.

♡

The minute I leave Suzy's, my phone rings. I can't keep the goofy smile off my face when I see it's Daniel ringing me.

"Hi, handsome," I greet him.

"Hi, gorgeous. Listen, I just received a phone call from the Cardiology Department at the Rigshospital. Andreas has been admitted there, but they didn't tell me why."

My good mood plummets immediately. "Oh, no. Are you on your way there now?" I ask him and pick up speed.

"Yes, can you meet me there, please?" It's impossible to miss the concern in his voice.

"Of course," I hurry to tell him. "I'll take a taxi and should be there in ten minutes or so."

"Thank you," he breathes out.

"Daniel, I'm your girlfriend, *and* he's my boss. Of course I want to see him," I tell him gently and cross the street to walk to a spot where there are usually a lot of taxis passing through.

"Still, I'm grateful. Okay, I'll see you soon, sweetheart," he says and ends the call.

Raising my arm, I try to catch the eye of a cabbie, and it doesn't take long before one pulls over. I open the door and quickly give him the address, and as he drives off, I pray that nothing horrible has happened.

CHAPTER THIRTY-FIVE

DANIEL

I'M PACING IN FRONT of the main desk at the hospital as I wait for a nurse to take me to see my uncle. Emma arrived at few minutes ago, and her support comforts me. She hasn't said much, but worry is etched on her face, and I pray that we will be able to get some answers soon.

Since Andreas has no other living relatives, apart from my mum, the staff didn't seem to have any problems releasing his information, but I wish like fuck they'd hurry up and take us to him!

I fall down on a chair next to Emma, and she grabs my hand immediately, intertwining our fingers.

Rubbing my arm, she says, "I'm sure the nurse will be back soon."

I look at her briefly and rub the stubble on my chin. "Yeah, you're probably right. But couldn't she have told us *something* at least before leaving us here?" Tension mixed with dread coils in the pit of my stomach, but Emma placing her hand on my cheek eases it a bit, and I smile faintly.

"He'll be okay, Daniel." She stares fiercely into my eyes, and I take heart at seeing the confidence there.

I open my mouth to respond but hearing my name called from behind us stops me, and I jump out of my chair and walk to the blonde walking towards me.

Wait a minute...That's not a nurse.

The woman is quite clearly a doctor, and I ask sharply, "What's wrong with my uncle?" Absentmindedly, I feel Emma rise from her seat to stand close beside me.

"Mr. Larsen, my name is Dr. Alice Christensen. Please allow me to provide you with some facts before I take you to him."

I cross my arms and narrow my eyes at her, waiting impatiently for her to get a move on.

"Your uncle appears to have suffered a massive heart attack. Some of the customers from his bookshop dialled 1-1-2 when he suddenly collapsed, and, luckily, one of them knew how to perform CPR. He was brought here swiftly, and while he is still very weak, he is stable for now."

Fuck.

"Okay, thank you. Can we see him now, please?" I ask her, and she gives me a small smile.

"I'll take you to him. He's understandably very weak but lucid. He needs rest so it'll have to be a short visit for now." She turns, and I glance quickly at Emma who seems to be close to tears, so I put an arm around her shoulder and we follow the doctor to Andreas' room.

When we reach the private room he's in, the doctor says, "Please go in and sit with him. But remember what I said: you can't stay long as he needs to rest." With that, she leaves us alone.

A pang hits me in my chest as I take in his sleeping form.

He's always been a bit on the skinny side, physically that is, but seeing him lying there, covered with wires, and what I can only guess is a heart monitor, he seems frail, vulnerable...older beyond his years. This is bad. I don't care what the doctor says, but this is not good.

Emma places a hand to my abs, half turning in my arms, and I realise that I have yet to move closer to him. I swallow the lump in my throat, reluctant to leave the safety of the threshold where I have easy access to the exit, yet I allow her to nudge me further inside until we're standing close together next to his bed.

This is the last place on earth I want to be right now, but I have no real choice: this man is my family, and I owe him so much for getting me to the point where I am today.

"The hardest choices in life are usually the right ones - only cowards choose the easy way out."

He told me that once, but here I am years later, hesitating to touch him even when I ought to know that he would want that.

Shit, I really am a chicken, aren't I? Well, that ends today.

I release my hold on Emma, and she takes a deep breath as I sit down on the incredibly ugly and uncomfortable plastic chair placed next to the hospital bed.

"Don't go," I whisper and turn my head slightly in her direction, but my eyes remain on the almost lifeless body lying before us. I can't tear my eyes away.

She wraps her arms around me and kisses me on my neck before she whispers, "I won't, I promise. But do you want a coffee or anything?"

"No, thank you. I just..." my voice breaks with suppressed emotion, and I wipe my damp eyes on my T-shirt. Clearing my throat, I try to continue without breaking down completely. "I just need you, sweetheart."

"You have me, honey. Always." She gives me a lingering hug, and I pull strength from her.

My girl...the one who once called me a white knight? Even though it was only said in jest, I have believed myself to be one. But *she* is the stronger of the two of us.

At the end of the day, *she* is the one person I will be able to lean on when I feel the world crashing down on me the way it is at this very moment.

I am never letting her go, and I hope and pray that she won't ever want me to.

Andreas begins to stir, and I put my hand on his, gripping it tightly.

"Prof? It's me, Daniel. We're here...Emma's here, too. Can you hear me?" Leaning a bit closer, I watch as his eyelids flutter, and it feels as if it takes an eternity before he opens them and turns his head slowly. Blinking, he coughs, and the wheeze snaps my heart in two like a twig that's being trod on.

"What...? What happened?" he asks me, voice weak and tired. I don't have any words right now. I'm afraid I'll start crying soon if I open my mouth to answer him, and I shake my head, unable to answer him.

"The doctor told us that you had a heart attack while at the shop, Mr. Andersen," Emma says quietly and comes to my rescue. She steps out from behind me and sits carefully down on the bed.

She puts a hand on top of mine, linking the three of us together, and I stare into her eyes, hoping that she can see how grateful I am for her presence.

"Aaah, I was afraid something like this would happen," Andreas sighs.

My head snap back so that I can watch him more closely.

"What do you mean?" I ask him. Gone are the tears threatening to spill from my eyes. A nagging suspicion begins to take root instead. "Uncle? What aren't you telling me?"

He lifts his other arm, trying to place it above our grip, but the movement is clearly too much for him, because it falls limply to his side, and he grunts.

He ignores my question and grumbles, "Well, this...this has definitely put a damper on my...my plans for the future."

I narrow my eyes at him, but before I can ask him any more questions, Emma butts in, "That's hardly important now, Mr. Andersen. Forget about your plans and please concentrate on getting well again, okay?"

She gives me a warning look, and I bite my tongue.

"I'm sorry, Prof. Emma's right, all that can wait until later."

Feeling his hand tighten on my own, he spits out, "No! It can't! Emma..." He turns to her, eyes pleading, and gasps, "Emma...You need to know this before...before it's too late."

Alarmed about the state he's getting himself into, I press the alarm button by the headboard of his bed to ring for a nurse while trying to calm him down and Emma stands from her seat and walks to the other side. Andreas' eyes follow her, though, and seeing the tears dripping on her cheeks breaks my heart into tiny fragments. It hurts to watch her torment.

"Please, Uncle, please calm down," I beg him and stand up quickly before I lean down so he can see the desperation I am feeling in my eyes.

"But, Daniel...," he protests feebly, and I know why he is panicking; I remember his plans about handing over the bookshop, his pride and joy, to Emma. It seems so long ago since he was standing in my kitchen, being all cryptic about it, when, in fact, it has only been a few short weeks.

"I know, Prof, I know," I whisper back. It seems that I'm finally breaking through to him, because he closes his eyes and lets out a defeated sigh.

"Just don't...don't forget, Daniel. Promise me?"

"I promise."

Emma is standing in the doorway, no doubt waiting for the nurse to come and help us, when Andreas calls out to her.

"Emma, dear?"

"I'm here, Andreas," she answers and scurries back to his side.

The last thing I thought I'd ever hear right now is my uncle's attempt to laugh, and yet, here we are, witnesses as he chuckles weakly.

"Did it really have to take...to take a heart attack before you started calling me by my name, Emma?" he breathes.

For a beat, he's greeted by silence, but Emma recovers quickly as usual.

"Well..." She looks down and takes his hand again before meeting his gaze, eyes shy all of a sudden. "I guess we're close to family now so I think it's time I dropped the formalities, don't you?"

My cheeks hurt from the wide smile I beam at her, proud as hell, and she blushes when she catches it.

Andreas nods slowly. "Indeed we are, my dear."

Finally, a nurse walks briskly into the room, and I try to cover my relieved sigh by coughing. I'm not really listening as Emma begins to explain why we rang for her...I'm too lost in my own misery to take in what the nurse says to her while she examines Andreas further.

I'm exhausted, and, for the first time in my life, scared as hell that one of the closest people in my life is going to die before it's his time.

CHAPTER THIRTY-SIX

EMMA

WE TOOK A TAXI home when the nurse practically ordered us to leave Andreas to rest, but I know we'll return tomorrow. Daniel didn't say a word at all, and I understand his silence; he was clearly in shock about the state of his uncle, and so was I.

I'm drained, emotionally spent, and I suppose it's no wonder, really, due to the events of the past 24 hours. Once we reach our home, Daniel remains silent and pays the driver, and we walk hand in hand upstairs. In silent agreement, I follow him inside his flat and quickly kick off my ballerinas and remove the hair tie holding in my wild curls.

I blow out a breath and wrap my arms around Daniel. His arms surround me and he presses his cheek against my hair, inhaling deeply.

"What a day," I sigh, nuzzling closer to him, and I love the way he squeezes me briefly.

Answering me on a yawn, he nods, and I take a step back to take him in.

"Are you hungry? I could order us a pizza or something else?" I ask him.

He smiles, every feature on his face exhausted, clear for me to see.

"No, thank you," he shakes his head. "To be honest, I just want to go to bed and hold you in my arms. Is that okay?"

I nod and kiss him quickly.

"Of course. I'll just get ready for bed, okay?"

"Sounds good," he replies and rubs his neck, a thoughtful expression in his eyes.

"What is it?" I frown, a bit concerned.

"Just wondering what we're going to do with the shop while Andreas recovers," he murmurs and lets his arm fall. "But let's worry about the details tomorrow, sweetheart. A good night's rest will probably help clear my head."

I nod and kiss him again. This time, though, I linger, the tip of our tongues meeting briefly, before I unwrap myself from his embrace and leave him to do my nightly routine.

Once I've removed all my makeup, I take a good, long look at my face now that it's free of its mask.

I know that Daniel doesn't really care for all the black, and he hasn't mentioned it in weeks now, but that hasn't stopped me from wondering if he still hates it. To be perfectly honest, I can't remember why I wear such heavy eyeshade anymore.

Perhaps it's just become a habit of sorts?

Or have I unconsciously seen it as my armour when out in public?

Either way, maybe it's time I start experimenting with a different kind of colour palette. I'll ask Suzy to teach me a few new tricks.

But there's a time and place for everything, and, right

now, my place is next to Daniel.

I hurry to brush my teeth - yes, I keep a toothbrush here - and then leave the bathroom.

I find Daniel lying in bed already, arms behind his head as he seems lost in thought once more. I leave him to it and quickly strip until I'm naked and then remove the blanket to crawl in. He breaks free from whatever it is that keeps the wheels turning in his head, and while his gaze is heated as always, the crease lines around his mouth are evidence of his tiredness.

I kiss the tip of his nose and say, "He'll be okay, honey."

"I hope so," he answers quietly and swallows loudly. There are shadows of fear in his eyes, and my heart hurts for him. I want to take away his pain more than anything else.

I caress his cheek with my thumb and whisper, "Rest, honey. We'll work through everything in the morning."

He nods and I turn my back on him so we're in our usual sleeping position: spooning. My favourite.

Shortly after, I can feel his hand brush away my hair, followed by his lips. He kisses the ten stars tattooed on my neck, causing my body to erupt in goose bumps as usual, and I sigh and kiss his hand before placing it above my heart.

"Goodnight, sweetheart," Daniel murmurs sleepily from behind me.

"Night, darling."

I doubt it takes even a full minute before we've both drifted off to sleep.

♡

The weekend passes in a blur, and although Daniel and I still spend our days together, between visits to the hospital and managing the shop, it feels as if we've hardly spoken more than a few words to each other. And don't even get me started on the lack of intimacy between us...it's at standstill, on an indefinite hold. To be honest, I'm not entirely sure why he's distancing himself from me, but I don't know how to approach him about it. I'm just as concerned about Andreas' health as he is, of course, and I do understand the worry and turmoil Daniel must be going through - I know how close they are - but...well.

I miss him.

Moreover, I'm getting more and more nervous about us meeting my brother. My feelings towards Steven have not changed the past month, but much of my years-long anger has faded.

His betrayal still hurts like a bitch, though, and I'm not sure I'll ever be able to forgive him for not believing in me.

For not protecting me once he learned the truth about Tom.

Will I ever be able to look my brother in the eye without the past coming back to spit in my face?

I hope so...If not for my own sake, at least for our parents'. The rift between us has probably hurt them more than I am able to comprehend, and I pray to the higher beings above that my future children will have a much better relationship with each other.

Wait, hang on...my children?

I'm sitting at *Goat and Cow's Tattoo Parlour* right now, scribbling down my thoughts in my ever-present journal when that last one causes me to stop.

Since when have I ever wanted children?

The answer is right there before me: since I met Daniel, and a slow smile creeps across my lips.

Well, then. I've come a long way since he literally stumbled into my life.

"Emma Davenport?" a female voice shouts from the desk, breaking me free from my inner musings, and I stand up.

"Yes?" I answer and approach the gorgeous brunette who called out to me.

"Kristian is in the back, ready for you," she tells me, and I turn my head in the direction she points before smiling at her.

"Thanks."

"You're welcome." She leans conspiratorially towards me. "I can't wait to see your tat."

I laugh and walk away, almost skipping, and the familiar excitement about *finally* taking the first steps to having the dream catcher tattoo inked permanently on my skin thrills through me.

I may not suffer from the nightmare each night like before, but I still want the reminder on my skin. But it also serves another purpose than taking my bad dreams away from me - every time I look at it, I will be reminded of the importance of chasing my dreams in the future.

Because now? Now I have the courage to follow them, make them come true.

When I see *who* the tattoo artist is, though, I stop dead in my tracks.

Shite...Of all the places in Copenhagen...

I clear my throat and knock on the doorframe, and he turns around. Once he sees me, his face lights up in a shit-eating grin.

"Emma, hi! It's been a while," he greets me and walks towards me. I don't even know what to say when he puts his arms around me and kisses my cheek.

Fuck, fuck, fuckity fuck!

Never in a million years did I think that I'd run into one of my past hook-ups, and especially not one who made it clear that he wanted more than just the one night we shared.

Just my rotten luck.

I pat him awkwardly on his back and he takes a step away.

"Oh, yes, hi...," I stammer and wish with all my heart that I could vanish into thin air right now.

"How are you?" he asks me and takes my hand to lead me further into the room to a leather bench.

"Good, good," I answer absentmindedly, hoping with all my might that he won't bring up the note he left on my kitchen counter.

"I was wondering if it was you when I saw your name on the calendar," he continues and sits down on the chair opposite me, turning to face me. "You never got in touch with me," he muses and rubs a fist over his heart. "Ouch."

I shrug and take off my leather jacket.

"I told you at the club that I only did hook-ups," I answer, avoiding his eyes as I sit down.

"True," I hear him grumble and sigh a little before venturing a look at him.

He's smiling sadly at me. "I guess I just hoped you'd break your rules for me."

Oh gosh, this is so awkward...I cringe and smile apologetically at him.

"Sorry."

An uncomfortable silence settles between us, and I turn my eyes to all the photos of clients getting ink hanging on the walls.

"Are you happy?" Kristian suddenly asks me, and I frown at him.

This is such a strange question coming from a man who didn't even spend 12 hours with me.

"What an odd thing to ask..." I avoid his question, tucking a few stray hairs behind my ear.

He smiles gently at me. "I guess I wasn't as drunk as you were when we met," he mumbles, and it causes me to narrow my eyes suspiciously at him.

"I wasn't *that* drunk," I protest and cross my arms defensively.

He looks exasperated at me. "Of course not. I'm not into necrophilia, you know; if I'd thought for one second that you were completely sloshed, unable to make your own decisions, I'd never have gone home with you."

Trying to unwind the tension in my shoulders, I nod. "I know. I didn't mean to imply anything...you were very..." Hesitating, I tilt my head. "...sweet," I finish, and even I can hear how lame it sounds.

Luckily, Kristian simply grins and then turns in his seat to grab a large notepad and a pencil.

"Any chance you want to have coffee with me after we're done here?" he asks me, catching me off-guard completely.

Oh, shit.

"Kristian..." I breathe and he waits patiently for me to either refuse or accept him. "I'm sorry, but...since our night together, I've met someone, and..." My voice trails off when he frowns unhappily at me.

He tries to cover it up, though, and gives me a lopsided grin before he sighs and fiddles with a few sheets of paper.

"He's a lucky guy," he mumbles and clears his throat.

"I hope he feels that way," I whisper, and the way Daniel

has been avoiding me the past few days enters my mind again.

"Well, if he doesn't know how to appreciate a woman like you, you know where to find me," Kristian says, winking at me, and I laugh for the first time that day.

Now I remember why I had sex with him; he's a really good guy.

After my laughter has died down, I smile back at him. "Thanks."

"Don't mention it," he assures me, and then inhales deeply. "Okay, you want to have a dream catcher inked on your ribs, right?"

I nod eagerly, happy to be back on track, and I begin to describe the design I want him to do for me, and he listens attentively to me. The sound of the pencil on paper is soothing, calming my nerves, and all I can think about is how significant a moment in my life this is.

I'm closing one door in my life only to open a window.

The first one is my past . . . the next is my future.

And I can't wait to face it.

♡

After I left Kristian, I went to the hospital to visit Andreas, bringing a game of chess with me. He has been complaining about being completely bored, so I thought this might cheer him up. Luckily, all his tests have come back looking better than we feared, but it'll take a long time before he'll be able to come back to work again.

I'm sitting on a chair beside his bed, pondering my next move, when Andreas calls my name and I focus on him. He seems to be in a contemplative mood today, so serious and definitely not as chipper as usual.

"There's something important I need to talk to you about," he starts, catching my attention further.

I lean back and stare at him more closely.

"What is it?" I ask him.

"Before I tell you, I want you to know that Daniel is already aware of this -- has been for a while, actually -- but I made him promise me not to mention it to you. So don't be mad at him for keeping this to himself, okay?"

"Okaaay," I answer slowly.

Where the heck is this going?

"Good. The thing is that I have known for some time now that my health wasn't as good as it used to be, and so I have been thinking that it might be a good idea for me to retire..."

"Retire?" I interrupt him. "But...what about your shop? It's your dream, your passion! You can't turn the key and close it for the last time!"

He raises a hand from the duvet covering him. "Now, now, don't worry about that. I'm getting to that part."

"Sorry," I grimace.

Me and my big mouth...

"As I was saying," he continues, a twinkle in his eyes. "I know you love the place, my dear, and I want to hand over the reins of running it to you."

A whoosh leaves my body, completely surprised by his words.

"Me?!" I ask him incredulously, pointing a finger at my chest. When he nods in the affirmative, I slump, completely taken aback by his generosity.

"But...I don't know how to run a shop," I reply feebly, thoughts running wild in my head. "I have no business degree, I don't have your experience, and I don't even live here!" Panicked, I get up from my seat to pace, ignoring his chuckle.

"Come now, Emma, you do live here, remember?"

I wave a hand at him as I concede, "Well, yes, for now I do, but my student visa won't be in effect in a year. What then?" I stop and put a hand on my hip. "And what about my parents? I know they miss me terribly, and *if*-" I turn my head in his direction - "...*if* I say yes, that'll mean they'll see even less of me in the future."

Andreas looks to the ceiling and rolls his eyes, an act so unusual for him to make that it almost causes me to laugh.

"Listen, Emma, I have considered all this - even talked it over with your dad, and..."

"You *what*?!" I shriek, mouth hanging open. "Wait, when? My dad hasn't mentioned anything about this to me at all."

My head is spinning and I feel weak at the knees of the enormity of what all this could mean.

"I phoned him a few months ago and talked it over with him," Andreas explains calmly. "He said that he would miss you, but like you've told me yourself when I once asked you why you chose to come to Denmark to study: England is not that far away. Your parents can easily hop on a plane from time to time to visit you. He also promised that he wouldn't say anything to your mother about this."

Releasing a breath, I mutter, "Right. Well, good thinking, because my mum would never be able to keep such a secret from me."

I think I need to have a little chat with dad later.

"He said something similar to me, actually," Andreas' amused tone interrupts my thought process once more, and I walk slowly back to his bed and resume my seat.

"Listen, Andreas, this is very generous of you...," I start.

"Don't follow that with a '*but*', Emma. I realise that this is a big surprise, and I understand that you can't accept it today. However..." He takes my hand in his and looks beseechingly into my eyes. "Please think about it. I know that there must be a lot of red tape and stupid bureaucracy you'll have to go through should you decide to take over the shop, but I'll help you. So will Daniel."

I frown at him. "What does Daniel say about all this?"

"He's absolutely fine with it. He has his own dreams and goals to follow...He doesn't mind it if that's what worries you?"

"Just a bit," I reply weakly, but the knots in my tummy loosen up a bit by Andreas' reassurance.

"For what it's worth, I have no doubt in my mind that he'll be overjoyed if you remain in Denmark, my dear," he tells me, a huge grin on his face.

"Well...Maybe." I shrug. "Okay, I promise I'll think about it," I say quietly and inhale deeply.

"You're quite good at keeping secrets, you know," I accuse fondly.

Andreas releases my hand and taps his nose.

"Oh yes, I know. I am very proud of myself, actually."

I smile at him. "But...if I say yes..." Tilting my head, I look questioningly at him. "What about you? Won't you get bored if you retire? What will you do?"

"I've always wanted to travel to France, Emma, so some village in Alsace will probably become my new home," he admits sheepishly, surprising me again.

"I see. I've never been to France," I muse and look out the window, not really seeing anything. I'm completely consumed with his offer.

"You and Daniel will have to come visit me," he says smugly, seemingly already assuming that he's got his wish, so I turn back to him.

"We'll see."

For now, that's the only answer I can give him, and I know he can hear the finality in my voice, because he nods and looks down at the chess board.

He moves the Queen forward and flips my King over. I know he's won.

"Check-mate," he states, and I shake my head, admitting defeat.

Perhaps in more ways than one.

CHAPTER THIRTY-SEVEN

EMMA

"DAD, HOW COULD YOU keep something like this from me?" I shout the minute, he picks up the phone. I haven't even left the hospital yet, but I'm too caught up in my rampage to give a toss about the disapproving look a nurse gives as I pass her.

"Hello, darling, how are you?" my dad calmly greets me.

"How *am* I?!" I splutter as I push the door open and turn left to get to the nearest bus stop. "I've just seen Andreas - my boss, Mr. Andersen, remember? It seems there's a secret you've been keeping from me."

My dad chuckles quietly. "I see he told you, did he?"

"Uh, yes! Honestly, Dad, this is not a minor detail such as, oh I don't know, who won the World Championship in football. This is huge! My future!"

"Hey, football is a very important matter, Emma," he replies, and I huff, exasperated.

"Dad!" I snap.

"Look, Emma, I realise that you're surprised, and I

understand that. But just breathe for a bit and think about it. You always tell your mum and me how much you love the shop, and your love for books hasn't changed, has it?"

"No," I mutter, sulking a bit as I slow down. Rubbing my forehead, I sigh. "Look, Dad, I'm just...well, I didn't see this opportunity coming at all, okay? I never dreamed that Andreas would propose such a thing, and the fact that he blindsided me like that? Well, he's a cunning old bugger, isn't he?"

"Oh, he is. But look at it this way: if you hadn't left Oxford and a similar opportunity presented itself...Would you accept it or not?"

My silence speaks volumes, because I know that I would jump in, feet first, if that was the case.

Dad goes on, "Exactly. Darling, please don't worry about your mum and me. We'll miss you, but we'll come visit you. We're not that far away, after all. Which reminds me..." He clears his throat. "When are we going to meet that young man of yours?" The amusement is now absent from his voice, leaving that certain 'Dad Tone' instead.

Oh, merciful heaven...

I close my eyes briefly. "Mum told you about Daniel?"

"She couldn't say much given the fact that you've been rather evasive about him whenever the two of you have spoken the last couple of weeks," he replies sternly. "Or that's what your mum tells me."

"Right, of course. I'll try to work something out and email you later," I hedge.

"Excellent. And I'll tell your mum and Nan about your new business venture," he informs me excitedly.

"Hey, I haven't accepted it yet," I answer, voice raised again.

"No, but you will. I know you, my girl."

I huff. "We'll see. Talk later, Dad."

"I hope so, sweetie. Don't forget to email us, you hear?" he reminds me.

"I won't. Love you, bye."

I push the red button and shake my head.

So that went well, eh?

I need to talk to Daniel about this, and it has to be now. Finding our last text convo, I type a quick text to him:

Me: We need to talk. Meet me at my place? X

His reply lights up my screen shortly after.

Daniel: Yes, we do. Sure. See you soon.

As the bus stops in front of me, I keep looking at the screen, wishing for his usual parting 'x' to appear, but it doesn't. With a sick feeling in the pit of my stomach, I enter the bus and find a seat in the back. My previous excitement has left me, and dread settles deeply within me instead. All the way home, I wonder if his feelings for me have changed.

That he doesn't love me anymore.

♡

DANIEL

"Shit." My crappy phone lost power just as I hit send, making me wonder if Emma got my reply to her text. I already know what it is she wants to talk with me about, though, because Andreas rang me this morning, letting me in on his plans to offer the bookshop to her.

I walk to her balcony door, watching the clouds gather in the distance while I wonder if she will accept it. The fact that she still hasn't said those pesky, albeit important, three little words I desperately long to hear is beginning to bother me more than it probably should.

I miss her.

I've been so busy since Andreas was admitted to the hospital last week that I've been utterly spent when I got home. Sorting out pending orders, taking care of customers, as well as trying to appease several publishers from the UK who demanded to speak with him alone, has been more than I can handle, and I know this. However, I want to prove a point to him and to Emma, I guess.

I am not weak.

I am not stupid.

I am not afraid.

I'm not so sure about the last part, though.

Even though the doctors feel confident that Andreas's heart troubles can become stable, better even, with medication, exercise, and a stricter diet than he's used to, I still fear that I'll receive a phone call from the hospital where they tell me that he has passed away.

Irrational? Maybe.

But it feels bloody realistic to me.

Lightning bursts across the sky, making me take a step back from the door in surprise, and I'm worried that Emma will get caught up in the storm that's about to hit us. Soon after, the rain starts pouring down, the sound of it falling making a racket the likes of which I can't remember I have ever seen before. All storms are violent, but this one is particularly nasty, and I can't shake the sense of foreboding that's holding me in its grasp.

I turn to walk to the kitchen but halt in my tracks as Emma practically runs inside, slams the door behind her, and pulls back her dripping wet hair from her face. She blows out a breath, chest heaving - she must have run from the bus stop around the corner - and she closes her eyes as she shakes her hair back.

Holy shit.

I can't breathe properly...I can't speak...I can't tear my eyes away from her.

She has never looked more beautiful as she does now.

Her mascara and makeup may be blotting her cheeks and neck, a complete mess, and giving her the most impressive pair of *panda eyes* I have ever seen, but I don't care.

Right now, she looks younger than she is, and as she catches my eyes, there's a vulnerability to hers I have not seen in a couple of weeks.

I'd like to think that I've been the reason for her joy and more positive attitude since we met.

Surely I can't be the reason why that vulnerability has returned?

She wrenches her arms free of her jacket, letting it fall to the floor, and stalks towards me.

What the...?

She stops right in front of me and jabs a finger in my chest.

"Are you breaking up with me?" she spits out, anger and hurt radiating from her entire being, and she's shaking from the cold.

"What?!" I ask, flabbergasted that she would even think such a thing.

"Because if you are, there's the door, Daniel!" she yells, her voice breaking on my name, and I reach an arm out to catch her hand. When she slaps it away, my own anger begins to simmer, though.

"Will you please calm down?" I ask her, gritting my

teeth.

"Calm down? What the fuck, Daniel?" She crosses her arms over her chest and dabs at a wayward tear dripping on her cheek. "What am I supposed to think? You've been so distant the past week, and I understand that you've had *a lot* on your plate, but you haven't even kissed me goodnight...What the fuck is that all about?!"

I take a step towards her and growl, "I'm worried about my uncle, okay? It has nothing to do with you!" Without meaning to, my last words come out as a shout, and she flinches.

"Considering the proposition he just dropped on me, I do actually think that it's my business -- especially when I seem to be crazy enough to accept it," she answers quietly, the fight having left her completely. The anger is gone, replacing it with hurt, and I sigh deeply, regretting with everything that I am to be the cause of it.

"You're staying?" I ask her quietly, not even daring to breathe for fear of her answer.

She sniffles and looks down at her feet. "Well, I was," she mutters. "Now, I'm not so sure."

"Sweetheart," I groan and move closer to her, placing my hand beneath her chin to bring her eyes back to mine. Although she's reluctant to do it, she does lift her head eventually, and my other hand comes up to cup her cheeks affectionately.

Gently, I wipe away the tears and ruined make-up and smile sadly at her.

"Why?" I ask her, and she blinks rapidly.

"*Why?!*" she repeats, and I nod in earnest.

"Yes, tell me why you're staying...I..." I hesitate, but force the words trapped in my throat out at last. "I want to hear you say it..." I swallow and take the final plunge, hoping and praying that I'm right about her. "I need you to say the words I have been longing to hear for so long."

She puts a hand on my wrist, leaning into my touch and closes her eyes briefly.

Please...I'm begging you...Put me out of my misery.

She takes a deep breath and whispers, "I'm still scared, Daniel..."

"Why?" I whisper back, so afraid that she doesn't love me.

"Because..." At last, her gaze meets mine. "Because it means you'll have the power to break me, and I'm not even whole yet...not entirely."

"Emma, sweetheart...," I beg, my desperation growing by the second. The raindrops become louder and louder - or maybe it's the sound of my heartbeat instead. I can't tell.

"I. Love. You," I whisper and close the gap between us by leaning my forehead to hers. "Haven't I proven that to you yet? You're the strongest person I know. You're not broken."

I need her eyes on mine.

"You're shredding my heart," I breathe and straighten my back. The tears brimming in her eyes almost bring me to my knees.

"That's the *last* thing I want to do," she sobs before she puts her arms around my neck. Smiling wobbly at me, she inhales deeply.

"I love you, too...," she says.

"Thank fuck," I groan and finally - *finally* - wrap my arms tightly around her waist before slamming my mouth down on hers.

Heaven.

Our tongues tangle, dancing the familiar dance, and I

can't breathe, but it doesn't matter. Her taste, her touch is all I'll ever need...She makes me feel alive. I place a hand on her arse and pull her flush against me. She gasps when I press my cock into her stomach, and I wrench my mouth free, panting wildly.

"Let me have you, Emma...please let me make love to you?" I beg her, and again, I don't give a fuck that she can hear how much I need to be close to her.

Eyelids heavy, she licks her lips, and I can't keep the groan from escaping my mouth.

"Are you sure?" she asks me, and there's no more uncertainty to trace in her voice...Only love.

"I ache for you, sweetheart...I want you so fucking much I'm afraid I'll embarrass myself and spill my need for you in my jeans," I chuckle, and she smiles teasingly at me.

"Oh, no, we can't have that." She leans up on her toes and whispers, "Kiss me again, please...I want you so much."

That's all I needed to hear.

My cock throbs with need for her as I lean down to ravage her mouth once more. She's just as hungry as I am, sucking on my tongue as she starts to yank my t-shirt free of my jeans and lifts it further up. I raise my arms in the air, briefly lose her mouth and pull it the rest of the way, and I toss it carelessly on the floor.

"Give me that mouth again," I demand as I pick her up, and she eagerly complies and wraps her legs around me. Her fingers grab fistfuls of my hair, pulling down, but the sting doesn't bother me. It only makes me wilder for her, and my teeth pull at her lip ring. She jumps in my arms and angles her head to the side, kissing me deeply. I walk to her bed and put her down, pressing my shaking body into hers, and as much as I'm drowning in her kiss, I need to taste her skin.

"I'll never get enough of you, Daniel," she pants as my mouth trails across her collarbone, my tongue licking her freckles there. "I love you so much, honey."

Bloody hell...this girl...

I lift up on my knees and reach my hands down to undo the button on her shorts, in a hurry to get my tongue on her slick heat, and I grab the ends and start to pull at them.

"Shite," I curse when the wet material doesn't budge. "Help me out here, please, sweetheart," I grin crookedly.

She giggles and our hands fumble for a while, and I can't keep the nervous laugh bubbling up in my throat inside.

"This is awkward," I grumble, annoyed. "How the hell did you get them on to begin with?"

Emma reaches a hand up to caress my cheek.

"Get the scissors in the kitchen and cut them open...," she tells me, and I stumble off the bed to do as she says.

"Sure you won't miss them?" I ask her as I get back, unbuttoning my jeans with one hand.

She licks her lips, her gaze hungry, and replies huskily, "Fuck them. I need to feel your cock inside me...now."

"God, I love it when you talk dirty to me," I breathe and start cutting open her shorts. As soon as she's able to, she kicks them off, picks the tattered pieces up and throws them on the floor.

When I discover that she's not wearing anything at all, her pussy bare for me to see, I growl, "You're killing me here. Have you been walking around all day like that?" I yank down my pants and boxers quickly and palm my balls.

She nods and lies down, bends her knees slightly and spreads her legs widely for me.

"Lose the top and your bra," I demand, basking in the power she is handing over to me. I'm running the show, and fuck if I don't love it. She does as I say and lies back down on the bed.

"Hurry up," she moans, her hands cupping her tits, but I shake my head at her.

"Oh no, I'm going to take this as slowly as possible...make you grow wild for me."

I lose the tight grip on my balls and sink down to my knees, reaching my arms forward to grab her hips, and I pull hard, making her slide down the bed. Immediately, she places her legs on either side of my head, and I move my hands from her hips to place them on her arse, digging my nails in.

I look down at her glistening pussy and lick my lips. I'm like a man lost in the desert, about to die of thirst, and she's the only one who's able to quench it.

Moving my head, I start to kiss, lick, and bite my way down her left inner thigh, my eyes locked on hers. It thrills me beyond measure when they never waver from mine. I repeat my devotion to her body on her right leg, chuckling huskily as she groans, raising her hips up, and silently asking me to go down on her.

"Getting impatient?" I mumble, voice teasing, and continue to take my sweet time, her arousal teasing my nostrils. I'm just as impatient as she is, of course...but I still want to savour her, draw it out a bit longer.

"Very," she pants and narrows her eyes at me. "If you don't hurry up, I'm going to get myself off." That grabs my full attention, and I look sternly at her.

"Grab the pillow behind you and *don't* let go," I tell her. She widens her eyes but again allows me to take control. "Good," I praise her when I have her right where I want her. I lean down and inhale her scent, close my eyes, and her thighs quiver around me. She's ready for me. I open my eyes again, and she gasps, no doubt seeing the need I have for her, and without breaking eye contact, I lick my lips before my mouth closes on her clit.

"Holy fuck!" she groans above me when I begin to lick her out from her clit, *down, down, down* to the puckered hole behind her...As always, pleasing her in this way makes me even harder for her.

I spread her arse cheeks more, letting her become completely exposed to me, and I can feel the tension in her thighs as she tightens them further. Her pussy is so wet for me, it's almost unreal...I'll never get enough of it.

I come up for air and put a finger inside her slick heat.

"My god, Emma, your pussy tastes better and better each fucking time."

Writhing on the bed, gripping the pillow underneath her head so tightly that her knuckles turn white, she chuckles throatily. "I love your mouth on me, Daniel. I need more...please..."

Spreading my finger gently inside her tightness, I reply, "My pleasure, darling..." I bend my head again. As I suck harder on her clit, I remove my finger only to run it down her slit until it rests lightly on her anus. We've done this a few times already, but this time it feels different...It means *everything*. I rub her hole easily, smearing it with her essence, and take my time letting her become used to it. As I lick her pussy, I push my finger slowly inside her hole, and when she moans my name in ecstasy, I can feel the pre-come leaking from my cock head.

Fuck...maybe I won't be able to make it last as long as I'd hoped.

Emma's whimpers become louder and louder as my finger picks up speed, pumping it in and out, and I can feel how close she is. Her excitement only spurs me on, and I lick and bite her clit harder than I've done before.

"Oh, god, Daniel! I'm going to...I'm..." she moans, her walls clamping down on my finger.

"Come, baby," I growl against her clit. "Come for me now..."

She screams, sobbing on my name, her hips moving frantically as she rides my face and finger, and watching her like this, horny as hell, letting go for me entirely...It's magnificent.

The minute her limp legs fall to my side, utterly spent, I release her clit and her hole gently from my grasp and lean over her to kiss my way up her body. She hums, and I can see a small, happy smile on her lips.

As I slip my tongue inside her belly button, I murmur, "If you fall asleep now, I think my cock will cry."

I look up when I hear her happy laugh and watch her eyes open.

"Don't worry, I'm far from done with you yet, honey," she says, and I can see the truth in her gaze: filled with love for me, yes, but the heat remains as well.

"Thank fuck," I groan and close my mouth over her right tit. I can see and feel her chest heaving as I suck her nipple hard, grazing my teeth over it.

"Oh...Daniel...What are you doing to me?" she breathes out when I lie down on top of her, covering her body completely, my throbbing cock resting on her stomach.

I release her nipple with a loud *pop* and place my legs on either side of her, straddling her.

"Loving you," I reply quietly as I stare at her. The tenderness that greets me makes me catch my breath, and when she raises her head to place a lingering kiss on my lips, her arms around my neck, the last thread of control snaps entirely.

Wrenching my mouth free, I sit up, grab the base of my cock and stroke it up and down a few times.

"Sweetheart, I won't last for much longer," I pant and grab her legs roughly to put them around my back, locking them in place. Her feet dig into my arse, pulling me closer. I look down as her fingers begin to rub her clit, and it only causes more pre-come to leak from the tip of my cock.

"I'm on the pill, Daniel," Emma says, catching my attention. "I'm ready when you are," she teases me, but she can't disguise how hot she is for me again.

I smile wickedly. "Well, then..."

Looking down again, I swirl my cock head around her clit, something that always drives her wild, and when her head falls back and she bites her lips, moaning loudly, I push inside her slowly. My head falls back in abandon when I feel her wetness surround me for the first time...the pleasure is overwhelming. Her heat is scorching in the most unfathomable way. My legs shake so hard and I need to *move*...I slam my cock inside her, and she groans, pushing her hips further against me.

"Holy shit, Em...You feel amazing," I pant, turning my gaze to look at where we're joined. Emma's fingers continue to play with her pussy, her other hand pulling at her nipple, and my speed picks up, growing wilder with each thrust.

"Fuck, so do you, Daniel," she moans. "I love feeling your cock inside me."

"Oh my god, Emma...What are you doing to me?" I repeat her words from before and stare into her eyes. The same burn coursing through me right now is reflected back at me, and I need to feel her lips again.

I lean down swiftly and take a firm hold on her chin.

"Mouth," I demand, and when our tongues meet again, I mimic the movements of my cock, letting her know in no uncertain terms how hot she makes me feel.

I end the kiss by licking the seam of her lips and place my mouth beside her ear. "I love you so fucking much, sweetheart."

As the words fall from my mouth, she cries out, and the tingling in my spine intensifies. I thrust one last time and still, spilling my load inside her. Dropping my weight on her, the tremors run through me, and I slide back and forth slowly as my cock gradually becomes slack.

She caresses my neck with open-mouthed kisses, tightening her arms around me, and I hum, sated.

"Thank you," I whisper and suck gently on her earlobe.

"Anytime, Preppy," she whispers, and I chuckle. Afraid I'll crush her with my weight, I lean to my side to allow her to catch her breath properly again.

I smile at her, perusing her face until my eyes rest on hers again. When I see the tears falling, my smile is wiped off immediately.

"Why are you crying?" I ask her, alarmed, my fingers wiping them away as fast as possible.

She sniffles. "Because I never knew it could feel like this..."

"*It?*" I ask her, confused.

She nods. "Sex. Hanky-panky. Fooling around. You know..." Sniffling, her lips pull up in a small grin.

No longer fearing that she'll run away from me, I kiss the tip of her nose while I press my stirring cock inside her again.

"That's because this is not sex, sweetheart," I tell her and lean down so that my lips hover above hers. She stills completely, her captivating blue-grey eyes taking me prisoner. "This is love," I continue. "I may not be an expert, but the way you just made me feel? As if I am the king of the world just for making you let go like that, opening yourself up for me completely?" She nods, a small smile forming on her lips. "Well...That says everything. And I'm not ever letting you go, Emma, you hear me?"

She closes the distance between us and kisses me, her breath and tongue caressing mine briefly before she falls back on the pillow again.

Smiling wickedly at me, she waggles her eyebrows at me. "Ready for round two?"

I grin.

"Oh, yeah, baby," I reply, and I roll to my back, taking her with me without losing the connection between us.

Placing her elbows on each side of my head, she threads her fingers through my hair and whispers, "But this time, I'm in charge."

Fuck. Me.

"Have at it, sweetheart," I growl.

Then she gets to work on my body, all the while I can see her love for me shine through her eyes.

CHAPTER THIRTY-EIGHT

EMMA

I FALL BACK IN bed, my heart hammering wildly, and panting I say, "You're going to break my vagina!"

Daniel chuckles, as breathless as I am, and slides down beside me. Reaching an arm across my belly, he takes a firm hold and pulls me closer to his side.

"It's your fault, sweetheart. If your body wasn't so irresistible, I'd have an easier time letting you rest."

I snort and slap his butt lightly. "Right, well, I'm far from perfect. My stomach's too floppy, and my arse is too full."

"Hey, no knocking two of my favourite body parts," he grins and snuggles closer to me.

I shake my head fondly at him and pull my duvet over my body. We lie in sated silence for a while, listening to the rain. The storm passed earlier, slowing it down, and it feels comforting to be here in our small cocoon, away from everyone and everything for a while.

It's just us.

Telling Daniel I love him was at first such a frightening

thought, but now that I've let those three little words out, I just want to shout them from the rooftops.

And yet...My sleepiness disappears abruptly when I remember that I have yet to tell him my story. I'm still scared that he'll see me differently, but it isn't as all encompassing as before.

I know I'm no longer weak.

I can get through this.

I sit up slowly and turn around to face him better. Placing my elbow on my pillow, I hold my head up while my other hand pulls slightly on the small smatter of hair on his chest.

"Daniel," I start, a bit unsure about how to go about this.

"Emma," he replies, voice serious, but I also hear slight amusement in his voice. I glance into his eyes but can't hold them for long.

Creasing my forehead, I try again. "There's something I have to tell you, and...well, it won't be pleasant."

He covers my hand on his chest with his, stilling my fingers. "You don't have to, sweetheart. I can wait."

Maybe you can, but I'm sick of waiting for my life to begin.

I kiss his chest quickly and smile sadly at him. Gone is the playfulness from earlier, leaving a concerned frown in his eyes instead.

"But I want to," I say quietly and take a deep breath before beginning my tale.

"When I was ten, my parents took us kids on a week-long vacation to Brighton. My brother wanted his friend, Tom, to come with us, and his parents didn't see anything wrong with it, so off we went. They rented a cottage that had a small, separate alcove attached to it where we children were meant to sleep. And my parents slept in the main house."

I lie down and Daniel turns to his side, facing me. He

clenches his jaw, possibly sensing how bad my story is, and I swallow.

"It was a beautiful place. We spent the first few days playing tourists, and I thought that it was fun having two older boys -- they were five years older than me -- watch over me. At first, I didn't think anything of it when I'd catch Tom staring at me with a funny look in his eyes from time to time. But then...on the second night, he came into my room - it wasn't close to my brother's - and he'd..." I close my eyes to prevent the tears from falling.

The nausea is back in full force.

Will the thought of him always make me sick?

"Sweetheart...," Daniel's voice breaks through, and I open my eyes. He looks torn, anguished...furious. But instead of making me lose heart, I take courage when, apart from those things, I also see his love for me.

"Please...I need to finish this," I beg him, ignoring the tears.

He grabs my hand in his, intertwining our fingers, and nods at me.

"So," I breathe. "At first, I wasn't completely awake, but when he turned me around on my stomach and pulled my knickers down, I tried to sit up to ask him why he was in my room, but...He put his hand over my mouth and hissed, *'If you scream, I'll kill you!'* before he gagged me with a cloth he pulled out of his swim shorts." I swallow the nausea that threatens to take me over. "The look in his eyes...it was so empty, cold...vacant. As if he wasn't really present. I started to cry when he straddled me from behind, but tried to keep my voice down because I truly believed his threat."

"Oh god, Emma," Daniel murmurs through his own tears.

I wipe a hand over my mouth and hurry to finish. "He kept my hands in such a fierce grip while he masturbated on top of me, all the while his harsh voice panted, and he kept licking my neck. He even tried to...to *kiss* me, forcing his probing tongue against my lips, making me gag. After he was done, he pushed a finger inside my vagina and...I swear, I tried to prevent him from doing that to me!"

Openly crying now, I bury my head in my pillow, the old shame rearing its ugly head, but Daniel pulls me into his arms.

"I kept pleading with him to stop, Daniel," I sob in his arms all the while he rocks me gently from side to side. "But every night, he'd come into my room...he'd do the same all over again. Over and over..."

I can't go on anymore, and Daniel lets me cry out my sorrow for the loss of my childhood.

When I'm finally spent, I lean away from him and look into his eyes.

"There's a bit more," I whisper, and his arms tighten around me.

"Okay, go on...finish it," he grits out and kisses my forehead.

"You're probably wondering why I didn't confide in my parents, but you have to understand one thing: when you're violated like that, you feel dirty...weak...and guilty. For the longest time, I thought that I was the reason for why he did what he did - after all, he kept telling me it was my fault - and I just felt so ashamed."

"But *did* you end up telling your parents about it? And your brother?"

I nod. "Yes, but not until five years later. I was really good at keeping secrets, and I'd ignore him whenever he came to visit Steven and lock my room; or I'd leave the house the minute I saw him, but...I became more and more withdrawn, started hanging out with the wrong crowd..." Sighing, I wipe the remnants of my tears away and look down at my lap. "I knew my parents were deeply concerned, and so was Nan, because the nightmares started soon after we came home from that trip. So I lied, of course. When my parents caught me coming home past my curfew one night, high as a kite, they fell apart. So...that's when I told them...and Steven about Tom and about what happened that summer."

I fall silent for a while, remembering that day as clearly as if it happened yesterday.

"What happened next, darling?" Daniel asks me quietly.

"My mum started to cry, and my dad...I've never seen him so *furious* before. But Steven...he..." I swallow past the lump in my throat. "He didn't believe me at all."

"*What?!*" Daniel jumps, and I look timidly at him. "That bastard! You're his sister, for god's sake! How could he not believe you?" His eyes are burning with outrage for me, and his body is shaking.

Drawing strength from his anger, I straighten my shoulders. "I don't know...Neither do my parents. Steven was away at university and didn't live at home at the time, and he just stormed out of the house that night, shouting that he'd come back when I admitted that I'd lied. I haven't seen him often since then, actually. And...I've never really talked about it with my parents, either. I think...once I straightened myself out, stopped doing drugs, I think we all thought that talking it through that one time was enough. But...well, clearly, we were all wrong about that part. I do know that my mum and dad had a meeting with his parents shortly after, but I've never asked what was said between them.

Daniel hugs me tightly to his chest, and I wrap my arms around his neck, never wanting to let him go.

"I'm so sorry, Em," he murmurs, and I kiss his neck.

He leans away from me and sighs. "So...what did you do? What happened to Tom? Did you report him?"

I shake my head. In some way, this is almost the hardest admission for him to ask of me.

"I couldn't go through with it, Daniel. Seeing as we were both considered children at the time, I doubt much would have come of it, other than a slap on his wrist."

He frowns.

"I know that I *should* have reported him to the police, honey," I whisper. "But...I didn't want to make a fuss. I felt that, what with the drugs and everything, I'd put my parents through enough already, and...I just wanted to forget altogether. Do you understand...?"

Please don't let go of me now.

A sigh of relief escapes me when he smiles gently at me. "I do," he concedes. "But god, Em...how can you even *want* to have sex after all you went through? I mean, all we've done..."

I grab his face and stare hard into his eyes, willing him to see the truth there.

"Don't, honey...I know it's probably completely fucked up, but I *love* sex...it's thrilling, exciting, hell...it's one of life's greatest pleasures!" I smile before I kiss him deeply, my tongue twirling around his, trying to convey the true depth of my love and need for him with my lips. We're both breathing hard when I end it.

"And making love to you...?" I whisper breathlessly, watching his intense eyes burn for me. "It's the *best* ever! If I could, I'd shackle you to this bed forever and ravage you over and over again."

His right hand finds its way to my arse, and my breath falters when he starts to massage it.

"So...," he muses as he licks my neck slowly. "You're not afraid of sex?"

"Definitely not," I pant. "There's probably some psychological explanation for that, but...oh..." I lose my train of thought when his mouth finds that sensitive spot below my ear.

"Promise me this, sweetheart," Daniel breathes in my ear as his other hand begins to roam my back, moving slowly up to play with the ends of my hair before he grips and pulls my head back even further.

"Anything, honey." I wrap my arms around his neck and trail them across his chin, nibbling lightly with my teeth until I suck softly on his neck. His hand flexes on my hip, and I can feel the tension in his muscles as he's holding himself back.

"If you *ever* feel that you're not up for it...that your head's not in the right frame of mind...? Promise me that you will tell me at once, and I'll stop, okay?"

I nod against his neck and press my body closer to his, my hardened nipples aching for his attention. "I swear, honey."

"Good," he sighs. "Fuck, I love you, Em," he groans. "I feel so repulsed by what you've gone through...And I'd like to kill that arsehole! I'll never let him come near you again."

He lifts my chin and we look deeply at each other. The love shining from his eyes makes me breathless, and I'm near to bursting with joy. His head descends, and our lips meet in a slow, sensual dance, until the passion consumes us. It builds and builds, stoking a fire within me, and our lips grow frantic, urgent. Daniel shifts, pulling me down beside him, and he begins to worship my body once more. Before I completely let

go in his arms, I rejoice in the fact that he hasn't left me.
Daniel's still here...He still loves me.
He doesn't think I'm disgusting or broken beyond repair.
And I trust him with all my heart.

♡

DANIEL

What I've learned so far about sex since Emma deflowered me a few nights ago:
1. Waking up to her mouth sucking my cock while her hands play with my balls, followed by her riding me, is bloody fantastic.
2. Shower sex is hot as hell, but a bit tricky - Emma assures me, though, that we'll just have to practice more. *Hoozah!*
3. Chocolate sauce and whipped cream is my new favourite food - at least when Emma's covered in it.

I feel raw, spent, used, and I absolutely love it. But aside from that, my mind continues to wander back to the night she told me about that filthy piece of scum, and the way her brother betrayed her makes my fists hungry to meet his jaw.

No, I'm not a violent man.

But that doesn't prevent me from wanting to give him a good arse-kicking whenever I think about it. And I do think about it...probably more than I should.

Today's when we're supposed to meet Steven, and Emma's been fretting over it for the past couple of hours. I watch her from my bed as she tries to pick the right outfit - she's fetched three different dresses from next door - and watching her standing there, only wearing some lacy underwear, face devoid of makeup, makes my mouth water.

Bloody hell, I'll never get enough of her.

As always, my cock stirs by the sight of her, and I glance quickly at my phone to check the time.

Still three hours...plenty of time.

I stand up slowly and move towards her, my own body naked, cock standing at attention. Pressing my body flushed to her back, I wipe the hair covering her neck away and breathe her in.

"You smell like lemons...," I mutter as I take a firm hold on her hips, preventing her from moving away from me.

"It's my new shampoo," she answers distractedly while she holds up a flimsy, black, very short, strapless dress.

"You're not wearing that one," I tell her firmly, almost forgetting my mission to devour her.

Sighing, she turns her head to meet my eyes, and she frowns at me.

"Why? It's a cute dress."

"*Because* it'll reveal too much of your delectable body...but don't throw it away," I mention as an afterthought, getting an idea for later.

"*Not* that you're allowed to tell me what to wear - *ever*," she says, narrowing her eyes playfully at me. I grin, amused by her stubbornness. "But you could be right...this dress would be more suitable for a night out clubbing instead of a lunch date." She hangs it in my wardrobe, and picks up a deep, emerald-green dress with small straps and a heart-shaped bodice instead.

"I like that one," I instantly tell her and then resume focusing on kissing her neck tenderly.

"Yeah, I think that's the one..." She leans her head back

on my chest and chuckles warningly, "Daniel..."

"Yes, sweetheart?" My thumb and forefinger find her right nipple, and even through the fabric of her bra, I can feel that it's already hard as a pebble.

"I don't think we have time for any...hanky-panky," she breathes and gasps when I yank down the cups of her bra, freeing her gorgeous breasts from their confinement.

"Don't worry, I checked the time," I whisper and push my cock closer to her back so that she can feel how hard I already am for her.

She groans as my lips trail kisses over the curve of her shoulder and back. "Don't you dare give me a love bite now."

"I wouldn't, trust me," I reassure her and then order her to turn around.

Picking her up in my arms, I walk her back to my bed and place her gently on her stomach.

"Tell me if you want me to stop, sweetheart," I whisper in her ear, and she sighs.

"I will."

Kissing my way down her spine, I nudge her legs open before settling on my knees. I lift her up by her hips and spread her legs wider. Running my flat hand down her side, I take in her new tattoo. It's breathtaking.

"Does this still hurt?" I ask her, trying to avoid touching it.

"It's still a bit tender, but nothing too unmanageable," she answers and puts her arms above her head to grab onto the headboard.

"I fucking love this tat, sweetheart," I tell her, and it's the god honest truth. The way it flows from her breast down her ribs and ends at her hip, almost looking as if it's blowing in the wind, the colours and shades in black and blue are breathtaking.

"I'm glad you like it," she whispers.

"It's stunning, Em..."

Now, enough with the talking...

"We have to be quick, I know." I pump my cock up and down with one hand while I check to see if her pussy is wet enough for me, running a finger lightly across it.

"Fuck, you're drenched," I growl, pinching her clit, and she moans.

"I'm always wet for you," she sighs and opens her eyes. "Please fuck me, Daniel."

I take a firm grip on the base of my cock and line it up against her opening. My lungs are fit to bursting, and I bite my lip as I push inside her. I dig my fingers into her hips as I begin to move inside her, almost instantly hitting her sweet spot, and I can feel her pussy gripping tightly around me.

Groaning, I pick up speed, pulling out slowly only to slam hard inside her welcoming heat, and she meets me eagerly with each stroke.

I remove a hand from her arse only to smack it, and she jumps when she feels the sting.

"My girl likes it rough, don't you?" I ask her breathlessly, and my hand takes another smack to it.

"Oh god, yes, I do," Emma shouts, and I lean over her back to bite down on her shoulder gently.

"God, you make my cock so hard," I growl in her ear. "Are you ready to get properly fucked now, sweetheart?"

"Yes, yes...*please*, honey, give me more...," she calls out, wetting her lips, eyes burning with lust.

"As you wish," I reply, sweat dripping down my back, and I pick up the pace.

CHAPTER THIRTY-NINE

EMMA

WE'RE STANDING NEXT TO The Stork Fountain, and I'm so nervous I don't know what to do with myself. Daniel's tight grip around my waist is soothing, but I can't relax. For the millionth time, I pull out my phone from my clutch to check the time.

"Relax, sweetheart, we're early," Daniel murmurs and leans down to kiss my cheek.

Pulling my hair free from my neck, I mutter, "Yes, I know. I just want this to be over and done with." Leaning back to look into his eyes, I bat my eyelashes at him. "At least Steven won't be able to think our relationship status is a hoax."

Daniel grins at me. "And why is that?" he asks me, turning me in his arms so I'm standing right in front of him.

I wrap my arms around his neck.

"Because he can't miss the love that's shining in my eyes whenever I look at you," I reply dramatically, and he laughs loudly.

Closing one eye, he grimaces. "That was one cheesy line, Miss Davenport."

I snort. "Yep, don't I know it? Hallmark card worthy, wouldn't you agree?"

He opens his mouth but doesn't get the chance to answer because Steven's voice interrupts our happy bubble.

"Oh, the boyfriend is here. Lovely," he mutters, and I grit my teeth before turning around to face him, a fake smile on my lips.

"Hello, brother," I greet him. Daniel pulls me close to his side, clearly stating his claim on me, and I reach out my hand to Steven.

Manners, remember?

"Emma," he says, an inscrutable look in his eyes. He looks the same: hair the same colour as mine styled to perfection, his navy-coloured suit designed specifically to him, I suppose. And his small, beady eyes hold no warmth at all. They never did when they turned to me.

We shake hands briefly and I turn to introduce Daniel to him.

"Daniel, this is my brother, Steven Davenport. Steven, meet my boyfriend, Daniel Larsen."

Steven nods dismissively at Daniel, not even bothering to say a proper 'hello', and, seething, I grimace inwardly at the arrogance oozing from this man who appears to be related to me.

But the thing is that this man may be my brother by blood, but he stopped being my family a very long time ago.

He can't hurt me anymore.

The realisation that I no longer fear him or his scathing words hits me right in my stomach, and I release a long breath, taking joy from it.

Daniel remains silent and gives Steven a chin lift, no doubt afraid that he'll say something not exactly prudent, and I bite the inside of my cheek to prevent myself from laughing at them both.

Men...so typical.

Women may be called the fairer sex, and men are still living in caves, it would seem.

Tucking my hand in the left back pocket of Daniel's cheek, I say brightly, "So! Where are we going to have lunch?"

Steven glances briefly at his gold Rolex glimmering in the sunlight.

"Actually, I can't do lunch after all," he informs us, catching me completely by surprise.

"What?" I ask him.

At least he has the good sense to look a bit embarrassed about ditching us like this.

"I'm sorry, Emma, but something came up, and I don't have time."

"Then *why* didn't you text me and cancel?" I ask him, frowning at him. I'm completely mystified. "If you couldn't make it, what's the reason for still meeting us here?"

Daniel can't hold back a snort and mutters, "He probably doesn't have the balls to face you, sweetheart."

Steven takes a step into Daniel's personal space, but it makes me proud to see that he doesn't back down at all.

"Excuse me, *Sir*," Steven spits out, "but why are you even here? This is a family matter, and you are most definitely not invited."

"Hey!" I butt in, my hand raised towards Steven, but he ignores me.

"I'm here because Emma asked me to come with her," Daniel answers calmly, but I can feel the tension radiating from his body. He's ready to pounce on my poor, unsuspecting brother. If I were the kind of woman who wanted a man to fight for her, I'd give him the signal to go right ahead and knock him down.

But I'm not.

I fight my own battles.

"Steven, will you please just *go*?"

He finally breaks free from Daniel's thunderous gaze.

"There's still something I need to talk to you about," he clips and glances briefly at his briefcase.

"Whatever it is, you can say it in front of Daniel," I tell him, finally letting my disgust for him out.

"This is a *family* matter," Steven protests warningly, and I take a step further and lean my head back to keep his shifting eyes on my hard ones.

"Daniel *is* family," I state. "So? Get on with it, and then leave me alone."

Steven ponders his next move and his shoulders slump a bit as he gives in.

"Very well," he mutters and opens the briefcase in his hand and takes out a letter.

"This is for you," he says quietly, all fight gone from his face, replacing it with sadness.

Confused, I hold out my hand to take it from him, and I can't help but notice that it has my name written on it. The handwriting is unfamiliar to me, and I have a horrible taste in my mouth even though it is entirely irrational.

I look back at him and wave the letter. "What is it?"

Daniel tucks me closer to his side, no doubt picking up on the trepidation in my voice.

For the first time since laying eyes on my brother, he seems unable to meet my gaze, because he looks to his right and swallows.

"It's from Tom."

I gasp, and I want to tear the letter into a million tiny pieces. My hand feels as if it's being burnt and the letter slips from my fingers, fluttering to the ground. Daniel bends down quickly and picks it up, putting it in his jacket pocket.

"What the hell, Steven?!" I take a step, fist clenched at my side, and if we weren't in public, I'd knee him in his balls for bringing something *he* has touched to me.

Steven sighs and rubs his forehead. "Listen, Tom's dead, okay, Emma? So just...well, do with it as you wish, but at least my task here is done."

Upon hearing this, I inhale deeply.

"How?" I whisper, my body rooted to the spot.

"Drug overdose," Steven spits out through gritted teeth, and he swallows hard.

Oh god...

"When?" Daniel asks, and I'm grateful at him for taking over now that I seem to have lost the ability to form real words anymore.

"Four months ago," Steven tells him. The hurt in his voice makes me spitting mad.

He's hurting, yes. But not for me...for him!

"I see you're still taking sides," I accuse, and I let the old hurt I have, so far, always been so careful to keep hidden from him out at last.

He cringes and looks down, remaining silent.

"That's it?" I ask him harshly, and he nods, still refusing to look at me.

"Well, then," I mutter and take Daniel's hand. "Have a nice life, brother," I greet him, and those are my final words to him.

I'm done with him for good.

"He was *mine!*" Steven suddenly calls after me, and I stop dead in my tracks, turning back to watch him, hardly believing the words coming out of his mouth. His beloved briefcase has fallen to the ground, and he's pointing at me, causing the people surrounding us to take notice.

"Why did you take him away from me?! Tom was mine!" His careful facade has completely disappeared as he's openly crying now. I stride back to him, getting completely up in his face.

"Are you telling me that you and Tom were lovers?" I ask him quietly. Daniel stands close beside me now and takes my hand, and I take comfort in his silent support.

Steven clenches his jaw and nods once.

"I didn't know," I whisper, and while my anger hasn't subsided, I do feel sorry for this poor excuse of man standing before me now.

"Why…why couldn't you just have kept quiet? If you hadn't told mum and dad about what he did, he wouldn't have turned to drugs, and he might still be alive," Steven spits at me, his eyes filled with nothing but hate for me. Snot and tears mingle as they draw lines down his face and jaw, and anger the likes of which I have not felt in a really long time takes possession over my body,

"How *dare* you?! What he did to me was sick, Steven!" I yell at him. "He *stole* my innocence, and I'll always hate the bastard for that! Don't you dare put the blame of his weakness on me!"

He wipes his nose on his jacket, but the tears are still flowing, and although he is visibly hurting for the loss of his love, I can't find it in my heart to feel any kind of sympathy towards him.

He has lost that privilege for good.

I take a good, long look at him, and I know that this is the last time I will ever see my brother again. Without speaking another word to him, I walk away, holding on tightly to the man beside me. Daniel's arm comes around my waist, and he kisses me gently on my cheek. He leads me to the train station, and the journey home is a complete haze. I don't know what I feel right now, but numbness is the last thing I expected.

Once we're back at my flat, Daniel leads me silently out to my balcony, and he sits down on one of my chairs before placing me on his lap. We sit like this, quiet, for the longest time, my thoughts running wild.

I should be sad that he's dead, shouldn't I? A young life is lost to a horrible addiction, and maybe I should feel a tiny sliver of sympathy towards him, but...

I hope he rots in hell.

Finally, Daniel's arms tighten around me, and he asks me, "Do you want to read the letter now?"

Gritting my teeth, I shake my head. "No. Burn it, please..."

He hesitates, and I turn to look into his eyes.

"I'm okay, I promise. I'm not sad that he's dead, and if that makes me a horrible person, then so be it."

"Are you *absolutely* sure?" he persists, scrutinising me. "Maybe you shouldn't do anything hasty right now...Let it rest for a while and then decide later on?"

Instead of answering, I move to stand up and walk the few steps to pick up my stash of cigarettes and the ashtray hidden behind my balcony door. As I walk back to him, I remove one, light it, and take a deep drag on it. As the smoke swirls between us, I put the ashtray on the table in front of us.

"Please give it to me," I ask him quietly, and he must see

how resolved I am, because he pulls out the letter from his jacket and hands it over without saying a word.

I point the tip of the cigarette to one end and watch, mesmerised, as the flame takes hold, before I place it in the ashtray. As we watch it burn, the tension in my body lifts slowly, and I feel lighter somehow. When there's nothing left but ashes, I put out the cigarette and take a deep breath.

Tom's hold on me is gone at last...vaporised into the thin air, cleansing me.

I reach my hand out to Daniel, and he stands up to walk towards me, and I gaze lovingly into his eyes when, instead of taking my proffered hand, he places his under my chin. His eyes are gentle, yet serious, and I try my best to reassure him and turn my head a bit to kiss his palm.

"He's gone, Daniel...And...I feel free of him at last."

Daniel smiles crookedly at me. "You're one remarkable woman, Emma Davenport."

I grin at him and put my arms around him. "Why, thank you, kind Sir." I kiss him soundly on his lips, and he chuckles.

"Make love to me, please...," I whisper and step up on my toes to reach his neck with my mouth, kissing it languidly, revelling in his taste.

His arms tighten around me, and his breathing picks up speed. He bends down and picks me up easily, and I wrap my legs around him as he walks us inside, away from prying eyes.

When he silently places me on my bed and begins to undress me, cherishing me with his mouth, his tongue, his hands, I lose myself entirely to him and let go.

No longer is there darkness, pain, or sorrow in my heart.

There is only hope, happiness, and laughter.

As he takes me softly, worshipping every part of my

body, I pour out all my love for him with my words and my touch.

One thought lingers as we come down from our high.

I believe in fairytales again.

THE END...OR IS IT?

So many of you have asked for more.
Well, here you go:

Turn the page and delve into the bonus chapters that take Emma & Daniel's journey a step further.

I hope you will love these extra scenes -

I have certainly enjoyed writing them.

NOTE

To my loyal readers:
Sometimes, there is a lot more to a story until you reach
The End.

Enjoy!

MEETING THE PARENTS - & NAN
SIX MONTHS AFTER EMMA AND DANIEL MET.

Chapter One
Oxford, England

EMMA

I'M BACK IN OXFORD for the first time in a year. Nothing's changed…The streets look the same like they always do: decorated to perfection now that December has arrived. People are lugging around all their shopping bags, some smiling with the anticipation that Christmas Day is only a few days away; others look haggard and bothered with the season, sour grimaces marring their features, and oozing impatience. I feel sorry for the latter.

My parents seem the same as always, though maybe somewhat happier than last year.

Nan hasn't changed, apart from looking slightly older.

Well, I guess *something* is a bit unusual this year.

I've brought Daniel with me.

And something else: *I* am not the same woman I was when I left home two years ago.

They say that time heals all wounds. I disagree. I think it is love that does that. Daniel is the reason I am a much happier, healthier person than I used to be.

I'm grateful for that, and I pray to the higher beings above that I will never take his love for granted.

Nevertheless, it's been a bit of a daunting experience for him to come here, I think.

I couldn't be happier that he agreed, though. Asking him to come with me was easy – but I never would have taken him for someone who suffers through fear of flying. He's become so confident in many ways the past couple of months, but maybe I have a tendency to forget to remind myself that underneath it all, he's a shy person, unused to meeting new people. I'm not arrogant, thinking that he's become better at overcoming his insecurities solely because of me. Being a student at university for the past three months has helped him face and move past a lot of things.

He's still my geek, though. And I wouldn't have him any other way.

♡

It's the 22nd of December, and although it's still pitch black outside, my internal clock tells me that it's no longer night but early morning instead. Daniel is still fast asleep, and I take comfort in the sounds of his faint snoring and the way his breath fans my neck.

My parents aren't so old-fashioned that they demanded we sleep in separate rooms during our stay, thankfully. I always sleep better at night when Daniel is near me, hence the reason we rarely spend any apart. It also gives me the perfect excuse to take advantage of his body if I wake up at night, turned on and in need of him.

Something that happens a lot, actually.

I glance at the bedside clock behind him and smile

slightly: only five-thirty am. Perfect. No one else will be awake for hours, and it gives me enough time for what I'm about to do. I turn on the light of the small lamp on my own bedside table and untangle my legs from the duvet. For once, I'm happy that I'm wearing PJs because there's a chill to my room that would have made me catch my breath if I'd been naked. Quickly, but carefully so as not to disturb Daniel, I get up and walk on my tip toes to the door and open it, sneaking outside as quietly as possible; I turn to the bathroom across my room. After having brushed my teeth and taken care of business – *why* do you always have to pee right after you wake up? – I walk quickly back. Daniel is still snoozing, his right arm outstretched, lying on my side as if he's been searching for me in his sleep, and my belly does a little flutter as I shamelessly take him in. The blankets are at his feet; he's wearing PJ's just like me to avoid the cold, only his are a simple black while mine are purple – an early Christmas present from my parents that they gave us when we arrived late last night. His face is calm in his sleep, his hair tousled and unruly, and he looks good enough to eat.

Damn...my own personal man candy. Yum.

When the cold in the room begins to seep into my toes, I walk back to him and gently remove his arm so that I can slide in beside him, only this time with my front to his.

Just as I'm about to lean down to kiss him, he grumbles, "Don't tell me you're wide awake already, please?"

I chuckle quietly and nuzzle my nose against his neck. The goose bumps rising fills me with happiness.

"Sorry, love," I whisper and kiss the sensitive skin below his ear. "You know me: I can never sleep for long."

He groans, his eyes remaining closed. "It's *dark* outside. It can't possibly be morning already."

"According to the clock, it is," I counter, and continue to nibble on his neck.

"Ugh...Impossible."

"How long are you going to keep your eyes closed?" I whisper and push him gently onto his back.

I take in the smirk on his face, and my stomach does that flip-flop again.

"I was kind of hoping that I'd convince you to go back to sleep if I kept them closed," he mumbles, still sounding far from awake.

"Haven't you come to terms with this about me yet? That I'm never going to be able to sleep in?" I snuggle closer to him and let my fingers trail through his chest hair peeking out from the V of his shirt.

"One can always hope." He opens one eye and grimaces slightly, probably because of the light behind me.

"Do we really have to get up already?" he groans and immediately shuts his eyes again.

I tilt my head and smile cheekily at him even though he can't see me. "By all means, you don't have to...As long as there's another part of your body that can *get up* instead, I'm happy to do the rest."

That gets his attention, because his eyes spring open immediately, and I lift my left leg and straddle him. Leaning down, I let my arms rest on either side of his face, and I look into his beautiful green eyes. Eyes that I noticed the moment we met. Eyes that can see right through me, and who immediately picks up on my mood when they gaze into mine. Eyes that speak to my soul.

Daniel grins as he takes a gentle hold on my arse. "I see...you woke up feeling frisky, eh?" He squeezes my bottom, and warmth spreads in my body with anticipation.

I rub my crotch against his and take pleasure when I feel a certain something beginning to rise to the occasion.

"Mm-hmm," I mumble, and move down to brush my lips against his. Daniel's eyes darken, and he moves his hands to my hips, pressing his cock into me, causing heat to rush to my very core.

"I gather you don't have a problem with that?" I whisper, my eyes fluttering closed when he places lingering kisses on my neck...as if we have all the time in the world to pleasure each other.

Technically, though, that isn't true, so I lean closer and kiss him in earnest, my tongue seeking his immediately. He growls into my mouth, and it's so sexy, so uncontrolled, that wetness gathers in my pussy.

Our passion will never fade, I'm sure of it.

He tilts his head before his hands cup my cheeks, his thumbs rubbing circles on my neck, and while I know he's letting me run the show for now, he won't be able to hold back for long.

I love him for it.

But he's also driving me kind of crazy at this very moment; the way his hips thrust gently up and down, up and down, his hardness torturing me endlessly is titillating and frustrating at the same time.

I need more.

I wrench my mouth away from his and pant, "I woke up wanting you to make love to me, but now I kind of want you to fuck me instead."

A sexy grin forms on his lips. "Not afraid that your parents will hear us?" His breath is laboured, he's just as turned on as me, and he squints at me as he starts to fumble with the drawstrings of my pants.

When he mentions my parents, I grimace and breathe deeply, trying to still the need in me for some wild lovemaking. Their room may be on the second floor while we're on the third, but that doesn't mean they won't be able to hear us if we're too loud.

"Shite," I mumble, but Daniel only chuckles at me, amusement taking over for a bit. He sits up, causing me to wobble in his lap, but he wraps his arms around me and I find my balance by holding on tight.

"You know," he mumbles and he looks into my eyes while his hands massage my arse. He's still breathing as quickly as me, and his cock pressing through the thin fabric of his pants and into my clit isn't exactly helping me turn it down a notch. "I'm kind of in the mood for slow."

Having him so close to me and looking at me with that hungry gaze of his always makes me give in to whatever he's in the mood for. I nod and let my arms fall to my side, and he smiles triumphantly at me as he starts to tuck my shirt free. Without making a sound, I raise my arms, and he lifts it up, his thumbs grazing the sides of my breasts as he does this. It causes my breath to speed up, but the chill from the room is a bit distracting.

Daniel notices the goose bumps and whispers, "Grab the blankets."

After I do as he asks, he covers up us both, creating our own personal tent in the middle of the bed, and warmth returns to my body soon after. It makes my heart melt at his sweet gesture. The light from the lamp is duller now, but I can still make out his features. His eyes zero in on my hardened nipples...they ache for his clever fingers...his mouth...his teeth.

He leans closer to me and our mouths are only a few

millimetres apart. He's moving achingly slow, teasing me by holding back, and I wrap my arms around his neck, silently begging him to close the distance between us.

"Remember to keep your voice down," he whispers, and I nod quickly. He looks down and pulls at the string on my pants again, and I lift up on my knees, wanting to help him free me of them.

He gasps when he finds me naked underneath them and watches, mesmerised, as his index finger slowly circles my clit. I watch him watch me so intently, and its turning me on like nothing else ever has.

No one has ever made me burn like Daniel does.

I bite my lip and try to keep the moan escaping my lips down.

I doubt I'm that successful.

"Fuck, you're so beautiful," Daniel breathes, and I remain on my knees so he can put two fingers inside my pussy. His fingers are magical, and I know he can feel how wet I am.

"Thank you," I whisper, and he raises his head. The passion in his gaze makes me shudder with longing to feel his mouth on me, and I put my hand on his shoulder, needing to feel his strong body underneath me.

"Never doubt it, sweetheart," he growls. "Play with yourself," he goes on to demand, tone rough with need, and I quickly lick my fingers and reach down to do as he wishes. His fingers leave my pussy, but only for a little while. After he's removed his shirt and tossed it behind him, his fingers push slowly back inside my wetness, and I gasp from the pleasure. Daniel's always watching me, murmuring deliciously dirty words to me.

"That's it, Em...let me see you get yourself off...fuck, that pussy is beautiful, so wet and turned on for me, isn't it?" There's lust in his voice, but more than that, there is love...a kind of reverence mingled with the lust, and it only makes me want to give in more often to him.

"Yes!" I gasp, still trying to keep my voice down, and I grip onto his shoulder with more force.

"You love it when I finger fuck you, don't you?" His fingers thrust inside me, and I start moving to the rhythm he is setting for me.

"Oh, yes," I whisper, and I have to close my eyes from the intense warmth coursing through me.

Tingles fill me as I keep playing with my clit, but I don't want to come just yet.

I don't want to stop, either.

"Kiss me, honey," I beg and lean forward to find his mouth. His kiss is ferocious, hungry, and he wraps his other arm around me, pressing my breasts to his front. His chest hair on my nipples, the friction on them is the breaking point, and I can't hold back any longer. His lips devour mine, his tongue matching the rhythm of his fingers thrusting deeply inside me, finding my sweet spot...it's all too much for me.

I cry my release into his mouth, and shudder violently as I come down from my high.

His kiss gentles, as do his fingers, but he keeps caressing me. His ministrations on my body are relentless, yet loving, and I wish I could stay like this forever.

I end the kiss slowly, not ready to lose his touch, but I have to come up for air at some point.

Daniel's satisfied smile is the first thing I see when I open my eyes, and I chuckle, my voice hoarse.

"That's just what I needed," I whisper, and he grins.

"I have to tell you that I fucking love when you let go by

my fingers."

I wrap my arms around his neck, sated and relaxed, and play with the hair on his nape.

"And I fucking love that you can," I reply and wiggle a bit, causing his fingers still inside me to hit that spot again, and it makes me shudder one last time.

"I've had a great teacher." He winks at me, and we laugh, yet keeping it low to avoid waking up the house.

I glance down at his lap, and the sight of his cock still standing fully erect almost makes me salivate. I lean back and begin to free it from its confinements.

"It's my turn to play," I mumble, and he hisses when I take a firm hold on the base.

"Tell me one of your fantasies as I suck you, Daniel," I tell him, and push him down on his back. I try to let him know with my eyes how serious I am. "I want to hear it."

"All my fantasies are about you," he pants as I stroke him from root to tip.

I smile at him. "I still want to hear one of them."

He must finally be able to see how serious as I am, because he nods slowly at me. His cheeks are flaming red, his lips plump and swollen from our kisses...He's never looked more delicious.

"Go on," I whisper, as I lean down to take the tip in my mouth.

He groans but does as I ask. "I want us to pretend we're strangers in a bar at a hotel," he whispers. "I want you to wear a short, black dress, and I want to...holy shit!" I've taken his delicious cock as far as I can, and hum as I start to play with his balls. He breathes deeply and spreads his legs wider for me.

He continues, "I want you to let me come onto you...to

chat as if we have never met...After some time, I want you to take my hand in yours and whisper in my ear that you have a room and that you want me to fuck you all night."

I press my thighs together, trying to alleviate the throbbing in my clit, and I keep our eyes locked: I'm already so turned on from his fantasy, and he hasn't even given me many details yet. Gently, I graze my nails on the underside of his cock, and it jerks in my hands.

Daniel swallows hard as I come up for air and lick the cockhead once more.

"I want you to tell me that you want to tie me up when we get to your room," he continues, and I stop what I'm doing, completely surprised by the turn this story is taking.

"I want to be at your mercy," Daniel whispers, and a thrill courses through me as I imagine the scene playing out in my head.

Shite, that would be hot.

Daniel fists his hands on the headboard behind him, his breaths coming faster now.

"You'll tell me to go down on you and lick you out at first, unable to move my arms or my legs," he whispers, and I have to play with my clit again.

I'm so massively turned on that I'm not sure I'll last before he reaches the end.

Greedily, I take his cock in my mouth once more, and he curses as he sees me reach down my tummy. He knows me so well...he knows how impatient I am.

"Fuck, I need to taste you, Emma...I need that sweet pussy in my mouth right now," he growls.

Wetness gathers between my legs, and I groan. I play with his balls more roughly now, just the way he likes it, and even let a finger wander back to caress his arse.

"Aaaah," he moans and then clamps a hand over his mouth.

I've never touched him there before, but it's something I've wanted to try for a while.

"It feels like heaven," he grunts, and he lifts his hips, giving me more room to play.

I can't stand it any longer, so I move around and lift my leg to straddle him from behind.

"Lick my pussy, please..." I resume sucking him off, my pace faster, more urgent, eager to please him. I press lightly against his puckered hole, and it pleases me when I hear him groaning again.

Firmly, he takes a strong hold on my arse and spreads the cheeks a bit. I can feel him blow on my clit, and it feels amazing.

"With pleasure," he whispers, and at last I feel his eager tongue on my pussy. I hum, and his cock jerks lightly in my mouth.

I don't know how long we keep doing this, but the familiar warmth in my body fills me more quickly this time. I let go of his cock, and as if he can read my mind, he turns me roughly before moving over me. I spread my legs as his mouth slams down on mine, and soon after, he thrusts inside me.

Our lovemaking isn't gentle. It's wild, rough, demanding...and just what I need now. I keep my eyes open as I meet his thrusts, needing to watch him unravel before me.

The orgasm tears through me even more fiercely than before, but our lips never leave the other's. Daniel stills, his arms around me shaking uncontrollably, before he settles heavily on top of me.

He kisses me languidly, slow and gentle, and I smile

against his lips. He opens his eyes and blinks at me before moving his hand to my cheek, his thumb caressing me.

"Wow," I breathe, and he smiles widely at me.

"You could say that again," he chuckles and then turns on his side and stretches. "I hope we didn't wake up the household," he mutters.

I shrug. For some reason, I don't care much about that part anymore. I cuddle close to him and kiss his chest, just above his heart. He lifts his arm so I can get more comfortable and grab the blankets from the floor with the other to cover us up.

"Well, if they did, there's nothing we can do now," I say, and draw random patterns on his chest.

He yawns loudly. "I guess there's no reason to worry about it unless they mention it."

I shake my head and we bask in the afterglow for some time.

"Did you like it when I touched your arse?" I ask him and look up as he snorts at me. His ears turn a bit red, and he's so adorable I just want to have my naughty way with him again.

"Are you joking?" Daniel glances down at me and turns to rest his hand on my hip bone.

"I fucking loved it," he replies, and I smile like the cat that got the cream. "It was so hot I thought I was going to spill my load then and there," he continues.

"I'll keep that in mind for future reference," I tell him and kiss him lightly on the lips.

Then I look at the alarm clock and almost panic.

"Oh gosh, we have to get up!" I shriek and jump out of the bed. "Nan will be here for breakfast any moment." I grab my pants and shirt from the floor and put them on, looking around for a hairband to tame my curls.

"What? It can't be that late," he grins at me.

I point at the alarm. "Our hanky-panky took over an hour, Daniel. So come on, get a move on."

He sighs and sits up on his elbows. "You're so bossy," he grumbles as he reluctantly removes the blankets.

Blowing him a kiss, I say, "You love me."

He stands up and grabs my arm as I rush past him, causing me to fall back against his chest. He wraps his own around me from behind, and I simply melt into him.

"Oomph," I breathe, and he removes some tendrils from my neck.

"I do," he whispers and then places a lingering kiss on my shoulder.

It makes me shudder as always.

Daniel squeezes me once and then release me. Taking a deep breath, I go in search of our bags to find some decent clothes to wear.

It's time for Daniel to meet Nan.

Chapter Two

DANIEL

I'D BE LYING IF I told Emma that I wasn't the least bit nervous about meeting her Nan.

I'm kind of scared to death because Ruth Davenport is a force to be reckoned with.

Even though I've spoken with her on the phone a few times over the past couple of months, and she's seemed nice, I know how important she is to my girl, thus making me break out in a cold sweat now that the day has finally arrived.

Nevertheless, I want her to meet me; to see who I am...what I mean to her beloved granddaughter.

Putting on my glasses, I check my appearance in the floor-length mirror standing next to Emma's old dresser. While my dress code has loosened up a bit since we met, I felt it somehow appropriate to wear my favourite pair of grey slacks, a simple white button-down shirt, and a dark-blue v-neck jumper. I want Emma's parents, and Ruth, to take me seriously.

They don't know it yet, and neither does Emma, but this meeting is more than important to me.

I want them to see that I mean it when I tell them that Emma is the love of my life.

I'm going to marry her one day.

Not tomorrow or maybe not even next year...but someday.

I can't wait.

For now, though, I need to get these nerves under control, or this visit will end up a complete disaster.

"You're looking very dashing," Emma whispers from behind me, and I smile at her reflection in the mirror.

"Thought it best to leave the funny t-shirts at home," I tease her, trying to avoid her finger poking my side.

She grins and steps around me to stand on her toes; she brushes her lips lightly across mine.

"No need to worry. They'll love you."

I inhale deeply and wrap my arms around her. She snuggles into my chest, and I rest my chin on her head as I stare, unseeing, out the window. It's been snowing since last night – hence the reason for our flight being delayed – and while it should probably soothe me, it doesn't.

"Don't take this the wrong way," I murmur, "but I can't wait for the official meeting to be over so we can spend the rest of our time here taking it easy."

She places her lips above my heart, and I take courage from her sweet gesture.

"I understand," she replies, and then leans away from me. I take in her appearance: she's wearing a dark-grey woollen dress with a V-neck covered in her favourite kind of silvery sparkles, and it stops just below her knees; it hugs her curves, and pride swells in my chest as I take her in. Her legs may be covered in some kind of leggings, but there's nothing frumpy about them; I know she gets cold during the winter months. Simple, black ballerinas are on her feet, and I'm a bit surprised she isn't wearing heels.

I peruse her face and am glad to see that she's gone a bit easy on the makeup for once: I love that she's not hiding herself as much as she used to. Her hair is hanging loosely down her back, and I revel in her beauty for a bit longer.

"You look stunning," I whisper, and smile when she looks down and her cheeks burn.

"Thank you," she says, and glances shyly at me.

I release my hold on her waist but take her right hand, lacing our fingers together.

I take one long breath again, and then announce, "I'm ready now."

"Good. Let's go downstairs so you can meet everyone properly, honey." Emma squeezes my hand and leads me out of the bedroom.

Here I go...like a lamb to the slaughterhouse.

As we walk down the two flights of stairs, I take in all the framed photos hanging on the walls. There are so many of them, and I wonder if the occupants realise how fascinating they are to someone like me who comes from such a different background. There are no real photos at my mum's place, just a few old ones from before my dad left us, depicting a happier time. I force the unhappy thoughts away and stop as one particular photo near the end of the landing catches my eyes. Emma stands on the step above, and I'm glad that she's letting me take my time.

The photo is of Julia, Ralph, Steven, Emma and Ruth, and it must be old, because I can barely recognise Emma: she looks to be maybe seven or eight years old, and she has her arms wrapped around the waist of her older brother, whose right arm is around her shoulders. The adults stand behind them, and it's taken somewhere outside – perhaps in the garden behind the house? It's summertime, and they all seem so...content. Without a care in the world.

My eyes return to the boy. Steven. The man makes my blood boil, but the child here? He looks...happy. Devoid of the sorrow and anger clouding him when we met. It's hard to grasp that he turned out to grow up to be a man not worth anyone's sympathy, but...I can't help but think it's a real shame even so.

"Do you miss him?" I ask Emma, my voice quiet, hesitant even. I turn to look up at her, but she doesn't meet my eyes. "I know we don't talk about him, and I understand why...but..." My voice trails off and I wait patiently for her reply.

Eventually, she sighs slightly and looks at me. Sadness clouds her features, and I want to kick my arse for even mentioning him.

"I miss what might have been," she answers shakily, and then shakes her head at me. "But I know that the reality is different, and there's no point dwelling on the past. I'm learning to let go, Daniel. Let's not talk about him anymore this Christmas, please?" She lifts her hand to caress my face, and I lean into her touch and nod once.

Murmuring from the kitchen interrupts the intimacy of our moment, and I try to make out who's talking.

"*Have you heard them have wild sex yet?*" a voice says, and I freeze on the spot. It must be Ruth, because someone shushes her loudly.

"*Nan, for god's sake...*" The deep voice can only belong to one person: Ralph, Emma's dad.

I groan and close my eyes before letting my head fall forward into Emma's chest. She chuckles slightly and kisses me quickly on my head before she reaches down to take my hand in hers.

"This is *not* funny," I whisper harshly, causing her to laugh louder.

"Oh, but it is. Come on, now. We can't dally here the rest of the morning."

I raise my head and can't help but smile back when I find the ghosts of the past have left her again. Her eyes shine with laughter, and without saying a word further, she moves past me, still holding on tightly to my hand, and she leads me into the kitchen.

"There you are!" Ruth exclaims from her seat at the far corner, and she moves to stand up, somewhat struggling a bit, and Emma walks quickly towards her.

"Nan, you don't have to get up," she says as she leans down to hug her.

Ruth huffs as she gets to her feet and waves her off, but returns her embrace warmly. "Oh, fiddlesticks, of course I do. When you meet a new member of the family for the first time, you make an effort. Now, stand back, please, and let me look at you."

Emma does as she says, but leaves her hands in Ruth's. Ruth looks closely at her granddaughter for a long time, unsmiling, and the nerves that had let me be while looking at the photos in the hallway hit me full force once again. But I stay in the background: there's something that tells me this moment between them mustn't be interrupted. I glance to the kitchen where Ralph and Julia have stopped preparing breakfast. They both have smiles on their faces, and warmth settles in my stomach.

Coming here for the holidays was the right decision for us.

My silent musings are interrupted when Ruth speaks again.

"You're happy, aren't you?" she asks Emma, head tilted to the side as she waits for her answer.

Emma nods. "Very happy, Nan."

Finally, Ruth beams. "Good. I can tell that you are, my dear, and that makes *me* happy in turn."

I let out the breath I didn't even know I was holding back

when she looks around Emma and finds me still waiting near the entrance.

"Come closer, young man, I don't bite." She releases one of Emma's hands and takes a step towards me.

I grin, still nervous, but walk quickly towards her, my hand stretched out towards her.

"How do you do, Mrs. Davenport?" I greet her, and she winks at me, showing her dimples.

"I'm very well, thank you, Daniel." We shake hands, and I'm a bit surprised when her grasp is firmer than I had anticipated. But I suppose it shouldn't be: she may look her age, but she's definitely not frail. She's wearing a black spencer, a light-blue turtleneck underneath it, and finally a blue cardigan.

"It's lovely to meet you, and please call me Nan. 'Mrs Davenport' makes me sound so old." She looks sternly at me and after I nod once, she turns back to her comfy chair behind her.

"Likewise." I shuffle a bit on my feet, unsure of where I should sit when Julia unknowingly comes to my rescue.

"Please take a seat, Daniel. Seeing as it's Christmas, Ralph and I are foregoing our clean living and are cooking a full English breakfast for you."

"And thank goodness for that," Ralph grumbles from his place by the stove where it seems that he's about to start frying the bacon.

Julia shakes her head fondly at him, and seeing them so relaxed and at ease causes the nerves to settle a bit more.

"I trust that you slept well?" Julia motions for me to sit down as she brings me and Emma coffee cups, and I take a chair at the dining room table. Emma walks to the chair to my left, her hand lingering at the nape of my neck as she walks past me.

"Thanks, mum, we did," Emma replies as she sits down.

"I'm glad. Emma told me that you prefer coffee instead of tea, just like her," Julia continues, "and it should be finished soon."

"Are you sure I can't help you with anything?" I ask her as I take the cup from her. "I'm happy to help."

Before she has a chance to reply, Ruth chimes in, "Oh, he's polite, Emma. I like that."

I smile briefly at her, satisfied that she seems to like what she sees of me so far.

"Oh, no, we've got this," Julia tells me and smiles warmly at me. "You just take it easy and relax."

She moves back to the kitchen, and I turn to Emma when I feel her hand on my thigh under the table.

I smile relieved at her when she winks at me.

This isn't so bad.

Emma looks at her dad. "Dad, are we going to the Lewis' farm to find our tree like we used to?"

He turns his head, a bit preoccupied with the bacon sizzling on the stove, it would seem, as he doesn't look at her for long, and nods. "Yes, of course. I've already phoned them so they know we're coming by later this morning."

Emma leans back in her chair and sighs lightly. "Good. I've been looking forward to it for weeks."

I love how content she is right now.

Ralph chuckles. "Now, let's try to not get too carried away this year, please. Our living room isn't *that* big." He removes some bacon and places it on a plate covered in a couple of napkins to let the fat drip before he gives her his full attention. "Though I am happy that you haven't become too old yet for going out with your dad."

She smiles warmly at him. "I'll never become too old for that."

"Good." He clears his throat and smiles briefly at Emma before he returns to the task at hand, and we sit in comfortable silence as Julia brings the coffee pot to the table.

"Here you go," she murmurs, and we both thank her.

I look at Ruth when I hear a clicking sounding from her chair in the corner: she has a large bag at her feet, and she picks up two rolls of yarn, black and yellow, as well as knitting needles. Seeing her begin to knit, I feel a small pang hit me in the heart. It's bittersweet to see her taking pleasure from a hobby that I remember vaguely my own mother used to have as well...before her life spiraled out of control, that is.

"What are you knitting?" I raise my voice slightly so that she can hear me. Emma has told me that her hearing isn't as good as it once was.

"Socks," she replies and looks briefly at me, her glasses hanging on the tip of her nose. "Ralph has never worn the ones you can buy in the supermarkets, so I spend a lot of time knitting new pairs for him."

"My mum used to knit," I blurt out, and immediately want to bite my tongue for not keeping that small bit of information to myself.

"I didn't know that," Emma says from my side, and I shrug shyly.

"Oh?" Ruth looks at me, and I turn my attention back to her. There's a lot of meaning in that single word: curiosity, yes, but also a tint of hesitation.

Instead of answering, I nod as I take a large sip of my coffee.

"Well, it's a nice kind of pastime, I suppose," Ruth goes on. "And I love to knit while watching a good crime show on the telly. But it's not for everyone: it takes patience...a good dash of imagination, too, in my opinion. I once tried to teach Emma, but she couldn't keep still long enough to learn it properly. Do you remember?" She looks fondly at Emma who grins at her, completely at ease beside me.

"I'll start knitting socks for you, too." Ruth looks at me briefly, understanding in her eyes, and then she picks up knitting once more, letting the subject go.

I'm grateful for that. But moreover, I'm touched that she offers to do that for me...somehow taking in that it means a lot to me.

"Thank you," I murmur, and she looks at me.

"Entirely my pleasure, my dear."

Julia comes over with plates, knives and forks and starts to set the table. The rest of the morning is spent relishing the delicious food, small-talk, and after an hour or so has passed, I no longer feel nervous.

I feel as if I belong here.

That this could eventually become my second home.

Both Ralph and Julia seem very interested to learn more about the bookshop, and I love watching Emma as she tells them, in great detail, what it's like and where she sees it going in the future. The pride and joy in their eyes make me happy. And proud as hell of what Emma has accomplished in a short amount of time.

Ruth takes great pleasure in teasing us – and embarrassing Ralph – by telling stories from her wild youth, and my cheeks ache from laughing so hard at a particular saucy story that involved skinny dipping with a young professor one summer back in 1935 in a lake near the grounds of the university she attended back then. Obviously, she was still a student, and they were almost caught by her fellow peers.

After we've all eaten way more than we probably should, Emma goes upstairs to change her outfit to one that's more fitting for cutting trees; her parents are loading the dishwasher, once again refusing my help, and I'm nursing my last cup of coffee for the day.

I turn to look at the gardens to my left, smiling relieved, when I feel a hand pressing down on my right arm. I look down at Ruth who, all of a sudden, seems more serious than she'd been before now.

"I know Emma has told you what happened," she whispers, glancing to the kitchen, and she lifts a hand at me, urging me to come closer. I lean towards her, trepidation filling me, because it doesn't take a university degree to understand what she's referring to. Her next words, however, take me by surprise.

"I love Steven, because he's my grandson. It's basically impossible for me not to," she smiles apologetically at me. "And my son and daughter-in-law love him, too, of course, because he's their child. So you must know how difficult it must be for them that he's not spending the holidays with them, and hasn't for years?" She looks beseechingly into my eyes, and I nod my understanding.

"We haven't seen Steven in years, but I try to keep in touch with him by writing letters to him – or, well, sending him *emails*," she spits out the word, and I can't help but smile slightly at the scorn that's easily detected in her voice.

She inhales deeply and look down at a piece of bacon resting on her plate, letting the tips of her fingers move it around in the cooling baked beans. She seems to gather her thoughts, and I wait patiently, even though I feel uneasy about her reason to tell me all this.

"Sometimes he replies back, but not often...I hope that I will live long enough to see Steven come to his senses, but we all know how fickle fate can be, and so I don't know if my wish will be granted. In case that I don't..."

Her hesitation is loaded with meaning, and I'm starting to comprehend how torn she and the rest of the family must feel, through no fault of their own.

It's Steven's fault.

"Daniel, I can see how much love you hold for Emma, and I see the same kind of love shining from her soul when you are near. I have no doubt that you are a match made in heaven, and I thank my lucky stars for bringing you to us."

Her words fill me with warmth, and I don't know what to say. She smiles gently at me, happiness mingled with sadness in her brown eyes evident for me to see.

"In case I never get my wish...Can I trust you to try to make it come true for me? Will you promise me that?"

I sigh and look down at my feet, taking time to really think her request through. I don't wish to make a promise I'm not sure I can keep.

Finally, I lean back in my seat and meet her gaze.

"I promise. I'm not sure I'll be able to, and I don't even know if there's any way for me to help, but...I'll try."

Ruth nods slowly at me while she stares out the window at the sun gleaming through the leaves of the trees. It stopped snowing a while ago, and I'm glad.

After some time has passed, she breaks the silence. "All any of us can ever really do is try our best, Daniel."

She turns her head to look at me once more. "You're a fine man, Daniel Larsen. I know you'll do what you can...and I realise that it's probably an impossible request I've made. Try to let it go for now, yes?"

Before I can answer, Ralph comes over to the table.

"What are the two of you whispering about?" he asks and rests a hand lightly on Ruth's shoulder.

She pats it lightly. "Oh, nothing, really. I just told Daniel that I plan on becoming at least 120 years old." She winks at me and I chuckle.

Ralph smiles at her, yet it doesn't completely erase the worrisome glint I see there.

"Well, if anyone can, it's you," he replies and looks at her plate. "Would you like some more to eat, Nan?"

Ruth shakes her head. "I'm about to burst, so no thank you."

He nods and clears her plate. Ruth watches him go and then leans conspiratorially towards me.

"Now, I am well aware that you young people swear by using emails, Facebook, and all that, but would you mind sending me a hand-written letter from time to time, telling me how you are? It would please me to no end."

I'm beginning to wonder if *anyone* is able to turn down this woman.

"It would be my pleasure," I assure her, and she grins at me once more.

"You're a good man, Daniel. You'll go far, I can tell. Now..." she points to her chair in the corner. "Could you hand me my knitting, please? Ralph has loads of socks so I think I'll start making you a pair instead. With any luck, you'll be able to bring them home with you when you leave at New Year's."

"Of course." Her gesture warms me, and I stand up and go to do as she asks.

When I pick up the bag and turn back, I find Julia and Ralph on either side of her, and Julia is hugging her tightly.

There are tears falling from her cheeks, and my heart cracks a little from seeing them. I acknowledge their need for privacy and pretend to look around on the floor for more yarn, giving them the time they seem to need.

A phrase I have often heard but never quite understood until now enters my thoughts:

"Family isn't whose blood you carry…It's who you love and who loves you back."

Indeed it is.

And this is my new family.

In time, I hope they will come to think of me the same way.

TATTOOS & TRINKETS

EMMA & DANIEL'S ONE-YEAR ANNIVERSARY

Chapter One

EMMA

ONE YEAR SINCE I met Daniel.
One year since I began my journey of healing.
And one year since I opened my heart up to the possibility of love.

Lots of things can happen throughout the course of a year, and this one proves the point. I don't believe in fate as such, but I can't help but wonder sometimes that if I hadn't been late for work on that fateful day, and if Daniel hadn't been the nephew of my boss, Mr. Andersen, if we'd ever have met?

It's not a thought that worms its way into my mind often, but, every now and then, I wonder…but then I stop because the thought of never having met him?

It's unbearable…heart-breaking.

Simply unacceptable.

It's a good thing that I still don't tend to dwell on all the negative stuff.

♡

I've been wracking my brain for weeks now, trying to

come up with the perfect gift for Daniel, and I think I've finally figured it out. The question, though, is if he'll think the same. Maybe it's a bit cuckoo, or just plain crazy, or too sappy, but I don't care.

Today is the day when I get a new tattoo – one that represents Daniel and how he makes me feel. Lately, he's hinted at having one done on his own body, but I honestly can't see this happening. He's just too sweet and geeky for that.

We woke up early as usual – well, I did – and after Daniel took his time making sweet love to me, he made me a special anniversary breakfast: pancakes with strawberries and cream. I was so touched when he presented me a jewellery box afterwards, and it turned out to hide the most exquisite silver necklace with a dream catcher attached to it.

I'm such a lucky girl.

Obviously, I couldn't help but attack him again after he'd put the necklace around my neck, and we ended up spending one of the best showers in the history of showers.

That man has always been quick to learn.

It's now ten am, and we're sitting on the bus, headed into town, and my tummy is swarming with butterflies.

What if he hates it?

What if he thinks it's stupid?

What if…what if…what if..?

I'm going crazy, trying to come up with something to say to distract my nerves, but my mind is drawing a blank. Or it just can't focus on anything else, at least.

"You're awfully quiet," Daniel says from beside me, and gently trails patterns on my hand with his fingers. They send a chill throughout my body, but I don't mind. They remind me of our strong physical connection as well as the emotional one.

I try to play it cool and keep my eyes turned to the window.

"I'm just thinking, I guess."

"About?" he prompts, and my lips lift infinitesimally.

"The last year - how we met - our lives," I muse, and sigh gently.

"Oh...that's deep." I can hear the teasing note in his voice and grin automatically as my eyes meet his.

"Oh yes, very. So are you excited about your surprise?" I ask him and lean my head on his shoulder.

I can never seem to get close enough to this man...and I love it.

I can feel him shrug slightly underneath my chin.

"I am, but also a bit anxious if you're going to like the one I have for you..." His voice trails off, and I squeeze his hand.

"I'm sure I'll love it whatever it is," I try to reassure him. "Either way, I'm just happy our anniversary is on a Sunday, so you didn't have to go to university, and that the shop is closed."

"Did you manage to track down that author you talked about the other day?" Daniel asks me. "The one who, according to you, no one really knows is a man or a woman?"

I grunt. "Nope, not yet...I really want him/her to let me do an interview I can post on my website, but, so far, no such luck, unfortunately. I think it's a man..."

"Why is that?"

"Because the way he writes...? It just has this male air to it that makes me believe that no woman writes like that." I shrug. "I'll keep trying, though. The problem with the big publishing houses in the UK is that they don't really take notice of a small, insignificant bookshop in Denmark. It's just the way it is. BUT…" I lean slightly away from him and meet his questioning eyes. "I did manage to find out that this mystery writer lives in Scotland. So that's something, I suppose. I just have to dig a bit harder."

"Hmm…It's annoying," Daniel grumbles, and I chuckle.

"I love that you asked, though. It means a lot to me that you remember these things," I add quietly, and there it is again; that warm, fuzzy feeling his caring always creates in my entire being.

He kisses my head quickly.

"I'm always interested to know what goes on in the shop," he reassures me.

"I know, and I love you for it. Have you spoken to Andreas lately?" I ask him.

He chuckles. "I meant to tell you that he rang yesterday afternoon before you got home. He asked, no, wait, more like *demanded* to tell you to call him soon. He said he misses you."

I smile and then straighten in my seat. The train station is our next stop.

"I miss him, too," I murmur. I glance at Daniel as we both stand up. "I'll ring him later today or tomorrow."

He pulls me along and, as usual, lets me walk in front of him as the bus stops, his hand resting lightly on my lower back – such a gentleman.

"Good. I say, he's getting rather grumpy on his old days," he muses.

I laugh loudly as we walk to the platform. "Is he? Maybe he just needs a hobby now that he's been living in France for a while and the novelty has worn off. Or some female companionship"

Daniel groans, and I wink at him.

"Please don't mention my uncle and *female companionship*

in the same sentence," he begs and pulls me closer to his side as we walk up the stairs to the right platform.

"Why? That man needs a woman," I tease him and wrap my arm around his waist.

"Maybe so, but it feels weird to think about him like that."

"How very old-fashioned of you," I gripe, but I guess I see his point. I can't even *think* of my parents and what they get up to now that they have the house to themselves without visibly cringing; it's just not natural.

"Anyway," Daniel interrupts the unwelcoming thoughts. "He also said that he hopes to come visit us this fall."

I beam at him as we stop on the platform. Our train has yet to arrive.

"That would be fantastic! We haven't seen him for months."

Daniel chuckles and leans down to brush his lips against mine, lightly tugging on my lip ring. It sends shocks of fire straight through my body to my toes, as always, and I can't wait until we're alone again.

"I thought you might be pleased, and told him that as well. Be sure to let him know that when you speak with him, yeah? It'll make him happy to hear it."

I nod. "I will, I promise."

"Good." He smiles at me, and it makes my heart warm when I see the happiness shining back at me.

A high-pitched whistle interrupts our conversation briefly. The train is coming closer, and we stand back as it slows and stops entirely. We wait for the passengers to get out before entering it ourselves, and then find a corner where we both can stand up without getting jostled too much by the other passengers hurrying to get to the city centre on this warm day.

As we stand there, Daniel's arm braced on the handle above me, I admire his good looks. I kind of like the beard he's growing, because it feels absolutely fabulous when we're intimate.

He doesn't seem to mind my silent perusal, and I have to confess that I enjoy the view often, completely unabashed. What can I say? He's handsome…it would be odd if I didn't do it.

"You're staring again," Daniel whispers, and I can see he has to fight to keep a straight face. His ears are turning red, and it's funny…in a good way, of course.

"Why, yes…yes, I am. I can't help it that you're so gorgeous I just want to attack you all the time," I tease, and he groans and shakes his head lightly.

"Shhh," he whispers, and I bite my lip.

I guess there's a time and place for everything, and a train filled with people eavesdropping is probably not it.

"Sorry…I didn't mean to embarrass you," I whisper, a bit uncertain if I tend to push it too far sometimes.

I look down at my feet, but am forced to raise my head when I feel his finger pressing in on my chin. Reluctantly, I meet his gaze.

"Hey, you didn't…and you don't, sweetheart. I'm very flattered that you feel that way."

"But?" I ask, confused by his reaction.

He leans down and turns slightly, his breath fanning my neck. The angle is such that the other passengers are unable to see what he's doing. When he places a soft kiss on the sensitive skin behind my ear, I shiver.

"But…whenever I feel your eyes on me, staring so

intently?" he whispers, and I nod slightly. "I start to get a hard-on, and I don't want people to see that."

"Oh," I breathe, and then chuckle. "That's not good, I guess."

"Well, let me put it this way: it makes it bloody difficult to keep my hands off you, and if we were at a place where we wouldn't be interrupted, nothing would stop me from ravaging you every time it happens…"

His voice has turned husky, causing a low throb to start in my core, yet I know that I'll have to be patient before having my wicked way with him again.

I lean up on my toes to whisper in his ear. "But what if we were at a place when it would be considered…odd to not give in to our desires with an audience…would it then be okay?"

His breath hitches, and I know he gets my point. The thrill of having other people watching us while making love has fascinated the both of us for a while now, but we haven't acted on it yet.

"Fucking perfect," he growls low, and then nips at my earlobe, not too gently this time. "It would be more than okay, Emma, you know that."

"We really do have to do something about it…and soon." The thought is so tantalising, so intriguing and forbidden, somehow. I'm sure my body will catch on fire soon if I don't force the topic off and away for now.

"Yes…we do." Daniel shifts on his feet and takes a step back. He clears his throat, eyes not leaving mine, and I can feel a flush erupt in my cheeks.

Trying to be discreet, I scan the faces of the other passengers the closest to us, but none seem to have heard our private conversation.

Thank goodness.

"So...Errm...Going to tell me where we're going?" he asks me, and I'm glad he's trying to change the subject.

I shake my head. "You'll just have to be patient and wait and see."

He sighs, but smiles while doing it.

"I'm good with that."

So am I.

♡

"You've got to be joking," Daniel murmurs, mouth hanging open, clearly baffled, as we stand in front of *"Cows & Goats Tattoo Parlour"*, and my heart plummets with disappointment, but I try to not let it show.

"Don't worry, you're not the one getting inked, Daniel," I grumble and release his hand. "I am."

"No, wait, you misunderstand me," he rushes to say, and takes my hand in his, pulling me back.

Back rigid, my eyes misting, I don't look at him, but say, "What, then? Your reaction just now speaks for itself."

"Sweetheart, please look at me." He tugs gently at my hand.

My eyes dart everywhere but at him, reluctant to do as he wishes. I never was a coward, though, so I finally relent on a small sigh and raise my head, meeting his eyes. He seems concerned, the corners of his mouth turned down.

Sniffling, I say, "Daniel, it's okay if you think it's a horrible idea, but I've wanted to have a tattoo that represents you and what you mean to me for a long time now. And I thought..." My breath hitches, not disguising the hurt I'm feeling right now, but I persevere. "I thought that having parts of it done today, on our one-year anniversary, would be a nice gift."

He frames my face between his hands and leans down to kiss the tip of my nose. Bending down in his knees so our eyes are almost perfectly aligned, he smiles wide at me.

Wait...what the what?

"It's the perfect gift, Emma," he whispers, and I frown, thoroughly confused.

"But...you didn't...I mean, just now, you seemed to think the opposite?"

He chuckles. "No, I didn't. You jumped to conclusions as usual."

I pout. "Did not."

"Did, too." He raises an eyebrow. "The only reason I said that is because I have an appointment with Kristian this afternoon."

I blink rapidly. "You've what?"

"Mm-hmm...Quite the coincidence, wouldn't you say so?" he teases me, and my heart is fit to burst with happiness now.

He did this for me.

"I'm sorry," I whisper, twisting my hands. I feel really foolish right now, and I know I need to stop this *'talking before thinking thing'* that most people seem able to master.

"For what?"

"For misunderstanding," I mutter, chewing on my lip ring.

Daniel shrugs. "It's okay, Em. But please work a bit on it."

I nod quickly. "I will, I promise."

"Good. Now..." He releases my face and takes my hand once more. "This is a wonderful surprise. Thank you."

I squeeze his hand. "You're welcome. Ready?"

He nods again. "Ready."

Hand in hand, we walk inside the shop, and the familiar excitement about getting a new tattoo – *Daniel's tattoo* – on my body sets in.

I know that there's no way these symbols will be done today; but it's a start, at least.

Chapter Two

DANIEL

I CAN'T BELIEVE THAT it's already been a year.
One year where I've been the happiest I could ever hope to be.
A year that has given me love and a home.
After we spent Christmas with Emma's family in Oxford, Nan has kept true to her promise: every couple of weeks, she sends me knitted socks, and while I don't exactly wear them – because that is too old-fashioned, even for me – I save them all in my dresser. I understand and appreciate her gesture. I've upheld my promise to her and send her handwritten letters or postcards when I can.
I know that Nan loves them, because she tells me often, and I have come to enjoy writing them.
Who'd have thought that meeting this spitfire of a woman would make me realise that while I may not have much to do with my blood relatives, that's not really important. People's actions speak louder than words. Nan's actions tell me that she has accepted me into her heart, and I'm grateful for it.
And now…now I'm ready to show Emma in more than mere words how much she means to me.
I can't say that I'm exactly looking forward to having my skin pierced with a tattoo needle, but, on the other hand, I have a high threshold for pain.
How bad can it be?
Maybe it's crazy, but I don't bloody care.
I only hope that she likes the words I've chosen.

As we walk inside the tattoo parlour – with the most ridiculous name I've ever come across – I take in how quiet it is.

"Hello?" Emma calls out, but no one answers back.

A faint giggle, though, comes from the closed door to our left marked *Office*, and I smirk when I hear a male voice curse loudly.

I open my mouth but then close it again, not really sure what to do now.

The soothing caresses from Emma's thumb circling on my hand draws my attention, and I smile down at her.

"Are you sure you've got the time right?" I ask her, and she nods.

"Yes. I even rang Kristian yesterday, confirming it."

"Hmm...I hope we're not interrupting anything," I muse, and she nudges her shoulder against my arm.

"Well, too bad. I've been so excited for this, so he'll just have to get out here and focus instead of playing around with the staff." She grins at me, and I can't hold back my laugh. I try to cover it up, turning it into a cough, when the door to the office opens and Kristian enters the shop, some tattooed girl in tow.

Smiling sheepishly at me, he comes closer until he stops in front of us.

"Sorry," he mumbles and places his hands in his back pockets, shifting on his feet. When I see the warmth in his eyes as his gaze zeroes in on my girlfriend, I stand a bit taller and place an arm around her shoulders.

I know that Kristian's a nice guy, but I don't think I'll ever be entirely comfortable that he holds a soft spot for Emma.

I'm a guy. I get jealous sometimes. It's just the way it is.

"It's okay," Emma teases him, smirking. "I hope we

didn't arrive at a too...err...explosive time."

Kristian bursts out laughing, and so does the girl he was with from behind her station at the entrance. They don't seem embarrassed anymore, and I guess there really isn't a reason for it; we're all adults here.

"Oh, not at all," he says, still chuckling and then comes closer to us. I'm forced to release Emma as he doesn't stop but instead invades our space, wrapping his arms around her. I almost let out a growl in warning when he decides to linger for longer than I like.

"We were all done," he says when he steps back, and I reach out my hand for him to shake. He turns his eyes to me and narrows them slightly.

"Daniel," he greets me, cordially enough, but I don't miss the clipped edge to his tone.

"Kristian," I murmur, putting a bit more pressure on his hand.

We stare each other down for a few seconds, and I guess he finally gets the message when his lips lift up ever so slightly and he takes a step back.

"Happy anniversary," he says, and Emma leans into my body. I relax my stance and nod.

Truce.

"Thanks."

"I must say it's been hard to keep you two in the dark," he proceeds to tell us, and I look down at Emma briefly before returning my eyes to him.

"You mean, about our appointments with you?"

"Yes. I'm glad I didn't accidentally blurt it out to either of you, though, ruining it for you. So, Emma..." He claps his hands and seems to kind of buzz with excitement while maintaining his professional persona.

"Should we get started?" he asks her.

Emma nods and smiles at me before we both follow Kristian to his work station at the other end of the shop.

"You know how it goes, Em," Kristian says and looks at her before turning to wash his hands in the sink behind him.

Emma removes her top and sits down on the bench. "Yep. I've got it."

Kristian dries his hands before procuring a pair of latex gloves from the drawer next to his station.

"Good."

He lifts his head and looks at me questioningly.

"Do you want to see the design before I get started?"

I nod, kind of nervous if the butterflies in my stomach are anything to go by, but the overriding emotion is excitement.

"Yes, please."

He hands me a drawing and my heart beats wildly in my chest when I reach for it.

"I hope you'll like it," Emma murmurs from beside me before I have a chance to look at it.

I lean down to kiss her lips.

"I'm sure I'll love it," I answer as I move back, staring intently in her eyes. I need her to see the sincerity behind mine before we get started.

When she smiles slowly after a few seconds have passed, I know that she understands.

"I love you," she whispers.

"I love you, too," I whisper back, but a groan interrupts our private moment.

"Will you two please stop all that lovey-dovey stuff?" Kristian gripes. "You'll make a renowned bachelor want to go in search of his own happily-ever-after. Sod it all to hell." He bats his eyelashes at us, blowing me a kiss in jest, and I snort at him.

"Just you wait," Emma says, pointing a finger at him. "One day, you'll meet a woman who'll knock you flat on your arse, and then you'll know what it's like."

He rolls his eyes at us, but I can see the teasing glint in them.

He ignores Emma's statement and lifts his chin, pointing at the paper in my hands.

"Tell me what you think of the design so we can get on with things, please."

I'd almost forgotten that it was in my hands, so I quickly look down. When I see it, I have to clear my throat for fear of being overcome by emotion.

The sun Kristian has drawn is the focal point of the design, and the yellow colour is beautiful, but it's the eagle in the middle that grabs my attention. It's in flight, wings spread wide, and you can see each feather clearly. Its eyes are alert, assessing...but warm, somehow. Underneath the images, there is a quote in swirling script that I don't know, but that speaks volumes:

To love is to burn, to be on fire.

Long seconds tick by as I keep repeating these powerful words silently in my head.

"Do you like it?" Emma's voice forces me to shift my attention back to her, and I swallow the lump in my throat and meet her anxious gaze.

"It's perfect, sweetheart," I state loudly, and she beams at me.

"I'm so glad," she says and grabs my hand.

I smile at her before taking one last look at the design.

"I'm not familiar with the quote," I murmur.

"It's one of Jane Austen's," Emma tells me, and it makes sense that she would choose a saying from one of the greatest female novelists in history.

Handing the paper over to Kristian, I tell him, "It's amazing."

He nods once as he takes it and then looks at Emma.

"I'm glad you both like it. I'll start with the eagle today, and depending on how it goes, we'll schedule your next appointment before you leave, yeah?"

Emma nods and turns around to lie facedown on the bench.

"Sounds good to me."

Kristian grabs his stool and sits down, pushing it forward. He turns on the lamp above and places it so it beams down on Emma's back.

"There's a chair behind you if you would like to sit down, Daniel," he says, and I look behind me to find it where he says it is.

As I sit down, Emma turns her head so that she can smile into my eyes.

"Thank you," I whisper as the buzz from the needle starts. "It's truly perfect."

Emma braces herself as Kristian tells her to hold still, and then the transformation of the design begins.

♡

It's been a few hours, and I think Emma's had enough for today. Apparently, so does Kristian, because he abruptly turns off the machine.

He cracks his neck and grabs a water bottle from the table

behind him.

"Let's stop now, Em," he tells her as he hands the bottle to her.

"But I don't want to," she protests, voice grumpy, and Kristian looks at me, telling me with his eyes that I need to run interference here.

I place my arms on the bench and rest my head there.

"Actually, I'm famished. I could definitely use a break."

She narrows her eyes at me, and I smirk.

"Liar," she mutters, but a loud growl erupting from my stomach belies her accusation.

Kristian laughs. "I guess that answers that," he says and grabs another water bottle. "Why don't the two of you go out, get something to eat, and then come back here so I can get you inked, Daniel?"

I straighten in my seat, sort of nervous now.

Emma chuckles. "Oh, I can't wait for this."

I pretend to scowl at her, but I know she sees right through it when she laughs louder.

"Just let me apply the lotion and get your covered up, Em," Kristian says, and while he applies plenty of the gooey substance on her skin, he instructs me on how to help Emma the next week or so.

It seems fairly simple, and I take the lotion from him along with a list of things we need to be aware of. I realise that Emma has done this plenty of times, but I haven't, and I appreciate how thorough he is.

"Okay, I'll see you in an hour or so," I tell Kristian once Emma is back on her feet and has had some more water.

"See you," Kristian replies, and then we're out the door.

"Anything in particular you'd fancy for lunch?" I ask her as we walk hand in hand down the street.

She shrugs. "Not really, no. Surprise me, yeah?"

"What about that pub near The Stork Fountain?" I ask her. "They do make some great Irish food there."

She smiles at me.

"Sounds great. Are you nervous about getting your virginal skin inked?"

I laugh. "First of all, I'm hardly a virgin anymore, and secondly…" I stop and tug on her hand. She moves closer and I wrap my arms around her back, pulling her into my embrace.

Her lips part and she breathes more quickly now.

"Secondly, I want you to fully grasp how much you mean to me, and having this quote on my body, above my heart?" I wait until she nods, her attention completely on me. "Well, I'm hoping you'll never forget how much I love you."

She wraps her arms around my neck. "I could never forget that."

I shrug lightly. "Even so, I still want it as a reminder."

"Okay, then. Let's get some lunch and then head back to get it done. I'm dying to know what it is!" She kisses me loudly on my lips, and I loosen my hold on her waist.

"Let's do that."

♡

Now that it's my turn to lie back on Kristian's bench in his studio, I almost wish I hadn't had such a big lunch. But then again, I know how important it is that I don't fall sick while here, and food as well as the soda I just consumed should prevent that.

Emma sits beside me, almost bouncing in her seat, and I smile crookedly at her excitement.

"You'll have to take it a bit easy on me for a while," I tease her, and she grins at me.

"Oh, don't you worry, honey. I'm very creative."

Kristian groans and I turn my head to see his hanging down, his shoulders tense.

"What now?" I frown, confused about his reaction.

"Enough with the sentimental love stuff, please!" he says and lifts his head. He points an accusing finger in Emma's direction. There's a smile on his face, though, so I'm not too alarmed by his reaction.

"I never thought you'd be one of those ultra girly girls, Em. All the innuendos, the *I love you's*...where's it all coming from?"

Emma raises an eyebrow and points a finger at me.

"It's Daniel's fault, really. I couldn't help but fall for his gentlemanly ways or his shy smile."

Kristian scratches the stubble on his chin, a calculating look in his eyes.

"So that's what it takes, eh?"

Emma rolls her eyes at him. "I'm no expert, Kris, but being a player and everything probably has the opposite effect if you want to find a serious girlfriend."

He holds his glove-clad hands in the air as if he's held at gunpoint.

"Hey, hey, hey...I'm not looking for love here. I was just curious."

"Mm-hmm," I muse and lift my arm, placing it behind my head so I'm more comfortable.

Kristian lowers his arms as he scowls at me.

"I'm not," he persists, and this time, I hold my tongue.

He takes a hairband from his back pocket and ties his longish hair back in a ponytail.

"Besides, I'll be leaving soon."

"Wait, what?" Emma asks, clearly taken aback by this news. "When? Where?"

"Relax, not *that* soon. I have plenty of time to finish your ink. But at the end of the year, I'll be heading to Scotland. It's time to do some traveling, and I've got an aunt there who emigrated twenty years ago or so. I'll be living with her for a while."

"Where in Scotland?" Emma asks.

"Something called Larkhall?" he answers on a question, and I can see the calculating look in Emma's eyes when I turn my head to watch her.

Slowly, she shakes her head. "I've never heard of it."

He smiles gently at her. "Most haven't, I suppose. It's not too far away from Glasgow. Maybe I'll find a *wee lass* to amuse me while I'm there."

"How very romantic," Emma teases, and Kristian waggles his eyebrows at her, clearly amused.

I intervene their jovial banter, because I really want it to to be over already.

"Well, best of luck to you, Kristian," I say.

He looks down at me as he pulls on a new set of gloves. "Thanks, man. Are you ready?"

I look at Emma one last time.

"Are you sure you don't want to see the design before he begins?" I ask her. I want to be one hundred percent sure of this before he gets started.

She nods eagerly. "I'm positive. Please, surprise me."

She takes my other hand resting on the bench, grips it tightly, and I take a deep breath as I hear the sound of the needle start up once more.

I hope this won't hurt too much.

♡

"I have to say you took that a lot better than I thought you would," Emma muses as we're back home and lying in my bed. I've removed my shirt because the sweat caused by the afternoon sun still clings to my skin, making me itch. The soft breeze blowing in from my open balcony door feels good on the soreness surrounding my new tattoo.

I yawn, almost entirely spent after the events of the day, and stretch carefully beside her.

"Thanks. I think." I give her a wry smile.

She snickers and kisses me gently above my tattoo.

"I didn't mean it in a bad way, Daniel."

I chuckle. "I know. I was just teasing you."

I shift on my side and take in the way she stares at the words now marking my body; she's hardly taken her eyes off it ever since Kristian finished it, and that says everything. They're the right words.

"I can't believe you remember what you said to me," she murmurs, sniffling a bit. Her lips tremble with emotion, making it clear how much those words, and the meaning behind them, have her enthralled. Pride swells in my heart.

Feeling a tad emotional myself, I look down at the words I told her a year ago:

"I love you, every single part of you – the light, the darkness, and the in-between."

"Words are powerful. You, of all people, understand, I think, and like I said earlier: I never want you to forget how much I love you."

Her gaze moves upwards, from my bare chest, to my neck, roaming my face, and I know she's thinking about it now. Placing a hand on my cheek, she caresses my stubble, and her eyes meet mine.

"I'll never forget, Daniel. I swear it."

"Good. Now…" I take off my glasses and place them on the bedside table behind me. I squint at her, resigned that I can't see her properly anymore. "How sore is your back?"

She smiles. "It's not too bad, but it does hurt a bit."

Thoughts running wild in my head, I muse, "Best get that creative mind into gear, sweetheart, because I plan on making love to you, then fucking you, before we fall asleep tonight. You up for that?"

She inhales deeply and sits up. Tucking her shirt free of her skirt, she doesn't answer my question, but carefully lifts her arms and removes the offending clothes. I lay back to take in the glorious sight before me as her bra-covered breasts are bared to me. I suck in a breath as she unclasps her bra, and she licks her lips before her hands start to play with her nipples. She leaves her short skirt and stiletto sandals on, though, and I bite my lip from seeing my gorgeous girl looking down at me with lust as well as love shining in her eyes.

It's almost enough to unman me already.

Almost…but not quite.

I groan as I unzip my shorts, and roughly push them down, kicking them off.

"I'll think of something," Emma says at last as she helps me free my cock from my boxers. It's not fully erect yet, but I know it won't take long.

It never does. Not when Emma is near.

"I'm sure you will," I pant, and dig my hands into her

waist, helping her settle on top of me. I can feel the wetness in her pussy through her panties already, and it turns me on beyond belief.

She leans down and gives me a languid, unhurried kiss. My tongue meets hers, eager but willing to take it slowly for now. Warmth spreads in my groin as she rubs her clit against my cock, and I moan into her mouth. I suck roughly on her tongue, and she hums, her breath quickening even more, and I remove my hands from around her waist to play with her tits instead.

She wrenches her mouth free, and we look into each other's eyes for the longest time.

The air is heavy, already filled with the scent of our arousal, and I thrust gently up, rubbing my cock against her.

"Happy anniversary, honey," she whispers on a low moan, her eyes fluttering closed, giving in to my fingers strumming their own tune on her body.

I sit up and blow on her left nipple, then lick it slowly. Her hips press down, and I can see her hand reach down to remove her skirt further.

"Happy anniversary, sweetheart," I growl.

Then I set out to show her, no longer with words, but with my body, that Emma means the world to me.

She always has, and she always will.

THE PROPOSAL
THREE YEARS AFTER EMMA & DANIEL MET.

Chapter One

DANIEL

I DIDN'T SLEEP LAST night.

I guess nerves about my plans for today got the best of me, and now I feel slightly sick to my stomach. I don't know why, because I've planned this particular day for weeks now.

I know what I want, and I'm going to get it.

Emma.

My wild, eccentric, cute as hell girl who doesn't even realise the impact she has on the people in her life. How her spirit and sass make people want to see her happy.

The way she has my uncle wrapped around her little finger is funny to watch. I know he thinks of her as family, and that she feels the same about him; and I can tell that some of her customers in the shop – like Mr. and Mrs. Sorensen – sometimes only step through the door to have a chat with her because they enjoy her company. But they seldom leave empty-handed.

My girl is great at what she does, and it causes happiness to soar through me when she tells me about her days. More often, they are great instead of bad.

However…I'm not too sure what she thinks about the whole marriage concept. I don't doubt her love for me, no. But maybe she doesn't believe in it like I do?

Another thing is that we really do need to find a bigger flat; we can't keep living like we do, and while our homes are right next to each other, we need more room.

I need more.

I've tried to show her several ads with flats to let – some have even been up for sale – but it feels as if Emma's been evading the subject every time I've spoken with her about getting a bigger place. I can't figure it out, and I'm tired of trying to.

Too many questions are running around a mile a minute in my head as I lie in her bed and take in her sleeping form. It's still dark outside, and we're bundled up underneath our blankets, trying to fend off the cold coming from the floors in her flat. Emma's sleep has been peaceful, and I'm grateful that her nightmares have been giving us a break for the past couple of months. They didn't over Christmas, which we spent in France with Andreas this year, and it definitely put a damper on our holiday spirit. The stress of running the shop must have been hitting her harder than I thought, and after she had a session with Katherine, her psychologist, she told me that taking it easier and to avoid stress would be the best course of action for her. She's kept her word, and the nightmares have ceased for a while…until the next time she forgets to take better care of herself, that is.

I let go of the unhappy thoughts. This is not a day for melancholy or even sadness. It's Valentine's Day, and I'm actually going to celebrate it with her this year. She better well enjoy it. Maybe it's not that original, choosing today to propose to her, but who gives a fuck? I'm allowed to be romantic on the most important day of my life.

Emma stirs beside me, and the butterflies erupt again, but I try to not let it show how nervous I am and simply kiss her on the back of her neck.

"Mmm," she purrs and turns slowly, eyes blinking the sleep away.

"Morning, sweetheart," I whisper and am about to kiss her when she covers her hand over her lips.

"Morning breath," she mumbles. "Be right back." She stretches lightly, and then backs out of the bed, giving me a perfect view of her gorgeous tits and the rest of her naked body.

"You know, one kiss in the morning before you brush your teeth won't kill us," I grumble after her, but she just waves me off and walks to the bathroom, closing the door behind her. Shaking my head, I lie back in bed and stare at the ceiling.

I go over the list in my head one more time.

The Ring? *Check.*

Flowers? *Check.*

Food? *Double check.*

I've stocked both our fridges with plenty of it, so I know we won't starve to death today, but I still have to prepare it in the picnic basket I bought the other day.

"You're looking mighty serious," Emma's voice interrupts my musings, and I smile and turn my gaze in her direction.

"I'm just thinking," I answer, and it's no lie. However, my thoughts aren't that preoccupied that they miss how she looks as she stands there against the doorjamb, the light from the bathroom cloaking her in warmth. My breath catches as I take in her beauty, and my heart swells in my chest.

This girl is mine...Only mine.

"Uh-uh." Emma waggles her eyebrows at me and then slowly walks closer, coming to a standstill beside me. "That sounds serious. What are you thinking about?"

"Just how beautiful you are," I answer truthfully and hold her gaze. "And that you're mine."

She smiles lovingly at me and leans down to capture my lips in a soft kiss before climbing up to sit on my lap. I wrap my arms around her and bury my hands in her hair, and I deepen the kiss when her breasts rub against my chest. Tightening my hands, I pull gently on her hair, and when she tilts her head back slightly, giving me permission to take control, I move my mouth away from hers. Trailing my tongue down her neck, taking my time to feed off her scent and skin, I marvel at the way she whimpers and sighs.

I know what my girl likes, and I can't get enough of showing her.

My cock throbs almost painfully, but I don't want to rush our lovemaking this morning. I crave her...I want her wild later, but for now...I'm going to worship her body.

"Daniel," she breathes as my mouth closes on her left nipple, and she pushes down on my cock. I kiss and bite her, not too gently, and she gasps loudly. It fills me with pride to get this kind of reaction out of her, and I try to soothe the sting away with my tongue.

I sit up and place my left arm around her back to brace her, digging my fingers into her hip, before I give her other breast the attention it deserves. Loosening my other hand from her hair, I leave a soft trail down her back, my fingertips following the curve of her spine, and I smile around her breast when I feel her shiver.

"It tickles," she giggles, but then whimpers softly as I

suckle harder on her nipple.

"Hush, now…I'm busy showing the woman I adore a good time," I mumble, moving my hand from her hip to her arse. "Fuck, I love the taste of your skin, Em," I groan as she rubs her pussy against my cock. "You intoxicate me."

"Oh, please…" She wraps her arms around my neck, and I look up at her flushed face, concentrating hard on not falling to pieces and give in to my cock's impatient demand: to flip her over on her hands and knees, and ram hard inside her. Not today…or not now, anyway.

"What, Em?" I ask her gruffly and look down at her clit rubbing my cock head. I grit my teeth, focusing only on her wetness on my skin.

"Please fuck me," she pants, and I shake my head.

"No fucking today, sweetheart. Only love. Look at me," I demand and turn my eyes to hers. They pop open and I can see the desire as clear as day shining back at me. "I'm running this show," I remind her, voice stern, and her gaze widens.

She nods slowly and licks her lips.

"Good. Now, lie down on your back and spread your legs for me. I need to taste you."

Quickly, I release my hold on her, and she does as she's told. I move up on my knees and watch her as I fist my cock, stroking it slowly from base to tip, and a rush down my spine warns me that I have to slow down.

I lie down on my stomach, my eyes never leaving hers. I place my hands on her inner thighs, pushing slowly to spread them more, and I inhale her arousal deeply.

"It drives me crazy to wait," she whispers, and I smirk at her.

"Oh, I know."

She snorts. "You're impossible. But I love you." The

adoration I see in her eyes makes me feel as if I can take on the entire world.

"I love you, too." I lean down and lick my lips, my arms shaking from the restraint I'm putting on my body's demands.

I watch Emma intently as she takes a firm hold on her tits, and my cock jerks. We're both breathing heavily, and I can't hold back anymore.

"Don't come until I tell you to, Emma. Understand?"

She nods. "Please, honey...please lick my pussy...I need you."

On a low growl, I lower my head and lick her clit, my tongue flat. Her hips thrust up as she cries out, and I apply more pressure on her thighs to keep her down.

"Fuck, Em," I groan against her wetness. "I'll never get enough of you." I grab her legs and place them on my shoulders, giving my hands the freedom they need to caress her body.

I take my time ravishing her, my mouth suckling on her sweetness, and my teeth scrape her clit lightly. I place my hands underneath her and lift her up, my tongue delving inside her pussy. I can hear her shouting my name over and over again, and I can feel my cock begin to leak.

Not yet, I chant over and over in my head, licking her out even more.

"Shite, Daniel, I can't hold back," she cries. I look up and take in the way her head thrashes from side to side.

"Shh," I croon and blow gently on her clit. Moving my right hand back, I glide my index finger through her wet folds, and I marvel at the feeling.

"I'm not done with you yet," I whisper as my finger wanders ever so lightly back to her arse. She moans and lifts her hips. She already knows what is coming, and she craves it just as much as I do.

I probe the puckered hole gently, groaning as I feel my finger slip in without too much resistance.

"I love your arse," I whisper and nip her inner thigh, leaving her pussy for now. "So tight, sweetheart…"

"Yes," she gasps. "I love feeling your fingers there," Emma moans, and she relaxes further against me. The flush covering her body is beautiful. Pumping gently in and out, getting her more worked up, I reach down my abs with my left hand, take a firm hold on my cock and I smear the pre-come over the tip.

"Fuck," I curse loudly as the tingle down my spine intensifies. I'm at my breaking point. "I'm going to lick you out now, Em. When I say *'come'*, you do that, you hear me?"

She nods, lost in the sensations my finger in her arse leaves inside her, and my mouth descends on her pussy again. This time, I don't hold back.

I feast on her sweetness.

I revel in her cries.

She owns me, heart and soul.

"Come, sweetheart," I command, mouth on her clit, and she does. Her body trembles wildly as my tongue works her towards orgasm, and my finger in her arse stills when she erupts. I take in how she fists the sheets, the violent tremors in her body, and I gently wipe my mouth against her stomach as I crawl up her body. Her arms relax, and her lips lift up in a catlike, satisfied smile. Her fingers find my cheek, yet her eyes remain closed, and I kiss the palm of her hand before lowering my mouth to hers. She kisses me back instantly, not caring in the least that she can taste her wetness on my tongue, and it only spurs me on more.

Groaning, I put my shaking hand on my cock and guide it inside her. My breath hitches when I feel her wet walls surround me instantly.

"Christ," I sigh as I move slowly inside her, and she lifts her arms and legs to embrace me, getting as close to me as possible. We look deeply into each other's eyes, revelling in the intimate act we both crave from each other so often, and my pace picks up when I hit her sweet spot.

"Harder," she groans, and I brace my arms on either side of her face.

"As you wish," I whisper, and then I fuck her…harder, deeper, longer than I thought I could, taking pleasure in her whimpers. Her lips find my neck as her hips thrust up to meet me, suckling on my skin, marking me with her teeth, and I lose it.

"So tight…fuck…so perfect," I grunt, kissing her wildly, our teeth and tongues clashing as we drink from each other. My mouth never leaves hers, not even when I come on a roar and still above her. Her own orgasm hits her just then, and my name on her lips has never sounded sweeter.

Moving slowly inside her a few times, I change my kiss as our bodies shaking lessens. Gently, I trail kisses from her mouth down her neck and torso until my mouth finishes on her breasts. Her hands caress my shoulders slowly, massaging them, and she breathes deeply.

"Wow," she whispers, and I chuckle.

"Indeed. Happy Valentine's Day." I give her nipples one last lick each before pulling out of her, and I lie down beside her. I reach my arm to wrap it tightly around her, pulling her to me so we're front to front.

"Is that today?" Emma asks me, her nose wrinkling.

She looks so adorable.

"Yes, it is," I answer and kiss her forehead. "I know you don't want to make a big deal out of it, but I have made plans for us today."

She groans slightly, and I laugh loudly at her resistance.

"I'm sorry," she chuckles. "But you know I don't give a crap about these things, Daniel. They seem so…superficial somehow. But…" She brushes her lips over mine. "It's a sweet gesture, and I can't wait to hear what you've got in store for us."

"Oh, I'm not going to tell you anything," I reply, tongue in cheek, and she narrows her eyes at me.

"You're not?" She looks a bit apprehensive, but she's still smiling, so I'll take that as a good sign.

"Nope." I remove my arm from her and stand up to stretch. I stop abruptly when I notice her gaze on my still semi-erect cock, and I point a finger at her.

"Emma, get your head out of the gutter," I pretend to sound stern, but who am I fooling? The wide grin on my face gives me away; I love that she can't get enough of my body. "I'm going next door to shower, and I suggest you do the same. I'll be back in half an hour, sweetheart."

I lean down to pick up my glasses on her beside table. I grab her neck and kiss the thoughtful frown marking her forehead before meeting her lips one last time. I let my tongue trace the seam of her lips but straighten when she tries to deepen our kiss.

"You better dress warm. It's going to be a cold day," I warn her as I move back from her.

Sighing, she gives me a salute, her eyes twinkling with mischief.

"Yes, sir," she replies.

Quickly, I put on my boxers, find the rest of my clothes

and keys, and then I leave her to take care of everything I need to make this day perfect.

Strangely enough, I'm no longer as nervous as before.

Hope and eagerness fill me as I enter my flat, and I rush to get ready.

Chapter Two

EMMA

"ARE YOU SERIOUSLY NOT going to let me see where you're taking me?" I sputter for the umpteenth time as we're walking, my eyes covered in a scarf. Daniel told me to wear it as we got on the bus to head into town, and after I gave in, anticipated and nervous, I was surprised when we got off the bus after only a short ride. We're now walking again, and I have no idea where we are.

"No, I'm not," Daniel's cheerful voice answers me, and his arm pulls me even more into his side. "Don't worry, I won't let you fall," he says, the teasing replaced with reassurance.

I huff. "I know, but still...it's weird." I can't hear any people around me, and the silence is nice. Not being able to see anything and trusting him completely at the same time is a bit odd, but it doesn't alarm me.

"Are we doing something kinky?" I blurt out.

"Shhh," he shushes me, and then chuckles before I feel his lips on my cheek. "No, we're not...yet."

Yet?

A delicious shiver runs through me, and my heart is galloping away in my chest.

It's so cold today, and I'm glad I'm wearing low-heeled boots; the air smells like snow, the frost stings my cheeks, and I tuck my chin further underneath my heavy woollen scarf.

"Are you cold?" Daniel asks me, a nervous note in his voice.

I shrug lightly. "Not really, but it's a good thing I'm

wearing the coat you gave me for Christmas. Otherwise, my bum might fall off."

He chuckles, and I can feel his hands give my arse a firm squeeze. I jump and squeal lightly, but it soon turns to laughter.

"I'm so glad it's Sunday and the shop is closed," I tell him and press into his side. "A walk in the fresh air is just what I needed...even though I can't see anything." I turn my head in his direction and raise my head up at him. Not being able to see him is strange, but I'm very excited about his surprise for me.

Valentine's Day may not exactly be a day we have celebrated before, and I doubt he'll be able to change my feelings about it, but I can't deny that this is very romantic.

"Are we there yet?" I ask teasingly.

"Smart-arse," he mumbles, affection clear in his voice. "No, not yet...but soon."

I nod, and I let him lead me for another couple of minutes. We remain silent the entire time, and nervous butterflies are swarming in my tummy.

Daniel may have planned a surprise for me, but little does he know that I have one for him, too.

I hope he likes it.

"Mind the step here," Daniel murmurs beside me, and I reach out my foot, cautiously taking the step down so as not to fall on the slippery sidewalk.

"There, one more step, and we're here," he encourages me.

Gravel replaces the asphalt we've been walking on so far, and I breathe deeply, taking in the woodsy scent of pine trees, wet leaves, and I can even hear a few birds chirping above us.

Curiouser and curiouser.

We walk for a while longer until Daniel at last brings me to a standstill.

"Okay, I'm going to remove the blindfold in a minute, Em..." His voice trails off and I reach out my arm, placing my hand on his shoulder when I feel his body standing close in front of me. I move my hand upwards until it rests on his cheek and let my thumb follow the soft stubble there.

"Are you okay?" I ask him quietly, and he nods beneath my hand.

"Yes. I'm great, sweetheart, I promise. I'm just a tad nervous, that's all," he mumbles.

"Oh? Why is that?"

"Shh," he shushes me. "No more questions, please."

I nod. "Okay...I can do that, I think."

My heart rate picks up like mad when I feel his soft lips on mine, and I drink from his mouth as he continues to kiss me ever so slowly.

As if we have all the time in the world.

As if he can't get enough of me.

I want to keep kissing him, but then I feel his hands behind my head, pulling at the knot on the blindfold, and I freeze in place.

His mouth leaves mine on a deep sigh. "Ready?" he asks me, and I nod resolutely.

"Ready."

"I love you," he whispers, a tremor in his voice, and I smile widely at him.

"I love you, too...more than you will ever know."

No sooner have the words left my lips until the blindfold is off my face, and I blink madly. When I see where we are, I laugh.

"Oh, my gosh!" I look around me, and then gasp when I

notice the balloons and confetti on the bench behind me. They are all the colours of the rainbow, bringing life to the glum day, and I turn around to stare at Daniel.

"You've brought me here?" I ask him, still smiling, and he nods.

"I thought it would be fitting. This is, after all, one of my favourite memories of the two of us together." He smiles at me, a naughty glint in his gaze, and I grin.

"Mine, too."

My mind fills with images of that day so long ago when he almost attacked me in the dressing room after I took him shopping for the first time. This park is where he made me grow wild with passion, not giving a rat's arse about being seen by innocent bystanders, but, more importantly, this is where he wormed his way into my heart and told me how I made him feel for the first time.

I inhale deeply. "Thank you, honey. This is perfect."

He places a big picnic basket on the bench behind us, and I just now notice that it's covered in blankets and pillows.

"But...how did you...?" I frown, completely taken aback at the grandeur of his gesture.

I look at him, and he must see the question in my eyes.

"Suzy helped me," he explains, and warmth fills my tummy. "I thought I would take advantage of her being home for a while, so I rang her last week."

"I was just about to say that you must've gotten help from someone, because there's no way you were able to carry all this on our way here," I tell him and then step into his arms. I tilt my head back, suddenly overcome with gratitude that this man...this beautiful, generous, thoughtful geek did this for me.

For us.

"I love Valentine's Day," I blurt, and his eyes widen in surprise before he smirks.

"Oh, really?" He leans down to brush his lips over mine. "I'll be sure to remember that," he murmurs against my lips. Then he steps back and points at the bench.

"Please sit, make yourself comfortable."

I bat my lashes at him. "Thank you. I don't mind if I do," I say in my best fake voice of Audrey Hepburn – my favourite actress – and he grins slowly at me. I pick up one of the blankets and wrap it around my lower body before I sit down. I look to my right to the picnic basket and sniff lightly.

"Is that…bacon?" I close my eyes and inhale more deeply.

Daniel laughs loudly, but stops abruptly when I lift a finger at him.

"Don't mock, Daniel…bacon is a serious matter, not to be taken lightly."

I open my eyes and wink playfully at him when I find him trying to wipe off the wide smile plastered on his lips. He nods once and comes closer.

"Indeed. Please forgive me. Yes, it's bacon…I've also got pasta and chicken salad, some different cheeses, some pâté, grapes, and a nice bottle of chilled Frascati for later. Oh, and freshly baked bread that Camilla picked up for me this morning."

I tilt my head at him. "So Camilla was in on your surprise as well? Hmm…what about George?"

Daniel scratches his head and grimaces lightly.

"Yes, him, too. He said he might stop by and take some photographs of us, but Camilla stopped that, thankfully." He frowns and scans the park behind him, as if he's expecting George to appear by magic, and I snort.

"One never knows with George," I concede and take off my mittens and hat.

"How true. Okay, are you ready for the next surprise?"

I stop opening the lid on the basket and look back at him.

"There's more?" I ask him, feeling slightly overwhelmed.

He smiles gently at me and walks the two steps separating us, and then stops right in front of me. "Yes. And this is the best part...or at least I think so."

My heart rate gallops wildly when I take in the seriousness in his gaze, and my breath hitches. This moment is significant. I can feel it. I can no longer hear the chirping birds from before or smell the food beside me: all my senses are focused on Daniel in front of me.

When he goes down on one knee, I gasp and put my hands over my mouth.

Wait...is he? But...oh, my...holy fuck!

"Emma Ruth Davenport," he begins and takes my hands firmly in his. His grip is a bit sweaty, yet firm. He takes a deep breath before blowing it out slowly, and his eyes are fixed on mine. I daren't even blink.

"I love you more than I can ever express. When we met three years ago, I knew almost from the start that I had found the woman I wanted to spend the rest of my days with. You saw me, the *real* me...and I swear it felt as if your soul spoke to mine. I never thought that I would be lucky enough to meet a woman like you; you were sassy, sexy, and so unbelievably sweet underneath all the layers you cloaked yourself in, but somehow...you let me in. You let me help you get free of the ghosts of your past, and I will always be grateful for that."

He pauses and takes a shaky breath, and tears fall from my eyes. I'm overcome by the beauty of his words, from what I can guess he's about to say.

"Sweetheart, you are my perfect match. You are my other half. Make me the happiest man on earth, please. Marry me, Emma."

I nod madly, tears clogging my throat, and release my hands from his. I lean towards him and take his face in my hands, kissing him over and over.

"Yes, yes, yes," I chant as I kiss him, laughter overtaking the tears, and he grins, kissing my lips vigorously. I welcome his tongue as it explores my mouth and tilt my head to give him better access. He groans as he pulls at my lip ring with his teeth, and I'm shivering…Not from the cold around us, no…But from the enormity of the situation.

"Wait, wait," he grins against my mouth, and I let him move back reluctantly.

Narrowing my eyes at him, I mutter, "I wasn't done kissing you."

His mouth meets mine again, and he gives me what I crave: his love.

Soon after, though, he kisses the tip of my nose, and whispers, "Don't you want to see the ring?"

My belly flutters madly. "Oh, yes, of course." My cheeks ache from smiling so much, and I release the tight hold around his neck.

He looks down as he fumbles around in his coat pocket.

"Daniel, please get off the ground," I say as I notice he's still kneeling in front of me. "I don't want you to get sick."

He stands up and does as I ask, and I wait for him to find the little black box as he sits down beside me. His ears are red, and his lips wet and swollen from our kisses. He's never looked more handsome.

"I'm not sure of the size," he says quietly as he pulls out the box. "You hardly ever wear rings, so…"

"I'll wear yours forever," I vow. "I'll never take it off."

The tenderness in his gaze makes my heart flutter with love, but then I look down to take in the ring he chose for me and it's impossible for me to hold back the gasp when I see it.

"I know it's a bit unusual, as far as engagement rings goes, but…I saw it and thought of you instantly," he murmurs, and takes the beautiful black vintage-style ring out of the box. I can't take my eyes off the square, black diamond surrounded by fiery white stones; it's made up of two bands instead of one, and it's beyond stunning. I give him my left hand and hold my breath as he puts it on my ring finger. It's a bit too big, but that's easy to solve.

"It's so gorgeous, Daniel," I whisper and new tears gather in my eyes. I raise my eyes to his and wipe them away quickly, not wanting them to cloud my eyesight: I want to see him properly and not look back on this day in twenty years, regretting that I can't remember the way he looked at me.

With Love. Adoration. Pride.

"It's perfect," I tell him and kiss him once more. "You're the perfect man for me, Daniel. I'll be proud to call you my husband, and not a day will go by when I won't tell you how much you mean to me. I promise you that."

He blinks rapidly and clears his throat before he takes my hand, placing a lingering kiss on the ring that now adorns it.

"I love you so much," I whisper. "Always and forever."

His gaze meets mine and his blinding smile mirrors my own.

"I adore you. Thank you for saying yes," he whispers.

"How could I not?" I ask him and then breathe deeply. "I have a surprise for you as well, actually, but it definitely can't top this one," I laugh.

"For me?"

"Yes. I spoke with Andreas a few days ago, and he had a proposition for us…"

He looks at me with wide eyes, and his eyebrows have almost disappeared underneath his wavy hair.

Adorable…just like always.

"His tenants have given their notice – they're moving to New Zealand, apparently – and he wants to know if we would like to become his new tenants."

He blinks and leans towards me. "His tenants? As in, us living in his house?"

I nod. "Yes. We need more room, Daniel. I know I've been evading the topic lately, and I'm sorry about that. I just wasn't sure what we could afford. But I ran some figures, and talked with the bank yesterday, and it's definitely doable. Especially considering the incredibly low rent Andreas is asking for. It's both near university and the bookshop…So: problem solved. Easy peasy."

He shakes his head slowly back and forth, clearly surprised.

"When? I mean, how soon until we can move in?" he asks me, excitement clear in his voice.

"Hmm. Not until July, I think…"

He laughs and then sighs before taking another look at the ring, and the way it sparkles in the light makes my lips tremble with emotion. I swallow the lump in my throat. I can't believe I'm engaged.

"I guess he always has this knack of meddling at the perfect time," he muses, crooked smile in place, and I shrug.

"He just wants to help us if he can," I answer, suddenly worried that he hates the idea even though he loves his uncle's house.

"Oh, I know…But you have to admit that his timing is

astonishing."

I grin. "Yes, I agree. So...should I say yes?"

"Bloody hell, yes!" Daniel shouts, and I laugh freely as he pulls me into his arms once more, kissing me intensely. I moan into his mouth, overcome with joy.

My ringtone interrupts us, and I pull back to rummage around in my pocket. When I see who the caller is, I grin at Daniel, holding it up for him to read it.

"I guess Suzy can't wait any longer," he smiles at me.

"You best get that. I'll prepare our food."

I swipe the screen quickly, and don't even let Suzy get a word in before I shout, "I'm engaged!"

"Woo hoo! Oh my god, Emma! Oh my god! I'm so happy for you!" She laughs with me, and even seems to sniffle a bit. "Wait until you see the dress I found."

My laughter dies down as I take in her words. "Wait, what? You've found a dress for me? How long have you known about Daniel's plans?" Daniel shakes his head at me, clearly as confused as me even though he can't hear her through the phone. Then again, maybe he can; Suzy has a tendency to raise her voice when she's on the phone.

"Oh, for months, of course," she laughs. "Not that Daniel asked me to help him out until a couple of days ago, but I've known where the two of you were headed for a while, so I've been dress hunting for you."

I shake my head affectionately. "Thank you," I whisper, touched that she would do this for me. "So...I guess you don't mind being my bridesmaid?"

Her scream almost makes me jump, it's so loud, and I giggle.

"Are you joking? Of course I don't mind! I can't freaking wait! This is the best news ever!"

I chuckle and smile back at Daniel when I feel his lips on my hand once more. I look into his eyes, and, upon seeing the love shining there, I say softly, "I can't wait, either."

'*I love you,*' he mouths at me, and my smile widens.

Maybe Valentine's Day isn't such a bad idea, after all.

AN UNEXPECTED SURPRISE
ONE YEAR AFTER EMMA & DANIEL'S WEDDING

Chapter One

EMMA

I FLUSH THE TOILET and close the lid before my feet give way, and I slump down on the seat.

I'm numb…cold…scared out of my mind.

This was so not part of the plan, but I can't avoid the reality any longer.

After having thrown up every morning for the past week, I don't need two pink lines to tell me what my instincts have been screaming at me for even longer.

Nevertheless, it's better to be safe than sorry. I bought three packages at the chemist last night, and there are two tests in each.

That makes it six tests in total, and they are all stating the same fact.

I'm pregnant.

I groan and put my head in my hands, trying to take deep breaths to settle my tummy. I don't know what to do, and I sniffle as a new round of tears roll down my cheeks.

Bloody hormones.

Am I sad?

Happy?

I can't stand the yucky taste in my mouth any longer, and stand up to brush my teeth, staring down at the tests in the sink. I don't know what I'm supposed to feel. Shouldn't I be happy? My legs still feel like jelly, and I lean heavily on the vanity before settling down on the toilet seat once more.

I'm not ready to face Daniel just yet, but I'm not given a choice to decide when I might be as a soft knock on the door causes me to straighten up. I wipe my nose quickly.

"Come in," I call out, voice soft.

I watch the handle as it presses down slowly and then Daniel's head peeks behind the door. When I see his concerned eyes, I want to throw myself into his arms and bawl like a baby, but I don't. I'm frozen in place, my hands clamped firmly between my thighs.

"Sweetheart, you've been here for over an hour. What's wrong?" He remains in the doorway, and all I long for is for him to come to me.

Please, Daniel…please come closer.

But I can't speak. I'm terrified of his reaction; of what this might mean for us. I don't doubt that he'll be a wonderful father, but what about all our plans?

I can feel the tears pouring down my face, and a sob tears its way from my throat. I can't see him clearly anymore, but at last, he unfreezes from his spot; he rushes closer and kneels before me.

"Emma? What is it?" His hands cover my face, and he tries to wipe away the wetness on my cheeks. "Please talk to me."

My body shakes, and my upset stomach leaves me lightheaded.

"Daniel," I sob. "I'm…I'm…"

Pregnant. Knocked up. I have a bun in the oven.
There are many ways to tell him the news, and yet my mouth refuse to say them.

Daniel kisses my tears away, his mouth lingering on my lips as he whispers sweet nothings, no doubt trying to calm me down even though he has no idea why I'm sitting here, crying like a loon, and unable to voice my distress.

"Please," he whispers, his voice tormented. "Whatever it is, you can tell me. We'll sort it out, I promise. I love you."

He puts his mouth on mine once more, his kisses more frantic now. I try to find the courage from within, berating myself for causing him harm by keeping quiet.

Fuck it.

I lean away from him and breathe deeply a couple of times, willing the tears to stop, and once his face is no longer blurry, I whisper, "I'm pregnant."

He blinks, and I swear he even stops breathing for a while.

One heartbeat…Two heartbeats…Three heartbeats…

I wrench my hands free and place them around his neck, sniffling as I try to take in the emotions waging a war in his eyes.

His hands take a firmer hold on my face, and there's a deep frown in place; for once, I can't read him clearly. He wipes my wild curls free from around my face, baring me to him completely, and I try to concentrate on my breathing. I do not want to throw up on him.

"You're pregnant?" he asks me, but it isn't really a question. His voice is too final, too calm.

I nod. My skin feels clammy and flushed.

"You're carrying my child?" His voice is gruff, and I don't think I've ever heard it like that before.

I nod again. "Yes." My lips are trembling, and I start chewing on my lip ring, overtaken with nerves.

The frown on his forehead clears slowly, and is that tears in his eyes? The light must be playing tricks on me, surely. But...if they're real, they give me hope.

"You're sure?" he asks me one more time, and I sniffle.

"Yes. Just look down in the sink." I tilt my head to my left, and Daniel cranes his neck to see the mess there, his hands remaining on my cheeks. His eyes widen before he looks back at me, a speculative glint in them.

"That's a lot of tests," he states, and for the first time today, a small giggle escapes me.

"I just wanted to be absolutely certain…" My voice trails off, and I shrug, hating the insecurity that settles deep within. I still don't know how he feels about this, and I *need* him to tell me soon, or I'll go out of my mind.

"I see." He sighs deeply and I take in the way his eyes rest on my stomach. Instinctively, I settle my hands over it, a strong sense of protection overtaking my nerves.

"Please say something," I whisper, and his head snaps up. I gasp when I see the blinding smile on his lips.

"You're really pregnant?" he asks me, voice disbelieving, but hopeful at the same time. I giggle again, frail happiness coursing through me.

"Yes. I am."

"Bloody hell," he laughs and puts his hands on top of mine. I interlace our fingers and hold on for dear life.

"You're happy?" I ask him, needing him to tell me in words instead of showing it. "This pretty much ruins our plans to visit Suzy in New York next year, but…" My breath hitches, yet hope blooms in my heart from seeing his elated gaze resting on our joined hands.

He leans forward until our noses are almost touching, and I try to hold his eyes even though it's a bit difficult when he's this close.

"Truly happy, Em," he whispers. "It almost tops our wedding day. Sod our plans," he continues, and then he kisses me.

Slow, deep, sweet.

This kiss is different from the thousands we have shared before.

There is a sense of reverence in this kiss...as if he's trying to tell me how much my words mean to him.

As if he's been waiting for this moment to happen for a while.

I tilt my head and open my mouth, inviting his tongue to come out to play with mine, and fireworks erupt in my entire body from the sweetness of our kiss. His hands move to my back, and when I feel him stand up, I wrap my legs around his waist and hold on tight, never breaking our kiss. He wobbles a bit, and I gasp when his lips leave mine.

"Hold on," he groans, and he carries me quickly out of the bathroom, through the hall and up the stairs. He stops halfway, though, and leans me against the wall, breath wheezing lightly.

"Look at me," he huffs, and I do as he says. I can't deny him anything, nor would I want to.

"Daniel," I moan when I see the fire burning for me, for *us*, looking back at me. A sense of urgency overtakes me from the strength of it, and I grab his neck and crush my mouth against his once more.

Gone are my doubts and fears, replaced with the familiar passion and heat that only Daniel emits in me.

"Hurry," I whisper, and reach down to unzip his pants. I

take a firm hold on his cock, freeing it from his boxers, and stroke it hard. He growls, thrusting his hips into my hand.

"Bloody hell, Em...what you do to me..." Daniel shifts and lays me on the stairs, fumbling with my belt before he pulls down my pants and knickers. I don't care that the steps dig into my back, or how sore I'll be once we're done fucking. I only care about the release Daniel can give me now.

I kick off my ballerinas as Daniel removes my clothes before he settles on top of me, and then he slams inside me. The intensity makes me call out his name, tilting my hips as I do. I need more. I crave more, just like always.

"Fuck, Em...you're so tight...so wet for me," Daniel groans and I pull down his head, seeking his mouth, my hips meeting him thrust for thrust. He braces above me, and I keep my eyes open to watch him as he loses control. His right hand leaves the step above my head and he reaches down to press his thumb against my clit. Wetness gathers in my core, and I groan as I feel the familiar fire course through me.

This may be wild and rough, but it is no less filled with love.

"Sweetheart, I don't...I can't..," he pants against my mouth, and I put my hand on top of his, rubbing my clit roughly as he picks up speed.

"Daniel," I moan, and kiss his neck, biting lightly. "I need you so much...I love you."

"I love you, Em...so much," he groans, and he fucks me even harder, hitting my sweet spot. I cry out and close my eyes as I come, my body trembling like mad. Stars burst beneath my eyelids, and I hear him call out my name as if from far away; soon after, he stills on a loud roar before collapsing on top of me.

We breathe heavily for the longest time, and I revel in

Daniel's soft lips trailing down my neck, then back up again, over and over. I don't think I can move, but my head tells me otherwise.

Sex on the stairs is definitely not comfortable.

"I'm sorry I tackled you," he murmurs against my skin, but I hug him closer to me.

"I liked it." I pull gently on his hair and he lifts his head to peer down at me. "But I need to get up now."

"Right." He kisses me gently before lifting off me, and I try not to giggle when he pulls out a handkerchief from one of his back pockets and begins to gently wipe away his come between my legs.

"That's so unromantic," I complain, and he chuckles.

"Yeah, you're right," he muses and straightens, pulling his pants back up. "I bet you don't read a lot about this part in your romance novels, eh?"

I shake my head and reach up my arms, silently asking him to help me.

"Nope, I guess not."

"Come on, sweetheart," he says and walks past me, my hands still in his. "We need a shower."

Stifling a yawn, I nod and trail after him, ignoring my scattered clothes. I'm all of a sudden so tired. It's only early evening, but all I can think about is how welcoming sleep sounds right about now.

I wonder if it's a boy or a girl.

The thought almost causes me to stumble as I walk up the steps behind Daniel, and I feel rather teary again. Motherhood isn't a factor I've ever truly taken into account...It's always seemed like some foreign concept, and while I've contemplated when Daniel and I would start our own family from time to time, something's always kept me at bay, letting go of the subject.

There are probably loads of things I need to read about babies, but for now, I'll simply relish the fact that Daniel is ecstatic about the news. I'm still scared out of my wits, but knowing how thrilled he is helps.

We'll work it out, I'm sure of it.

Chapter Two

DANIEL

I*T'S LATE, AND* I can't sleep.

I'm going to be a father.

A little boy or girl will be calling me Daddy one day.

Bloody hell.

I had a sneaky suspicion that Emma might be pregnant; apart from suffering from some hefty mood swings the past month or so, it is, after all, the most obvious conclusion to draw when your wife rushes out of bed every morning and throws up for a week. If she hadn't bought all those tests, I would have done it myself.

I turn to lie on my side in our bed and look at Emma's sleeping form, chin in my hand. Carefully, so as not to wake her, I remove the duvet covering her, and I place my right hand on her stomach. The bedside lamp is on, the soft light caresses her features, and I can't help but smile when I hear her soft snores. She'll deny that she does in fact snore, and a lot, but I know the truth, and I take great pleasure in teasing her about it all the time.

Smiling, I look back on my hand resting on her stomach, and the enormity of the situation grabs hold on me once more.

"Wow," I whisper and lean down, my eyes on Emma's navel.

"I can't wait to meet you, Pip," I continue and place a soft, light kiss there, afraid that I'll wake her up if I linger.

"Pip?" Emma's sleepy voice makes me turn my head and I smile apologetically at her.

"I'm sorry I woke you." I kiss her belly once more, and I

can feel the intake of her breath when I put my head on her stomach. Softly, she trails her fingers through my hair, and I sigh, utterly content in this very moment.

"What if it's a girl?" she asks me quietly, almost on a whisper. "Pip is more a boy's nick name, I think. Not that I have any real knowledge about such things."

I shrug and turn my head to meet her eyes. "Well…maybe. But we can't just keep saying '*it*'. That's so…impersonal, don't you agree?"

She nods and sucks on her lip ring, a thoughtful look in her eyes now.

"True," she purses her lips. "What about Bee?"

I frown. "That's too girly."

She chuckles. "Okay then…what would you suggest? It'll be months before we'll find out if we're having a boy or a girl. We have to come up with something for…well, it."

Kissing her belly once more, I take some time to think it through. And then a splendid idea takes hold on me, and I look back at her.

"How about I'll just call it Pip, and you'll go with Bee? At least for now."

A smile tugs at the corner of her lips.

"I suppose we could do that for a little while," she agrees, and I smile at her.

I don't know if it's possible for pregnant women to have that certain glow about them so early on in their pregnancy – and we don't even know how far along Emma is yet – but as I lie here, taking in her soft smile, and the calm she exudes…I think there's something to it.

"You're so beautiful," I whisper, and she beams at me.

"Thank you. You're quite handsome yourself. Adorable, too."

I grunt, and I can feel my ears getting warm.

"Men aren't adorable," I mutter. "That word belongs to babies and puppies. But not to hot, sexy-as-sin alpha males like me." I waggle my eyes at her when she snorts.

"Ah-ha. Okay."

"When will you ring your parents?" I change the subject and move up to lie next to her.

She frowns. "I want to wait until I've seen my doctor first. Is that okay with you? Keeping it between us for the time being?"

I rub at the anxious line between her eyes and smile gently at her.

"Of course it is. Whatever you want to do, I'm fine with it."

She turns so we're lying front to front, and I put my arm around her, tucking her close. She snuggles closer, head under my chin, and I rub soothing circles on her hip and bottom.

"I'm sorry I freaked out like that," she whispers, and I squeeze her.

"Sweetheart, it's okay. I think it's perfectly normal to react like that, especially given the fact that we haven't talked about starting a family." I hesitate, unsure whether I should reveal my thoughts to her, but we don't keep secrets from each other, so I continue, "I was a bit scared, too."

"You were?" She starts running her fingers through the hair on my chest and I nod once.

"Yes. I mean, this was...unexpected. I couldn't be happier, though. You have to promise me to take care of yourself, Em."

She looks up at me and frowns.

"You say that as if you think I wouldn't."

I push down in bed so we're face to face, and I brush my lips over hers once before I place my hand to rest against her neck.

"You know how you get when you're too stressed," I murmur, and her frown clears as she nods her understanding. "That's our child you'll be carrying for the next long while…I need you to listen to your body and rest when you need it. Can you do that, please? For me?" I look down briefly and place my hand on her belly before meeting her eyes again. "For little Pip or Bee?"

A crooked smile forms on her lips and she nods again.

"Of course. Anything for you."

"Good." I kiss the tip of her nose and close my eyes on a deep sigh, the events of today finally catching up with me.

"I'm still scared," she admits on a whisper. "What if I'm rubbish at being a mum? What if the baby doesn't love me? What if…"

"Emma, please…," I chuckle and open my eyes to reassure her that she couldn't be more wrong. "You'll be a wonderful mum…our baby will love you unconditionally, and do you know why?"

I wait until her eyes rest on mine once more before I continue. "Because *you* will love our baby with every fibre of your being, and so will I. I don't know much about children, but I'm pretty sure they can sense a person's emotions early on. I have no doubt that Pip or Bee will fall madly in love with you, just like I did. Every day, I fall a little bit more in love with you, Emma. Even if you do snore like mad."

Her eyes narrow on me, but she can't stop the smile grazing her lips.

"It's a good thing you have a way with words, Daniel, or I might not let your last comment slip so easily." She leans up on her arm and I move back to give her more room. I'm not sure what she's up to, and I look questioningly at her. Swiftly, she tucks the duvet from my body, throwing it on the floor, and I gasp when she takes a firm hold on my cock.

"What are you doing?" I ask cheekily, and she rolls her eyes at me.

"As if it wasn't obvious. I'm going to suck that arrogant grin off your face by paying attention to your delicious cock, and then I'm going to sleep. Are you okay with that?" She leans down and places a kiss on my chest, before she bites down on my left nipple. As she moves further down my chest, I groan as I feel her fingernails scrape my balls lightly, and my breath picks up speed.

I love that dirty mouth of hers.

I wrap her long hair around my fist, giving me a perfect view of her face, and spread my legs for her.

"Fuck, yes, that's more than okay," I pant when her tongue licks the tip of the head, and I can feel my cock harden further.

"Good." Keeping her eyes locked with mine, she closes her mouth over my cock, and the last conscious thought in my mind is how much I love this woman.

And that I can't wait to see what the future holds for us.

Epilogue

DANIEL

5 years later

LOOKING DOWN AT MY infant daughter sleeping in my arms, a lump forms in my throat.
Holy mother...I'm a father!
I swallow and turn my watery eyes to my wife resting on the couch beside me. She looks exhausted, and I can't say I'm surprised. Getting used to breastfeeding every few hours each night must take its toll, but seeing as I can't help her in that department, I can at least provide some relief whenever our daughter is fidgeting, but not for food.

We came home from the hospital only a few days ago, and we're still trying to get used to the changes Eliza will undoubtedly cause.

But I have faith we'll manage.

We always do.

Lots of things have happened in our lives the past few years.

Emma taking over *Andersen's* Books proved to be rather challenging because she was still at university at the time, but we were able to keep it afloat throughout her final year, resorting to only hiring other students to help us out when we couldn't handle everything ourselves. But then came the hurdle of sorting out Emma's citizenship, and let's just say that the Danish government was not exactly easy to please.

Again, we pulled through, and the day when Emma became my wife followed shortly after. What with me being a typical guy, I dreaded that she'd run amok planning it.

I should have known my girl wouldn't like something flashy and big, though, because after I'd proposed and she'd said yes - and once we'd settled down after our subsequent sexathon - she asked me if we could simply get married at City Hall, her parents, her Nan and Suzy the only ones attending from her side. When I'd no doubt looked as if I didn't take her seriously, she'd laughed at me and said, "I don't need the big, fancy wedding with a couple of hundreds guests that I don't even know. I just need you."

So there...as usual, she got her way.

I know she's happy because she tells me so almost every day, but she still suffers from nightmares every once in a while, and it breaks my heart to see her like that. I do wonder if burning that letter from Tom plays a part in why she has them, but we'll probably never know for sure. However, her nightmares only occur when she's highly stressed out - being a shop owner is no easy feat, you know - so we try to slow things down whenever they start up again.

I look back at my daughter and tuck her closer into my arms. This one was a bit of a surprise, to be honest, but a welcoming one, of course. I've taken leave from university and will stay at home with my family for the next six months, and then it's time to finish my Ph.D. in English History & Literature.

"Don't be too hard on your mum, wee one," I whisper to her and kiss her head, careful not to wake her.

"I don't think she's able to answer that quite yet, honey." Emma's sleepy reply makes me turn my head, and I look at this woman who I adore with everything that I am.

"Maybe not," I whisper and stand up to place Eliza in her crib beside the couch, before I walk back to Emma and tuck in behind her. I pull her into my arms, spooning her, and sigh happily, a bit tired now.

"Shouldn't you try to rest a bit longer?" I whisper and kiss her neck.

"A text from mum woke me up," she answers sleepily. "She wanted to know if she and dad can come visit us in a week."

"If you think you'll be up for it, it's fine with me."

She stretches languidly, her arse pushing into my crotch, and I grit my teeth.

Not being able to have sex with her for the next month is going to be hell.

Emma chuckles and reaches a hand behind her until she finds my cock.

"Something tells me that you're feeling frisky," she teases me, and I shrug even though she can't see me.

"I'm always turned on when you're near me," I grin, but gasp when her hand takes a firm hold on it and begins to stroke it slowly.

"Sweetheart," I warn her, and she sits up carefully before kneeling before me.

"Hush," she whispers huskily and kisses my cock head through the fabric of my boxers. "I know you're kind of suffering these days...Let me do something about that."

Without waiting for me to answer, she yanks my underwear down and frees my cock. She hums deeply and licks her lips before her head descends upon it and her mouth closes over the tip, sucking gently.

I hiss loudly. "Fuck, Emma, I've missed your mouth."

As she begins to suck me off in earnest, I place a hand on her cheek, and gaze lovingly into her eyes that never leave mine.

My girl. The strongest person I know.

I'm the luckiest man on earth, and I thank the deities above for putting me in her path all those years ago.

I'll treasure her always.

EMMA

"So, my dear, how does it feel to be a mother?" Andreas asks me, his voice amused.

I chuckle into the phone resting on my shoulder as I give Eliza her last bottle before her afternoon nap.

"Well, it's challenging, to say the least, but wait until you see her: she's absolutely perfect," I answer, unable to wrench my eyes away from the little bundle of perfection lying in my arms.

"When are you going to visit us again?"

"How does next month sound to you?" he asks me, and I smile widely.

"Perfect. Just email me some dates that work for you, and we'll make sure that the guest room is ready. Oh, and I do hope that Gabrielle will come with you?"

The smile is evident in his voice when he answers me. "I'll see if I can persuade her to join me."

"I'll try to get a hold of Suzy and Garrett, too. Perhaps I can convince them to leave New York as well, make it a big gathering," I muse.

"That would be lovely," Andreas replies excitedly.

Eliza begins to fuss, and I quickly say, "Listen, I have to go, but we'll talk soon, okay?"

"Of course. Give that beautiful girl a big kiss from me,

Emma. Talk soon, bye."

As we ring off, I lift my darling girl up to let her rest on my shoulder while I rub her back soothingly.

The past three months have passed in a blur, but having Daniel home has been such a blessing. It'll be strange once he returns to university to finish his degree, to not have him home every day, but I'm so proud of him for pursuing his dreams.

He'll become a wonderful teacher.

When I think back on the conversation I just had with Andreas, I murmur to Eliza, "Your uncle will visit us soon, sweetie. Won't that be fun?"

She burps loudly, and I take that as a *yes*.

Andreas thrives in France, and the fact that he has a lady friend now - a retired nurse, actually - pleases me to no end. He's still a bit of a mystery to me, and hasn't divulged anything about his past, but I've long ago accepted that there are parts of him that he wants to keep to himself.

If there's one thing I've learned in the past five years, it's that you can't force someone to open up their pasts to you. And that's okay, actually. I know he'll let me in when he's ready.

Rocking Eliza gently in my arms, feeling her weight settle on me, I whisper, "Sleep, darling. Mummy's here..." Shortly after, I can hear her light snoring, and I stand from my rocking chair to walk to our bedroom, placing her in her crib where she can sleep for the next few hours.

And while she does, I plan on having a lot of fun with her daddy.

As I leave our bedroom, I turn on the baby monitor, determined to hunt him down to have my wicked way with him, and I must be in a nostalgic mood, because I can't keep my mind from wandering down memory lane.

Five years since I met Daniel...and so much has happened.

Who'd have thought that I'd fall for such a geek? That he'd tip my world on its axis, causing me to fall head over heels in love with him by simply waiting patiently for me to give in to his stubbornness?

Even after all this time, he still makes my heart race and my belly erupts with butterflies when he smiles at me; waiting the past few months with being intimate since I gave birth to Eliza has been sheer hell. For the both of us, I think.

I absolutely love my life with him, and I wouldn't change a thing.

Well, apart from the nightmares, that is.

Sometimes, when things seem to overwhelm me, I make an appointment with Katherine, and although she doesn't hold all the answers, I always feel more balanced and confident in myself once I leave. I do hope I'll be able to stop seeing her altogether, of course, but, for now, I'm okay with the fact that I need her help. Or her advice, at least.

Suzy knows everything Tom put me through when I was just a girl, and I actually told her the whole story the day after that dreadful meeting with Steven. It felt liberating...even though it hurt at the time. We ended up consuming two bottles of wine, crying in each other's arms, and Suzy stayed the night at my flat. We had the meanest hangover ever the morning after, but I wouldn't change that, either, because it meant that Daniel cooked a full, English breakfast for us. A course he's become very handy with over the years.

I never hear from Steven, and I've told Mum and Dad why, of course. No more secrets, no more lies. They understand my reasons, but are saddened by them as well as conflicted; Steven is their son, after all, and you can't stop loving your children, no matter what they do. At least you shouldn't.

Should I not have burned that letter? Maybe not. But I can't do anything about that, and, to be honest, I very rarely think about it anymore.

When I took over the bookshop, I was so frightened of failing, but after I took some business classes, I slowly got the hang of it. Luckily for me, Andreas helped out a lot as well, providing me with invaluable knowledge about the business, but he maintained his distance like he said he would. It can't have been easy for him, but I respect him for it. It took some sweat and tears - no blood, thankfully - but now, five years later, I'm proud of where I am. I've even made a couple of deals with a few independently published authors to try to sell their books in my shop, and I truly hope that it'll be a great success.

Lately, though, I've also had the beginnings of a story of my own swirling inside my mind, and I've made so many notes, plotting and outlining it, that I feel I am finally ready to start writing it.

Exciting times ahead, eh?

But first...Where is my hubby?

I walk downstairs to look for him in the library - always a good place to start - and find him sitting at his desk, phone in hand.

"No, mum, I can't come see you today," he answers, voice flat.

When I hear who the caller is, I grimace and walk quickly inside the room and stop beside him, rubbing his shoulder in comfort.

That awful mother. Still hasn't changed at all.

I know that it's not my place to say anything, but I really

wish that Daniel would stop taking her calls. But I suppose he isn't ready for that yet.

Instead, I move to stand behind him and begin to work out the knots in his shoulders.

"Well, then, I'll talk to you another time," he barks into the phone and after he's ended the call, he tosses it carelessly on his desk, sighing deeply.

"I'm sorry, darling," I whisper, and lean down to kiss his cheek, but he doesn't answer. Instead, he swivels around in his chair, grabs my hips, and yanks me down to straddle him. Surprised by his swift movements, I gasp, but it's soon swallowed by his hungry mouth devouring mine.

"Daniel," I sigh when he wrenches his mouth free and his lips trail hungry kisses down my neck, his hands moving my skirt aside, and I move up on my knees so his fingers can find my pussy.

"Christ, I need you, sweetheart," he growls and, without warning, yanks my thong aside and plunges two fingers inside my slick heat, causing me to moan loudly. His thumb presses down hard on my clit, and I ride his hand, lost in the familiar passion only he is able to give me.

"Fuck me, Daniel," I gasp, my hands pulling at the zipper on his slacks. "It's been too long."

He sits back further in his seat, giving me room to free his cock, and I almost cry when I lose his fingers inside me. His lips are swollen from my kisses, and there's sweat on his forehead.

Mmm...delicious.

When I find that he's gone commando today, I hum, approving his idea, and I look into his heated eyes.

I miss his glasses.

I move back slightly and yank my top off, followed by

my bra, and his mouth closes in on my right nipple.

"Oh god, I want you inside me," I pant and, without losing his mouth on my breast, I sit up and then down again, his hard cock filling me completely.

We groan in unison as I begin to move, slowly at first, then faster and faster, until Daniel grabs my arse to set the right pace, angling his hips so the base of his cock hits my clit with every thrust.

"Oh god, oh god, oh god," I chant, panting, and I pull at his hair.

"Mouth, sweetheart," he grits out, teeth clenched, and as always, I do as he wish, slamming my lips down on his, sucking on his tongue to the rhythm of our lovemaking.

The pleasure is scorching me like always.

I'll never get my need for him stilled...it's all-consuming. As it should be.

Just as I'm close to unravelling entirely, he stills and moans my name in my mouth. His cock jerks as he spills his load in my pussy. I cry out in utter bliss. I lean forward to kiss him deeply again, our tongues twirling gently, and I wrap my arms around his neck.

Ending the kiss on a satisfied moan, I snuggle closer to him and wait in silence until my hammering heartbeat has settled down, and I revel in his hands caressing my back, my hips, my arse.

I kiss him on his neck and whisper, "Thank you," emotions clogging my throat.

He chuckles. "Not that I necessarily disagree, but why?"

"For this life. For making me believe in fairytales again. And for always being here for me, even when the darkness sometimes comes calling, knocking me back on my feet."

Daniel tightens his grip around me and whispers,

"You're welcome, sweetheart." I can sense that this moment is just as emotional for him as it is for me, and I brush my lips across his once more, keeping my eyes open the whole time.

We sit like this for a while, kissing, his cock still inside me, as I think back on the day he came into my life.

Meeting him was the best thing that ever happened to me.

He taught me to trust again...he taught me the true meaning of love.

But, above all, he taught me to believe in dreams again.

And for that, I'll always be grateful.

THE END

SUZY'S STORY, *"Fool for Love"*, *is available now! You can buy your copy on Amazon.*

ACKNOWLEDGMENTS

What a fantastic year this has been.

There are so many people to thank for helping me while I have been on this very emotional journey, but I have to start with the girls - my fairies - of my street team:

Ladies...you are funny, loving, quirky, and filled with so much spirit and sass that I wish with all my heart that we could all meet in person one day. Thank you for being there for me whenever I was filled with doubts, and thank you for always being ready for a good laugh. (Remember the "m" word discussion? ;-))

Michelle H. - love you loads, my book bestie - Clare, my American sister, and Autumn, my #pervpartnerincrime...Your words of wisdom, and your faith in this story have completely blown me away. You have helped me become a better writer, and I thank you for every comment, weird sticker, and uplifting message, all urging me to persevere and see this adventure through. I love you all to bits!

Michelle T., Natasha, and Dina: thank you for being part of my beta team. I value and appreciate all your feedback as well as taking the time out of your busy lives to read this book, and I love how much Emma & Daniel's story has moved you. Thank you so very much. You rock!

A special shout out to Ella Stewart of EscapeNBooks Blog for just being the way she is: kind, caring, funny, passionate...You are beautiful. Never forget it. (Pssst...and a great "pumper"! ;-))

Thank you so much to the indie community - authors, bloggers, PR Companies, readers - for welcoming me with open arms, taking me under your wings, and for offering me advice and guidance whenever I need it. I truly appreciate it.

To my very own Suzy: we have known each other for over 20 years, and there may be times when we are too busy and do not get the chance to chat properly, but when we do? It is the best! I would not be where I am today if I had not had you in my corner. You are my soul sister...my family...I love you, always and forever.

I would be a horrible person if I did not mention the unwavering support and love my family has shown me throughout my life.

To my parents: thank you for always having faith in me even when it was not always easy - I love you.

To my grandmother, Ruth: wherever you are, I hope you are with Granddad, and that the two of you are having fun.

To my husband, Lars: you are my heart. I love you and our life together, and I cannot wait to grow old with you.

AUTHOR BIO

Karen Ferry is a thirty-something writer, wife to a quiet, laidback man, and mother to a gorgeous, stubborn, redheaded girl who keeps her parents on their toes.

Karen tends to have a short fuse if she does not get a proper caffeine fix first thing in the mornings, but she is, in fact, a gentle person deep down.

Karen loves Italian food and wine, travelling, and spending time with her family. When she is not writing, she reads -- her favourite genres are New Adult, Contemporary Romance, Erotica and Romantic Suspense. She can never get enough of romance. Or of too many book boyfriends, either.

Even though Karen is Danish, she has always felt more at ease writing stories in English, and she has not read a book in her native tongue in over ten years.

She can be very outspoken and a complete fan girl of other authors online but will probably be very shy once she meets you in person.

You can learn more about Karen and her future projects here:

Website: https://authorkarenferry.wordpress.com/
Facebook: https://www.facebook.com/authorkarenferry
Twitter: https://www.twitter.com/authorkarenferr
Instagram: @authorkarenferry
Pinterest: https://www.pinterest.com/authorkarenferr/